SKULL
X
BONES

Other Anthologies Edited by:

SKULL X BONES

Edited by

David B. Coe
&
Joshua Palmatier

Zombies Need Brains LLC
www.zombiesneedbrains.com

Interior Design (ebook): ZNB Design
Interior Design (print): ZNB Design
Cover Design by ZNB Design
Cover Art "Skull X Bones"
by Justin Adams

ZNB Book Collectors #44
All characters and events in this book are fictitious.
All resemblance to persons living or dead is coincidental.

Kickstarter Edition Printing, December 2025
First Printing, December 2025

Print ISBN-13: 978-1940709864

Ebook ISBN-13: 978-1940709871

COPYRIGHTS

Illustration by Ariel Guzman

Table of Contents

SIGNATURE PAGE

David B. Coe, editor:

_____

Joshua Palmatier, editor:

_____

Steven Harper:

_____

Alex Bledsoe:

_____

Alan Smale:

_____

E.J. Delaney:

_____

Violette Malan:

_____

Adam Stemple:

_____

Nemo Herndon:

_____

Alena Van Arendonk:

_____

Gloria Wickman:

_____

R.S. Belcher:

_____

Jennifer Brozek:

_____

R.M. Olson:

_____

Misty Massey:

_____

C.C. Finlay:

_____

Justin Adams, artist:

_____

Ariel Guzman, artist:

_____

Greg Uchrin, artist:

_____

Half Life

Steven Harper

Right around lunchtime, my office door opens and a pirate walks in. Not a Captain Hook kind of pirate. This pirate is dressed in a smooth gray suit with a blood-red tie and matching pocket square. He has a beard, but it's carefully-manicured scruff, and instead of an eyepatch, he's tucking a pair of designer sunglasses into his jacket pocket. No pegleg. No hook.

You should know up front that this isn't a pirate story. Or rather, it isn't *just* a pirate story. It's also a witch story and a vampire story and my own story. It's also a story about the end of the universe.

"Larry," I say to the pirate.

"Wanda," he replies. "I need your help."

I sigh. "Again?"

"Again."

Another sigh, this time with eye roll. "How many times are you going to lose your heart before you learn your lesson?"

"I didn't come for a lecture, Wanda," Larry says, now with a little heat. "Are you going to help me or not?"

I grimace. The rent is due, and although my office is a tiny storefront with Ikea furniture, it doesn't come cheap. My only indulgence is a drooping potted daffodil, my favorite flower. They die but always come back.

The sign on the glass door says, 'Wanda Silver: For Hire.' I'm what you might call a fixer for…specialized clientele. Supernatural clientele. I'm not a vampire or a witch or a fairy myself. I just work for them. It started a few years ago when my brother Eric was turned into a vampire—don't worry, he's still a nice guy—and I learned there's a whole underground of supernatural creatures in the shadows, creatures who sometimes need a little help from someone in the mortal world. It opened up a whole new world for me—and my business.

I soften my tone. "Have a seat, Larry, and tell me what happened."

A smile lights his face and he drops with easy, masculine grace into the chair across from my desk. "No one does the job like you, Wanda."

"That's because no one else has this job. And I'm not cheap, remember. So, what beautiful woman stole your heart?"

"It's a complicated story," he hedges. "One better told over a drink?"

I don't do flirting, even with handsome pirates. I fish a flask from my desk drawer. "Sure! Want some?"

He makes a face. "Your holy water? A nun would turn that away."

"Keeps the vampires at stake's length." I take a slug, even though Larry isn't a vampire. Like I said, he's a pirate.

See, about three hundred years ago, Cut-Throat Lawrence was an ordinary pirate captain going up against an ordinary Spanish galleon. Except the Spanish galleon turned out to be a warship in disguise. It sank Larry's ship with a wave of its cannons, and Larry was the only survivor. He washed ashore near the Miskito Coast, alone and on the run. Then his fortunes changed. Larry met an old Mayan priest with a mad-on for Europeans. In exchange for Larry's promise to sink as many European ships as he could get his cannonballs on, the old Mayan bent Larry over an altar, cut out his heart, and put it into a magic box.

Yeah, ew.

The heart is still beating. It keeps Larry alive, theoretically forever, though if anyone destroys his heart, he'll push up daffodils like the rest of us.

Cut-Throat Lawrence went back to pirating, and in no time at all, killed his way up the ladder until he was a captain again. When the Golden Age of Pirates ended, Larry discovered another form of piracy—capitalism. Piles of gold and really long investment periods do wonders for your bottom line.

I stow the flask. "Your loss. So 'fess up—what happened with your heart?"

"You have to promise not to yell. Your voice is particularly...piercing when you yell."

"Piercing?" I yell, and Larry winces. With a cough, I bring the volume down. "I won't yell. I didn't yell when you gave your heart to Sandy Wikolewski. Or to Gwen McPherson."

This is Larry's latest thing—dating apps. And he falls in love faster than a middle-schooler with a hot teacher. After the fourth or fifth date, he gives his latest the box with his heart. Usually, she flees screaming. But a few women stick around, and occasionally one of them uses the heart for extortion. *Buy me a yacht or suffer the worst heartbreak ever,* and so on. He needs to get it back, which is where I come in.

Larry still looks reluctant. He's steepling his hands between his knees and his left leg bounces.

"Look, if you don't tell me, I can't help you."

"It's…Henrietta Rumple."

I recoil. "The witch?"

"Not just any witch. A witch *queen.*"

"Henrietta Rumple isn't *a* witch queen. She's *the* witch queen. Calling her a witch is like calling a thunderstorm a refreshing shower."

"My weakness for the fairer sex is forever my undoing," he says without a hint of regret. "And I thought a woman who was long-lived might understand—" He gestures at his own body. "—this."

"So, you saw her a few times, decided it was true love again, and gave the witch queen your heart. What is she demanding?"

He looks away, and I narrow my eyes. "What's going on, Larry? Why is your heart in jeopardy?"

"She's not demanding anything. Things just aren't…working out with us. I don't feel it anymore."

This is new. Larry's never fallen *out* of love before. Huh. "I take it you want me to break up with your girlfriend for you and get your heart back."

"That's about it."

"Why can't you do it yourself? It's embarrassing, but everyone goes through it."

"Embarrassing. Right." His face reddens. "Look, I've swung from a mast with a knife in my teeth. I've swum away from sinking ships through shark-infested waters. I've lain on an altar with a mad priest holding a knife over my chest. But the thought of breaking up with Henrietta Rumple terrifies me."

I think about that. "Fair."

"So will you do it?"

"Anything for you and your debit card, Larry." I get to my feet. "Off we go."

"What, right now?"

"May as well get it over with."

Henrietta Rumple lives by the ocean in what looks like a quirky vacation cottage with a wooden deck and two beach chairs out front. A stone jetty stretches into the water and crooks to the left to make a little shelter from the roiling water. In it is a motorized inflatable dinghy. Off-shore, I can just make out what seems to be a yacht. Some rich guy deciding to slum it in a non-tropical part of the ocean. I park my little Ford while Larry eyes the cottage nervously.

"I'll wait in the car," he says. Predictably. Well, this is why I get paid the big bucks.

I trot up to the cottage door and ring the bell. A moment later, a soccer mom opens the door—streaked hair pulled back, trim-ish figure, white t-shirt, blue beach shorts. Small kitchen behind her.

"Wanda!" she says brightly. "It's been ages. What brings you by?"

"Hi, Henrietta. Could we talk? I've got a case you can help with."

She widens the door. "You aren't a vampire, so come on in."

The moment she closes the door behind me, the interior of the cottage changes. Instead of a small, practical cottage kitchen, we're standing in an airy space with a chef-level stove and an island you could beach a whale on. Henrietta leads me to a breakfast nook that would seat eight. Generous windows look out over the beach. Tea and cookies are already sitting on the table. Steam rises from the teapot as Henrietta pours. "Instant tea" means something else to a witch.

"Speaking of vampires," Henrietta says, "how's your brother doing? Eric, isn't it?"

"He's well," I reply. "I don't see him much these days. Lucas and being a vampire keep him pretty busy, I guess."

She stirs sugar into her tea. "You don't sound happy about that."

"Well, no," I reply with a note of melancholy. "He's my little brother, the only family I have, and he's basically disappeared from my life. I'm lucky to get a text a week. I miss him."

"That's a shame." Henrietta sips. "It takes time for young people to learn the importance of family, and it's painful for the rest of us in the meantime."

She's not wrong. Eric's continued absence is a hole in my big-sister heart. My head knows that he's a twenty-something adult with his own un-life, but my emotions haven't caught up. It all happened so fast. Four years ago, a vampire named Lucas turned Eric into a vampire when Eric was seventeen and dying from leukemia. I hated Lucas for that, even though he ultimately saved Eric's life, and Eric really was—is—in love with him. Eventually the three of us had it out in the world's weirdest family row. But that's a story for another time. Short version is, Lucas and I came to an understanding as reluctant in-laws, and Eric promised he'd call more often. He kept his word for less than a month.

I try the tea. Chamomile with a hint of lemon. Soothing. "Anyway, this case."

"Of course. How can I help?"

"It's actually a little sensitive," I hedge. "It involves Larry."

Her eyebrows knit together. "Larry? Are you investigating him for someone?"

"Nothing like that. But...you still have his heart, don't you?"

Small smile, and she leans in conspiratorially. "He gave it to me last week. Isn't that adorable?" She goes to a drawer and takes out a small wooden box. Blocky Mayan carvings crawl across the surface. "It's right here. A pirate's heart."

Before I can say anything, she opens the box. Inside is a wet, bloody human heart. It's beating, pressing a little against the sides of the box. I hear the *lub-dub* and smell warm, raw meat. Ew.

"A pirate and a witch," she says, skimming a fond finger over the heart. "Who would've thought?"

"Yeah." My stomach roils and I'm wishing I hadn't had that tea. Okay, only one way forward. Band-Aid, rip. "Here's what's happening. Larry would like it if you returned his heart."

Her expression goes flat and she snaps the box shut. "What?"

"He's really sorry, but he needs to ask for it back."

"Is he breaking up with me?" Her voice rises and now I know what Larry means by *piercing*.

"I'm afraid so. If it helps, he says it's not you, it's him."

"And that little weasel couldn't tell me this *in person?*"

My neck hair prickles and a taste of ozone tangs the air. I spread my hands with a weak smile. "You know Larry. Fearless when it comes to piracy, but a big, fat chicken when it comes to angry women."

Henrietta's hands clench around the box and her body quivers like a tuning fork. Thunder rumbles in the distance, and I start planning escape routes.

And then she relaxes. Her face clears and the rumble fades. "Ugh. I should have seen it coming. That's Larry—hot but flighty."

"Famous for it," I hastily agree. My own heart stops leaping around my chest. Henrietta can be a grownup after all. Good. Great. Easy rent money. "I can take that box to him, if you like. Save you both the trip."

"No." Her tone is hard again.

Uh-oh. "No?"

"I'm not another notch on his figurehead," she not-quite snarls. "He gave me a gift, free and clear. I won't give it up."

Ah. I get it now. "What do you want for it?"

She laughs with a hint of gingerbread cackle. "What makes you think I want something?"

"Just tell me, Henrietta. I'm only mortal and my time is limited."

"Too true. I'm in the same boat, you know."

This surprises me. "You are?"

"I'm long-lived, thanks to a little tinkering, but one day I'll die, just like any other woman. I might get two hundred more years, but that's it. Even magic has its limits."

"And the heart?"

She caresses the box like a cat licking its paw. "Larry has immortality. I want it, too."

Oh, boy. Oh, geez. I shake my head, careful to add a dash of sympathy. "Larry's an outlier. The only way a mortal can become immortal is by becoming a vampire. If it's vampirism you want, I can—"

"I don't want vampire immortality. Vampirism changes you. I want to remain myself."

"There's no other way to—"

"There is," she interrupts again. "The Cup of Hebe."

I roll my eyes. "Yeah, sure. One sip from the goblet of the goddess of youth and you're immortal. You think you're the first person to look for it? It doesn't exist. Everyone knows that."

"It *does* exist, and Larry knows where it is. He's an immortal pirate who's traveled every inch of every ocean." She draws the box back to her. "Tell him I'll trade his heart for that cup."

"But—"

She's gone, and I'm standing outside the door. I hate when people do that.

Back in the car, Larry is waiting with badly-disguised impatience. "Well?"

I tell him, ending with, "Do you really know where it is?"

Another pause. "Yeah. It's on an island. Three days' sailing."

"But?" There's always a *but*. It's some kind of law.

"But no mortal is supposed to have the Cup. It grants *true* immortality to the first mortal who drinks from it."

I wrinkle my nose. "True immortality? As opposed to fake immortality?"

"Immortals can die," he clarifies. "Or rather, we can be killed. Vampires and stakes. Fairies and iron. Me and my heart. As long as I'm at least a little alive, I'll recover from just about anything. But if you take my heart out of that box, I'm done. Hebe's immortality keeps you coming back forever. It's a step away from godhood. Forbidden."

I think about that for several heartbeats. True immortality. Huh.

"How do we get to this island, then?" I ask casually.

He looks at me sidelong. "You're staying on the case?"

"You don't have your heart back yet. I have a rep to keep up."

"Thank you, Wanda. I mean it."

"Just bring your debit card."

He leads me down to the jetty and the dingy moored there. I didn't realize it was his. He helps me board, starts the motor, and heads into the ocean. The water is choppy, and the dinghy skips from wave to wave. Thank all powers that I don't get seasick, or I'd've heaved my guts. Wind pulls my hair, and the motor growls like a werewolf on a bender. It's kind of fun.

"Are we taking this all the way to the island?" I shout over the noise.

Larry shakes his head and points at the distant yacht, which isn't so distant now. It's sleek and modern and—wavering? As we close the distance, the yacht changes before my eyes into an actual pirate ship, complete with sails and rigging, a mermaid figurehead, and a grinning Jolly Roger flapping in the breeze. Wow. I'm still staring when Larry brings the dinghy alongside and boosts me up a rope ladder. I clamber on board, smelling tar and salt breezes. The sails are down, and the ship pulls a little at its anchor. Wood creaks. Larry comes over the gunwale with ease and grace, looking out of place in his gray suit and scarlet tie.

"Is this your original ship?" I ask.

"*The Gray Phantom.* I've kept her up. A glamor keeps people from noticing she's old-fashioned."

I look doubtfully at the empty deck and the complicated rigging. "This is amazing, but I don't know squat about sailing, and you're just one pirate. How will—?"

In answer, Larry takes a silver navy whistle from his pocket, trills a few shrill notes, and shouts orders in some weird version of English that makes no sense to me. The rigging leaps to life. Ropes snake about, sails burst upward, the anchor sucks itself up to the hull. Larry takes up a position at the big, spokey helm thingie. I clap my gaping mouth shut and join him.

"How?" I ask.

"Ghosts of my original crew. Story for another time." Then he gives me a look. "What are you thinking, Wanda? You're wearing your thoughtful face."

"I'm thinking that this morning I ate a greasy McMuffin at my desk in my office, and this afternoon I'm sailing on a ship manned by ghosts and looking for a cup of immortality because a pirate literally gave his heart to a witch." I grin. "I love my life."

His eyes narrow. "That's it?"

"That's it."

Actually, that's a lie. But I don't tell him that.

As promised, it takes us three days. I spend it exploring *The Gray Phantom* and learning a tiny bit about sailing a pirate ship. Larry even lets me steer. Navigate. Whatever. I find a stash of clothes that are a little outdated but still serviceable, which I appreciate because my own clothes are getting whiffy. There's a skirt and sweater ensemble from the fifties, a pantsuit from the seventies, and some workout gear with leg-warmers from the eighties. Probably from old girlfriends. I hold up the pantsuit. This lady is probably pushing eighty now. I wonder where she is and what she's doing and how she'd react if Larry came back into her life, still young and dashing.

Just thought I'd say hi, Phyllis, and see how you're doing.

What will it be like to be eighty and plump and wrinkled? How will it feel when Eric comes to the nursing home? He'll stride through the door, still young and agile and sharp around the edges while I slowly lose focus and fade away.

Who are you again, dear? My memory isn't what it used to be.

I get a sick feeling that has nothing to do with the motion of the ship and take a pull of holy water to distract myself. But Eric still hovers at the back of my mind.

Meanwhile, the invisible pirate ghosts do everything for us. They sail the ship and clean up and cook some pretty good meals. At first, it's weird having plates and food zing toward the table, but I adapt.

The fourth day dawns unusually warm and sunny and the ocean is a crystal blue. Larry points at a smudge on the horizon. "The island."

He hands me a telescope, and I focus in. "Is that…a Greek temple?"

"Hebe is a Greek goddess and we *are* in the Aegean."

"Wait—what? When did—" I stop myself. "You know, never mind. Just tell me what we do next."

Harry hesitates, and I narrow my eyes. "What is it?"

"I can't help you," he says. "You'll be on your own."

"Meaning?"

"Immortals can't set foot on the island or touch the goblet. Hebe's law. And…" he hesitates again. "And you could die."

"Die? What do you mean *die*?"

"There are three trials—the trial of the body, the trial of the head, and the trial of the soul. No mortal has ever gotten past them. You're not intended to."

"And just what do these trials involve, pray?"

"No one has ever come back to say, but I've heard daemons are involved." He gives me an apprehensive look. "Look, the more I think about it, the more I think we should just turn around and figure out another way to get my heart back from Henrietta. Maybe we can steal it or trick her out of it or something. I don't think she'd kill me, right? But even if she does…" He trails off. "Well, I've already lived way longer than anyone has a right to."

"What do you do with yourself, Larry?" I ask, pointedly turning my back on Y'all-Gonna-Die Island. "It's got to be lonely on this ship."

He gives a humorless smile and adjusts his collar. He's wearing a polo shirt and boat shoes. Apparently, he likes pirate ships but not pirate clothes. "Here's where I'm supposed to say the sea is my mistress and she keeps me happy. And she usually does. I never feel more alive than when I'm sailing with a fresh wind behind me and the horizon ahead. I've explored every port in the world a dozen times over and I still find something new. But yeah, it does get lonely. It's why I chase romance."

"Maybe you should stop chasing romance and look for something else."

"Like?"

I shrug. "Try a found family. Henrietta, for example. I think she still likes you. The romance might have died, but the relationship doesn't have to."

"Hm." He coughs. "So, about the island of death—"

"I'm going."

He can't hide his surprise. "You are?"

"I'm the fixer, right?"

"Oh. Well…thank you, Wanda." He sounds sincere and looks like he's going to lean in to kiss me. Ick. Even after my little talk, it seems to be the only way he knows how to relate to women. I step a little sideways, pretending I didn't notice what he was up to, and he pulls up short.

To cover, I say, "So let's go, Captain!"

Now Larry is in more of a hurry, as if he's afraid I might change my mind. He sails us in to a couple hundred yards offshore and the ghosts drop anchor. In short order, I'm aboard the dinghy and put-put-putting toward the beach, my borrowed pantsuit fluttering in the breeze. The only thing I have with me is my water flask. Ahead of me, the beach sand is smooth and has a pink tinge that makes me think of blood spoor. Having a vampire for a brother does stuff to your world view.

I beach the dinghy and look around. Lovely vacation spot. Gentle lapping waves. Perfect sun. Grove of emerald trees that climb gentle foothills to a green mountain. Ruined Greek temple partway up.

Soda bottle near the waterline.

The hell? I pick it up. Cold. Taped to the side is a note:

Drink it all, keep it down.

Is that a riddle? I wonder. The note changes.

No.

Okay. "Is this part of the trial?"

Yes. Drink it all, keep it down.

I shrug, crack open the bottle, and chug. Sweet and fizzy. Perfect for the beach. Just then, a strange hissing noise starts up, and I turn uneasily back toward the beach.

Cockroaches swarm the sand. Billions of cockroaches.

It's a good swarm. More of a horde, really. Thick carpet of carapaces and wiggling legs and waving antennae. Slithering, chittery kind of noise that slides over my skin. The horde heaves and undulates like a single, gross living thing. It covers the twenty or thirty yards between the waterline and the overly-obvious path leading into the trees. Tall and unclimbable rocks book-end the beach, so there's no going around. Every suburban girl organ in my body is screeching from the top of a chair. The body trial. I have to get through *that?*

The note on the side of the bottle says *Yes.*

I puff out my cheeks. Fuckity snicket. Well, I didn't get this far to only get this far, right? Cockroaches aren't deadly. They don't bite. They aren't poisonous. *You can do this,* I tell myself. *It'll be gross, but not as gross as that time you helped Bitsy Olechowski clear poop fairies out of her basement. On three, then.*

And I sprint ahead. Cockroaches crunch like kid cereal under my shoes, and right away I feel thousands of tiny bug feet skittering up the legs of my pantsuit. In no time, I'm over-swarmed with roaches. They crawl down my back, up my chest, under my arms. Feathery antennae probe my ears, nose, and lips. I'm still running hard. *Crunch* crunch *crunch* crunch. My stomach twists with nausea, and the soda roils. *Keep it down.* That's the test, then—don't barf. I clamp my mouth and imagine swallowing a cork.

I can hardly see through the cockroaches covering my face and crawling through my hair. I'm halfway across now, leaving gooey footprints behind. More than halfway. Three-quarters. Almost there.

Turns out gooshy cockroaches are slipperier than anticipated. One foot goes out from under me and I fall toward the horde with a little scream, which means my mouth pops open. I hit the ground with the biggest, wettest *SMUNCH* this side of a nightmare and instantly my mouth is full of squirming bugs.

I scream again, which helps me spit out most of the bugs. But not all. I can feel them writhe and wriggle on my tongue and against the inside of my cheek. The soda is coming up again. *No!* I taste high fructose corn syrup tanged with stomach acid. *No!* I blast the rest of the bugs from my mouth and clamp it shut again. I went to college—I can hold my barf. I shove myself upright. Cockroaches slide off me. I shake like a dog, and a bunch of them whirl away. I run again, the insect legs still pricking my skin in a million places. I'm almost crying now with the effort of holding everything together.

And then I'm through. It's just sand under my shoes. I shake and brush frantically at myself, and it takes me a second to realize that the cockroaches are completely gone. Vanished. Even the squishy bits. But I can still feel them on my skin, and I know what my next nightmare will be. The soda bottle is still in my hand.

"Okay," I pant. "Body trial: passed. Next?"

No answer. Forward, then.

The soda bottle is empty, but I keep it anyway because you never know. I trot down the trail into the trees. They're hung heavy with dark olives, and the grove thickens until it's hard to see between the trees. Leaves block the sun. Ahead, the trail divides and I pause. Which way? There's no signpost or anything. I peer down the left fork and see that a little ways ahead, the trail divides again. Same for the right fork. Now I get it—a labyrinth. The head challenge.

Good. I'm due an easy one.

I trot down the right trail, and when it forks, I take the right trail again. And then again. Labyrinths are simple. All you have to do is follow one wall. It might take a while, but you'll eventually find the—

"Moo."

I spin. Behind me, predictably I suppose, is a minotaur. I make a little gurgling sound. Seven feet tall. Mountainous shoulders, bulgy biceps, huge hands. Bull's head, wicked horns. Hooves for feet. And hung like a—

Well, you probably know.

"Moo," the minotaur says again. He didn't make a mooing sound. He actually *said* "Moo."

I'm rooted to the spot. No way I can outrun this thing, or outfight it. I'm cold all over and my heart is a drum in my chest. What do I do?

The minotaur picks me up with both massive hands around my waist. I struggle, but it's useless. The smell of rotting meat is on the minotaur's breath.

"I'm gonna ask you a riddle," he says, "and you're gonna answer."

"Uh…isn't this mixing myths?" I ask.

He shrugs like a gathering avalanche. "Gods aren't creative. You wanna do this or not?"

"What if I don't?" I squeak.

"Been a long time since breakfast," he replies, and squeezes. It's like being crushed by steel girders. I gasp, unable to budge even one of his fingers.

"Ask the fucking riddle," I manage.

"Good. Listen up. *I have no hands, yet hold you tight,*" he says, singsong. "*Born of shadow, shaped by night. I have no voice but make you scream. Tangible but still unseen. What am I?*"

"Can't I just negotiate the maze?" I gasp.

He squeezes and my ribs creak. "Sundial's ticking. What's your answer?"

I smash the bottle against the side of the minotaur's head with all my strength. It shatters. Glass flies everywhere. The minotaur's grip loosens a tiny bit in surprise, but not enough for me to squirm free. He blinks. There's no sign I hurt him in the slightest.

"Really?" he says. "Guess I shouldn't be surprised. That Theseus guy tried to cheat, too. No more tricks, now. Answer the riddle."

Fuck. Now it's really starting to hurt. "I might be able to figure it out if my guts weren't being crushed by a cement mixer," I croak.

"You're not meant to figure it out, doofus. You're meant to be folded into a pita for my lunch. Mortals ain't meant to have the cup."

Shit, shit, shit. I try to think, but I've never been good at riddles, and it's getting really hard to breathe. Sweat runs down my face. *I have no voice but make you scream.* What the fuck is that about? My thoughts run in circles like terrified cats. The fear is—is—

"Fear!" I shout. "It's fear!"

"Well, shit." The minotaur drops me and I go to my knees, sucking air. "I spent all morning on that one."

I pull myself to my feet. "Sorry to disappoint."

"Meh. Or maybe 'moo.' Come on—I'll show you out. This way, then left."

I'm having a little trouble adjusting to the whiplash. One moment I'm in deadly danger, the next I'm having a polite walk-and-talk with a myth monster. I better not wake up and find this was all a dream. It's been too much work. Suddenly I'm thirsty. I take a swig from my flask and stow it again. Holy water slakes your thirst as good as regular.

"Do you get a lot of mortals looking for the Cup?" I ask as we walk.

"Depends on what you mean by *a lot.*" He snorts to clear his nostrils and I try not to cringe. "Most people land on the island without knowing what the deal is. But they run like hell from the cockroaches. Maybe two or three a century are actually here for the Cup."

"And no one's found it yet?"

"Nope. Couple have gotten this far, but the third test's a real killer. And don't ask—I can't tell." He wipes his nose with a furry arm. "You mind a question?"

"Long as there's no squeezing involved."

"Why are you here?"

I look at him, genuinely puzzled. "To find the Cup of Hebe."

"Bullshit." He snorts again. "And I know my bullshit. This is way too much trouble for a handful of cash. So why are you *really* here?"

I don't bother asking how he knows I'm being paid. Instead, I stare straight ahead. "I really, really need the money."

"Okay, have it your way. Anyhoo, there's the way out." He points to another opening in the trees, then turns and heads into the labyrinth without a backward glance.

"Thank you!" I call after him.

"Moo."

On the other side of the opening is a wide, velvety lawn that goes all the way to the side of a steep foothill, the one with the temple. The grass looks cool and inviting, and I'd give my left pinky toe to just stretch out on it for ten minutes. But in the center of the lawn maybe ten steps ahead of me is a stone altar covered in intricate carvings of people painted in lifelike colors. As I get closer, I can see they're moving, and I recognize some of them. There's Pegasus, the winged horse, bucking Bellerophon off his back. And there's Otus and Ephialtes, tricked by Artemis into spearing each other when they try to take over Olympus. And there's Icarus, a terrified look on his face as the sun melts the waxy wings off his back and he plunges toward the sea. All examples of hubris. Too much pride. Hint, hint.

On top of the altar is a plain goblet. Carved of stone, rimmed with gold, pocked and chipped. This is a goblet that's seen a lot of wild parties.

I look around. Nobody and nothing. It can't be this easy, can it? I reach for the goblet.

"Hey, sis."

I spin. Eric is standing behind me in the shade. Shadows darken his red hair into a deep auburn, and his blue eyes burn in a foxy, familiar face. He's wearing his habitual jeans and hoodie. The last time I saw him alive, he was stick-thin and wasted from the chemo. Now he's dead and strong and healthy, if a little pale. A thrill goes through me.

"Eric!" I wrap him in a hug. His cheek is cool against mine, and he returns the embrace perfunctorily, as if a public hug embarrasses him. Teenagers.

He shrugs and gives that half smile that makes him so adorable. He'd've been a real ladykiller—gentlemankiller—in a few years. Now he's eternally stranded at seventeen, which means he's doomed to mere cuteness for eternity.

I remember where I am. Is Eric part of the test? Snatched up and brought here to distract me? "What are you doing here?" I ask cautiously.

"One minute I'm in the crypt with Lucas, the next I'm here," he says resignedly. "The life of a vampire, I guess. What are *you* doing here?"

"Taking this." Before anything else can happen, I grab the goblet—and wait. No lightning forks the sky. No monsters appear. No Indiana Jones traps swallow me up. I look inside the Cup. A few drops of daffodil-gold liquid roll around the bottom like mercury. And they're *mine*. This is the real reason I came here.

"I'm not giving this up so a witch will help a pirate," I say savagely. "For once, I'm doing something for *me*."

"But why?"

"You should know that, Eric. You should know *me*. But you barely do anymore."

"I'm a different person now, sis. I'm—"

"A vampire, I know." My voice climbs into piercing range. Why am I talking about this? I should be demanding to know who brought him and why. But my emotions barrel ahead without me, and a burst of long-held anger spills out. "Lucas saved your life, but he wrecked our family!"

"It would be even more wrecked if I had died," he calmly points out.

Anger is in the driver's seat and I'm shaking with it. I'm angry at Eric. I'm angry at Lucas. I'm angry at the whole fucking world. "If you had died, I could have grieved and moved on. This—" I wave the Cup at him "—this is a half life. You're not alive, but you're not dead. You aren't part of my life, but you haven't left it. Half life. How the fuck can you—can *anyone*—expect me to live like this?" I'm shouting now, barely aware of what I'm saying.

"You think that cup is the answer?"

"I'll live forever, Eric." I bring the volume down and find I'm crying. "We can be a family again."

He grabs me in a hug, a voluntary one, but my legs have gone weak, and I drag us both to the ground. Eric doesn't let go. Four years of tears streams out of me, wetting his hoodie. I cry until I'm hiccupping and snot runs out of my nose. Once I'm spent, we sit next to each other in sibling silence. I cradle the Cup in my lap. Gold gleams at the bottom.

At last Eric says, "I won't live forever, you know. All vampires die eventually. Lucas says that after three, four hundred years, we get…tired. Bored. The tired ones spend one last night of debauchery before…"

I wipe my face with the back of my hand. "Before what?"

"They watch the sunrise." He sighs. "It'll happen to me one day. So, if you drink, you'll outlive me. By centuries. Millenniums."

"Millennia," I correct absently.

"You know how the stories go," Eric says. "Immortals watch everyone they love age and die. They disconnect and live lonely lives."

"I'm *already* lonely, Eric. Half life, remember?"

"So, change. Make some friends. Take your own advice to Larry and do the found family thing. You need to know more people than just me." Eric puts his chilly hand on my back. "And I'll change. I promise. We'll do a midnight snack together every week. How about that?"

I turn away. "You've said that before."

"I mean it this time. You don't want the Cup. Not really."

At those words, a couple-three things smash through me all at once. The world flips over, but I'm still on solid ground. I *get* it now. I get everything. How the trial of the soul works. Why no one ever takes the Cup. Why the Cup is forbidden. I clamber to my feet, breathing clarity like cool spring water. Eric stands up, watching me with those piercing blue eyes.

"You're right. I don't really want it." I carefully set the Cup back on the altar, as if moving too fast will shatter my newfound lucidity. Relief fills Eric's eyes. "I guess when it comes down to it, I knew it was wrong to come here in the first place."

Small smile. "You always were the smart one."

"I need a drink." I pull out my flask and waggle it at him. "Want some?"

"No, thanks."

I sip thoughtfully and say, "You're not Eric."

He blinks and for a moment I think he's going to deny it. But then he says, "What gave me away?"

"Eric always flinches away from my flask. You didn't. Eric wouldn't know about my found family advice to Larry. You did." I take a third pull.

"Well, damn. Hebe won't be happy. Ironic, right?" Fake Eric sighs. "Look, mortals aren't meant to have the cup, and the test of the soul is literally impossible to complete. There's no way to win. If you fail the test, I kill you. If you pass the test, you won't want the cup anyway. I thought you passed it just now when you set the cup down. But you're still planning on taking it, aren't you?"

I nod, my lips pursed shut.

"I'm going to rip your throat out now. It'll be quick, promise. I'll even give you a coin for Charon so your ghost doesn't hang around." Fake Eric cocks his head. "Any last words?"

I shake my head. What is there to say?

"Then let's do this." Fake Eric's face runs like soupy mud and reforms into bat-like features. His body expands until he's seven feet tall and covered in brown scales. His arms become spindly, and they end in foot-long claws. Behind him, a spiny tail hisses through the air. Looks like Larry was right about daemons. Shit. As promised, it swings those claws straight at my throat.

I spray it with a spit-take of water. Holy water.

The daemon screeches and melts like ice cream in a hot car. It screams and screams. I clap my hands over my ears to stop the horrible sound. As its body dissolves, it draws back its arm lightning-quick and swings for my neck before I realize what's happening. The claws slice through the air and I feel a prick at my neck. And then it's gone. I'm alone in the clearing, panting and sweaty and wrung out. But it's over, and I won. I fucking won. Feeling victorious, I pluck the Cup from the altar. The drops of nectar roll around the bottom. Eternal life is mine for the taking. I raise the Cup to the sky in a mock toast.

"To you, Hebe," I say to the empty air, "the one who tried to kill me so I don't live forever."

No answer.

I bring the Cup to my lips...and pull it away.

"Kidding!" I say to the air again. "I figured it all out, and I'm not drinking. But I *am* taking the Cup with me. Contract, and all that. Besides, I passed the tests."

The earth shakes. The olive trees shudder. A crack runs down the distant mountain and speeds toward me.

"Shit!" I run for the labyrinth. The ground shakes harder, and I have to work to keep my balance. I'm trying not to panic. How will I find my way back through?

Then the minotaur is there, running beside me. "What the fuck did you do?" he bellows. "The whole island is coming apart!"

In answer, I hold up the Cup, then trip. The minotaur catches me in one meaty hand. The trees are snapping and the ground is groaning.

"You got a way out of here?" he yells.

"The beach!" I yell back.

Still holding me, the minotaur charges ahead as cracks appear all around us. He whips through the twisty maze with the ease of long practice and bursts out onto the beach with the cracks following close behind. The water is choppy, but the inflatable dinghy is still there. The minotaur throws me like a basketball and I land in the bottom. A second later, the dinghy lurches as the minotaur lands next to me.

Off my startled look, he says, "Did you think I was going to sacrifice myself to save you? More bullshit. Go go go!"

The mountain is crumbling, devouring itself and the island with a dragon's roar. Frantically I start the motor and slam it into high gear. We zip away as the island tumbles into the sea.

Larry's a little startled when a minotaur climbs onto his ship, but he sets the ghosts to sailing us away, me with the Cup clutched in my hand and my eyes on the spot where Hebe's island sank.

That evening, the three of us are belowdecks on *The Gray Phantom,* devouring a celebratory dinner of roast pork—the ghosts are smart enough not to serve beef—and I give Larry the long version while the Cup sits in the center of the table. Larry toys with his wine glass. The minotaur chugs from a beer mug the size of a small barrel. He and Larry have been getting along great over dinner, and I'm glad. I think it's been a long time since Larry had a male friend. Also, the ghosts have scrounged up a minotaur-sized pair of pants, for which I'm grateful.

"So why didn't you drink the nectar?" Larry asks me.

"He may have been a daemon, but that doesn't mean he was wrong," I say. "I think I'm better off trying to have a full, short life rather than an empty, infinite one."

"Hear, hear!" The minotaur says, banging his mug on the table.

Larry turns to him, looking oddly hopeful. "What about you? You want me to drop you somewhere?"

"Nah." The minotaur wipes his mouth. "I have a different idea."

"And that is?"

"Ship's awful empty. I think you need a first mate."

Larry grins a pirate's grin.

And soon enough, we're back home. The minotaur elects to stay on the ship while Larry and I hit up Henrietta on shore. She lets us both into the kitchen and gives Larry a hard stare. Larry has the grace to look abashed. The tea things are on the table, and we sit.

"Do you have it?" she asks without preamble.

I set the Cup on the table next to my cookie plate. Henrietta stares at it like a famine victim seeing a roast chicken. Entranced, she reaches for it, but I pull it away.

"The box?" I ask.

Without taking her eyes off the Cup, Henrietta produces the box and slides it over to Larry. He snatches it up, peeks inside, and gives the world's heaviest sigh.

"Never, ever again," he mutters, and this time I believe him.

Henrietta, meanwhile, peers inside the Cup at the golden drops. "This will do it, then?"

"Immortality guaranteed," I say. "No half life."

"There are no words," she whispers, and raises the Cup to her lips while Larry watches with an unreadable expression.

"But…" I interrupt.

She pauses to glare at me. "Why is there always a *but?*"

"I think it's a law of the universe," I say. "*But*…have you thought this through to its logical conclusion?"

"What conclusion might that be?"

"The conclusion that hit me after the trial of the soul. The conclusion that persuaded me not to drink the nectar myself. The Cup isn't forbidden because the gods are control freaks. The Cup is forbidden for our own good."

"What does that mean?"

"That nectar will make you truly immortal. Unkillable. Undying. Forever."

"That *is* the point," Henrietta says.

I lean forward, my eyes boring in on hers. "Drink, and you live a hundred years. A thousand. And then a million. More time passes. One day, the last member of the human race dies, but not you. Other life dies out, but not you. Eventually, the sun engulfs the earth, destroying what's left, but not you. You cling to a hunk of dead rock and try to kill yourself a thousand different ways. None of them work. More and more and more time passes. The universe falls in on itself. Galaxies collide. The stars die. But not you. You're the only thing left in a black, empty universe. That's what forever is." I gesture at the Cup. "If you drink."

Henrietta goes motionless. I sip my tea. Larry hesitantly takes a cookie, then sets it down again. A thousand thoughts chase themselves across Henrietta's face. At last, she puffs out a hard breath and shoves the Cup back at me.

"I hate you," she says, without rancor. It doesn't seem to be in her to hold a grudge, even if she is a witch. "Especially when you're right."

"Eric says the same thing." I take the Cup back, relieved on her behalf.

"What are you going to do with it?" Larry asks. "It's awfully dangerous to leave lying around."

"I'll think of something. It's what I do." I raise my teacup. "Now, a toast."

They take up their own teacups. "What are we toasting to?" Larry says.

I look around the table at the pirate and the witch and out the window toward Larry's yacht with its minotaur first mate…and smile. "To found family."

"Hear hear," says Henrietta with a smile of her own. "Now how about you all stay for lunch? I'm dying to meet that minotaur."

That evening, I stop in at my office and set the Cup on my desk. Everything looks so…normal. Ordinary desk. Ordinary chairs. Ordinary daffodil drooping in its ordinary pot. I stare at the Cup for a long time as the shadows lengthen and the street lights come on. Finally, I raise the Cup in yet another toast. What would immortality taste like?

"To eternity," I whisper.

Nah.

I tip the Cup over the daffodil pot. Three golden drops sink into the dirt. The pot glows for a moment, and the daffodil perks up. The flower becomes fresh and new, and the soft smell of spring daffodils wafts through the office. Delight fills me and I smile at the thought that this bit of beauty will be the final thing at the end of a dark universe.

The front door opens. Of course. Something always needs fixing, and the supernatural doesn't keep banker's hours. I turn.

"Hi! How can I…"

The words fade. Eric slouches in the doorway, his red hair blazing in the hard light of the street lamp.

"Hey, sis," he says. "Um…I saw you were gone and you didn't answer my texts and I was worried you might be…well, anyway, I kinda missed you. You want to get a midnight snack or something?"

I give him a long, completely mortal hug.

No Prey, No Pay

Alex Bledsoe

"The code is more what you'd call 'guidelines' than actual rules."
—Hector Barbarossa

I always sleep well on a ship. The constant motion bothers some people, but to me it's soothing, like a child being rocked. The fact that I now slept on a pirate ship didn't change that.

The shout of "All hands, on deck!" though, definitely harshed the mood. I jumped out of my bunk, threw on my clothes, grabbed my sword (I carried a short Killmaster Drawing-Room Special for use in the close-quarters-fighting pirating often entailed), and rushed to see what was up.

My friend Jane Argo, six feet of broad-shouldered menace with a high, giggly voice, had hired me to fill in for her first mate until someone could break him out of jail. It was a simple enough gig, since Jane was definitely in command and never had to give an order twice. My job was to take those orders, break them down into manageable tasks, and distribute them among the crew.

This lack of ultimate responsibility, along with the sea air and the fun of raiding cargo ships from Outagamo, made this almost a vacation. Our ship, the *Battista*, was acting as a privateer on behalf of Langlade, currently at war with Outagamo.

The crew had gathered around something at the forecastle and I saw Jane's distinctive hair over the tops of their heads. I pushed my way through until I reached her.

"What do you make of this?" she said without preamble.

This was a dead body on the deck. I recognized him as Big Tommy Acuff, an able seaman and fair swordsman, who had given me no trouble so far. Not that he would in the future: the flesh from the entire middle of his body, from his sternum down to the tops of his hip bones, was gone. It looked for all the world like he'd been gnawed to the bone by some carnivore, except that we were in the middle of the ocean and, as far as I knew, sharks didn't climb on deck. And our rats were nowhere near that motivated.

I knelt and looked closer. Across two deck planks was a singular track, larger than my two spread hands. It was a three-toed print, like a gigantic chicken. I glanced up, hoping to see some huge bird circling the ship. But the skies were bare of anything but clouds.

This was much closer to my usual job as a sword jockey, hiring my fighting arm and expertise out to solve crimes, find missing people, and clean up trouble. So much for my working vacation.

"Based on what we've got here," I said as I stood, "it looks like some huge bird killed him. But the bird big enough to do that, and leave that print, would have a hard time doing it without attracting attention. I assume nobody saw or heard anything?"

There were general mumbles and head shakes. On another adventure, Jane and I once encountered a monstrous, many-tentacled sea creature shackled to the bottom of a derelict ship, and Jane still bore the scar on her thigh from its grasp, so I knew sea monsters existed. But this was something new in my experience.

Or was it? Also in my experience, very human killers weren't above disguising their work as something done by an animal, mythical or otherwise.

Then a voice said, "We all know whose fault this is."

We all turned toward the speaker. Malachi was taller than Jane, and therefore considerably taller than me; he was long and lean with wiry brute strength.

"And who might that be?" Jane challenged.

He nodded at her and said insolently, "I said back in port that you were bad luck. You're not a sailor, and you're not a pirate. You have no business commanding this ship. You're just a sword whore."

I didn't have to see Jane's face to know the way her eyes narrowed and her lips turned up; I'd seen it many times when someone challenged her. She stepped close to Malachi and said, "When you call me that, sailor…smile."

"I didn't vote for you."

"And yet you signed on."

"And I still wouldn't vote for you."

"Are you calling for a new vote now, then?"

Pirates were a lot of things—dishonest, disloyal, violent, dangerous, and quite often really smelly—but in one sense they were a real improvement over the many kingdoms and empires that dotted the world: they ruled by majority. The crew signed on to an agreed-upon set of rules, and a captain could be replaced any time he or she lost the confidence of the crew. Anyone could call for a vote, but if they lost, they had no protection from the captain's wrath. Which meant they had to be pretty damn sure they had the votes.

Malachi knew he didn't. In a low, defeated voice, he answered, "No, captain. I would not. Not today."

"Then shut the hell up, sailor." Jane turned to me. "Put someone in the crow's nest full-time, Mr. LaCrosse. And post watches on deck, to *watch* the deck."

"Aye, captain," I said.

"And when you've done that, come see me in my cabin." The crew parted to clear her way toward the quarterdeck.

I turned to the second officer, a grizzled one-eyed veteran named Poe. "Mr. Poe, you go up in the crow's nest. Yell good and loud if you see anything odd."

"Aye, sir," he said with a half-salute.

"You're sending the one-eyed guy up to keep watch?" Malachi harped.

"Poe's one eye is three times the equal of any man's here." I poked him in the chest. "And four times yours, Malachi."

"Yeah, well, a bunch of us think you shouldn't be giving us orders, lubber."

Ah, the old insult. "Lubber" as in landlubber, as in someone who had no business on a working ship. It wasn't the first time I'd heard it, usually muttered behind my back, and ordinarily I wouldn't have paid it any mind. But a man was dead, and it was no time to let the crew see anything that could be taken for weakness. Plus, Malachi was just a dick.

So I punched him right in the dick, as hard as I could.

He made a little squeak and doubled over. I shot an uppercut into his face and felt it through my arm all the way to my neck; throwing that kind of punch was for younger men with springier bones. He toppled backward, and the crew stepped aside to let him thud to the deck. No one moved to help him.

I kept my face neutral, even though my hand was already throbbing. "Anyone else going to question orders?" I asked calmly.

Again the chorus and headshakes of "no"s.

"Good. Now if you'll excuse me, the captain wants me. Oh, and someone throw a bucket of something into Malachi's face. Water, rum, piss, I don't really care what."

They stepped aside for me, too. I knocked on Jane's cabin door, waited for permission, and went inside.

She sat behind her chart desk, one bare foot propped up on it. The other leg was stretched out while her cabin girl unlaced her boot. The girl was about ten and took the place of the usual cabin *boy*; Jane saw no reason a girl couldn't fulfill this role and had picked her up running wild on some island before I came on board. Her name was Nell.

"Thanks, Nell," Jane said when her second boot came off. "Now excuse us for a minute, will you?"

Nell gave a smart salute. "Aye, captain."

"Cute kid," I said as I sat.

"I've had cabin boys, but they all want to get glimpses of me undressed."

"Do you mind?"

She giggled her distinctive, high-pitched laugh. "Ten years ago I would've given them a show. But I'm too old and married for that anymore." The humor left her face. "But what the *hell*, Eddie? Did you see that mess?"

"Whatever did it must've made at least a *little* noise. I doubt Big Tommy just went along quietly. Why didn't somebody hear something?"

"Maybe somebody did, but they were too afraid to intervene. Now they're too embarrassed to say anything."

"Or maybe this is all a set-up to make a regular old murder look like a sea monster did it. What do you think?"

"I think for someone to strip a man down to the bone like that would both take a while and make a bigger mess. Where did all the meat go if nothing ate it?"

I had no answer.

"What do you know about the dead man?" Jane asked.

"Big Tommy? Good sailor, fair fighter. Never caused me any trouble, never did anything grand. Just always where he was supposed to be, when he was supposed to be there, doing what he was supposed to do."

"Where was he supposed to be last night?"

"I didn't assign him to the watch. Did you?"

"Not me."

"So why was he on deck, then?"

She grinned and winked. "That sounds like a question for a sword jockey to puzzle out."

"You're a sword jockey, too."

"Not on board the *Battista*."

"If I do two jobs, do I get double pay?"

"Depends on how well you do them."

"You really need to work on your motivation, Captain."

"Like you wouldn't do it anyway. You couldn't let go of a mystery like this if I threw you overboard tied to an anchor."

She had me there. Jane and I go way back, so she knew how I worked, and that I usually got results. And in this case, it was either a sea monster, or a human culprit, and it shouldn't be too much trouble to figure out which. After all, we were on a ship; the killer couldn't exactly skip town.

I went back on deck. The sun was bright and sparkled off the light chop. I looked up at the crow's nest, where Poe stood watch; we exchanged salutes. I spotted Malachi, recovered now, half-assedly gathering line. He did everything half-assedly; this was not new. But the way he glared at me before quickly looking away was, so I knew I'd need to keep tabs on him. Few things were as dangerous as a self-pitying coward.

In fact, he seemed as likely a place to start as anyone else. I walked over and leaned against the rail near him. He said nothing, but began to wind the rope more energetically. I watched for a moment before I said, "Do we have a problem, Malachi?"

"No, sir, Mr. LaCrosse," he said without looking at me.

"I disagree. I'd say a dead man with his midsection gone counts as a big problem."

He looked up sharply as he got my meaning. "You don't think I had anything to do with it, do you?"

"You seemed to have a lot of opinions earlier. You might be trying to force the issue of captain's competence by making things harder for her."

"By killing Big Tommy?"

I shrugged.

"I was just messing around. I didn't mean anything by what I said."

"That's not what it sounded like."

He stood up straight, again trying to use his height to intimidate me, but careful to hold the coiled line over his crotch. "I signed the Articles of Plunder. I understand what that means. Article 3 says anyone can call for a vote to replace the captain."

"But only with cause. Do you have any, beyond just not liking women giving you orders?"

"I'll keep my own council on that for now."

"Then how about this: tell me what *you* think killed Big Tommy."

He looked out at the sea. A whale breached, sending up a magnificent spray that made rainbows before it dissipated. Its calf followed suit with a much smaller spout. "There's a lot of strange things in the ocean, Mr. LaCrosse. A lot of weird animals, weird…beings."

"Anything specifically?"

He shrugged. "Beats me. If I knew, I'd tell you, because I don't want to be next."

"You think it'll happen again?"

"I think if it snuck onto the ship, ate half of Big Tommy and snuck off without getting caught, it'll come back when it's hungry again. Wouldn't you?"

That made sense. What would happen tonight? Would the creature—if there was a creature—strike again? There was only one way to tell.

I went back to stand beside the helmsman, my usual post when I was on deck. It gave me a good view of the deck, as well as three-fourths of the ocean around me. The helmsman, Dolly, looked up from the wheel and said, "Afternoon, sir. How's your morning been?"

"I bet you can guess."

She laughed, exposing missing teeth. "Heavy lies the head, eh?"

"That's what the head gets paid for. You didn't see anything unusual, did you?"

"Steady as she goes all day."

"What about last night?"

"Slept like an old, snaggle-toothed baby."

I left her to her job and continued my survey, which proved fruitless. When the deck crews changed for second watch, I ducked into my cabin for a quick nap. My goal was to spend third watch, when the attack must've happened, on deck.

But I didn't.

When I woke up, it was full morning again.

I jumped out of my bunk. *What the actual fuck?* I never overslept, and I never slacked off at my job. I threw on my clothes and ran on deck, just in time to see two things: Jane emerge from below deck, looking as sleep-befuddled as I felt, and the crew gathered around something just as they'd been the previous morning.

No one had called all hands, so the crowd was limited to the deck crew. And we were tacking east, right into the sun, so for a moment I was blinded. I shielded my eyes and felt Jane stop beside me.

"What the hell, Eddie?"

"Beats me. I slept through the whole night. I never do that."

"Me neither. I'd planned to come on deck before dawn."

We exchanged a look. I wasn't young, and Jane wasn't always diligent, but we were both professionals: neither of us would have overslept.

We pushed through the crowd and found another body, this time one of the long, lanky Sapphire Coast girls, Klanna by name. Her midsection was intact, but from the hips down her legs were picked bare, to the bone, including her feet, and she'd bled out during the assault. But evidently, she hadn't made a single sound.

And on the deck next to her, *two* bloody bird prints this time.

"Mikonawa," someone said, and others repeated it in murmurs.

"Okay, what's that?" Jane demanded.

A man with a shaved head covered with tattoos looked up. "On my islands, the mikonawa is the night bird. It eats the souls of the unjust."

"Uh-huh. So Klanna here was unjust?"

He shrugged. "The mikonawa knows."

"What does it look like?" I asked.

"A mighty black raven with sharp teeth in its beak."

"And it eats souls?"

"So we're told as children."

"But this ate her legs. And it ate Big Tommy's midsection."

"Perhaps their souls were in different places."

I couldn't argue with that logic. Most of the crew was on deck now, many of them yawning as if they'd also slept hard and heavy all night. I said loudly, "Hey, how many of you slept through the night last night? I mean solidly, without waking up to pee or anything?"

The entire first and second watch, and way too many of the third watch, raised their hands. Something was going on here.

Jane saw it, too. "All right, back to work. Get the body ready for burial. Gollina?"

Another of the Sapphire Island girls stepped forward.

"Are there any special rites she needs?"

Gollina nodded. "I'll take care of it."

"Thanks. Eddie, in my cabin."

I followed her. When the door was shut behind us, she said, "So except for being exceptionally well-rested, we still have no idea what's going on."

"That's not quite true. We have an explanation for why nobody's heard anything. Something is coming aboard and putting us all to sleep before picking out one of us to kill."

"'Something' like a bird? A big bird?"

"Something with a bird's feet."

"The mikonawa?"

"Unlikely. Whatever's happening here, it's not mythological."

"We've been moving constantly. Is it moving with us?"

"If it can swim or fly, why wouldn't it?"

Jane rang the bell for Nell and sat behind her desk. "If it's a creature, sure. But what if it's one of the crew trying to make it *look* like a creature?"

"Then we have a pretty smart murderer on our hands, one who can make the whole crew fall asleep before killing someone. What do Klanna and Big Tommy have in common?"

"Nothing. Klanna was new to the crew, Big Tommy has been with me since I took command. Those Sapphire Island girls don't mix with the rest of the crew much, and if they're smart, the rest of the crew don't push the issue. They poison their fingernails so the slightest scratch is lethal."

I didn't know *that* about the Sapphire Islanders, so I made a mental note to be extra polite around them.

Nell came in, curtsied, and said, "Yes, Captain?"

"Get the brush and do my hair. I didn't have time this morning before I had to go on deck." Jane turned to me. "We have to stay awake tonight."

"Yeah. Have the cook put on extra coffee."

But we didn't need it. Jane and I stayed up with the third watch all night with no trouble, and nothing happened. No one died, no mysterious bird tracks were found. Exhausted, we rendezvoused in her cabin after six bells, when the sun was up enough to count as daylight.

"That was pointless," she said as Nell pulled off her boots. "Have we outrun whatever it is?"

"I wouldn't bet on it," I said. "Maybe it doesn't attack when it knows someone might see it."

"That's pretty sly for a bird."

"Isn't it, though."

There was no activity for the next four nights, and we'd begun to believe that, horrific as it was, the two attacks were all. Maybe we'd sailed from the creature's territory, or else it had discovered another ship with meatier fare.

On the morning of the fifth day, we sighted a three-masted Outagamo schooner and gave chase, overtaking it almost at once. They put up a good fight, but once we boarded them it was short work. The captain, a surly man with a truly epic mustache, reluctantly surrendered when his defeat was clear. No doubt the image of Jane Argo towering over him with a sword in each hand, shrieking her battle cry, helped that along.

We stayed tied up to the other ship until we'd transferred anything valuable to our own hold, then assigned a crew of our own to be in charge of sailing it, and the prisoners, back to Langlade. It was decided they'd depart the next morning, when the wind would be in their favor.

I can only credit the day's action and intrigue with why it didn't occur to me that our visitor might return for the new flesh. Certainly, I should've suspected it when I woke up to a persistent bladder and realized I'd slept through the whole night again. But when I heard the deck bells frantically ringing, I knew instantly what had happened.

I was just behind Jane as we came on deck. "Report!" she yelled, and second mate Poe rushed up.

"Who'd we lose?" she demanded.

"No one of ours. But three of the prisoners, all officers, including the captain."

"On the other ship? Show me."

We swung over on ropes. The other captain's cabin was a crimson, flesh-scattered mess. The only identifiable part of the captain's body was his mustache. His exposed skeleton was still bloody and stained with bits of ragged meat. The other two men were equally picked clean all over. Apparently, whatever attacked them felt it had the time to finish, which it didn't when scavenging on deck.

"Holy shit," Jane whispered. Both of us had seen our share of death, but this was unpleasantly new.

I knelt over the captain's big leg bone. There were notches and cuts in it, like someone had de-boned him with a knife. But that would've taken even more time, or more assailants, than there seemed to be.

"Look here, captain," Poe said. A line of those big bird tracks went bloodily back and forth among the corpses.

"Our death chicken strikes again," Jane said.

"Except for one thing," Poe said. "The cabin door was locked, and I had the only key. I discovered all this when I came in to check on them at daybreak."

That complicated things. I mean, I could've picked the lock to get in, but I would've had a hard time *un*-picking it when I left.

"This is some bullshit," Jane said, seething with anger. "Poe, you're now acting first mate. Eddie, this is your sole job. Find out who or what is doing this and stop him. Her. It. Whatever."

"Aye, Captain," I said with a salute. There was a small idea tickling me, but it wasn't close enough to the front of my brain yet.

Jane departed, but I stayed to look more closely at the room. If the assailant or creature didn't go through the door, how did it get in? There were the big stern windows, but to reach them he/she/it would have to climb up from the ocean along part of the hull that curved out, meaning those claws visible in the footprints would've scraped the wood. I leaned out to check but saw no signs of anything.

The other option, of course, was that it *flew* in. After all, it did leave bird tracks.

There was a missing element here. The attacks were animalistic, as were the tracks, but the skill and stealthiness spoke of human intelligence. Was someone really going to all this trouble to frighten us? What would be the motive?

Jane had bigger problems. As she swung back onto the *Battista*, she was met by a contingent of the crew, led by Malachi. He wasted no time. "Captain Argo, we're calling for a vote to replace you."

Jane was unfazed. "Oh, yeah? On what grounds?"

"That you're cursed by whatever has been doing this killing, and it's not going to stop until you're gone. According to Article 19 of the Articles we signed, the presence of a curse or spell on the captain removes his—I mean, her—authority."

I joined her with my arms folded, trying to provide moral support. Not that she needed it.

"We've sailed together for a long time, fellas. I've personally saved more than a few of your asses from ending up under the waves. When did I supposedly pick up this curse, huh? Or did one of you put it on me?" She met every eye in the crowd, and no one, especially not Malachi, could hold her gaze. "Uh-huh. According to that same article, an actual magical practitioner has to discern the curse's reality. I didn't know we had one of those on board. Have you been holding out, Malachi?"

Malachi turned red but said nothing.

"Right. Now get back to work. Whatever's going on, we'll have it sorted out soon enough." She looked back at me and winked. "Eddie here is on the case, and nothing gets past him."

Her confidence in me was inspiring, but this wasn't an easy puzzle. Some giant flying bird with the power to put entire crews to sleep before settling in to peck away at the meat of its victims?

If I'd been on land, I could've ridden to a nearby (or faraway, for that matter) city and consulted someone smarter, a mage or a wizard or even a scribe. But here there was only me. Jane was at least as smart as I was, but she knew everything I did, and neither of us had figured this out.

But there was one question I had to ask. When we were alone in her cabin, I said, "Jane, who's the newest crew member?"

"Malachi, Delongio, Snarf, and the Sapphire Island girls all signed on before we left Langlade."

"And they're the most recent?"

"Yeah." Her eyes narrowed. "Does that simplify things?"

"Maybe. I don't think the Sapphire Island girls would sacrifice one of their own just to throw us off the scent, do you?"

"No."

"And Malachi's an idiot and a rabble-rouser, but I don't see him being involved. I don't know Delongio and Snarf that well."

"Snarf's the old man with one arm."

"Oh, yeah. Gets teased about swimming in a circle."

"But Delongio…there's nothing obvious wrong with him. In fact, I don't really know anything about him. I do know he doesn't have chicken feet, though."

Now came my biggest leap of logic. "At least, not all the time."

She looked at me as if *I'd* sprouted chicken feet. "I know you don't mean what I think you mean."

"I knew a woman who could change her appearance so quickly and drastically that she might as well have been a shape-shifting monster."

"Where was that?"

"Grand Bruan. I was there just before King Marcus Drake fell. He had a sister who hated him and could transform herself into almost anyone. Some of it was acting, some make-up, but…I don't know, it took me a lot longer than it should have to figure it out."

"So what do we do? Lock up Delongio?"

"No, but we keep an eye on him, especially at night. And we stay the fuck awake."

Which I did. The first two nights nothing happened, and if Delongio—a swarthy, stocky man with colorful beads in his beard—noticed the extra scrutiny, he didn't let on. The Outagamo ship sailed for port in Langlade to register the capture, and the *Battista* continued to cruise looking for more ships to raid.

But the third night, everything changed.

I was fully nocturnal now, sleeping all day and then wandering the deck at night. If anyone asked, I was following, with feigned annoyance, Captain Argo's orders. All sailors understand that you don't question the captain, only obey, so they nodded with sympathy.

It was a clear, moonless night with a wide sky of stars. Seven men were on deck, three of them just because it was too hot to sleep below. Delongio sat watch at the forecastle deck, bored as only a veteran can be. If he suspected I was watching him, he gave no sign. I was pretty good at following people on land—it was a basic sword jockey skill—but it was much harder to do it on a ship, where no one could really hide for long.

At some point past midnight, though, something happened.

I stared out at the glowing waves of plankton left in our wake. Above the sloshing, the ripple of sails, the creaking of wood, I heard…something else. Or maybe it wasn't above all those normal noises, but below it. It was somehow musical, a woman's voice almost, sad and keening and…

And then I woke up.

I was seated on a barrel, my head down on my folded arms at the deck rail. The sky was light in the east, and as I looked around, I saw that the half-dozen men on deck also looked as if they'd just woken up as well.

I jumped to my feet and quickly ran the length of the ship, checking on each man. Then I reached Delongio.

Or, once again, what was left of him.

This time all the skin and muscle had been eaten from the middle of his chest up. With his skull exposed, he looked surprised, as I'm sure he did when the flesh was still there.

Guess it wasn't you after all, pal, I thought, and turned to greet the frantic, sleepy sailors just catching sight of him.

Jane was not a happy captain when she found out. "I'm about tired of all this," she seethed. "I've got a mutinous crew and a monster on board. What next, scurvy?"

"Not a monster," I corrected. "A siren."

"A what?"

"A siren. A creature that sings sailors to their doom."

"But they lure them into the water to drown, or make their ships crash. They don't gnaw them down to the bone."

"Are you sure?"

"Okay, even if you're right, we're nowhere near land. Don't they sing from rocks or cliffs or something?"

"You're taking legends as facts down to the details. What if it's one of those things where there's a core truth that got embellished over time? Instead of beautiful women singing sailors to their doom, it's some creature who sings them to sleep so it can feed?"

Jane thought this over. "Then we've got one on board."

"Yeah. I think we always have. But I believe I can catch it tonight, if it comes out to feed again."

"How?"

I told her my plan. She gave me a skeptical grin. "That's not much of a plan."

"Want a better plan, pay me more."

There was, unfortunately, a more immediate problem. Malachi, despite my warnings, was still sowing the seeds of mutiny among the crew. It wasn't a majority yet, but it was growing, and I knew that one really dedicated asshole could sow a lot of mistrust in a crisis, and this definitely was that. Even now, I could see him whispering something to a deckhand who then turned to glare in my direction.

I technically might not have been first mate any longer, but it still felt like my responsibility to do something about it. So I took a page from his own rule-obsessed playbook.

I drew my sword and called out, "Malachi!"

He turned pale under his tan when he saw the sunlight glint off my sword blade (which I'd positioned to make sure he'd see that). "Aye, Mr. LaCrosse?"

I strode toward him. Other sailors stepped quickly aside. "Under Article Five of the ship's Articles of Plunder, subsection six, I charge you with fomenting mutiny and demand satisfaction right now."

He turned even paler. I knew two things about Malachi: he was a dick, as previously noted, and he was an awful swordsman. When we attacked ships, he struck with a pair of knives, usually when his opponent's back was turned. That was fine for piracy, but not so good when you had to meet your opponent face to face.

An amused crewman passed him a battered and slightly bent sword. Malachi looked at it like it was a dead squid.

"You want to challenge the captain, go right ahead," I said. "But this campaign behind her back is a coward's way, and I won't put up with it." I put my sword's tip right in front of his nose. "So let's dance and let the sea take the loser."

"N-now, wait a minute, Mr. LaCrosse," he said as his sword clanged to the deck. "I-I-I don't know what you mean, I wasn't—"

I flicked my wrist and slapped him with the flat of the blade. His scruffy beard kept the edge from cutting him. "You're right, you weren't. And you're not gonna. Subsection nine under that same article makes it clear that organizing a mutiny behind the captain's back is a plank-walking offense."

He swallowed hard. "I, uh…hadn't read that one."

"You should always read what you sign, idiot. Am I clear?"

I held his gaze for a long moment, gratified by the fear I saw in it. Then I turned on my heel and strode away. I was aware that he might use this occasion to jump me with his knives, but that would require more balls than I knew he had.

One problem solved, at least for the moment. Now all I had to do was stop whatever had been coming aboard and feasting on the crew.

We sighted a pair of ships during the day, but they were too far away and moving too fast to catch. So the crew was already irritable when it got dark and I readied myself to finally meet the monster.

I rolled up two balls of beeswax and stuffed them in my ears, muffling most of the sound. In return, I had the unpleasant noise of my own blood and heartbeat, and that annoying click when I moved my jaw. The sudden cessation of the ever-present ocean sound was disconcerting, and my brain wanted to act as if I was now on comparatively silent land, which my legs disputed. I almost had my first experience with seasickness before I got used to it.

I took a spot at the very back of the quarterdeck, where I could see the whole length of the ship. A waxing gibbous moon hung high in the sky by midnight, casting hard shadows from the sails and masts. The lookouts strode the boards, but I couldn't hear the usual creaking of their steps or nattering of their complaints. The third-watch helmsman, a young man called Kulu, gave no indication he even knew I was there.

As time passed, boredom made my mind drift. Then I suddenly realized that there was no movement on deck. A quick scan revealed that everyone had fallen asleep where they were, a few just curling up in the middle of the deck. Kulu was draped over the wheel, his body holding it on course. The wax had done its job, though; I was wide awake.

I crept forward as slowly as I could, trusting to reflex to keep me silent. Somewhere on the ship, the chicken-footed siren monster was preparing to select its dinner.

I stayed in the sails' shadows and was halfway across the deck before I thought to look up. My heart thundered like the drums at a Hortonian funeral.

Perched on the topmast boom, with the moonlight casting its shadow on the canvas below it, was an enormous bird. As I watched, it stretched its wings, shivered, then folded them back. I knew it was probably singing and, to be honest, I was dying to hear its song, but I remembered that I might literally die if I heard it and fell asleep.

The silhouette of its head was not at all birdlike, though. It had long hair rather than feathers, and as best I could make out, delicate feminine features. I'd seen some strange and unlikely things in my life—goddesses in human form, the last of the fire-breathing dragons, and even that enormous squid-creature chained to the bottom of a ship—so I could believe this was a real siren.

And I had to do something about it.

It helped my decision by fluttering gracefully down to the deck. It landed between two sleeping sailors, a young boy and a middle-aged woman. It walked from one to the other, possibly pondering the taste.

I didn't wait for it to decide.

I rushed out of the shadows and drew my sword at the same time. There was no option for discussion or negotiation: this thing had killed six people, so far, and was about to make it seven. I was in mid-swing when it turned toward me and I saw its face.

Fuck me.

It was too late. I took off its human head, and its bird body went into convulsions that sent it over the side. The head rolled toward the drain on the deck railing, but I caught it in time. I picked it up by the hair.

And looked into the startled, now-dead eyes of Jane's cabin girl, Nell.

That pretty much ended the voyage of the privateer *Battista* under Jane's command. The crew, no doubt nudged by Malachi, considered the whole thing

Jane's fault, since it was her cabin girl who turned out to be the monster. The ballot wasn't even close; I was the only one who voted for her. So we returned to Langlade, and most of the crew left. Including me.

As we watched the crew file down the gang plank, Jane tried to talk me out of it. "Oh, come on, Eddie, I'll get a fresh crew and we'll be back out in a week. It'll be fun, I promise."

"That's what you said about *this* trip."

"Well, it was, wasn't it? One more story you can tell that girlfriend of yours while you're sitting around that tavern."

"Yeah," I said, but couldn't muster a laugh. All I could think of was the head of that little girl rolling across the deck. Where had she come from? How had she learned to disguise herself? And did she really shape-shift, or did she just affect our minds so we *saw* her as a little girl? There would be no answers, though; it was just one more mystery for the sea.

"Nah, it's not for me," I said. "I'm a land crab. I do my best work on dirt and rock."

She offered me her hand. "Well, thanks for saving our asses."

I shook it. "It's what heroes do," I said with a wink, and walked away to the fading sound of her high-pitched, tittering giggle.

Caesar at Sea

Alan Smale

"The scum are still gaining on us." Gnaeus Piso closed an eye and squinted with the other, his head tilted, as if this would somehow bring the four pirate ships across the blue waters into sharper focus.

Gaius Julius Caesar, twenty-six years old and brash, shook his head. "Did you not promise me this was the finest galley to sail the Aegean?"

"Finest, aye. I hardly said fastest." His irritation clear, Piso—*navium magistri*, master of ships of their small flotilla—strode aft along the trireme's deck to bark orders to his helmsman, sail crew, and rowing master, all of whom he found more congenial than the young Roman. He had made his contempt for Caesar's soft hands and patrician manner clear before they had even set sail from Rome's port, Ostia. And Caesar was just a passenger, making his way to Rhodes. True shipmen hated *passengers*.

Gaius Caesar frowned and took stock. The three ranks of oarsmen stacked beneath them in the lower decks were already rowing at the highest pace the *hortator* could get out of them, and the canvas sails above him were straining likewise. Little chance of Piso getting more speed out of this benighted vessel by merely ordering it to be so, and the *Juno* was already pulling away from the bireme and two low cargo vessels they were supposedly escorting. The circumstances surely demanded a different strategy.

Caesar took one more look at the pirate vessels bouncing on the waves, visibly closer since last he'd looked, and stalked to the stern, where Piso was now shouting at his helmsman. This was not improving the wobbles in the

Juno's wake. The youngster looked as terrified of Piso as he was of the pirates, and the shipwright who stood nearby was glowering at the magister.

"See here," Caesar began, "this approach is preposterous."

The shipwright and helmsman now both turned to glare at *him*, and Piso merely waved a hand as if swatting away a fly.

Remembering the class of men he was addressing, Caesar changed his tone to one of authority. "Gnaeus Piso. Attend me. And you two as well." Aside from the ship's magister, Caesar hadn't bothered to learn any of their names. He didn't care who they were. He just needed them to listen. "We cannot outrun the pirates. Their ships are *designed* to overhaul fleeing triremes. You are merely exhausting our crew, and we need them to catch their breath and be ready to fight in—" He glanced back at the pirates. "—twenty minutes, perhaps less."

Piso spat. "Fight, is it? We have thirty marines aboard, and scarcely ten more of the sailors, plus ourselves. What's forty-something to their crews?"

Caesar tutted in exasperation. "This galley alone has three hundred men aboard."

"The *slaves*?"

"And our other ships?" Caesar gestured at the bireme and cargo cogs. "Another two hundred, all told?" Now he pointed at the four ships that were gaining on them relentlessly. "As for the enemy's vessels: they appear to be *hemioliae*, war galleys. Two decks. Fast and nimble because they are small. Seventy-five crew apiece, maximum. We *outnumber* the bastards."

Piso eyed him as if he were mad. "You would arm the slaves? Unchain those barbarians, they'd up and kill us all, and do the pirate's work for them."

"Not if you offer them their freedom." It was so obvious. Any sane Roman slave would take his chances and fight for his freedom, rather than be re-enslaved on a pirate ship or, if he turned on his Roman masters, become an outlaw, a fugitive.

The pirate ships were looming ever closer. "We cannot escape," Caesar repeated. "We must stand our ground and fight."

Piso chewed at his moustaches, and for the twentieth time, glanced up at the pennant fluttering atop his mainmast. "Maybe we'll yet outrun them."

"You're waiting for a miracle, perhaps?"

"The auguries were good when we set out. Fine livers, never seen better. The gods may soon be planning to smile upon us."

"Or they may be waiting for us to help ourselves. Listen: those men in hot pursuit are Cilicians. Strong men, of hardworking farming stock, but poor and desperate. They can *smell* the riches in these vessels. Such men will not tire."

"And what would a young pup like you know of it?"

Caesar was hardly young, at least in his own eyes. He drew himself up to his full height. "My father was governor of Asia." And would next have been a consul of Rome, if not for the bitter swirl of republican politics. "I myself served with Marcus Minucius Thermus in Asia, and Servilius Isauricus in *Cilicia*."

"On land," said the shipwright, as if that were all that mattered.

Yes, on land. And to be sure, that had been Cilicia Pedia, the flat Roman province in the east, not Cilicia Trachaea, the mountainous and lawless region to the west that was infested with pirate lairs, but these dunces would not know the difference. And yet Gaius Caesar had served with distinction in multiple theaters of war, even winning the Civic Crown for his actions during the siege of Mytilene, helping to put down a rebellion against Rome. "Land or sea, I still outrank you all."

The shipwright laughed in his face. "Is that a fact?"

The four pirate ships had now divided into pairs to outflank Piso's pathetic flotilla. Close enough that Caesar could pick out individual rogues aboard, see them leaning forward in anticipation, even see the swords in some hands and the bows in others.

Meanwhile, back amidships, the trireme's marines were busy donning their leather armor, while others were still appearing from belowdecks carrying sheafs of spears. Used to the metal armor, mail shirts, and large scutum shields of the land legions, to Caesar the marines looked ridiculously ill-equipped.

But they were running out of time. "I am taking control of this vessel, and those in our care. Slow your rowers' pace to allow our other ships to catch up. Hold the line and allow the men a moment's respite while we strike the sails and turn to meet the foe head-on. This trireme is heavier than one of their galleys if it comes to a collision, if we get the opportunity to ram. Then we must coordinate our forces to repel boarders—"

He had half-turned to scan the Roman cargo vessels, to ensure that their marines, too, were preparing—and so he failed to see the punch aimed at him until it smashed into his jaw. The blow sent him reeling, and he landed on the deck on hands and knees, dazed.

"Pompous shit," said magister Piso.

Caesar spat blood onto the wood beneath him and pushed himself unsteadily back up. Having struck him down, Gnaeus Piso was now pointedly ignoring him again.

In a fair fight, armed and armored, Caesar was certain that he could dispatch this villain promptly. In a brawl with fisticuffs, the result was less clear. And by the looks that the helmsman and shipwright were giving him, he could expect no assistance there.

Enough of these curs. Caesar spied the centurion that led the marines by the vine staff in his hand and the plumed helmet under his arm and strode over. "You, there. Are your men seasoned in battle?"

The centurion barely spared him a glance. "No, I won't follow your orders either. Get lost. We're busy."

Caesar gave it up. "Well, then. At least allow me the honor of wielding a sword against the foe?"

* * *

Engaging the pirate galleys head-on and with their full crews armed and ready, the Roman vessels might have prevailed, or at least made a noble stand. Overhauled from the rear and in this state of disarray, the battle was lost from the start.

The pirate galleys were indeed *hemioliae*, nimble and built for the sprint, barely larger than the Romans' bireme but much faster in the turns. They'd struck their sails and were still overhauling the Romans on oars alone. And all four ships ignored the cargo vessels—at least for now—and angled in toward the trireme.

Caesar could have predicted these tactics—kill the big dog, then bag the puppies—but nobody had asked him.

The first pirate galley came in from the rear port side at a shallow angle, smashing through the trireme's ranks of oars. Under the centurion's command, Caesar and the rest of the marines in the forward line heaved pila after pila, the heavy Roman spears, across the short gap between the vessels. However, given the heavy swell and with both vessels swinging, they scored few kills.

Next came a wave of arrows from the archers on the second galley's deck. Three of Piso's sailing crew and two of the marines went down with arrows in their limbs or torsos, and after that Caesar stopped counting the dead and wounded.

They were so focused on hurling spears at the first two attacking vessels that when the third one swooped in to ram them at the starboard bow they had almost no warning. Caesar lost his footing and skated ignominiously across the deck on his rear end, picking up splinters that would be hell to remove later.

The pirate ship bounced back and away from the impact. Its ram was blunt, its intent not to penetrate the hull but to open the trireme's seams with the stress of the impact. From the way the *Juno* wallowed and listed suddenly, Caesar could tell this objective had been achieved.

Piso still strode back and forth, bellowing orders that were undoubtedly stupid, but no one could hear him over the cries of the military men and the hoots and hollers of the pirates. The *hortator* was shouting, too. Above the din, the piper was still valiantly chirping some kind of martial tune and the drummer was banging away, setting a pointless beat that few of their oarsmen could keep time with; those slaves on the port side had likely sustained heavy injuries when the galley smashed their oars, and those to starboard must have been knocked clear off their benches by the ramming.

Resistance now was an exercise in futility. Caesar peered through the chaos, trying to see where their bireme had gotten to, and the cargo ships. The fourth pirate ship had turned to impede the bireme's flight, one of the cargo ships was ponderously attempting to flee against the wind and making little headway, and the other appeared to be going around in a circle for some reason. Maybe the oarsmen were panicking? No, Caesar saw there was some kind of fire onboard that its men were trying to put out. Had the pirates flung across a pot of burning pitch?

Caesar ducked as a large metal object flew past his head—an iron grapnel— and slammed into the deck twenty feet from him. Other grapnels were flying from the pirate ships on each side, pulling the vessels together. Wasting no time, pirates were already leaping onto the trireme's deck. The centurion and his remaining marines—ten, twelve?—rushed forward to do battle.

Caesar saw no good reason to do likewise. Instead, he backed up, sword in hand, and found Piso right behind him, similarly armed but white-faced and slack-jawed as the shock of his situation sank in. Beyond him, the helmsman's body sprawled across his rudder, two arrows jutting out of his back. The shipwright had disappeared, gods knew where.

The trireme lurched again as the second pirate ship banged into it, hauled close by men tugging at the grapnel ropes. More of the sea wolves clambered up over the bulwarks into the *Juno*'s stern.

By now the trireme's marines were all down, either slain or on their knees, empty hands out to their side in surrender. Slavery for them, then.

For a moment, time seemed to pause. From the rear boarders, a man who could only be the pirate captain stepped forward. He was dressed similarly to his fellows—rough and dirty dark tunic, boots, scarf—but he was larger and a little older, with more swagger; Syrian by his looks, and his eyes were keen as he surveyed the deck.

"My name is Ashur," he said, his blunt, accented Latin spoken in a voice that carried clear across the deck. "Order your cargo ships to heave to, and there need be—"

"To Hades with you, and a pox on all your men!" Piso screamed, and spat on the deck. "I'll do nothing you say, you scoundrel!"

Ashur blinked at him. "You are in no position to bargain."

Piso snarled and raised his sword, but Caesar had had enough. He turned and lunged once, fast and efficient, and, as his blade slid into Piso's belly, jerked it hard to the right, half-disemboweling the man where he stood. Tugging the sword free, he next hacked into the man's throat and shoved the rapidly dying magister down onto the deck.

Caesar had no use for fools, and since he obviously wasn't about to kill any pirates today, he needed to take his battle-rage out on *somebody*.

He wiped his sword on Piso's cloak, slid it back into its baldric, and stepped up calmly to face the pirate captain. "My apologies. You were saying?"

* * *

Captain Ashur was not unreasonable in victory. His terms were simple: the crews of all four Roman ships would surrender and yield up their weapons, then do exactly as they were told, on pain of death.

Neither the bireme nor the first cargo ship had suffered significant damage in the fray. The pirates would take these ships as prizes, retaining enough of the Roman slaves to row them to their stronghold. The second cargo ship was charred along its port hull and listing badly: the captive Romans would transfer its cargo onto the pirate ships. Once this was achieved, the surplus Roman crew would be cast into this second, now otherwise empty cargo vessel, and set adrift. Ashur had no need for additional slaves at this time, and no stomach for further deaths.

Caesar readily agreed. He gave the appropriate orders to his ship captains, and ensured they were carried out. By now the trireme was awash, a floating wreck, its top deck perilously close to the water level. Its surviving slaves were swimming in the waters around it or clinging to the hull, and Caesar made it a priority to fish these men out and get them warm and dry.

The cargo loading and cleanup took the rest of the afternoon, and as the sun dipped toward the horizon, Caesar was the last living man off the ill-fated trireme and its consignment of corpses. As he clambered onto Ashur's ship, he side-stepped the swarthy pirate waiting to tie him up and strode across to Ashur. "Thirsty work," he said companionably. "I suggest we break into one of the amphorae we loaded into your third hold. One with a Falernian vintner's mark, perhaps?"

Ashur looked him up and down. "Wine, is it?"

Caesar gazed out over the waves. Most of the pirate ships had already set out eastward, along with the bireme prize. The cargo cog was raising sail, preparing to follow. The second cargo vessel, overloaded with Romans and deprived of its sails and most of its oars, wallowed a few hundred yards away. As he watched, the pirates' *hortator* on the vessel he was standing on called the oarsmen to order. The drumbeat sounded, and oars dug into the waves.

"Why not?" Caesar said. "It is, after all, a fine evening on the water."

* * *

Despite his arrogance, Caesar readily recognized his own errors in judgment and worked to correct them. Aboard the *Juno*, he had not troubled to befriend those around him, due to an army man's natural snobbery against *nautas* and the knowledge that he would share their company for just one short voyage. That mistake had cost him dear. Had he impressed the *Juno*'s crew more, especially the sail master and centurion, he might have succeeded in wresting control from Piso at the very start and more effectively repelled the pirates' attack.

Now, though, Caesar made a point of learning every name he could, and being as cooperative and entertaining a prisoner as possible, while still maintaining his *dignitas* and, where necessary, tactfully emphasizing his superiority over them. Having recognized his nobility, it was understood that they would attempt to ransom him, and Caesar knew that between them, his family, friends, and *clientes* would be good for the money. His living body would be worth as much to the pirates as the cargo they'd stolen and he was keen to ensure they returned it to civilization in good working order.

They were rogues, to be sure. Coarse men of the seas and fields, and not all Cilician: as motley a batch of renegades as ten countries in the Levant could put together. But what Gaius Caesar was not expecting was how much he came to like and respect them.

* * *

"News from Rome," Ashur said, striding across the beach and back into his camp.

Caesar was still toweling off his chest and neck from sparring with Ashur's lieutenants. As all fighting men must, the pirates religiously practiced their swordplay and other battle skills while ashore, and after Caesar had baited and mocked them congenially for a few days, they'd allowed him a blunt sword to join the exercise. Initially he let them win, to put them in good cheer, but by now he was holding his own. Most of the time, anyway. "I thought as much," he said.

Ashur cocked an eye at him. "How so?"

Caesar gestured at the midmorning sun over the crags behind the beach. "Two weeks is long enough to get a fast ship to Rome and back again, with a little left over for your spies to make enquiries. And I saw the small cog that tacked into the next bay over, last night at dusk, and how you all studiously ignored it. Then you set off at dawn, alone." Caesar tossed his soaked towel onto the sand, and pulled his tunic back over his head. "It's rare that you go anywhere further than the privy by yourself."

Ashur gestured toward the wicker stools in the shade of a sail, draped over an array of stout poles, and they sat. "My spies weave quite the tale about you. One of the odder mixes I've heard, and some of it strains belief. But I'd prefer to hear it from yourself."

"Double-checking your sources, eh?" Caesar took a long swig of water. "Smart. Never trust a spy. They'll always tell you what they think you want to hear."

"Just so." Ashur gestured again. "In your own words, then."

"Very well." Caesar sipped more water and collected his thoughts. "Even though I find bragging loathsome, I shall tell it to you straight, with neither embellishment nor false modesty. My father, also a Gaius Julius Caesar, was a military tribune and praetor, governor of the province of Asia for many years, though he is now sadly deceased. My family, the *gens Julia*, traces its lineage by direct descent to Aeneas, first hero of Rome, and ancestor of Romulus and Remus." He glanced sideways. "Aeneas, as I'm certain you know, is a son of the goddess Venus."

Ashur stared. "You claim...*divinity*?"

Caesar waved his hand. "Merely a distinguished heritage. Anyway, my mother Aurelia is also of consular rank: a daughter and granddaughter of consuls, with her brothers likely to also rise to the consulship, if indeed they have not already, the elections were due...I see they have, while I have been locked away from polite society."

Ashur was nodding. "Even now, Marcus Aurelius Cotta serves as consul in Rome."

"Splendid. I despise the man, but mother will be pleased. Anyway. For myself, I am at the beginning of what I am convinced will be a long and distinguished career, unless you lose your wits and slay me."

"I'm still considering it."

"But, speaking of the gods...I have served as *flamen dialis*, high priest of Jupiter in the city of Rome—that surprises you, eh? Me, too—but it's a high honor, with some visibility, conferred upon me by consul Lucius Cornelius Cinna."

"The would-be dictator?"

"The same, but far from the most recent. Doubtless, even a misbegotten wretch like yourself is familiar with the name of Lucius Cornelius Sulla? Sorry the names are so similar."

"Of course," Ashur spat. "Sulla? Trouble."

"Trouble indeed. The latest and strongest in a line of tyrants trying to knock the lawful Republic off its perch for his own gain. I sometimes wonder whether Mother Rome can survive such continual assaults. I grew up during the Social War, when Rome was at war with itself. Preposterous. And then came Cinna, and Marius, and Sulla...but you did not request a lecture in politics."

"Nay." Ashur considered. "What think you of Cinna?"

"That...is complex," Caesar said. "And it is obvious why you ask. Your spies have told you that I am married to his daughter?"

"Aye."

"The marriage seemed strategic enough at the time." Caesar felt a pang at this casual dismissal, for he genuinely loved Cornelia, in a way that men did not often love their political wives. He missed her terribly, every day.

But, no need to reveal such an exploitable weakness to Pirate Captain Ashur. "As for Sulla, he is trouble, indeed: after marching on Rome in a far-from-bloodless coup he assembled a proscription list of his enemies and worked through them, having them slain. My name was prominent on that list, due to my association with Cinna. And so, I obviously fled Rome in preference to having my throat cut, my bones smashed, and my body flung into the Tiber."

Ashur was leaning forward. "And despite that, you still believe yourself worthy of a ransom?"

Caesar raised his hand, palm out. "Hush, man, my tale is not done. A deal was brokered. My extended family, other prominent members of the *gens Julia*, and the Vestal Virgins, all interceded on my account."

The pirate's eyebrows went up. "Vestal Virgins?"

"Long story. But as its end result, I was merely expelled from Urbs Roma, and so pursued a military career in Anatolia—Asia and Cilicia in particular—in search of further distinction, which I quickly accrued. I did attempt a return to Rome along the way, but Sulla is…unpredictable. He constantly claims he will stand down, retire, and write his memoirs of all things, then does not, and the next morning a dozen more corpses of senators and equestrians wash up by the riverside. So, off I went again. I was traveling to Rhodes to study rhetoric with Apollonius Molon when I was…persuaded to become your guest."

"Rhetoric." Ashur was greatly amused. "Explains why you talk so much."

"A necessary skill in these modern times. Anyway: Sulla is growing ancient, over sixty, and surely cannot last much longer. And once he drops dead, then back I'll go, to serve Rome in a political capacity as best I can."

"Interesting." Ashur was studying him. "Simple words, but the passion in your eyes when you say them? Daunting. I might not like to oppose you."

Caesar grinned tightly. "No. And so, your verdict? Am I worth a ransom, according to the tales from my own lips and those of your nefarious spies?"

"You surely are. A man with powerful friends, and descended from the gods, no less?" Ashur eyed him shrewdly. "I am thinking, perhaps, of demanding twenty talents of silver."

Caesar scoffed. "Twenty? Ridiculous."

"Sulla would act to prevent such a ransom?"

"By no means. Sulla is irrelevant to this particular matter, but…*twenty*?"

"Ten, then?"

Caesar shook his head. "You misunderstand me, Ashur my friend, and I am embarrassed for you. So timid an ambition? Disappointing."

Ashur blinked rapidly, which for a man of his stoic personality was equivalent to leaping up and pacing around. Twenty talents of silver…four hundred and eighty thousand sesterces? That, in itself, was a fortune likely beyond his imagination.

Caesar waited. Eventually, Ashur said: "Your suggestion?"

"Fifty."

"Fifty *talents*?"

Caesar nodded. "Let us talk tomorrow about how it shall be raised and delivered; I have already given this some thought. But, Captain: if Rome is to pay so much, you must tell me something. Share with me some further information from your network of scurrilous rogues."

"What do you want to know?"

"The latest news from Italy and Iberia."

"*War* news?"

Caesar nodded. "The best kind."

* * *

Rome was currently at war on not just two fronts, but three. Pompey, sometimes called Pompey the Great (although not by Caesar), had been in Iberia for several years, quelling the rebellion of Quintus Sertorius, and seemed doomed to remain there for several more. At this, Caesar nodded in satisfaction. "Still out of the way, then."

Meanwhile, an army commanded by praetor Publius Varinius had been assigned to put down the slave revolt led by Spartacus the gladiator. From humble beginnings—literally a kitchen revolt—Spartacus's army had grown to tens of thousands as more slaves and disaffected Roman civilians from the provinces flocked to his banner.

Finally, the long-running enmity between Rome and the Kingdom of Pontus had once more erupted into war, and this third wave of the conflict looked likely to also consume the lands of Bithynia and even Armenia. The Roman consuls Lucius Lucullus and the very same Marcus Cotta that was uncle to Caesar had been sent east to lead the war against King Mithridates VI.

Caesar rocked back, eyes gleaming. "Well, well. Isn't *that* interesting."

"It is?"

"To be sure." Caesar studied him. "The Kingdom of Pontus borders the Black Sea, to the north of the Galatian and Cappadocian regions. Cappadocia borders Cilicia. Bithynia is nearby, with the province of Asia beneath, all bound within Anatolia…"

"I know all these lands," Ashur said, with some impatience.

"Of course you do." Caesar leaned forward. "I have heard that sometimes Cilician pirates venture into the Black Sea. Is it so? Have *you* ventured so far?"

"Occasionally. Others, more so. Many among us prey on Armenian merchants."

Caesar eyed him thoughtfully. "I have heard that some chieftains in your swarthy pirate federation have sympathies, perhaps even alliances, with Mithridates and his allies? And, in addition, Pontus is a much closer neighbor, and it would surely be in your best interests to favor Bithynia, since they control the mouth of the Black Sea…no?"

The Syrian captain was shaking his head with some vigor. "By no means. Those Pontians are cowardly scum, and too chummy with the Parthians for our liking. Pirates will take Mithridates' money, but he gets precious little for it. More to the point, their ships offer rich pickings." He looked almost apologetic. "Roman ships are more often our victims, as you must know, from your navy's frequent attacks upon us."

"And yet…Rome buys your slaves."

Ashur ducked his head. "Just so, and often the Roman senators themselves are, well…" He rubbed finger and thumb together.

"Bribed."

"Sweetened."

"Well, well," Caesar said again. "You're not Rome's natural enemy after all, then. And how much less urgent would Rome's ardor become if you ceased to attack their ships altogether?"

"Well, that's not about to happen."

Caesar waved that away, as if Ashur's response was of no importance. "As you say. Anyway. What is the going rate for fighting men, in these parts?"

"The what?"

Caesar leaned closer. "Ashur, my friend, my question is simple. How many ships and mercenaries might fifty talents of silver buy us?"

* * *

As all good deals are, this one was simple. Caesar would raise his own hostage money. Fifty talents: a fortune. Twenty of those talents for Ashur and his crew, after which they and all other pirates would consider Caesar a free man, but he would neither depart for Rome—after all, he was still at considerable risk, there—nor continue on to Rhodes.

No, Caesar would stay at sea and…reinvest the other thirty talents in Ashur's business enterprise, so to speak.

More precisely: his ransom money and the inducement of future rich pickings would buy Caesar a pirate fleet, with himself as commander and Ashur as his admiral.

Next, Caesar and Ashur would set out to convince the Cilician pirate fraternity to leave Roman vessels strictly alone. But the ships of Mithridates of Pontus, and his allies? Open season on those.

If Caesar could help to win one of Rome's biggest wars where even Rome's consuls were failing, as a free agent, and resolve the Cilician pirate issue at the same time, well: certainly he could write his own ticket for his political future in Rome.

The fact that he'd be sticking his thumb in his uncle's eye, and another much more important thumb in Sulla's, would just be an added bonus. With a bit of luck, Sulla would be so angry that his heart would fail. For that matter, it would also be thumbs in the eye to Crassus and Pompey, Caesar's main competition for any real power in Rome in the future…

He was going to run out of thumbs.

"It's perfect," he said. "Gods willing, within five years, we might finally vanquish Mithridates and win a war that Rome has been fighting for nearly two decades. I will enter Rome as a hero. And you, my friend, will be a very rich man."

"Unless," Ashur said darkly, "we're both dead."

* * *

Six months later, as the sun blazed down on the deep blue waters of the northern Aegean, five trading ships of Pontus attempted to flee from a pirate fleet almost twice their number.

The contest was unequal. The six nimble hounds of the *hemioliae* danced around the traders, nipping at their heels and bombarding them with arrows. The three larger vessels, a trireme purchased with honest coin and two biremes captured in skirmish, were the bulls that would come in at the end to gore the trading vessels and finish this.

Aboard his new trireme, Caesar watched the unfolding scene with a keen interest. He had signal flags ready to hand, to be hoisted up the mast at need, but he did not think he would need them. Their victims today were not well-trained military, and there would be little need for a fine-tuned capture strategy. Ashur and his men knew their business, and it was a pleasure to sit back and watch them set about it.

Indeed, such was their fearsome reputation by now that three of the traders struck their sails and surrendered without a fight, thus ensuring their crew's lives would be spared—though not their liberty. The smallest of the remaining ships, Ashur ruthlessly demolished with a firestorm of burning oil from the right and left, turning it into a blazing torch. Corralled by the biremes and taking fire, the largest cargo vessel fought on until Caesar ordered his trireme to thunder through and ram it.

He braced himself and, at the moment of impact, gave a shouted command. The giant Roman corvus spike dropped and slammed down into the deck of that Pontian vessel, locking the craft together and providing a wide boarding ramp for his pirates to stampede across onto the enemy ships.

Today, Caesar himself did not join them. Today, it was only a Pontian fleet, fat and rich and of little real challenge. He would watch from his captain's chair as the work of mop-up and plunder proceeded, sipping water and wine and taking quick notes on a wax tablet with a stylus.

It was much more satisfying to be the hunter than the stag, and even more satisfying to sit and dramatize such hunts with evocative and politically-tuned prose.

* * *

Cornelia Cinnae boarded the pirate flagship *Caesaris Fortuna* just after sunset, off the rocky western coast of Crete. Despite the evening warmth, she was trying not to shiver, from apprehension as much as the dusk breeze.

Caesar stood as she was ushered into his cabin, his heart beating even faster than it did during naval actions, and stepped forward with much less certainty than he did up on deck. "My love. Welcome to the *Fortuna.*"

Kastabalan, one of Caesar's lieutenants, who had guided Cornelia thus far, bowed and backed out of the room. Before the door had even closed, Cornelia fixed him with a look. "Too busy to come and greet me yourself?"

"I rarely leave the ship. Given the steepness of Sulla's bounty on my head, not to mention Mithridates…" He shrugged, affecting modesty.

"Not even awaiting me on deck? Thus leaving me to wend my way alone through this den of thieves?"

"Upstanding men around you, one and all. Thieves, certainly, but I trust you were in no way insulted?"

"Some muttering, only, by persons unidentified," she said. "I overhear that I am bad luck aboard a ship, by virtue of my sex."

"*Nautas.*" He lifted his hands. "Sailors are the same everywhere. They'll get over it."

His back was as ramrod-straight as her own. As if, after two years, neither knew how to react to the other. He swallowed. "And how is my daughter?"

"High-spirited. Runs everywhere. Breaks everything, just like her father." At his blink of surprise, Cornelia added, "She *is* five years old, now."

"I suppose she would be. And…what of matters in Rome?"

"Good grief, Gaius, you idiot." At last, Cornelia's face split into that infectious grin he loved so well, and she spread her arms. "For heaven's sake, come and kiss me."

The tension thus broken, they both strode forward eagerly, and collided rather than merely embraced. There was kissing, then, and more than kissing, and the latest scuttlebutt from Rome had to wait a while longer.

* * *

"A life of piracy seems to have treated you well." Her hand drifted across his bare chest as they lay on his cot, limbs still entwined.

Tenderly, he pushed her hair back from her eyes. "I suppose the sea air is quite brisk. Healthier than the miasma of Rome, I'll be bound."

"Ah, Rome." She cocked an eye at him. "You are, of *course*, the talk of the town, to a quite nauseating extent. I, your mother, and many an ambitious senator, have seen to that."

"And my Commentaries are being read?" After the first year, Caesar had sent his *Commentaries on Naval Warfare* to Rome, along with a bag of Bithynian gold to subsidize their copying and promulgation. They described his military successes in lavish detail.

"And reread. Sulla initially banned their publication, you know, and tried to have them destroyed—"

"Oh, Gods."

"—which obviously helped a great deal. Resistance to his tyranny continues to increase. He talks of retiring six times a year now instead of merely twice. Anyway, in addition to the scrolls, I ensure that details of your adventures are regularly read out in the Forum." She looked at him sideways again. "I lately heard that in addition to your seagoing exploits, your rogues have sacked and plundered Amisus?"

"Ami*sos*." The Pontic coastal city went by its Greek name. "And also Kotyora?"

"Ah yes, that one, too. Such a funny name. And after racking up quite the Pontic and Parthian death count, your fleet had to fight its way out of the Black Sea through the Bosphorus and Dardanelles to safety."

"Just so," Caesar said, satisfied. He had, of course, greatly exaggerated all these exploits when he had written up the details, but there was a kernel of truth to most of them.

"Your exploits are entirely eclipsing those of Lucullus, in his efforts on land against Mithridates. And people say that his successes were only possible because of your dominance of the seas, and occasional plundering forays ashore."

Caesar half-grinned. "How gratifying."

"And you are now insufferably rich?"

That was true beyond any shadow of a doubt. But he just waved self-deprecatingly. "I have not done too badly out of it all."

"Splendid. For I have quite expensive tastes, you know."

He nodded. "And Rome knows that not a single Roman vessel has been attacked by Cilicians for nearly two years?"

"Yes, Gaius."

"And that seven months ago, when a fleet of Roman grain vessels came under attack by the forces of Pontus, my ships came to their aid and forced the raiders to retreat?"

"Yes, yes, yes, Gaius; everybody knows everything." She looked at him thoughtfully. "There is one thing that *you* do not know, though. And I am uncertain whether to tell you."

"Because?"

"Because it may lead to trouble."

"Good trouble or bad trouble?"

"A matter of definition, I think."

"And for me, or for Rome?"

"Those are exactly the right questions," Cornelia said. "There is…a certain man, who is requesting your assistance. Though, it is possible he has misunderstood your motives." She put her finger under her chin, rather endearingly, feigning deep thought. "Or, or: perhaps he merely knows you better than you know yourself. Even though the two of you have never met."

Not Crassus, then, nor Pompey. Not that either of them would demean themselves by asking him for help. "Enough riddles, Cornelia. What man?"

"A fighting man, rather uncouth." She smiled, sphinxlike. "A man whose name makes the whole of Rome tremble."

* * *

Two months later, and before Caesar went up on deck, Cornelia stopped him. "Gaius…my father was a revolutionary. A man of ridiculous ambition and lust for power."

Caesar nodded. "He was, at that."

"And it killed him, in the end." She studied him. "Perhaps it was too much to hope that my husband would not have the same ambitions."

"And the same lusts," he said, slyly.

"Do not flirt," she said somberly. "Not right at this moment."

"Very well." He looked her in the eyes. "Would you wish it differently? Is this the wrong path? Because, if you disagree…?"

"No." Cornelia took a long, deep breath, and patted him on the arm. "This is the right path. I am certain of it. I am certain of *you*."

Caesar's hand covered hers. "Thank you, my love."

* * *

A meeting at sea, forty miles south of the boot of Italy, at noon. Cunningly arranged after a long back-and-forth of messages, requests, refusals, further negotiations, and finally, terms and conditions. Trust was hard to come by under the circumstances, for either party.

But after all that, when the small trading cog came alongside the *Fortuna*, and Spartacus himself shinned up the rope ladder and hopped over the bulwark with conspicuous agility, he came alone.

A fighting man indeed, a warrior's warrior; his shoulders and chest rippled with muscle. Caesar himself was tall, yet Spartacus topped him by several inches, and wearing sandals rather than Caesar's sea-boots at that. Caesar was fair-complexioned, though now tanned from his life on the ocean waves, while Spartacus looked like what he was, an olive-skinned barbarian, a Thracian of the Maedi tribe.

Caesar was patrician, of course, and Spartacus merely a gladiator of the most common stock imaginable. But it was difficult not to feel daunted by the man. Especially as he now led an army of somewhere between seventy thousand and a hundred and twenty thousand rebels that had already crushed Roman armies led by Varinius, Gellius, and Lentulus, and was currently leading Crassus's legions a merry dance.

And so, Caesar bowed to the man. "*Salve*, Thracian."

The man cocked his head. "*Salve*, Piratus."

Caesar glanced past him into the merchant boat. "No entourage, I see?"

"Do I look like a man who needs one?"

"You do not."

"I was promised safe passage."

"And you did not even demand hostages," Caesar murmured.

Spartacus swept his gaze across the *Fortuna*'s deck. "I'm assuming that wasn't a mistake."

"By no means. Just a friendly suggestion, to bear in mind in the future."

By agreement, Caesar's nearest pirates were forty feet away and not visibly armed. And Caesar had no doubt that even with just the knife at Spartacus's belt that appeared to be his only weapon, the Thracian would be able to take down any number of pirates before snapping Caesar's neck and leaping back into his boat.

"I plan no treachery. I'm interested to discuss your proposal. Will you sit? I can have refreshments brought."

Spartacus remained standing. "You already know it. Help my army give the slip to bloody Crassus. Ferry us over to Sicily. We can pay, of course. Once we're there, more slaves and citizens will flock to our banners. Bulk up my army even further. Then we'll stand a chance."

Caesar, a good judge of character, already had little doubt that Spartacus would be able to hold Sicily against Crassus, unless the Roman general had truly overwhelming force. "Your ultimate goal, then, is to march on Rome?"

"Only if I must." Spartacus shook his head in frustration. "We are not all agreed. Some of us want more plunder. More destruction. More of the mad life we already have. Others, me included, would be happy to just get away. Lead those who want to go up North, into Gaul. Disappear. Farm, or...I don't know. Just make a new life where I never have to see any bloody Romans again." He cleared his throat. "No offense."

"Small ambitions, then," Caesar said carefully.

Spartacus stared. "Yours are larger, sitting out here in your boats? And you're saying what, exactly: that you'd *prefer* me to march on Rome?"

A blunt man, this Spartacus. A man who said exactly what he was thinking, with no honey added. Caesar rather liked him. "My motivations must be clear by now. I am furthering Rome's struggle against Mithridates. I have amassed a considerable naval force and used it solely in Rome's defense and to the detriment of both Pontus and Parthia. I have entirely eclipsed the efforts of Lucullus and my uncle in this regard."

"All right. So what?"

"So, you should not imagine that I do not love the Republic."

"While hating Sulla."

Straight to the point again.

"I hate no man," Caesar said. "I merely need Sulla to die, ideally in as painful and humiliating a way as possible, so that I can go home as well."

"You'd give up all this?" Spartacus said ironically, waving around him. "Can't quite see you going off to farm."

"Oh, I'm certain my military life will continue. I've developed quite a taste for it."

Enough dancing around. If this Thracian could be direct, so could Caesar. He took a deep breath, realizing that he was…afraid of Spartacus's ridicule?

Well, out with it. "I propose that we join forces."

That rocked Spartacus. He recoiled, then looked Caesar up and down once more. "What?"

"Listen, man: however far you get from Rome, do you really imagine you will ever truly escape it?"

"Maybe."

"No. Rome will pursue you to the ends of the earth. You must win, or die in the attempt." Being direct was rather fun. Caesar might get used to it. "And, while Sulla clings to power, the same is true for me. So. Let us win this together."

Spartacus's brow furrowed. "I don't get it. What do you suggest?"

Obviously, still not direct enough. "I command eighty thousand pirates, with a taste for plunder and high living. You command a further hundred thousand, let us say. Both forces have proven their valor in countless battles. And so, let us fight side by side. March on Rome. Kill Sulla and lift the iron hand of his despotism. Bring back order to the Republic."

Understanding dawned. "And power for yourself?"

"Of course. Consul permanently, I should imagine. The precedent has, after all, been set. And equal power for you as well, should you desire it. You could not be eligible for a consulship, of course, but there are other ways." He paused. "Though based on your words, power and authority are the matters furthest from your thoughts."

Spartacus just grunted.

"At a bare minimum, freedom and a pardon for you, and all who fight with you. Land grants, perhaps. Good Roman farming country. Your troops would need to stop raiding Roman towns, though." Caesar considered. "Then again, might that faction amongst you who love the fight want to raid in the East, instead? Anywhere in the Levant, really. Parthia, even? Hispania, or the North? Who do you hate as much as Romans?"

The Thracian looked at him. "No one. Uh, no…"

"No offense, yes, yes, I understand."

"And yet…" Spartacus gazed out over the waves, considering. Caesar waited patiently, also looking out over the sea. From here, he could almost see the coast of Italy. Almost.

He cleared his throat. "Well?"

Spartacus's eyes swung back to meet his. "You offered me a drink, before, yes?"

"I did."

The gladiator nodded slowly, then finally sat. "I believe I'd like one now."

Of Scourge & Skulduggery

E.J. Delaney

It sounds glamorous, being a pirate. Me, I'm in it for the money, and perhaps the endorphin hit of pulling off the perfect raid, but I reckon two of the crew are glam-bangers. That's Ryder, our siren, whose moniker is a shout-out to Winona Ryder; and Bago, the counter-suggestive, also a WR-derivative (via the portmanteau 'Winonabago'). Ramdolf is another who might lean that way, but her life off-ship is spent mostly in the gloom, so it's hard to tell.

The rest of us? Shrug. We're the usual hodgepodge of misfits and loners—as glamorous as gout, probably. Truth is, I don't know them that well. They come when Kurohana calls, and when the job's over we go our separate ways. Doc l'orange has a real-world practice somewhere. Tats is a barkeep over in shanty. Dee, I think, earns her crust as a martial arts instructor. Or maybe a garbo? The details fade, like everything unrelated to the work. I write you these notes and stopper them up inside empty rum bottles. (If you're reading this, Z., then either I'm dead or I've dosed too much on the Dutch courage.)

Glamorous? Hardly. But the coin is good and the life runs hot in my veins. I'm first mate on a schooner whose exploits are whispered in back-alley dives and corporate palaces from Antwerp to Zamboanga, from Zurich to Abidjan. Buccaneers "R" Us, Sis. I know you'll have long disowned me, but perhaps you can be a little proud, too—if not of what I do, then at least of how well I do it?

Evidence those new e-spruiks with Kennedy ♡. (Symbol for a last name? I'd pucker me a second hole if not for the picto-branding in 💀 *Duggery*.)

Cheesy as all get-out! But a vegan actress scoffing up roadkill? Doesn't that make you wonder?

Well, Z., you need flabber your gast no more. Have a tot and I'll talk you through it…

* * *

"Amber, report."

The voice in my earpiece is gruff yet precise, which is Kurohana's trademark (never more than three syllables, articulated in wood-grained kanji). I know I won't be able to make her out; still I let my gaze rove across the restaurant. The crew are at their stations, remarkably unobtrusive given the refined backdrop. Dee and Tats scrub up well as waiters. Krull is tucked away in the kitchen. Ramdolf stands out a little, but then she always does, blinking and ill-at-ease in the real world. She's sufficiently awkward that we can pass her off as Doc's teen phone-twiddler.

"All set," I murmur; then, to the open channel, "Monday, eyes peeled."

"Ha-effing-ha." Monday gives me the finger, pushing in the vicinity of her meta-glasses.

"Figuratively speaking," I clarify.

"Figuratively speaking, you can park your tailbone on a steam whistle."

Monday, it's fair to say, is the other person who looks somewhat out of place in five-star surrounds. A blind goth-girl with punk-collar guide dog? An actual panda bear would hardly raise more eyebrows. And yet, attention slides off her. It's the uneasy juxtaposition, I suppose: on the one hand, young impaired female; on the other, widowed corpse bride with trimmings of extreme violence. Experience has shown that she can go pretty much wherever she chooses. Ocular deficiency notwithstanding, she's proven herself the perfect lookout.

"Eyes peeled," I repeat. "Nostrils diced; ears cauliflowered: it's all the same to me."

"Tongue basted?" Bago suggests.

Hashtag barks, a restrained *ruff* that I hear both through my earpiece and from across the room. Monday reikies the peach fuzz on his crown.

"Go for it, Winnie B. Hash says he'll rip your balls off. Also, lobes on the target: two o'clock, thin as a twig."

I check the window reflections. Sure enough, Kennedy ♡ is on her way in.

"Ryder, last call. Ramdolf, are we prepped?"

"Manifestation queued, components in alignment."

I switch to Kurohana's private channel. "All systems go, Captain."

"Proceed."

"Hoist the mainsail," I tell the others. "Ready the hooks."

The Maître d' leads Kennedy to her table. As per the dossier, it's a secluded, lonely-looking affair: lunch for one, setting for two; an unfulfilled fantasy born of childhood rom-coms and suppressed rainbows—too much investment in her heteronormative screen image. She skims the menu, orders without taking it in.

We launch the *Duggery*.

Like all vessels of its kind, the ship appears out of a misty nowhere: first the keel, then the hull and decking, printed in ethereal layers cascading from Ramdolf's phone. Once the quarterdeck is instantiated, there follow the bilge and bulkhead, the bowsprit, masts and rigging. Each copy is unique to the mission at hand, each iteration purpose-actuated within a rippling metagestive field.

Additional aspects code themselves congruent with the crew: gunports by Dee; scuppers alongside the Doc; a forecastle extending beyond the swing doors to where Krull scrubs crockery. The one inconsistent feature is the locked cabin from which Kurohana issues her directives. This nags briefly at my awareness—that it should exist in want of its progenitor—but then the pixel fairies darn helm and rudder around me. The rigging shifts; Monday is revealed glowering down through jibstays, gaff and boom, glassy-eyed atop a mezzanine crow's nest. Hashtag's tongue lolls in a phantom squall.

Oblivious, the restaurant staff go about their business. The customers, too, evince no awareness of the shadow play we've unleashed; the niche reality-show playing out in their midst. While Kennedy 💟 drowns herself in carbonated melon juice, we of the *Duggery* bob and roll upon superimposed waves, the configuration set to exemplify our subliminal tinkering, but for now just a test of our sea legs. Ramdolf hauls on the virtual halyard until the pig-stick tops the masthead, unfurling a flag that only we can see.

"Manifestation realized. Subcon overlay confirmed."

"Ryder," I order, "you're up. Let's give the people what they want."

The people, in this instance, being Kennedy 💟's talent agent, a bottom line–feeder slyly covetous of the burger endorsement thrice offered and as yet twice refused by her client.

"Aye-aye," Ryder acknowledges. "Clear the deck. Bat-ten your pantaloons. Prime-grade rumptydooler coming through."

The raid goes like clockwork. Ryder approaches from Kennedy's blind spot, pacing the deck, promenading; gusting by in a heady first impression of nautical shorts, sandals, cropped blouse, and pixie cut. Even as she moves beyond reach, she falters on the half-step, turns, fixes Kennedy with the full, fleeting force of the goddess Androgyna's coy regard—just a glimpse, a partially formed smile stillborn in its intentions. Her expression is at once open and contrite, wistful with longing, as if to mark what could have, might have, should have been in this Sliding Doors moment.

Then she about-faces. Not a word! Just a doubling-down on the vacillation—a hitching of her clutch bag, adroitly orchestrated to expose the burger tattoo in the small of her back—before whisking herself away, the breeze of her passing turned salty with regret.

Kennedy half stands. She's hooked, hesitant.

"Got her," Ramdolf announces.

And there it is. A second ship has ghosted to life in our meld: a shapely little sloop, two-sailed in watermelon pink, drawn from Kennedy's neural telegraphy. Its tantalized ki rides high in the meta-field.

"Ryder," I direct, "once more, with feeling. Tats, Bago, reel her in."

Finessing the flow, Ryder slows, stops. She has come to a glass-tanked crossroads, no less a slave to destiny, it would seem, than the doomed lobsters agitating within. Kennedy wavers, herself teetering on the verge of motion.

For an instant, the permutations lie perfectly balanced. Then Ryder initiates a collapse. She breathes deeply; the *Duggery*'s sails billow in perceptual accord. Then, catching Kennedy off-guard, she squares her shoulders and strides for the door. The sloop yaws. It surges on a synaptic swell, telltale of Kennedy's heart as she hurries forward, tacking frantically from potential to action, forsaking her table. Too fast, she—

Slam! Tats collects her on the corner. Ornamental fern fronds scatter. Dishes erupt from upturned palm and wrist. Kennedy sprawls across Bago's table. From breaking free, pursuing with reckless abandon, suddenly she's folded prostrate in too-close proximity to an overdressed, over-jowled beta male, her face planted in a marinated white-bean salad (the stricken vardøger of her own order).

"Stage two," Ramdolf confirms. "Contra-suggestive latched and holding."

It's a flawless grapple. Force and counter-force draw the sloop near. Kennedy struggles back to her feet, casting about, babbling apologies; fending off Bago's understanding, his overtones, his off-putting and distinctly hetero not-*Ryder*-ness.

We give no quarter.

At my command, Dee swings aboard the sloop. That's what it looks like through the meld, anyway. To anyone without Ramdolf's embedded tech, she merely deposits a gourmet burger—so placed as to evoke the once-glimpsed tattoo—then sets to work with napkin and murmured assurances, sopping up bean chunks. Kennedy shudders. From the giddying highs of the swell, it's a dumping comedown: salad up the nose; Bago, bland and bloated, buzzing *in situ* like a half-swatted fly. Her desperation snags upon the burger. Associations shift, transforming it from food object to commemorative icon (the missed chance, the branded loss), coloring the endorsement offer with shades of yearning.

Tipping the balance.

As the scourge plays out, Dee steers Kennedy toward the restroom— running the gauntlet past Monday, whose unseeing appraisal constitutes the pitiable yet also somehow judgmental, scare-induced "what-if?" cherry on top. (Monday, I've found, acts like a blunderbuss to the head, accentuating a mark's helplessness then implanting the impulse to *do something*—if not here, then *soon*. I message Kennedy's agent. She'll re-float the deal first thing this afternoon.) Acquiescence catches; Kennedy hiccups. If she can't have happiness, what use are her principles?

The sloop bobs deep now in the doldrums of the meta-field, its colors struck, mast bare; its crew of one submitting to the fate we've decreed. Hashtag lets out a mournful whine.

"Cleaved to the brisket," I affirm. "Where there's prey, there's pay, ladies."

I take a swig of grapeshot. Satisfaction spreads warm across my chest: job done, raid notched—burger endorsement all but secured.

Ramdolf nixes the meta-field. The *Duggery* fades and takes the sloop with it, back into the now and nether. As the subliminal overlay dissipates, I find myself faced with the specials board. My vision fills with looped flourishes of chalk: macaw-colored cursive declaiming, *moula, moula, moula!*

* * *

Sometimes when I set my thoughts down like this—here in my one-bedroom above the Suds & Duds, riding the churn of a dozen coin-fed tumblers—I picture you here with me, Z., arguing back, playing devil's advocate.

Why chase after treasure, you chide. *We had all we needed, Amber: allowances, godmother trust; inheritance in the offing.*

"True," I'll admit (my voice more tangible, if less steady than your scribbled echo). "But money's just a way of keeping score. Those things I said I'd do— standing up for Mother Nature, bringing down corporate marauders; holding the bastards accountable—well, just wait until Kurohana hangs up her tricorne. The *Duggery* will be mine soon—her crew, the industry contacts. I'll have the clout to take whole companies to Davy Jones!"

And in the meantime, what, you're a petty fixer? A gunwale for hire?

Disappointment smolders in your eyes, reflecting my own features in miniature: false worship; pacts betrayed.

"Don't look at me like that."

But you let loose a frown censorious beyond your years.

Why the actress, Ambs? What happened to you, that all you can pitch me is a backroom swindle, even in letters you're too cowardly to send?

Your Komodo dragon gaze falls upon the shelf at my back. I feel the weight of emptiness there, the rum bottles marshalled but not yet discarded.

What aren't you telling me, Amber?

* * *

The day of our thirtieth raid dawns red as a pomegranate. I'm up early, running contingencies, ironing a plaid pantsuit with flared trousers and plunging neckline. In the shop below, a lone washing machine grumbles its way through bilge-sucking overtime. My earpiece spits to life.

"Amber." Kurohana spares just the one kanji for preamble. "Report."

"Prepped to embark, Captain. The 'x' limits us to sloop capacity, so I've stood down Doc and Monday."

"Prognosis?"

"Unimpaired, at least so far as securing the swag. Two bidders, in-person only." I tilt the iron back; it emits a dissatisfied snort. "So long as our intel's on the mark, there shouldn't be a problem."

"Cons?"

"Well, we're left vulnerable. Restricted access, no full schooner." I push at a wrinkled uncertainty. "But that's just egg for the omelette. If it has to be now, we don't have much choice."

For an inscrutable second, Kurohana doesn't respond. Then she carves out her customary edict:

"Proceed."

Her sign-off is half kiai, half sanction. A westerly chill seeps into the laundromat and up through the floorboards, its premonitory ache lodging in my bones.

We've been commissioned by Hanakuro Pharmaceuticals to attend today's auction at Porter's and ensure that lot number twelve—an Inuit shaman's hood fashioned from walrus pelt—falls to their representative. What they want it for, I can't imagine. Nor why they'd anticipate two other parties setting to in the thick of the bidding, battling with dainty paddles. (Chief Executive Oneupmanship, presumably.) In spite of our diminished crew, the job should be straightforward: manifest the *Duggery*, jimmy the hammer-fall. Yet, something about it brushes at my neck hairs.

Propitious as a red-headed wig, I mutter.

But the time for Jane Austen has passed. I've taken the down payment, vouchsafed the raid. Qualms or no, we can't back out now.

Double-checking that the iron is switched off, I don my steam-infused pantsuit and make for the helm.

At first, everything goes to plan. Krull doubles for Monday, sporting the credentials of a Tribal Historic Preservation Officer and tucking herself away in a discreet alcove up back of the punters. Ramdolf and I pose as PAs (for

Bago and Ryder respectively). Dee and Tats are still on-books with the catering company, so Ramdolf has hacked the roster to have them circling amongst the clientele, tuxedoed and anonymous behind trays of rose cuvée and moneybag hors d'oeuvres.

We blend in, consult the catalogue, cast the occasional bid. Bago feigns interest in a Danilo Donati gold-trimmed Ming the Merciless costume, only to catch the fever and almost blow his wad dueling mano a mano with a serious collector. Tats curtails the frenzy by sidestepping a feigned collision and elbowing him in the back of the head.

"Bago," I warn, "stop dicking about! Ramdolf, are we prepped?"

"Queued and aligned."

"Stand by."

I check our position against those of the Hanakuro Pharmaceuticals man and his two rivals. Bago and Ryder sit square in their eyelines.

Our strategy is simple: Ryder, having spent the morning foreshadowing her siren effect with stolen glances and micro-flirtations, will bid early. She'll feign dismay whenever a non-HP bidder gazumps her, approval when they refrain. Even as she drops out of the race, she'll up the ante, fostering the Hanakuro rep's bids. Bago, meanwhile, will hitch his counter-suggestive wagon to the non-HP bidders. His unpalatable desire for them to win, plus their own burgeoning preference for Ryder, should clear the decks for a successful raid.

Such, at least, is the theory. Practice, in this case, proves less than perfect.

"Sold!" the auctioneer proclaims.

A virtual jukebox strikes up, all sultry down-shuffle and brass moxie. Lot number eleven, comprising Nancy Sinatra's sequined minidress and boots from her 1966 "Made for Walking" music video, walks itself off into someone's collection.

"Raise the mainsail," I instruct. "Hooks at the ready."

"Ki-scourge initiated," Ramdolf acknowledges.

Lot number twelve is unveiled: one shaman's hood, tatty and tusked in the downlights. As the auctioneer begins her spiel, our private second reality mists to life and the *Duggery* takes form: hull, keel, bilge, poop deck; rudder and rigging. No crow's nest, though, and no scuppers. We're not at full complement, and the ship reflects that.

"Manifestation complete. Subcon overlay confirmed."

"Complete" seems something of a misnomer, given the absence of captain's cabin and half the quarterdeck. We're limping more than fearsome, but we've still the heft to latch-and-grapple the non-HP bidders.

We launch, simultaneous with the auctioneer.

"What shall we say then?" the woman coaxes. "Inuit aficionado or John Lennon wannabe, let's start the bidding at fifty gold pieces, with me…"

No sooner have the marks' lifeboats shimmered into being—two sleek corporate jobs, set adrift in Ryder's direction—than the raid turns to albatross soup.

Monday would have snarled us due warning. She'd have smelled, heard, tasted trouble; *felt* the disaster coming. Hashtag, bless his floppy ears, would have growled his disquiet well before the maggots emerged. But Monday isn't here. She and Hash are off on a bender somewhere, or whatever the equivalent is in Monday's worldview: shanty-town life drawings, probably, in spray-paint on brick. Krull is our lookout, which, in hindsight, was like bringing a cutlass to a cannon fight. I'd have been better off leaving Tats behind.

Or me.

The crux of the debacle is that there's a third bidder, a rogue element we haven't accounted for. She springs her ambush with minimal fuss, sweeping her hair loose and raising a paddle lacquered in sleepy-eyed disinterest. She wears tan suede and a seductive, tomb-raiding expression.

"Who *is* that?" I demand. "Krull?"

"N—nobody," Krull stammers. "I mean, she's not in the dossier. All she's done is sit there and look around."

"Until now!"

The lady flaunts her paddle again, winks at Ryder. A nasty idea starts muscling in on my prefrontal cortex.

"Ramdolf, scan for—"

"Venn incursion!"

Ramdolf's yelp is loud enough that I don't need the earpiece. She fumbles her phone. Somewhere behind us, a champagne glass hits the floor.

Another ship has sprung to life! Unlike those engendered in a mark, this is a full-fledged brigantine, all square-rigged sails and apple-on-black pennant, projected atop the *Duggery* and competing for virtual spume. Oppugnant meta-fields register, react, take rambunctious issue with each other, our meld rocked by the crackling kiss of proximity, if not the resultant tell divulging who, among the auction's attendees, might be crewing the interloper. The name *Forbidden Fruit* smolders at its prow.

The auctioneer crooks an eyebrow. "Madam is perhaps enamored of a rival house's listings? Returning to the matter at hand…"

All at once, my mind is a jellied terrine. Amongst the pirate fraternity, the *Fruit* isn't so much a legend as a short-fused, powder-keg bogeyman: First Gen code-riders who robbed the real world blind and retired with their spoils to live lives of perfect revelry. The word at Taverners is that they dust off their bandanas only at nostalgia's beck or when New Generation upstarts encroach upon their territory. Any raid too fixated on glory, any crew grown too big for its britches, risks courting the *Forbidden Fruit*.

Superstition, I've always thought. But now—

"It's the *Hubris*…" Ramdolf intones, part awed, part disbelieving. That she refers to the ship by euphemism speaks to how much she's been thrown off-kilter. "I can't shake them. They've got us in a Bermuda Reuleaux."

"Keep trying," I order. "Bago, Ryder, stay the course. If they jag the walrus pelt, we're up Pinniped Creek."

The auction rumbles on. It's a lurching affair now, the bidders' lifeboats heaving this way and that as both ships try to latch-and-grapple them. My gut rolls in sympathy. It's my first raid sans Kurohana's direct oversight, and everything's gone pear-shaped!

How is the *Fruit* even here? We had difficulty enough conjuring a sloop, yet they've snuck in the crew to manifest a brigantine?

I cast about, striving to identify the captain. Is it the auctioneer; the woman in suede?

"Tats, find out who's jinxing the marks. Dee, same with our guy. Take them down, understand? Tray to the brachial; garotte them with your dreads; whatever. No holds barred."

Sloughing all pretense, Dee and Tats ready themselves for combat, eyes and bodies straining at the bit. But they've no clear target. There must be another siren in the room, and a counter-suggestive to trump Bago's impact; but whoever they're masquerading as, our FF counterparts are good. Monday might have sniffed them out, but without her we're sailing blinder than blind.

Taking on water. Losing the battle.

"Going once at five hundred…"

The brigantine fires its guns: a seven-cannon broadside that rocks the *Duggery* and sends us staggering. Our grapple ropes slip free.

"Krull, where's it coming from? Who's running them?"

But Krull can't answer me. When we search her out afterwards, we find her slumped like a voodoo doll, a broken champagne flute stuck deep into her neck. It's like stumbling upon a freshly congealed Pro Hart: dead eyes and desperate hands; O-neg rose cuvée clotted where she's tried to staunch the bleeding.

"Going twice…" the auctioneer cautions.

Ramdolf confirms: "Ki-force failing. We've lost subcon. Reverting to the now and nether."

We fire a salvo of our own—Dee in impeccable beatdown—but it barely amounts to a spite check. Obscured in her nook, Krull is bleeding out; and I've brought us here without the Doc. The hammer falls. We're dead in the water.

"Sold, to the Lady of Autumn!"

* * *

When first I took residence above the Suds & Duds, the machines would keep me awake—so far from home, the boundless horizon compacted like scrap metal, squeezed into a space no larger than our guest bathroom. I'd toss and turn through the early hours, anything but lulled by the slosh and grind and tumble belowdecks.

Nowadays, I can't sleep without them.

Silence, it transpires, is its own form of keelhauling. Pills don't help, and there are times late at night when the washers run dry and the dryers lie starved of jocks and socks. In the aftermath of the Inuit shaman's hood fiasco, I purloined one of the old DR35s and had Bago and Dee lug it upstairs for me. It squats now next to my rollout mattress. I drift off staring into its porthole, feeding it coins from my nightmares.

We went to Krull's funeral at Saint Nick's, all of us save Kurohana. It was mainly just her mum and brothers, and people from her day job, none of them in on the side-hustle. I had to invent some guff about a book club, to which Ma Krull nodded and said *that explains the Robert Louis Stevenson tattoo*. Her voice was so bleak, I felt like jumping down next to the coffin and letting them shovel on dirt two-for-one. Hashtag gave a piteous, snuffling grunt; then Tats, in deference to my book club angle, improvised some Jim Hawkins. Monday lobbed a black rose onto the russet heartwood.

Abandoning Krull to the worms, we withdrew to Taverners for a liquid send-off. Shots at half-mast. Wordless, clinkless toasts.

The thing is, Z., we're on the hook for the botched raid. (*Dishonorable*, was Kurohana's assessment, phlegmatic as ever but drawn beyond the three-syllable limit. She's given the client their money back, but that's just the first step toward making amends.) As per the Code, our next job for Hanakuro Pharmaceuticals will have to be gratis: whatever they ask for, full commitment. And come what may, we'd better deliver.

Do you remember in the nursery, Zadie, how we used to play Ludo, and our own special version of Squeak Piggy Squeak? And how I couldn't bear losing? The trick, I've discovered, is to choose your game carefully. (That's two years' wisdom right there: ninety-nine bottles of rum on the wall. The ultimate tot-à-tête.)

Now, though, it seems there *is* no choice.

I've put the word out for a new cabin boy. (Between cycles of the DR35, I wonder what we even need one for; but then, if we *didn't*, what was Krull doing at the auction?) Our reputation took a hit at Porter's. Still, I've had a few nibbles. One girl in particular looks promising. She's a bit like you, Z.—same set to the jaw, same duck-in-jodhpurs prominence of backside. I don't know if that makes me want to take her aboard or send her packing.

"Glutes" she calls herself, which at least means she shouldn't be as *gluteless* as Krull. (Gallows humor.) I'll vet her with Monday, I guess—uncanny ratification, plus a lick from Hashtag. Then I'll have her sign the articles.

Brine of Jerusalem, my head hurts. One more job. One last raid until I've served out my agreement and Kurohana hands over the *Duggery*. One final reckoning.

I know I'm only talking to myself, but give Lady Susan scritches from me, won't you, Z.? Spill a shandy on the patio.

Whatever luck you can conjure, we've dug a hole deep enough I doubt you'll ever be able to fill it.

* * *

Our penitence raid takes the *Duggery* beakhead-first into uncharted waters. It is equal parts audacious, bold, and cunning; delusory and egregious; foolhardy in the extreme. The tale, no doubt, will grow in the telling, but even at base level I can't quite believe what we're attempting.

Ten minutes until Butterbiscuit gives his speech. That's Cormorant D. White to his friends—career Republicrat and soon-to-be Governor of Westmont. As he accepts that great honor, yada-yada, blah-blah-blah, we're to latch-and-grapple not *his* emotions but rather those of the voting faithful, sublimating their support into a fanatical, consumeristic embrace of HP's shiny new placebo pill. There are 1,500 people in the live audience, hundreds of thousands more tuning in online. If we pull this off, we'll render the *Forbidden Fruit* as old-hat as Abe Lincoln.

And it *should* work. For all that can go wrong, the metagestive odds stack up: first a dose of counter-suggestion—cutaways of the defeated candidate; tears from Bago, hobo-like and nursing a week-old lettuce—then a switch-to-siren with Butterbiscuit triumphant; Ryder in irresistible closeup, her dress a silk-wrapped pennant exhibiting the black hellebore flower of Hanakuro Pharmaceuticals. While Cormorant leads the national prayer-to-orgasm, we'll implant a craving strong enough to suck billions into HP's coffers.

"Monday," I prompt, "how's it looking?"

"Dark," she growls. (Her face is stony behind Ray Charles metas.) "Very dark. But it *smells* like a rosewater pity party."

She and Hashtag are stood with a little boy in a wheelchair, near enough to Butterbiscuit's own children that the cameras show glimpses of them whenever they hone in for the wholesome family shot.

"Impediments?"

"Bodyguards, SS crew. Nothing we didn't taste coming."

At which Bago affects a sorrowful contemplation of his Boston Bibb:

"Alas, poor Yorick! To have known her, Horatio..."

"Stow it," I snap. (If nothing else, I've grown brusque enough to succeed Kurohana.) "Ramdolf?"

"Queued, aligned."

She's posing as Doc's daughter again, three rows back and slouched over her phone as the preliminary speakers go about their prattle. (Doc, apparently, is not without influence, having been called upon early in the campaign to nip an embryonic scandal in the bud.) Dee and Tats are in the press corps. Ryder hangs off Butterbiscuit Jr.'s arm, her pennant dress hidden for now beneath a long coat the hue and luster of eggplant. Glutes is filling in as harried dogsbody to one of the campaign high-ups.

I click to Kurohana's private channel. "Shipshape verified, Captain. We're ready to launch."

"Proceed."

At her terse go-ahead, I cue Ramdolf for action. We're in position, meta-field defined but not yet activated, the *Duggery* champing in the next paddock over.

Montrose Hall stirs on its piles. The MC throws to Haisley Hickenlooper, Cormorant's horse-ranch running mate.

Timing is everything. I've analyzed Hickenlooper's campaign speeches, every quirk of body language and oratory. In consultation with Ramdolf, I've raked over the entire recorded history of gubernatorial introductions in the states of Westmont, Brask, and Floribama. The trick will be to instantiate the *Duggery* in advance of Butterbiscuit taking the stage, yet late enough in the piece that we can carry off the raid before State Security weighs anchor.

"*…we kept faith!*" the lieutenant governor-elect asserts. "*And tonight, Westmont has spoken—clearly, firmly, and with purpose…*"

My pulse twinges, thick with misgiving as I gaze upon the assembled Cormorphants. When I took to the flintlock and cutlass, it was to seek reparations; forcing those billionaires to walk the plank who preen and primp on other people's misery. Yet here I am, prepping to fleece an already well-shorn, gormless flock. It's the Code, I know, and the means to an end, but even so.

"*…I am prouder still of the man I now have the privilege of introducing…*"

I catch a flash of tan in the crowd. It's only a waning A-lister—a grizzled old method actor too set in his ways to switch garb for the canyon-red, diamond-blue argyle—and yet my throat hitches. I think back to Porter's and the mystery bidder, the *Forbidden Fruit* firing point-blank into our midsection; to Krull, six feet under, flute-shivved for profit.

"*…Cormorant D. White doesn't traffic in outrage. He doesn't chase applause. And when Cormorant D. makes a promise, he keeps it—even if no one is watching…*"

I crane my neck for any sign of Kurohana. She must be here somewhere, a ki-actuator around whom the *Duggery* will take shape. I know I'd feel better if I could spot her, just this one time. There's Doc and Ramdolf, Tats and Dee; Monday, Hashtag; Bago and Ryder. But—

"Looking for someone?"

The whisper in my ear—no, from just *beside* my ear—is girlish and familiar. I jerk to port and aft, muting the earpiece.

"Glutes? Joseph's tits, we're about to launch! Get back out there, before we manifest a galley at the helm!"

"This is wrong, Amber."

She peers at me, slightly wide-eyed. Memories of adolescence come flooding back—dreamy teen slumbers routed at cock's crow and bounced into submission by a one-girl horde of indomitable sisterliness.

I blink hard. "Zadie?"

It can't be her—you. I mean, you're all I've thought about these last two years (back at the family home, finishing your studies) but there's no way you could have followed me; no way, even if you did, that I wouldn't have recognized you.

She's a ringer; that's the only explanation. An almost-lookalike weaseled aboard to distract me from—

From—

"*…and belief in our common future, that I present to you the next governor of the great state of Westmont…*"

"Mary, mother of Mayhem!" I unmute my earpiece. The channel is awash with queries, curses. I look to Ramdolf and find her wriggling about, near wetting her pants trying to pick me out over her shoulder. I cut through the babble: "Go! Go! Haul anchor!"

"About time," Monday grouses. "What were you waiting for? A telegram from God?"

"Stations!" I reiterate. "Bago? Ryder?"

"Ahoy," Ryder checks in. "Dolled up and ready for rig-running."

Bago lets his jowls sag. "'I was at the Butterbiscuit raid,'" he prophesizes, "'and all I got was this lousy lettuce.'"

Fake-Zadie grabs me by the scapula. "You don't want to do this, Ambs. It's obscene! Maid Marian and Sheriff of Nottingham imposter porn." She shakes me with real vigor. "This isn't you!"

I think back to our childhood. Maybe she's right.

But what I am just now is a pirate. I'm first mate on the ☠ *Duggery*, her hull and bulkheads rolling out from where Ramdolf sits; her deck, masts, and sails borne on invisible mists.

Ryder sheds her coat. As Butterbiscuit crosses the threshold, she glides forward and links her arm through his. Jilting Cormorant Jr., she escorts the governor-elect to the rostrum. Mrs. D. White stiffens but her husband has no option. He waves kinship to the audience, embarks upon his speech. Ryder takes a chaste step back, fading maybe five per cent into the shadow of his limelight; the rest is pure siren allure. Though not the focus, her pennant dress and hellebore flower round out every frame.

"Metagestive overlay implanted!" Ramdolf heaves a sigh of relief. "Counter-suggestive minimal but holding. Hooks on the primary L-and-G."

"*...for your fierce integrity. I could not ask for a better ally in the work ahead...*"

Fully deployed, the *Duggery* is a sight fit to giddy the chandeliers, not that anyone save the augmented can see her. She skims over unperceived whitecaps, bowsprit dislocated (evidence one errant cabin boy), but her ki nonetheless majestic, lashed like Gulliver to a fleet of Lilliputian dinghies and rowboats—drawing them closer, suborning each captain to fly the flag of Hanakuro Pharmaceuticals.

"Call it off," Fake-Zadie urges. "Those placebo pills? There'll be deaths, Amber. Old biddies chucking in their meds for a one-pop party trick."

"*...who would show up, who would listen, who would lead. And I am humbled beyond measure that your answer was...*"

"Here they come," Monday warns. "Slow and Steady, on the move."

Ramdolf *thocks* her tongue. "Venn overlap confirmed. We've got a three—no, a four-master. State Security colors. The *Texas Angel.*"

This isn't unexpected. Even the most starry-eyed SS captain couldn't help but notice us ploughing into their meta-torial waters. Still, it does momentarily knock the wind from my sails. The galleon is enormous: a bombastic, dread-inducing mishmash of lateen and square rigging; of shrouded masts and swivel guns; cannon like shark teeth. As the ship bears down, its grim-faced crew fan out amongst the crowd.

"Tats, Dee," I warn. "Incoming. Ramdolf, ETA on captivation?"

"With this many grapples, who knows? A couple of minutes?"

"Roger that." I'm not sure we can hold out, but it's bullion or bust. "Bago, Doc, buy us some time?"

"Aye, will do."

Doc rises to an apologetic stoop and begins squeezing her way past knees and feet, her hair a flaming match head. Bago, born to such legerdemain, commences a restless lobbing of his lettuce—up and down, higher and higher, making himself a target.

"Aye, aye, always with the eyes..." Monday bends over Hashtag, stroking and patting him as if muttering half in Morse. "We'll just stand here feeling pretty, shall we?"

Fake-Zadie clicks her fingers at me.

"Ambs, snap out of it! Can't you see? You're not in control." She hits me with the stare again, same as when I was sixteen and she thought I'd gone gaga for Lucas Penry. "It's Hanakuro Pharm. Has been all along. Hanakuro; Kurohana. Hellebore; the Black Flower. Come on, Amber, that's not even subtle!"

"*…to the folks who didn't agree with me on everything—but saw enough in this campaign to give me a chance…*"

Cormorant drones on, and I'm there in Zadie's eyes: gray as goose-feather where I trace my own silhouette. Beyond, Tats and Dee barrel into the first rank of Texas Angels. We fire off our cannons. The galleon lurches, returns fire.

"What—are you saying?"

"I'm saying there *is* no Kurohana. You're a puppet, Ambs—in bed with HP and being suppositoried up the Jack Sparrow! Don't you get it? *You've been raided.*"

My stomach twists. "No…"

"First job out, subliminal broadside. The *Duggery* was your ship, but you lost her; lost yourself. I knew something was wrong when you stopped writing home." She shakes me some more. "Raided, Ambs! And ever since, you've been dancing a blaggard's hornpipe, monkeying about while the organ-grinder cranks your handle."

The mixed metaphor is Zadie all over, but it *can't* be her—you.

Raided? The *Duggery*?

Up on stage, Butterbiscuit continues smarming to the converted. The hubbub at his feet has drawn some attention but nothing, as yet, that can't be attributed to high spirits. Off to one side, Doc calmly chloroforms one of the Angels. We fire our guns. Someone tackles Bago.

"What—organ—grinder?"

"The captain, of course. So-called. Jeepers, Ambs, last time you were this out of it, you'd just spooked Willoughby and gone headfirst into the paddock gate." Her face swims in triplicate, mimicking yours from when I came-to that day. "Amber, you have to cut loose; sever the ropes. Take the helm back! Listen to me, Sis: *there is no Kurohana.*"

I don't believe her. I'm first mate; she's just the cabin boy. We're raiding the governor-elect's acceptance speech, a State Security galleon bearing down on us. Pilate's panties, Krull *died* last mission. What Glutes says can't be true—or I'd have spent the last twenty-four months with a spectral fist up my second eyepatch, parroting, puppeted, betraying everything I stand for.

"Who?" I manage.

"Monday."

I don't believe her.

Bago is down now; they have him in a chokehold. Butterbiscuit throws in a joke, his words reassuring as the crowd cranes its collective neck. The Texas Angels swing, cutlasses between their teeth, from one ship to the other. Cannons puff. Dee and Tats put the hurt on.

Monday, a turncoat? A blind Machiavelli bluffing, gruffing it out, tugging on my strings; setting us up?

I don't believe her...

"Look at me, Ambs."

...but I do believe *you*. Even before you drop into my lap, wrapping your arms around my neck and claiming, "Squeak, Piggy, squeak!" Before I switch to the captain's private channel and demand, "Monday, report!" and it's Monday who bites back at me, not in jagged kanji but with her usual skunk-spray. I *know*, Little Sis. I know that you are you; that I've been living a scourge. I feel the grapple lines hewn deep into my flesh.

I know what to do to free myself.

* * *

There was a limerick; do you remember, Z.? In that ratty old book I picked up at the Willow Creek jumble sale. (No cover, no frontispiece, but chock-full of tales and treasure maps; snippets too thrillingly salacious for prude-raised teens.) I read it so many times, the pages would fall open there, my thumbprint marking the tannin. You said it was disgusting, but I still caught you checking it out a few times—five sordid lines scrawled across the printed text as if by a libido-starved castaway:

There once was a pirate most ugsome,
the vilest of slubberdegullions;
she scuppered her ship
just to suck on some dick;
going down, thus she drowned in high dudgeon

It's funny, don't you think, the extent to which chance discoveries—random little influences—can shape the course and currents of a life? How, spared only for charity, that filthy ditty in its binnable trappings could lodge and take hold (a kind of suppressed *idée fixe*)? How prescient it would prove? How, in the space of a moment—in the hallowed chamber of Montrose Hall, no less—such a verse might recrudesce in glorious, buccaneering counter-refrain?

How a girl once lost might dare reappropriate her dreams?

* * *

"Change of plans," I declare, muting Monday from the open channel. "Ramdolf, where are we on entrancement?"

"Eighty-four, eighty-five per cent. Eighty-six…"

"Belay that, if you please. Ryder, Bago: Opposite Day, maximum prejudice. It seems HP have been buggering us sideways. Let's repay the courtesy."

"Sure—thing," Bago gurgles. "Just—the one—snag…"

"Dee, get Bago clear. Tats, full sail on the diversion."

"Aye-aye."

"What about me?" you ask.

I cast narrowed eyes to Monday. She's hanging the jib, fiddling with her earpiece. I hail her directly:

"—day," I rasp, pulling the old faulty connection caper. "—wrong with… hear me? I'm—…Glutes with…—ment…—you copy?"

Then I turn to you. "Ask Doc for the postscript. Kick to the head, Z. Teach that treacherous dungbie a lesson."

"Aye-aye, Big Sis!"

With a grin half Christmas morning, half trick-or-treat, you scamper off.

Puckfoisted no longer, we re-rewrite the raid.

"…*I don't mean slogans on bumper stickers. I mean honesty. Dignity. The right to…*"

It's pure pandemonium now, but less spongy, somehow, than any previous 💀 *Duggery*. The overlay shifts around me. The captain's cabin re-forms. For the first time in two years, I truly take charge.

First, the distraction: Dee goes roaring after Bago, dreadlocks wild as she wrestles him free of a Texas Angel. Heads turn. Tats sucker-punches a second Angel, steals her aubergine cloak; points an accusing arm at Ramdolf:

"There! The insurgent navigator!"

Ramdolf jerks in her seat. Pouncing on her reaction, a dozen vengeful Angels swarm the aisle. Butterbiscuit carries on:

"…*to my wife, Lydia, who bore this campaign as surely as I did, your love is my—hmmmph!*"

The sentiment is hard to maintain, in part because Ramdolf is now being dragged away, struggling like Gollum to keep hold of her precious decoy phone. (The real one is built into her shoe. "They missed it," she'll tell me, "by *that* much.") In part because—

Ryder kisses him. Even as Cormorant D. preaches the importance of family values, she steps up, HP logo to the fore, and molds her body to his, locking lips, consummating the siren's call. Their smooch sends ripples through the metagestive field—an outraged contra-suggestive linking Hanakuro Pharmaceuticals once-and-for-damning-all with infidelity and betrayal.

Butterbiscuit pulls away, but only briefly. Ryder sheds her pennant dress. She tears it loose (revealing a lace corset and little else); hurls it to Bago before lunging in for a second, more lustful kiss. Bago, who has himself been stripping, dons the dress over his Y-fronts, then scoops up the Boston Bibb and hurls it, insult to injury, straight into the face of Mrs. Butterbiscuit.

"Counter-suggestive by two," I murmur. "Now, let's stick the landing…"

The dinghies, I note, are being drawn close to the *Duggery*, their ki bound by our deplorable new latch-and-grapple. There'll be no sales upsurge for HP's placebo pill, no nefarious black-rogering of the market. That ship has sailed, sunk.

But the raid isn't over. We may have thrown Hanakuro the stink pot, damn near holed them; but there's still positive energy to be harnessed, our escape to manufacture…

I reach into my bag, fingers curling around the cap gun I've smuggled past security. (Resin and acetate, shaped like a spare hair-clip. The scanners didn't bat an eyelid.) I bare my teeth to the wind.

"Now, Zadie!"

You've grabbed the pepper spray from Doc. With near malicious glee, you skip up to Monday, pluck loose her glasses and let her have it. I brandish the hair-clip blunderbuss, leap onto my seat; pull the trigger: *bang, bang—bang!* Three shots, barrel to ceiling. Bittersweet smoke wafts up around me. Doc cracks the fire alarm.

Ramdolf gasps: "Captivation at—one hundred—per cent!"

The crowd stampedes. Montrose Hall voids its bowels: Republicrats, press; the Texas Angels and the boy in the wheelchair (A-lister propelled); Haisley Hickenlooper and Butterbiscuit Jr., all the rest. I watch as Tats trips one of the cameramen, purloining his Two-Eighty, redirecting its feed. As we crest the subliminal wave and sink back into the now and nether, the abiding image imprinted on a slack-jawed, grappled populace is of Monday, eyes streaming, an apparent innocent left abandoned in the exodus, floundering, groping blindly for Hashtag.

I allow myself a hangman's smile. *Simon says don't be a patsy, Amber.* I'm back in command, my ki liberated, raid reclaimed. The *Duggery Redux* has struck her first blow.

Little black pills? Not on my watch.

If I'm reading the room correctly, guide dog donations are about to hit a new high…

* * *

…and so, to the now and nether, in the dead of night back above the Suds & Duds: we come full-circle; the story, thus told, bites its own tail.

What next? you ask—two simple words, but as full of love as any brace of syllables can be. I bask in their glow; in your presence. The last rum bottle sits between us, emptied to its dregs as we toast my autonomy, the renewal of our shared history; the downfall of Monday, Kurohana, the Black Flower in all its iterations. Your ki enfolds me where for so long there's been only shipwreck.

"Well," I consider. "First of all, new digs. I'll miss the rough and tumble but it wouldn't do to just let them come for me."

You nod. My duffle bag is packed, the DR35 unplugged. Hashtag lies stretched out at my feet, his nose pointed at the door.

And after that?

"Oh, you know…same old shizzle and grift. There's mistakes to right—two years of misspent youth to undo—but I think the crew will stick with me. They're good eggs at heart; up for the fight."

You proffer a salute that would cheek the pants off a monkey.

Glutes, reporting for duty, suh!

I should tell you no. What's coming won't be safe, not by a long shot. As your big sister, I really ought to send you home. But then, we've seen how that turns out. Might is right, and the corporations still rule Brutannia: HP first and foremost, but a hundred more; a thousand. That part of the plan hasn't changed.

Resist their raids. Respond in kind.

Pillage. Plunder. Wield my ki like the pirates of old.

"Cabin boy, eh?" I brush an insolent curl from your forehead. "Well, I dare say some deck-scrubbing would do you good."

Black-spotted dick it would! I was thinking more first mate. You know? Seeing as how the incumbent's got her hands on a tricorne?

"Compromise," I offer. "We're short one lookout. Pay negotiable, Labrador included. Must have experience pulling the new captain's chestnuts from the fire."

You twist your lips in musing regard, drop your chin toward Hash.

Dog's tempting.

"Us against the world, Z. All the fat-cat rump that's worth kicking. What do you say?"

Fine, you concede, and a shaft of moonlight catches upon your feral little incisors. *But only until we tear them a new one the size of Pandora's Box.*

I cradle my glass, envisaging a ki-tulip of loss, growth, and resolve.

I think of home, of comfort; of Ma Krull and burials at sea, the endless wash of bitter placebo. My heart gives a heavy flap—from deepest despair, the Jolly Roger set to unfurl. I tell you:

"Deal."

The Judgment

Violette Malan

"I find there is insufficient evidence to convict the crew of the *Sea Dancer* of piracy."

"You're telling us they're not the pirates?" Vont Degler closed his hands into fists so tight his nails dug into his palms. He didn't hear the murmurings around him over the sound of the blood pounding in his ears.

Emlin Starhand, the Mercenary Brother hired by the Lesonika city council to sit in judgment on this case, lifted his silver-gray eyebrows. "No. I am telling you there is not enough evidence to convict them of piracy." His narrow smile said he wasn't sure he was being understood. "For a conviction, I would need more evidence." He stood, signifying the judgment was over.

"So, if these aren't the pirates, then who is?" Degler didn't see who had asked the question, but he was glad someone had.

Starhand stopped and turned back, flipping his gray-streaked braid back over his shoulder. "You could always hire me to find out."

Degler took a step toward the Mercenary. "What if—"

"Softly, softly. People are looking."

Degler tried to pull his sleeve out of Zoew Illkie's fingers, but his first mate only tightened her hold. He pressed his lips together and said no more. She was right. This was not the place to draw attention. No one argued with a Mercenary's judgment, though Degler could see unsatisfied faces in the watching crowd.

"That's it, Cap'n. Let everyone else go out first. Relax."

This time Degler did yank his arm away. She wasn't his mother. Telling him to relax. What next?

"It's a disappointment," Zoew said as they walked into the nearby tavern. "But not altogether unexpected."

Degler threw himself into a corner seat while she signaled for the waiter. "What does that mean?"

Zoew shrugged and lowered her voice as the waiter approached them with two mugs. "We didn't manage to get the 'evidence' on board." She smiled at the waiter and tossed a coin on the table top. Of course she was right. If they'd been able to get some of the goods they'd stolen onto the Nomad ship, that would have been all the evidence anyone could need. Their security was just too blooded good. "We should have known a Mercenary Brother would be scrupulous," she added.

Degler grunted. Sure. That was why people agreed to use them as judges: no one more impartial. "If it had been the council…" he shook his head and took a sip of his beer. But no, he thought, grimacing. The ale tasted more bitter than usual. Half the council were merchants, unwilling to try the Nomads for piracy because it might endanger trade, and where would they get their oh-so-precious fressian drugs then? Spineless simpletons. With a Mercenary House in the city, it was easy to get them to take over a chore no one else wanted.

"Someone's been paid off," he murmured. He wondered if he could get a rumor started.

"You saying a *Mercenary Brother* accepted a bribe?"

"No, of course not." He hated it when Zoew looked at him as though he was stupid. "All I'm saying is, someone on the council got paid to back out of the hearing, to hand things over to the Brotherhood."

All his careful planning, useless. He'd found people were willing to believe the Nomads could be pirates, but clearly it wasn't going to be so easy to have them convicted. No point in relying on courts, or mainlanders. No he'd have to do this himself. There was more than one way to teach those blooded Nomads a lesson.

"I'll have to put an end to them myself," he said. His mate didn't answer. "You disagree?"

Zoew looked at him steadily in that way she had. Finally, when he was beginning to lose his temper, she spoke. "No, of course not," she said. "You're the captain."

* * *

Sonra Lor slammed the door of her cabin and threw herself down on her bunk.

"Temper."

She glared at her husband and first officer, but when Paden only lifted an eyebrow, she took a deep breath. Without a Crayx in the Midland Sea, she couldn't tell what he was thinking.

"This is so frustrating," she said, and even without a Crayx she knew he felt the same. "Thought all we had to do was get back to the ship…"

"What did the wine merchant say to you?"

Sonra gritted her teeth. She'd thought the hard words and harder looks thrown at them in the streets were the worst that could happen. "Oh, took his cargo, what he'd ordered anyway. Then it was all 'We'll talk later, when all this is blown over and the pirates are caught.' Expect others will say the same."

Paden nodded. "Idiots. If don't make new orders why would we come back?" He stood and stretched, pushing his hands against the ceiling of the cabin. "At least no one tried to stop us from leaving. The Mercenary's judgment did that much for us."

"Not sure that's a good thing." Sonra sat up. "Who's doing this to us? Who would accuse us of piracy? Long Ocean Nomads have been trading with landsters for generations, always had good relations—" Or so she'd thought.

Their reputation was gone, stolen from them just like goods stolen from a ship. And maybe even harder to get back.

* * *

"They're leaving on this evening's tide." Zoew told Degler. Only one or two of the Nomad's regular clients had put in new orders. The Nomad's status—whether they were pirates or not—wouldn't be as important to these merchants as a steady supply of the drugs they needed for their businesses.

"Heading where?"

"Stanisun is supposed to be their next port of call."

"Through the Canakal Narrows then, farthest end of the Midland Sea."

"What are you thinking?"

"If they never come back, what will people think?" Degler watched Zoew's thoughts shift over her face. He saw her get his point.

"Everyone will be sure they're the pirates," she said, "getting away while they can."

"Exactly. So, the first order of business," he told his mate, who watched him with careful eyes, "is to get to Stanisum before them."

* * *

"There's a boat coming out to meet us."

Sonra shielded her eyes. This was unusual. Stanisun wasn't even in sight. "Weapons ready?" She touched the *garwon* she wore strapped to her leg. They had to be prepared when travelling without a Crayx.

"It's Macedin Haraanot, though don't recognize the boat." Paden lowered the farseer he'd held to his eye.

"Fine and good," Sonra said, relieved by this appearance of a regular customer. "But why come out before we've told him we're here?"

She and Paden waited at the rail until Haraanot pulled up alongside in a two-man pleasure yacht painted a startling scarlet. Sonra signaled for the boarding ladder to be lowered, but the old merchant waved it away.

"I will not be boarding," he called. "I am here only as a friend to warn you not to approach the city. Turn around and flee while you still can."

Sonra's stomach sank and she gripped the rail.

"What's going on?" she asked the merchant.

"Two days ago, a Captain Degler came ashore with news of the trial in Lesonika. How the Mercenary Brother who was a judge did not declare you innocent, but only said there was not enough evidence to convict you. Degler said that everyone respected the Brother's decision, but they all knew you were the real pirates. I tell you as a friend, the law is waiting to arrest you as you come ashore. Better you do not enter the harbor at all. If you enter the city, you may not be allowed to leave again."

"Who's this Degler?"

"His ship is the *Far Voyager*. A small trader, but he is well enough known that people are listening to him. A few of us have spoken for you, but not as many listen to us as listened to him."

"We thank you for the warning," Sonra said formally. "Wait a moment, and we will give you your cargo." It was a small enough thing to do considering what the man had saved them from. Though when the small chest was brought up on deck, she had second thoughts.

"Will having this get you into any kind of trouble?"

Haraanot had a murmured conversation with the younger man helping him. "I do not think so," he said after the other man had nodded. "I told people I was going for a sail with my son, and now we will run back in and tell everyone that we have seen you. No one will suspect us."

That was good strategic thinking.

"But tell me, how can I get a message to you to let you know it is safe to come back?"

Sonra exchanged a look with her husband. Even unable to speak mind-to-mind he would know what she was thinking. Paden nodded. "We have a House in Navra Port." Sonra swallowed, hoping she did the right thing revealing this. Could they be putting their landlocked kin in danger? "A message there will always reach us."

Paden watched their client sail away. "Degler. Means nothing to me. Ask among the crew."

Sonra rubbed her face with her hands. "Why do this to us?" She looked up at Paden.

"Could it be someone we no longer trade with? Disgruntled clients?"

"It couldn't be—never heard of this man. And besides, who would go to so much trouble?"

* * *

"What's old Haraanot saying?" Degler knew the man, even though he'd had no business with him himself. Zoew looked over her shoulder at the merchant standing with his son in a circle of dockside hangers-on.

"He says he saw the Nomad ship just this side of the Narrows, but it wasn't heading into port."

Degler couldn't believe it. What had changed their minds? "Then we've got to follow them."

"But we don't know where they're going."

"They're going to Navra—they always go there. We'll overtake them. Now."

Zoew followed him to his cabin, where she found him sitting with his head in his hands. "Cap'n, just why are we doing this?"

He lifted his head. "Is that what the crew is asking?"

"No, Vont, it's what *I'm* asking." She so rarely used his given name it was serious business when she did. "The crew's happy as long as we make money." She sat and pulled the cork from the bottle of beer on the table. "But I deserve to know."

Degler nodded. "They tried to keep all this from me."

Zoew frowned and poured them each a mug of beer. "What, exactly?"

He gestured around them. "This. The ship, the sea, the crew. My life. They tried to keep this from me."

"How?" She took a sip, watching him as he relaxed and picked up his own cup.

"I was one of them once. The *Nomads.*" His nose wrinkled as he said the word. "They put me ashore when I was eleven. Just sent me away, after I'd lived my whole life on board. I'd never even stood on land before."

"But why?"

Degler hesitated. "They told me I was a bad fit. *I* didn't fit in. *Me.* I was a child. This is what I was born for—do you know a better sailor?

Zoew shook her head. "So, this is revenge?" She needed to stay calm. *He* needed her to.

"You might say that." He took in a deep breath through his nose and let it out through his mouth.

She nodded. "I can work with that. But what about the crew? In case there's talk."

Degler smiled. "There's an easy answer. Remind them the *Sea Dancer* hasn't been able to offload much cargo. Think of all the goods that could be ours."

She left grinning. That was something the crew could get behind.

* * *

Zoew's fear that they wouldn't catch *Sea Dancer* before she entered the Narrows proved to be correct. According to some fishermen they found catching barbudos, they were at least a day behind the Nomad ship. Once through the Narrows and into the main body of the Midland Sea, the wind was against them, blowing sporadically through the Herculat Strait as winter approached. Degler wasn't discouraged, the wind would be against the Nomad ship as well, and his *Far Voyager*—lighter and faster—sailed particularly well against the wind.

Two days later the lookout finally sighted the distinctive pale green sails of the *Sea Dancer*. By this time, the massive rocks of the Herculat Strait itself were almost in sight.

"All hands on deck. Take your stations. Let's see how well they sail when we take out a mast."

* * *

"That's the *Far Voyager* all right," the lookout said. "Saw it in Lesonika harbor."

"So, *these* are the people who accused us? Still doesn't tell us why."

Sonra lifted her face and narrowed her eyes. "Wind's dying." It normally did as the sun rose or set. Not a problem unless you were relying on it to get you through the Straits before the tides changed.

"All hands to stations!"

At that moment, their wind faded away completely—but not that of the *Far Voyager*. That ship came on, even as the *Sea Dancer* crew twitched sails, and the helmsman jiggled the wheel to get the wind back. Would the other ship catch them? It was still moving toward them, though more slowly now. Sonra stood on the rail to see them more clearly. The other ship was finishing its last tack, but would that put them near enough—

The other ship turned, showing her their open gun ports, and then Sonra saw a flash, felt a massive shove as the rail under her cracked, and the next thing she knew she was flung into the air. Only remembered there were no Crayx to help her when she hit the water.

* * *

"They've got him." Degler lowered his glasses, but kept looking at the boat they'd sent out. He'd seen the one who went overboard wore a scaled cuirass and he remembered that those who did always wore their braided hair long enough to wrap around their waists like a belt—which meant that the rope-like length of hair down their backs could serve as a loop that could be hooked by a would-be rescuer.

"You see the others just left him," he pointed out to Zoew. "Wind picked up and they're gone."

"Left *her*," Zoew said. "It's a woman."

* * *

"Who accuses us? Will you tell me that? Rumor, that is who." It had taken several minutes of choking up seawater before Sonra realized she was not aboard the *Sea Dancer*. "Where are the victims? Even the Mercenary Brother had to acknowledge that there is no evidence against us."

"Well, there wouldn't be, would there, if you did the job right." Zoew Illkie, apparently the first mate on this ship of fools, was seated across the table from her.

"But why accuse *us*? If someone feels we cheated them, all they have to do is take us to the tribunals. I tell you, we are not the pirates."

"Who said we thought you were pirates?" Finally, the man who was obviously the captain spoke up. He had a fine tenor voice, totally at odds with his square, stocky build and his frowning face. A strange smile flitted over his face. Suddenly Sonra had the feeling the man knew perfectly well the *Sea Dancer* crew were not pirates, because he was the pirate himself.

She rubbed her forehead with trembling fingers. This made no sense, what did Vont Degler want from them? "You would never have gotten this close to us if there was a Crayx in the Midland Sea."

"There are no Crayx!" The man slammed the top of the table with both fists. Sonra flinched back before she could stop herself, startled by the man's sudden violence. His mate put her hand on his arm and he subsided. "These fancy fish don't exist and you don't communicate with them mind to mind!"

Sonra frowned and leaned back on her stool. "Why is this so important to you? What matter if we delude ourselves? Or if this is just our strange religion?" She knew that there were people who thought this about the Long Ocean Nomads, and tolerated what they saw as unusual beliefs.

"Because you're frauds. The beasts don't exist and you use them as an excuse to keep shipping out of the Long Ocean. And," his hands formed fists, "to rid yourselves of people you don't want, to abandon children on shore. Unwanted and rejected. Like you abandoned me."

Then Sonra understood what was really going on. This man was one of the land locked, a Nomad lacking pod-sense, the ability to hear and become one with the Crayx. The Nomads had several land-based havens for their pod-deaf kinsman, who thrived as agents of their more mobile kin. A pod-deaf person on board a Nomad ship was a danger to everyone—themselves most of all—and most were happy to leave.

Evidently this man was not one of those.

"You believe this," she said, looking for more clarity. "You believe you were abandoned for some *other* reason? Nothing to do with the Crayx?"

"Jealousy. Envy. I was too smart, too quick to be tolerated by the smaller minds on the ship where I was born. So, they used this nonsense of the Crayx to rid themselves of me, as they do with everyone who threatens them. I would have become captain, I would have changed all that crap and they knew it."

Insane, Sonra thought to herself. "But wouldn't have been given to the land until you were at least ten years old. Have seen the Crayx yourself, with your own eyes."

"There are no Crayx! I never saw any because they don't exist. Don't think you can try that trick again. You don't have a whole ship of people to back you up."

The full force of the other man's reality dawned on her. "You *are* insane." Imagine believing that an entire crew, adults, oldsters and children, would unite to make you believe in something that didn't exist, and for the sole purpose of getting rid of you.

"Oh, that's right, the boy who doesn't agree with us must be mentally twisted, deficient."

"This is revenge." Sonra gripped the edge of the table. "This isn't about piracy at all."

"Not about piracy? Pirates are thieves and despoilers. They tear people away from their homes and families. They steal people's lives the way you stole my life! You took away everything that I had! What is that but piracy?"

"Captain, sir." A wide-eyed sailor stuck his head into the door of the cabin. "The *Sea Dancer* is still in sight, almost like they're waiting for us."

"Send up a signal flare." Degler got to his feet, dragged Sonra out on deck, and had her climb on the top of the captain's cabin. "Can they see us? Is anyone looking this way?"

Zoew, looking through the glasses, nodded. "There's a man on deck looking at us. He's lowered his telescope. He's doing this." With her glasses still to her eyes Zoew made a come-hither gesture with her hand. "Now they're turning away."

"You see." Degler pulled Sonra down to the deck and shook her. "You see how quick they are to abandon you?"

"He's saying 'follow me,'" Sonra said, smiling. "Follow me if you dare." She looked between captain and mate, but Degler had already made his decision.

"After them."

"But, Captain, what if they go through the Straits?"

"Don't be an idiot, man," Zoew stepped between the captain and the sailor who'd spoken. "We can catch them in Navra."

Can you? Sonra thought to herself. Can you indeed?

* * *

The space they'd shoved her into was too small to be a cabin, but too large to be a sail locker. Sonra sat on the stool they'd put in with her and tried to be patient. The way the ship moved now told her they had passed through the Straits and were nearing the open sea of the Long Ocean. Soon. Soon, everything would be well. The latch clicked and Zoew came in with a second stool and a tray. From the smell, fish chowder and boiled potatoes. She handed Sonra the tray, took a seat facing her, and gestured at the meal in invitation. Sonra nodded her thanks and picked up the spoon.

"Why did you really abandon him?"

Sonra carefully chewed and swallowed before answering. "We didn't. At least," she shrugged, "not the way he thinks. The Crayx really do exist, and we Nomads really do communicate with them mind to mind—and with their help we can speak mind to mind with each other. We call it pod sense." She took another mouthful of chowder. It was delicious.

The other woman nodded. "I'm from Navra. I've heard the stories. Besides, why create such an elaborate make-believe? But what about putting Vont—the captain ashore? Why did that happen?"

"Every so often a child is born without pod sense, just as every so often a landster is born with it, though they might never learn they have it, with no Crayx nearby. It doesn't always appear at the same age, but never after puberty. It's dangerous for people with no pod sense to stay aboard. For all of us."

Zoew let her eat a while in silence. "I don't see it," she said finally. "Why dangerous? None of us have it, and we can all manage a ship. Without any mind reading."

"Imagine a storm, or an attack by pirates, or the Mortaxa across the Long Ocean. Linked, we can move as one being, knowing where each of us is. The person who can't connect with the rest of us—it's as if, in that moment, they don't exist. They can get killed in the confusion. They can be overlooked and forgotten. They can get in the way without meaning to, and we can't protect them." Sonra put the spoon back on the tray. She wasn't hungry any longer. "I haven't experienced it, but we all know stories. For their own safety, and for ours, we put them ashore in one of our havens."

"And that's what you did with the captain."

It wasn't a question but Sonra answered it anyway. "That's what would have been done, yes, though not by my pod personally."

"And that's why he hates you."

"That's what he says. Though he must realize that we're only one ship—and not even the right one—so what does destroying us gain him?"

* * *

"Sir, if they were putting in to Navra Port they'd have changed direction by now."

"What?" Degler took a look through the telescope. Zoew was right. His heart beat faster. They were going out into the Long Ocean.

"Captain," Zoew said. "If the crew haven't already noticed, they will soon."

Degler could hear the vibration in her voice. If she was this nervous, what must the crew be feeling? "Call assembly, I'll speak to them."

* * *

Degler stood on the foredeck looking down at the assembled crew. Everyone except the man at the wheel and the lad on lookout stared back at him.

"I hear some of you are worried. What I don't know is why. We're not feeble land men! We've proven that. We've been pillaging around the Midland Sea for months, and no one even suspects us. Are we going to be scared off by a bunch of fish-worshipers? Are we going to be frightened away from the best and biggest cargo we've ever seen by their lies about the magical 'Crayx?'" He spat when he said the word, and then pointed ahead where everyone knew the other ship to be. "That ship is full of fressian—worth its weight in gold—and it should be ours."

The crew had been yelling "no" to Degler's every question, and at this last statement they cheered, some throwing their caps into the air.

* * *

"Any sign?"

Paden shook his head, then said, "No," aloud when he realized that Kolara, one of the navigating twins, had not been looking at him when she asked the question. Life was so much more complicated without the Crayx.

"The lookout thought she saw something, but she can't verify," he elaborated.

"Got to follow us," Kolara murmured. "Got to." She turned toward him. "With respect, it's a crazy plan," she pointed out, not for the first time.

Paden nodded. "Got a better one?"

#Soothing##Calm#

Paden felt everyone on board take a deep breath and relax. The Crayx were here. Now everything would be all right.

* * *

"There, I told you. Is the sea any different here?" Zoew was jollying the crew along. There were still a few nervous types afraid of passing through the Straits—the initial enthusiasm following the captain's speech had started to cool. Zoew knew most of the nerves were caused by their heading straight out into the Long Ocean, not along the coasts where the few who passed the Straits usually stayed. "The captain's never been wrong yet."

"We're not any closer to them," one of the sailors muttered under his breath.

Zoew knew who it was, but, pretending she didn't, spoke her response into the air. "You know who the captain will blame for that, so get back to your jobs."

A few hours later Zoew knew they *were* getting closer. The wind was with both of them, but the *Far Voyager* had just a little more sail. Enough to give them the advantage. Soon, she was sure of it, and so were the others. She sent for the captain and blew her whistle.

"All hands on deck. Everyone in position."

Everyone scrambled to their posts. Degler stood next to the wheel, opening and closing his hands, itching to take it over himself. But the man handling it was good, not better, but good. And the captain needed to be free to move about the ship, give orders.

"Fire a warning shot."

The cannon ball barely missed the stern of the ship. At first nothing changed, and then the other ship began to lower sails, preparing to heave to.

* * *

#Here#

Sonra relaxed for what felt like the first time in weeks. Knew she was sharing her relief with every one of her Pod. *Never going to the Midland Sea alone ever again*

#Laughter##See what we can do#

What have you learned This was Paden.

*One of the landlocked**Thinks he was abandoned, his birthright taken from him**Doesn't believe in the Crayx*

#Interested##Saddened##What can we do#

Has this happened before

#Unhappiness, homesickness, even bitterness, of course, but adjust##Never disbelief#

*Has stolen people's trust in us**What shall we do if we cannot trade**Wait**Speaking to me*

"We're catching up. Your sailors are no match for me." The smile on Degler's face faded. "You don't seem worried."

"What's the worst you can do? Kill me?"

"Oh no, I know of something far worse. What do you think it's going to be like for you and your people when everyone thinks you're pirates?"

"Couldn't convince them before, what is different now?"

"When we catch your ship, we're going to trade cargos and sail your ship back to Lesonika with all the evidence aboard it that anyone would need. Everyone will know you for the pirates and thieves you are, and no Long Ocean Nomad will ever be able to trade here again."

"What about my people? Can tell the truth."

"After I've put you all ashore at the first place I can find? I don't think so. Any who don't like the idea are welcome to go overboard." He frowned at her. "You still don't look worried."

"Will all go overboard, and Crayx will save us."

Degler grabbed her by the front of her cuirass. "There are no Crayx, you crazy woman. You'll all drown and to the ocean bottom with all of you." He pushed her back and looked over the rail at the *Sea Dancer.* "Well, well, what do we have here?"

Sonra watched her ship suddenly jerk around, as if in a harbor and swinging on her anchor. She was now broadside to the *Far Voyager*, sails flapping impotently.

Tell me this is you

#Of course##Relax# Paden's plan flashed through her mind.

"Bring us up alongside! Cannons to bear."

Sonra gritted her teeth. She trusted that her crew knew what they were doing, but wasn't so sure Degler's crew could manage to come alongside without damage to someone. Grappling hooks and lines drew the two vessels together.

Someone get the bumpers out

Teach your grandmother

#Leave it to us#

The sides of the ships kissed, but only the Nomads knew it was the work of the Crayx. Degler leaped across, and signaled to Sonra to follow him.

Time to surrender Paden thought.

This better work

"Captain Vont Degler, as captain of the *Sea Dancer* I officially surrender." The smug look of joy and triumph almost made her change her mind.

#Patience##Trust#

Better work she thought again.

* * *

Degler looked around him at the faces of the Nomad crew. Most of them didn't meet his eye. He felt as though he'd grown inches in the last few minutes. He'd won, and it felt every bit as good as he'd dreamed it would.

"These are my ships officers—"

"Doesn't matter. None of you are going to be sailors ever again." Degler walked up and down as if inspecting them. All wore the scaled cuirasses. "Where are your arms?"

"Put our *garwons* in the weapons chest." The man who had moved to Sonra's side pointed to a small locker at the aft end of the ship, under the wheel. Degler nodded. He could feel the smile on his face and he left it there. There might be other weapons on board, but these were the only crew who routinely went armed.

"You told me I would never be a sailor, and look where we are now."

They all looked back at him, eerily with the same set expression. As if they were listening to something only they could hear. The hairs on the back of his neck stood up. This is what they'd done before, his parents, his family, his *crew*. All pretending to be listening to something, all with the same expression on their faces.

"Pay attention—look at me! You didn't trick me before and you can't trick me now."

He didn't notice that the strange eddy that allowed the two ships to ride side by side had slowly died away. A murmur of sound came from the crew of the *Far Voyager*, then grew to a roar.

"Captain, look."

Degler glanced over the side. A darkness seemed to be rising from the depths of the sea. "No," he said, shaking his head. Finally, the dark shadow formed a scaled back, a very large, very long scaled back. A tail flicked out of the water just as a long horsey snout covered with pale green scales rose to loom over the rail.

"No." This time Degler screamed. "NO! Impossible. I don't see anything. There's nothing there! Nothing! It's a trick." He covered his eyes with his hands and, sobbing, fell to his knees. Zoew knelt down beside him, put her arm around his shoulders, and looked up at Sonra.

"They're real then."

The Nomad captain nodded. "Want me to ask them to do anything? Shoot water? Swim in reverse direction? Prove I can speak to them?"

Zoew licked her lips. "No… What happens to us now?" The crew of the *Far Voyager* had all retreated to their own ship, held immobile by the Crayx. Zoew tightened her hold on her captain. "He had his reasons. They seemed good to him," she said. "He's no danger to you now. Let me look after him."

Loves him Paden said.

If you say so Sonra was not so convinced. "There remains the little matter of the piracy charge."

* * *

"And you found this ship crashed on the shore of one of the Canbari Islands?" Emlin Starhand held the paper that contained the list of goods found on the shipwreck a little farther away from his eyes. Two women had come to the Mercenary House asking for him. The Nomad captain he remembered, Sonra Lor, and the other one—not another Nomad—had introduced herself as Zoew Illkie, captain of the *Far Voyager*.

"The westernmost one. There is a natural harbor near where we found it, and it's possible they were trying to reach it, but the storm blew them just enough off course for them to end up on the rocks," Lor said.

"We passed the wreck ourselves, on our way into the harbor for water," Illkie agreed.

"And found us already there for the same purpose."

"And this was all you found there? Some cargo?" Starhand looked from one to the other.

"And maybe not all of it," the Nomad captain said. "The hold was open and partially full of water."

"There certainly weren't any bodies that we could see," Illkie added. "But naturally this very mixed bag of stuff made us think of the pirates, and we thought it fairly obvious that this must have been the pirate ship that's been causing so much trouble."

Starhand scanned the list again. "And you brought this to me?"

"You're the one who sat in judgment," Lor said. "We thought it best to come to you."

"And we can testify about the other ship," Illkie said. "So no one can say the *Sea Dancer* is just bringing back stuff they stole in order to clear their names."

"I see." Starhand laid the paper on the desk top, looked up at the two women, and smiled. He decided it wasn't important to believe them. "I'll make the necessary reports."

"Thank you," the two women said together.

[The right to have a character named after Zoe Willkie was a Kickstarter perk purchased by John Senn. Zoe, I'll bet you thought I was making you a bad guy.]

The Sea Wolf

Adam Stemple

There is no God but Allah, and Muhammad is his prophet.

With those words, I became *mumin*, a believer. Well, not just the words. There was also the clipping of my yard with a cramped wire, but I don't like to talk about that. I mean, would you?

Why did I do it?

Because I was born a wolf, and a wolf I must be. A sea wolf, where the waves take all evidence of my depredations and leave no sign nor scent for the hounds to follow. It is far better to be a privateer than a pirate, so when our new Calvinist king took back my letter of marque, I had no choice but to turn Turk. The Sultan gave me a name I couldn't pronounce, affixed it to a new letter of marque, and I set about hunting the folks I used to work for.

Yes, yes, I'm admitting I was a pirate. Why deny it? I have already been convicted and sentenced to hang. Now, stop interrupting and let me tell my story.

Pirating the Barbary way is different from the English way. My ship was a galley now, powered more often by oars than its single sail. And the only cannon she had was bronze cast and fixed to the bow. But what the Turks lacked in firepower, they more than made up for in fierceness. My crew were mad bastards, every one, and they loved me. I was as bloodthirsty as they were, and I had *chosen* their religion, making me damn near holy in their eyes. Suffering that wire is no jest for a grown man. And any man who didn't immediately love me for my faith was won over when they found I was freer with the liquor than the lash. A drunk crew might be less effective when it came to battle, but I'll tell you a secret: we pirates don't want a battle. People get killed in battle, and no one wants that. And not just because no man wants to die. It cuts into your profit, as well, for you can't enslave a dead man. A healthy, young Frank will fetch a fine price in Algiers. So, put one across the bow and put your crew—frothing, murderous, and bristling with weapons—all up on deck, and most merchantmen will strike their colors rather than fight.

All except the damned *Sárkány*.

Things had gotten quite hot in North African waters, so we were hunting amongst the inlets and islands east of Ancona, where there is no shortage of fresh water and convenient escape routes when warships appeared. The *Sárkány* was not a warship, but she was a sleek vessel, and cut through the waves handsomely. Normally, I would search out fat, merchant pigs stuffed with goods to sell. This ship looked incapable of carrying a lot of cargo, but I had other ideas for her.

"Capture it, Amir al-Bahr?" my chief mate, Hamid, said when I told him my plan. He was a short man, and older, legs bowed from long years balancing on a ship's planks. His brown face was all nooks and crannies, his mouth a dark slash with a red clay pipe stuck in it that looked grown there. His stout arms spoke of a time when he likely was chained to an oar, but I had never asked him if this was true.

"Yes. I have long wanted to swive my former people in their own waters." Hamid grinned at that, for he was a violent and dirty old frig. "And for that, I need a ship with more sails than the one we have."

"We cannot row to England?"

"No. Past Tangier, the waters are no longer constrained by close shores. The waves build till they are higher than the Pyramids."

"Bah! We have rowed to Salé. It is past Tangier."

"Aye. But we clung to the shore like a barnacle."

He knew this was true but frowned anyway. "There are no shores to cling to on the way to your homeland?"

"The Spanish coast has more warships than ports. We must away to sea to safely pass them by."

And while all this was true, the real reason I wanted the *Sárkány* was that I missed *sailing*. Whipping slaves to row you a hundred yards from shore didn't compare to sailing the deep blue. Give me a wind off the beam and all my canvas spread to catch it, no land to lee and none on the horizon neither. I missed that more than I missed my foreskin. The *Sárkány* looked small enough to take, but big enough to make the journey I wanted her for.

"And will it make us rich?"

"Yes, my greedy little friend, it will."

It would not. The people who get rich pirating are the sultans and kings who back big privateering expeditions targeting Dutch convoys or Spanish treasure ships. And they're rich already. But no one wants to hear that.

We slipped from the cover of a small island's headland and pounced on the *Sárkány* like a lion on a wounded antelope. No ship in these waters could have escaped us then, but the *Sárkány* didn't even try. No extra canvas was spread to catch the shreds of wind as we closed in. No guns fired on us as we caught her with grapple and rope and stormed over the sides; Janissaries first, disciplined and fierce in their red robes and tall white hats, then the sailors in a jumble of weaponries and colors. No one met us at the rail with boarding pikes and grenadoes. No one defended the deck with sabres and wheellocks, or fired at us from the tops with blunderbuss and musket. In a few silent minutes, the ship was ours.

My men spread out to search the vessel. But they didn't do it in their usual mad dash, ripping open doors and hatches with abandon and dragging out whatever was inside. They moved cautiously, softly, the still silence of the empty ship subduing them in a way no battle's aftermath ever had.

"I do not like this," Hamid said, nervously chewing on the end of his pipe.

"A ship without a fight? What could be better?" I said it heartily, for the men were a superstitious lot and read signs in everything. They were as like to see an abandoned ship as a curse as a gift. I certainly considered it a gift, but couldn't deny that the empty silence was unnerving. But I was already thinking of the ship as mine. And I don't give up what's mine.

Still, I worried over what could have cleared the ship of its inhabitants. *Sickness?* I caught no stench of plague or rot on the breeze, but one never knew. The deck was cleared for action and blood-stained planks spoke of a fight. But it was old blood. *Better than sickness,* I thought.

There were no bodies.

"Amir al-Bahr!" a sailor called from the stern. I turned to see my pilot, Petros, a Greek boy we had captured a few months ago. He was more use to us as a pilot than a slave, as his father had been a fisherman and he knew these waters as only someone born upon them could. He had been wasted as a fisherman and took to the pirate life like a shark to the ocean. Now he stood by the *Sárkány*'s pilot, who was poised strangely behind the ship's wheel. As I approached, I saw why: he was dead. He only stood because his hands were tied to the wheel, preventing him from falling over.

"Cut him free," I told Hamid. "And throw him overboard." The corpse was desiccated, as though the man had been drained of fluids before he died. Or perhaps that was why he died. "And do it quietly, before the crew come back from belowdecks."

I turned my back to the strange corpse and looked over my new ship. She was a small two-master, a brigantine no more than sixty feet in length. On the gundeck, she carried only eight cannon and, up top, a handful of deck guns. I would need to refit before I could pirate with her. Add some bow chasers. See if she could take heavier guns below.

I will have to rename her, I thought. *Perhaps something French to tweak the noses of my former employers.* I chuckled to myself as it came to me: *Chasseur de Loups. The Wolfhunter.*

Only, I am the wolf.

I heard a commotion from belowdecks and, for a moment, feared my men had been ambushed. But then a call floated up from the open hatch, "Amir al-Bahr! You will want to see this."

I heard the splash of the dead pilot going overboard as I followed the voice down the hatch. Belowdecks was cramped, as the boat was shallow-drafted, but still had a gun deck. It smelled only faintly of wet men in close quarters, which meant the ship had been empty for some time. A crewman led me past the cannon to an odd scene at the bow. A deathly-thin young woman knelt on the boards, facing down the length of the ship. Her arms were raised like St. Andrew on his cross, manacled wrists held upright by chains hurriedly nailed into the deck above her head. She wore a noblewoman's dress, embroidered skirts and puffy sleeves, though it looked worse for wear.

"English?" she asked sharply. "You are English?"

Her vowels were Muscovy thick, but spoken more melodically than that aggressive language.

"I am."

"Oh, thank the Lord. I am rescued from these dreadful Mahometans!"

I stepped forward and to the side, so what thin light available belowdecks illuminated her face. Though she had the thick lids and canted brows of the Eastern Khans, her skin was strikingly pale, as though made from the alabaster of the ancient Greeks. Black hair stretched from a pronounced widow's peak into a long wave that reached her waist. Her lips were thin and bloodless, her eyes dark as a moonless night.

"My dear lady, I am afraid you are not rescued quite yet."

"Will you not do the Christian thing and release me from my bonds?"

I chuckled at that. "I will not. For I am one of the 'dreadful Mahometans.'"

"Truly?" She sighed and slouched back as far as her chains would allow her. "Then what is my fate?"

"Well," I said, stepping forward once more and crouching down so we were eye to eye, "I don't know as of yet. Why don't you tell me what happened here?"

"We were set upon by pirates! My men fought bravely but they were overwhelmed." She sat up straighter as she spoke.

"Your men?"

"Yes, I am Ambrusne Piroska, daughter of Princeps Ultrasilvanus the Voivode of Erdély, and Ispán of Fehér County in my own right. I am sailing for Genoa to marry."

I seized on one of the few words she had spoken that I understood. "So, Countess, your husband-to-be, is he a rich man?"

She almost smiled when she realized where I was going with this. "A very rich man, my Lord."

My smile was wide. "Then your rescue is assured. Assuming he will pay to have his wife delivered…?"

"He will pay a great deal." She paused to stare hard at me for a moment. As she was unarmed, chained, and half my size, I managed not to draw back in fear. "If I am delivered unharmed. He is also a very powerful man, and known to have a great appetite for vengeance."

If I was afraid of men's vengeance, I would hardly have been a pirate. The "paying a great deal" part was far more persuasive.

"Of course, Countess." I smiled my most reassuring smile, the one with not too many teeth showing. "Let's get you out of those chains and into a cabin."

As the chains came off, she rubbed at her chafed wrists and slapped at her legs to get the blood back into them. There was something theatrical about the way she moved, as though she knew she was being watched and wanted to make sure we saw what she was doing. But I had little experience with noblewomen, and thought perhaps that was how they did most things. Are they not always surrounded by people? Maids, handservants, suitors, and the like? Regardless, touching every part of herself made me wonder what kind of body she hid under her voluminous skirts and if, after getting a few good meals into her, I could charm her out of them before journey's end.

If the men are thinking the same, I may have some trouble keeping her unharmed.

"Where are the pirates now?" I asked her, for on the ship, my crew and I were the only pirates we had found.

"After the capture, we were hit with storms and sickness. Many men died. As is the custom among the ignorant and uncivilized, they blamed the sole woman on board." Her frown encompassed all men. "They chained me here and left."

I could see the men near me starting to think that might not be the worst idea. "Superstitious trumpery," I said quickly and offered her my arm.

She ignored it and marched to the ladder, her legs weak from confinement but her back straight, for she was of small stature and could stand upright even in the cramped confines. As she began to climb, she turned to look back for the briefest second, a tiny smile on her lips. The light pouring down from the open hatch made her already pale face go even whiter. Suddenly, her dark eyes looked cavernous, her smile a death's head grin. She looked like a skull perched atop a clothier's mannequin, a facsimile of life dressed in taut flesh and finery.

But then she took another step up, the angle of the light shifted, and she looked like what she was once more: a scared girl putting on a brave face for the pack of murderous ruffians that surrounded her. *Again,* I remembered, for if her story was true, we were the second pack of ruffians she had run afoul of. I castigated myself for allowing my mind to become as oppressed by the empty ship and strange prisoner as my superstitious crew.

I told Hamid to escort her to an empty cabin and set a guard. "If you can find any you trust with her virtue."

"It will take some thought."

Meanwhile, I dropped anchor and set about putting my new ship to rights. I took what men I could from the galley. The Janissaries refused to leave it, as they had been assigned there, and they are completely without nuance or compromise where their orders are concerned. But I had enough to sail the *Chasseur de Loups,* and if it came to battle, I would hammer my opponent from afar with the brigantine cannon and send the galley in close to board. It seemed a clever enough plan, but sure as I sit here awaiting the gallows, I know the gods take special joy in shitting upon clever plans.

I assigned Musa, another convert, and the only man besides me who had served on a European ship, as boatswain, and he instructed the others on how to handle two masts' worth of square-rigged sails rather than the one lateen-rigged piece of cloth we had on the galley. My gunner Ramazan leered gleefully at the multiple guns belowdecks and assured me he had enough men to man them.

"Both sides!" He mimed explosions with both fingers. "I will sink two ships at once for you, Amir al-Bahr."

I like to think I'm a good enough captain to keep myself from getting trapped between two hostile ships, but I gave him a smile for his enthusiasm.

I set the rest of the men to cleaning above and below, swabbing the dried blood off the planks and ejecting water from the bilge that had gotten deep with no one to man the pumps. Finally, Petros had some letters, so I put him over the side on a hanging plank to paint my new name on the hull. By nightfall, the *Chasseur de Loups* was ready to sail.

We did not, with such an inexperienced crew, try to sail at night. Instead, we left the anchor down and settled in. I am a light sleeper, and with the light of the waxing half-moon shining on my face through my new cabin's window, I hadn't slept at all when the screams started.

There were three cabins on the *Chasseur de Loups,* one fore and two aft. The fore cabin was split to house four officers, the two aft were the captain's cabin—actually a suite of well-appointed rooms I was enjoying far more than my meager accommodations on the galley—and a spare cabin for visiting dignitaries or important passengers. The screams came from the spare cabin, where Hamid had placed the countess. I reached it in moments.

The door was open, and I smelled the iron tang of blood from inside. By the light of a single lantern, I saw the countess sitting up in bed, the quilt pulled up to her chin, her mouth in an "O" of surprise. On the floor before her were the two men set to guard her, their throats sliced open, their bloody knives by their hands.

"They burst in," the countess said, her voice shaky, "and started fighting."

"Hamid!" I shouted. He appeared at my shoulder. I could hear the crew gathering behind him. "I thought you picked reliable men."

"My best, Amir al-Bahr." He peered down at the dead men, furiously chewing his pipestem. Pointed at the lefthand corpse. "Nebi was even a eunuch. He would have no interest in her."

"He was fending the other one off," the countess said decisively. She gave a theatrical sigh. "He died a hero. I will pray for him."

"As it was a Christian that gelded him," I said, "I doubt he wants your Christian prayers."

Was it rude to speak to a lady this way? Of course. But I have grown tired of the hypocrisy of religion. I have seen them all and been no small number, as well. Catholic, Protestant, Muslim, Hindoo, the Sky god of the Khans, the old pagan gods of the Slavs and Norse. Every one of them used to excuse the worst excesses a man can perform.

You look at me askance, for you think you know how many men I have killed. I assure you, your number is low. And not just men, but women and children, for there is no reasonable distinction between them. But I kill because I am a hunter, and death is how a hunt must end. And I make no excuse. I have no care how my prey judges me.

"Pick new men," I told Hamid. "*Reliable* men."

"Yes, Amir al-Bahr."

I turned to the crowd that had gathered and spoke to them in Sabir, the lingua franca of the corsairs. "If this happens again, I will trade you for the oar slaves."

It was a spurious threat, but it let them know how displeased I was. Two brothers from Tunis stepped forward immediately and swore to Allah that they would keep the woman safe. "Or may we never reach paradise."

Having seen the atrocities these two gleefully performed, I doubted paradise was their destination regardless of whether they succeeded at this duty or not. But I let them stand guard and the rest of the night passed uneventfully.

Dawn came with a wind off the beam to send us whisking south out of the Adriatic and around the boot of Italy. From there we would sail west to Tunis to arrange messengers to Genoa to set up a ransom and exchange. *If I could get the men to understand that they couldn't control three sails per mast without climbing up into the riggings.*

"The ropes are right here on deck, Amir al-Bahr." Hamid spoke slowly like *I* was the fool. "I will show you…"

"I know very well how the lines work!" It had been a frustrating morning. The ship wallowed when she should have been doing ten knots. *A wind wasted soon turns.* It is like a scorned lover that way. I feared it would birth a squall if we didn't show it some respect and put some canvas up to catch it. "Signal the galley to tow us 'til these fools learn how to sail. Musa!" I shouted. "Make 'em learn."

He grinned without humor and picked up a pin to "start" the men who were slow climbing into the riggings. Before too long, we were underway, but only because the galley was now towing us.

"At least we're moving," I said to no one in particular.

The setting sun was ablaze on the horizon when the storm hit.

We cut the rope to the galley before we pulled it under. The *Chasseur de Loups* spun wildly as men ran around pulling on lines ineffectually. I left Musa to get the deck crew under control and climbed into the riggings myself. I had started my time at sea in the riggings, though on ships far different from this one. Personal demonstration turned out to be what the men needed, and soon enough I had them brailing up the main sails so the wind wasn't thrashing us as badly. Musa eventually got the lines set correctly and by midnight we were running before the storm instead of being whipped by it. But the battle with wind and wave continued, as we had been driven far west and risked running aground on unfriendly shores.

Somehow, we met the dawn still afloat. With a calmer wind pushing us away from shore, I sent most of the men to their hammocks and went to bed myself. Rising at midday, I got the report from Hamid.

"Three men gone, Amir al-Bahr. Washed overboard by the storm." He gave me their names.

"Ibrahim? I saw him an hour before dawn. I sent him below to rest."

"He must have stayed up top to help."

It was passing strange, as the storm was mostly blown out by then. But I had sent the man below because he was exhausted. And a ship is a dangerous place for an exhausted man. In that state, he could have easily fallen overboard.

"The galley?" I asked.

"No sight of it."

I hoped they had survived, but there was nothing I could do about it now. "They know where we're bound. They'll meet us in Tunis."

"And if not?"

"Then we'll meet them in paradise." I gave as good a smile as I could. It seemed to hearten the man. "But we are sure to find them in Tunis. We'll be there for some time while our envoys arrange the ransom." I was already dreaming of how I would spend the money hiring on men who could actually work the lines and be useful in the tops. "I'm going to check on our prisoner. Get some rest, Hamid."

The countess was awake and sitting at the small table nailed to the floor of her bedroom. An untouched plate of fruit and dried meat sat before her. Though the floor had been well-scrubbed since the two crewmen's deaths, I still smelled blood.

"Not hungry?" I asked.

"Not after that night." She frowned at the food, then me. "I thought we were going to turn full over."

"A small blow, nothing more." Despite her professed lack of appetite, she looked better than when we had unchained her. Less pale. Cheeks fuller, not just skin stretched over knifing cheekbones. *Her husband might pay extra, we're delivering her so hale.* "Would you like to come enjoy the afterdeck with me? The weather is quite pleasant now."

She shook her head. "I am not quite recovered from last night's excitement. Perhaps tomorrow, Captain?"

I gave her a courtly bow. "I look forward to it, Countess."

Then I went and stood on the aftdeck with a steady wind behind me and an open sea before. And despite the storm and the deaths, I was content. I was sailing.

Two nights later, the next incident occurred.

The moon had gone down, so I was sleeping soundly when Petros burst into my cabin, shouting madly in Greek. As I do not speak that language, I had to wait till he calmed enough to regain his English.

"Wings," he finally said, the first word I understood. "Wings and shadows. Smoke and darkness."

While the first words made no sense, "smoke" got me out of bed in a shot. Sailors fear nothing more than fire. But when I got on deck, I saw no flames.

"In the tops," Petros said, pointing up at the sails. "I saw it in the tops."

I followed his gaze and saw nothing but slack sails and stars. "Saw what?"

He shook his head. "Wings and shadows, Captain."

We were a bit far from land for birds to come perch on our masts, but it was not unheard of. Tired albatrosses or migrating hawks are wont to grab a rest if one is made available. And of course, gulls are not shy in menacing a fisherman's catch. But Petros would know that. I was surprised at his terror at spotting one.

"A night bird is nothing to fear," I said, trying to sound more like a caring father than an exasperated captain.

"It was no night bird." He pointed at a dark lump on the deck below the mizzenmast. "It grabbed Murad and bit him, then threw him aside."

I approached the lump and it indeed resolved into the corpse of Murad, a boy of no more than fourteen, and the only crewman who had taken to the riggings with any alacrity. His body was broken and mangled from the fall.

I turned back to Petros and grabbed him by the shoulders. Gave him a shake. "Murad shouldn't have been up in the riggings at night by himself. Clearly, he surprised a bird roosting on the mast and this tragedy occurred."

"But I —"

"Whatever you think you saw, that is the only possibility that makes sense."

He stood in thought as the logic of my words warred with what he had seen. My words must have won, because he finally nodded. "Yes, Captain. You must be right."

Now, if I could only convince myself.

I settled Petros down and had Hamid pick men to wash Murad's body and sew it into his hammock. Then I went to my cabin to fetch the astrolabe. Back on deck, I took some readings, then returned to consult the charts. We were two hundred nautical miles from Tunis, which should only take a few days depending on the winds. I went to sleep confident that we would be able to reach port soon, offload our passenger, then sit back and wait for the specie to roll in.

But the wind was gusting and indecisive the next day, only holding steady when all hands were watching Murad put over the side—his face turned toward Mecca, of course. After that, it seemed every time we set our sails to the wind, it shifted. Eventually, it settled, becoming light and westerly, leaving us tacking slowly into it, a difficult maneuver that my inexperienced crew handled poorly. An evening reading showed we had made only five miles to windward. Clouds covered the moon, but I still couldn't sleep.

Is this ship cursed?

The ill wind continued for a solid week. I could have turned around and run for Ottoman-held Greece, but if the wind turned again, I would give up the meager gains I had earned for nothing.

Meanwhile, the *Chasseur de Loups* was hit with a raft of suspicious accidents. Normally surefooted crewman Kemal fell overboard. The marlinspike Sunduk was using to separate rope somehow ended up in his eye. Musa's head got torn nearly free of his body by a tangled line. We lost ten other men in ever stranger ways. If we lost many more, we would be unable to sail the ship at all.

I never saw the countess leave her cabin or touch the food served her, but by the end of the week she was plump and pert, her cheeks rosy with good health.

Naturally, the crew began muttering that the last group of pirates had been right and the countess had cursed the ship. Hamid came to me with their concerns.

"We must put her over, Amir al-Bahr." I thought the clay of his pipe would crumble to dust, he worked it so feverishly. "Or we must take the ship's boat and leave."

I didn't disagree. *But surely the last crew tried the same?* I no longer believed the countess's story of a pirate attack and then abandonment. And since she was the only one alive by the end, it stood to reason she was to blame. *Save the pilot*, I reminded myself, who somehow managed to chain her below and tie himself to the wheel. *Much good it did him.* But he was not me, and I knew that in three days I could call her to account. Until then, I feared any action against her would only accelerate our doom.

"We need to stay the course, Hamid."

He didn't like it, but I was the captain, and he trusted me. He talked the crew down, and we returned to crawling our way toward Tunis.

We lost him the next night, impaled by an unsecured boarding pike.

Impotent anger is the worst kind. I was furious, but knew in my soul that anything I did besides blithely sailing west would only hasten the deaths. I could do nothing about the murder of the closest thing I had to a friend on board. My crew was also incensed, but unlike me, they had a convenient outlet for their rage.

Mutiny.

But I could see it building and, by the time they came for me, I had gathered an armload of pistols and the boarding pike that had killed Hamid and locked myself in my cabin. "The first dozen through the door get shot!" I shouted. "And I'll take my chances with the rest."

They knew how good I was with a wheellock and left me alone. I could hear them trying to sail, but without Musa or me giving orders, it was hopeless. The ship floundered while I broke apart the tables and chairs in my cabin and nailed the resulting wood over the windows and reinforced the door.

If I had tried to sleep that night, it would have been impossible. There was too much screaming.

The fools tried to take her at night. I planned on doing the same, but I had good reason.

When I left my cabin in the morning, all pretense of accidental death was gone. My crew were spread across the deck, some in pieces, some whole but with their necks torn out. There was less blood than one might expect from so many bodies, but still plenty to once again stain the planks red. I threw the bodies overboard without ceremony. Whether they were bound for paradise, hell, or simply a final nothingness, no words from me were going to affect their soul's final disposition. Then I scrubbed the deck clean and went to check in on the ship's only other denizen.

She sat atop the covers, smiling at me without showing her teeth. *Like a serpent*, I thought. "Good morning, Captain."

"And an ill one to you, Countess."

She shot me a moue that I am sure I would have found enticing under other circumstances. With my hands still red with the blood of my erstwhile crew, I felt nothing but disgust.

"There is no need for rudeness, Captain." She patted the bed beside her. "Why don't you come in and sit beside me."

"I shall stay here, if that's no bother." I stood in the doorway. In the light.

She shrugged. "It makes no real difference. You can come to me willingly, and I promise you an ending you will enjoy. I have seen you leering at me." She gave me a genuine smile then, even more disturbing than the first. For this one showed her eyeteeth, which were long as a panther's and twice as sharp. "But either way, you will be dead ere the moon rises."

Considering what she had done to my crew and the crew that had come before, it was a more than fair offer. But instead of accepting, I made a counteroffer. "If you take the ship's boat," I said, "and leave, I promise not to follow."

I meant it. As angry as I was, I was also calculating. *There is no profit in predators hunting each other.*

She cocked her head for a moment, as though considering it. Then she laughed. "Oh, I shall miss you, Captain. You are funny."

There was nothing more to say. I tried to set the sails on my own, but I didn't do any better at it without a crew than they had without me. When the sun reached the horizon, I locked myself in my cabin.

That night was the longest of my life. She clawed at the doors, battered the windows. She went below and scratched at the floor, then went overhead and stomped on the deck above me. She screamed in frustration, cooed in supplication, and threatened me with the most vile degradations if I didn't let her in. Perhaps it is as they say, and her kind can't enter a place uninvited. Or perhaps she knew we were days out from land and was enjoying toying with me like a cat with a mouse. Either way, I survived 'til the morning.

"You look tired," she said innocently when I stood at her door. "Did you not sleep well?"

"I make you the same offer as yesterday: leave now, and I will not follow. I will not hunt you." I tried to look at her sternly, but was suddenly afraid to meet her gaze. "I am an excellent hunter."

"It is an interesting game you play. So interesting, that even if I believed you, I would stay just to see how it ends." She sighed. Theatrically, of course. I knew now the reason for it. *She mimics the habits of mankind, for they do not come naturally to her.*

It helps her to hunt, you see. It's not the way I hunt, but I respected her method. And given how many bodies I had recently sent to the bottom of the ocean, I couldn't deny its effectiveness.

When I didn't answer her, she gave me a bored shooing motion with her hand. "Away with you now. I shall see you tonight."

I spent the day sharpening the butt end of the boarding pike.

That night was no better than the last, though I was now more certain that she couldn't enter without my invitation. But not so certain that I went to sleep. The morning broke with me bleary but unbowed.

"I would like to make you an offer," she said without preamble, standing on the bed and bouncing slightly. One would almost think her a child, if not for her womanly form. That form filled out her dress much more than when we had first found her, chained and emaciated. Of course, to think her even human, let alone a human child, one would also have to ignore the two long teeth she now just let hang out of her mouth, there no longer being any reason to conceal them.

"And this offer is?"

"Why, it is the same as yours. To wit, leave now and I shall not follow. You will survive where none ever have before." She grinned wickedly. "I, too, am an excellent hunter."

I gave her a short bow of respect, for it was true. But I did not accept, though it was a good offer, and I believe most men in my place would have taken it. But even if I believed her—which I did not; it felt more a tactical ruse to get her prey out of its hiding-hole—it is as I have already told you: I do not give up what is mine without a fight. So, I refused her and told her we would end things tonight. I even took a little joy in the surprise on her face before I shut the door and returned to my cabin with nothing to do but wait.

And that night, when I saw the full moon rise through a crack in the boards over the windows, I took hold of the boarding pike, pointed its sharpened wooden end toward the door and said, "Come in, Countess."

* * *

I can see you have questions, "How can he expect me to believe this?" being top among them, I imagine. But also, "If it is true, how did he defeat her?" Both questions shall be answered, though not in the way you think. Instead, let me explain why I have told you this long and unbelievable tale. Once you know that, all will become alarmingly clear.

First, I have told you this tale to teach a lesson, both to you—though it will come too late—and to myself, for I need reminding now and again. The lesson is this: listen when a person tells you who they are. By omission or plain statement, they usually do, yet we so often ignore or misinterpret the message. By her name and lineage, I should have known what the countess was. But I was distracted by the new ship and the promise of riches, and didn't react until it was almost too late. For me. It was far too late for my crew.

And you, who sits there blithely taking my confession while I have told you—from the very first!—who and what I am. Yet you do not hear, or don't care to listen. And now the full moon's light is shining through the bars of this prison cell, and it is too late for you to do either.

For that is the second reason I told this tale: to delay my execution until the moon is full and up. There is no time left for you to ask why. You will know all too soon. You already gaze at the back of my hand and wonder if it was that hairy this evening when you entered my cell. I will answer that. No. Neither were the nails so long. You see my face now, how my jaw elongates and my ears grow tall and pointed. How new musculature strains against my tunic so that it is close to bursting. When it does, you will see a chest covered in dark fur.

So now you know both that the tale is true and how I defeated her. It is as I said from the first: I am a wolf.

And when the full moon rises, I hunt.

Unmoorings

Nemo Herndon

They say Tetlow the Serpent went down fighting to the end.

Like a harpoon-riddled Sea beast, or so goes the story these days. Like some vengeful behemoth, a hardened thing more scar than flesh baring its teeth in a blood-soaked grin, a force of nature wronged. There he stood with his head held high, cutlass in one hand, spent flintlock in the other, a navy man-of-war circling closer like a tightening noose. There were one hundred—no, two hundred—no, *three* hundred men on the enemy vessel, seasoned pirate hunters all. Cannons thundered and muskets barked gunpowder smoke. It was an ambush in the storm of the century, a spinning waltz amid razor winds and cloud-kissing waves. They got him in the end somewhere off the Strait of Ciona but the Sea made a feast of them both. Tetlow had sworn an oath long ago, had the curse carved into his ship's wheel: *Let he who slays me follow me down.* When dawn spilled like fire across the horizon, there was nothing left but driftwood and the dead bobbing in tranquil silence.

The tale gets taller all the time but I keep listening, waiting for the truth to trickle through. Weaving around woozy sailors and wobbling chairs, I catch the newest embellishments fresh from the docks. Tetlow fought one-handed, I hear. He leapt across the Sea's frothing maw and challenged the other captain to a duel. He lined up a shot and killed three men standing in a line. The navy ship went up in cerulean flames that grew higher and hungrier in the rain. Someone raises an empty mug, shakes it in the air impatiently, and I rush to fill it again. There's a merchant shipping crew taking up a couple of the corner tables tonight, arrived so recently they still smell of salt and spices.

"And the soothsailor? They brought one, didn't they?" someone asks when I get there. The others hiss and splash him with their drinks to ward off the Sea's attention.

"Don't talk about it," they warn him. "A jinx at Sea and a jinx on the tongue."

"Of course they brought one."

"An old man, I heard. Fished him out of a storm—"

"Don't talk about it!"

"Hell of a way to go, I say." They toast to Tetlow's memory like they wouldn't have been his favorite prey. He always had that effect on people, even the ones who only knew him as tavern talk. But there's a dark current beneath all the chatter. Every smile is strained and anxious. There's something even the youngest, most clueless and loose-lipped among them hesitates to say. Everyone wants to ask, but nobody will.

He's dead, right? He's really dead?

It's fine to wonder. It's expected to tell stories, to lie, to spin fantasy from threads of rumor. But it's dangerous to ask. Men like Tetlow never die right at Sea.

The door creaks, held open by callused fingers. Cold night breeze slithers off the harbor and floods the tavern. Talk gets tamer when navy sailors come strutting through, a man in an admiral's gilded tailcoat tucking a bicorne hat under his arm. I think about trying to slip out when nobody's looking, ripping slits in my long, heavy skirt and running until I can't see the lights of the harbor anymore, but I don't get a good chance. The admiral marches to the back of the tavern where I'm stacking dishes, his stare unwavering.

"The proprietor's out," I tell him, wiping my hands on my apron. "Be back in a bit if you don't mind waiting. Can I get you something?"

"Perhaps you can," he says. A thin bronze chain dangles between his fingers and a pendant sits in his open palm. Waves, strange stars, and piscine horrors surround a compass rose in place of directions. The needle at its heart quivers in a nasty mix of thick, ichorous liquid, scarlet water, and black sand. Sea's Bile, they call that, scraped from cliffs where She's tongued the rock smooth over centuries. I let out an impatient huff, pretending I don't know what he's holding or what it means. He watches me like he can hear my hammering pulse.

Two of them by the door. Five more wandering the tavern. Swords at their hips. I'm faster but if they brought a compass, they might've brought other things, too.

"You know why I'm here," the admiral says.

"I'm afraid I don't, sir," I say. I need a weapon. A frying pan. A kitchen knife. I pace behind the counter and he follows with his eyes, the compass needle dragging back and forth wherever I walk. He wears a tactician's calculating expression, a steady gaze and assured smile that stirs uncomfortable memories.

"My name is Francis Aylward. I've been given the unpleasant task of sinking Tetlow a second time."

All the sailors pretending they weren't eavesdropping start talking again, low and somber like a funeral. I refuse to look Aylward in the eye. "What went wrong the first time?" I ask.

"Don't waste my time and I won't waste yours. I need a soothsailor."

A hiss. A splash. Nobody's quite brazen enough to sully his coat but the floorboards are soaked. He scowls at the dark liquid puddle he's standing in.

"Look around. I'm sure you'll find one," I say. I've talked my way out of this before, but the admiral looks too certain. He snaps the compass shut.

"You'd be paid for your trouble," he says.

"Not enough gold in the world for the kind of trouble you're asking for."

His smile wanes with his patience. "I'm not asking, Amis."

Laughter rises from the nearest tables. *Amis? Serpent's Fang Amis? Admiral needs his eyes checked.* He was small, sure, they all agree on that, small enough to be mistaken for a lass—the last mistake many a sailor ever made. Now they're telling older stories of Tetlow and his faithful dagger Amis, that quick-handed creature who could empty a man's pockets and slit his throat before he realized anyone was there. Thick as thieves, those two, always eyeing the same spot on the horizon, always moving in unison like two bodies sharing one head and one heart. But Amis went first, they say, long gone by the time Tetlow took a man-of-war down with him. Nobody can agree on when or where or why, so they weave their own reasons of heroic sacrifices and daring last stands on distant shores.

But Aylward knows. He dares me to say otherwise. I'm a seasoned liar but I know the look of a man whose mind is made up. He's not walking out of here without me. The tavern floods with stories, the air thick with *Amis, Amis, Amis.*

You'll be back, Amis. You always come back. Nobody here, now, says that. I hear it anyway.

I keep my voice low, beneath the tenuously jovial atmosphere. "Kill me, then. I'd sooner die than go back to Sea."

"Not even for an official pardon? Your whole past wiped clean?" Alyward presses. I shake my head. "Then for closure. You've waited years for your chance and here it is."

"I wasn't waiting for anything."

"You would've left if you weren't. Gone further inland, at least, where you couldn't hear Her." He leans against the counter and waits. I think about running again. Vaulting tables, ducking fists. Leaving the tavern red in my wake just like I used to. There was a time when I wouldn't have hesitated. Instead, I take off my apron and leave it folded on the counter. My skirt feels too clean. There's grime caked to the hem but it's dry and crusted, land filth instead of briny dampness. Aylward puts his hat back on. He doesn't linger and he doesn't look back, knowing I'll follow.

I make him wait. A round of drinks for the whole tavern lifts the mood and drags out a few shanties. I soak up the candlelit revelry one last time. They've already moved on from Amis, claimed me dead and buried on a deserted island where Tetlow surely stashes his treasures. Wouldn't that be fitting? All of his most cherished possessions in one place. Someone's ripped down the notice that used to be in the doorway, a warning about the *Blue Lady's Favor* with a hefty bounty for anyone who brings her captain in alive. There'll be a new one in its place tomorrow, sterner in tone, no bounty offered. *Avoid at all costs,* it'll say instead, but it won't matter. Some people can't be taught not to put their hands close enough for a snake to bite.

Like me, I think. *I never learn.*

* * *

"They say you warmed Tetlow's bed."

I'm at the docks bright and early with a burlap sack slung over one shoulder, squinting through the sunrise. Aylward leans against the railing of his ship, poised unavoidably beside the boarding plank. What is it about captains, I wonder, that makes them feel they're owed every piece of a person? "Hell of a way to greet someone who's doing you a favor," I say. The Sea hisses. She rushes between the stilt legs of the docks and gently rocks the ship. A wave bucks against the hull and foam splashes my legs as I climb aboard. I could take that as a greeting or a warning. Aylward's crew rush back and forth across the deck, making final preparations before we set sail. I hear some praying to whatever gods they're leaving ashore. One pinches a handful of soil from his homeland out of a pouch and flicks it overboard in offering.

"I'm wondering why you parted ways," Aylward says. He follows as I pace, inspecting the vessel that may very well become our grave. Sailors scurry out of our path when they see us coming. They keep their distance like I'm a viper that slithered aboard. "Personal or professional differences seem unlikely. Your loyalty was legendary. Then again, they say the sign of true love is letting go."

He doesn't really believe that. He's prodding, trying to see what makes me wince. His edges aren't sharp enough to get anything more than a scowl out of me. "You know what makes a person a soothsailor?" I ask him.

"Almost drowning at Sea."

"So they say. I think we really do drown. She's still got some of me down there."

"Ghosts can't come ashore," Aylward says.

"Not quite what I meant." I stroke the ship's railing. The *Fortunate Voyager,* Aylward called her. She's lovely for a navy ship, aged oak with a dark sun-dried finish, but she pales in comparison to the *Blue Lady's Favor* and her ornate engravings. "Did you get what I asked for?"

Aylward nods to the last of the cargo disappearing into the hold. "Three full casks of sprite's tears. Tetlow's weapon of choice, I can't help but notice."

"He always liked a spectacle," I say. The Sea's gunpowder, some call it. It catches on blood, not sparks, and water makes it worse. Those eerie flames entranced Tetlow. The azure glow, the coldness of it, just how long it could leave a man screaming before it finally killed him.

A barrel sloshes as it's rolled up the plank, the side marked with an "X" of blue paint. The sailor pushing it looks at me and then looks again, flinching. I recognize him from the tavern last night. He thought he recognized my voice but now that he's looking, taking in the tattered coat and unbuttoned undershirt, the shape of my face with my hair swept back, he's trying to make sense of me. Did I pad my blouse last night or am I binding my chest now? He's looking for a lie but there isn't one.

Aylward nods sharply, urging him to stop gawking and keep moving. "I see you brought some things of your own."

"Just the essentials."

"Leviathan bonedust?" he guesses. He joins me at the railing, looking out at Sea. Here, She's sparkling and tranquil, gilded by the rising sun. It's a sight worth savoring.

"So, you've done this before," I say.

He shakes his head. "I've escorted a soothsailor but that was for an execution, not an exorcism. Do you have much experience?"

More than most soothsailors will ever get. When I sailed with Tetlow, I helped hold his prey under so it didn't come back up. We robbed both the living and the dead. "Bit late if I don't," I say. "Shouldn't you have asked last night?"

"You know Tetlow well. That's more important."

I don't like how he says that. "If you'll excuse me, I'm going to get settled in. It's a long way to the Strait of Ciona."

"You'll come back up the moment we spot the *Blue Lady's Favor,*" Aylward says.

"I'll come back up when it's time and not a second earlier. Whoever made this mess lost their soothsailor that way, I guarantee it."

We used to watch him do it. We'd line up on the deck as Tetlow traced the curses carved into the railing, an ill-fated navy ship drifting closer. They always kept their soothsailors in the open, loosely surrounded sometimes, as though that would make a difference. He'd pick out the nervous wretch long before my eyes could make sense of anything through a faraway blur of uniforms. That would be his first shot for the battle to come, his arm steady and his aim true even as the *Blue Lady's Favor* swayed and shuddered underfoot. He'd cock his head, close one eye, and count down under his breath. It sounded like the crack of thunder. We would hear screaming far away, see red blossom across the deck.

"What a shame. Now they have to try and take us alive." He'd laugh, and we'd all laugh, untouchable.

I find a spot on the horizon, a molten shimmer atop the churning waves. I imagine the *Blue Lady's Favor* and Tetlow at the helm, smiling like a dare. He'd tried to teach me to use his pistol once but I didn't care for it. Too loud, too slow, too much trouble when my first love was the knife, but I'd liked how he felt folded against my back with his hands over mine. I point with my thumb extended, one eye closed as if that might fix my shaking, jittery aim. A shot between the eyes could never fix this anyway.

I can feel Aylward watching. "I'll be down below if you need me," I mutter, leaving like a scolded dog. This time, he doesn't stop me. I wonder if he's having second thoughts about whether I can be trusted, if I'll follow through when the time comes, but we both know it has to be me.

Love is letting go, he says. *Do you believe that?* I ask the Sea.

She ebbs and flows, lapping at the hull of the *Fortunate Voyager.* I don't know if She hears me or if She cares. Some say we're her favorites. Some say she hates us most of all.

You keep letting me go. Maybe you shouldn't. I wipe the salt from my cheeks. Down in the hold, surrounded by shadows and the groans of the ship, somebody whispers my name. It's not Her. Not Aylward. Not any of the sailors on board. I wedge myself into a corner hoping I'll feel safer with walls at my back, but nowhere is safe on the water. It could be him. It could be a day that's already passed, as clear and painful as it was when I lived it. Ghosts have voices that carry and the Sea is full of echoes. Tetlow had a way of haunting people and places long before he died. I hold my breath.

I knew you'd come back to me, he says. My lungs ache like they're full of water.

* * *

They say every man has an anchor. Sometimes it's a dream and sometimes it's a burden, but it's always heavy and always with him. It keeps him moored where he must stay and it lifts when he must go, and every man must go eventually. It's only the wicked whose anchors grow so heavy they could drag their whole crew down with them, and it's only at Sea that a thing as inevitable as death could be drowned. That's one version I've heard, anyway. It's the kind of thing they argue about in churches and academies. Sometimes I think nobody's meant to be at Sea, that She's picking the worst of us to punish the rest, and sometimes I think that's surely beneath Her. Maybe She isn't trying to keep us at all and it's only our fault when we stay, but I like to think She's understanding or knows what pity is, at least. She's spat me out twice now, after all.

"Twice?" the navigator asks me.

We're all down here, him and the boatswain and the quartermaster, huddled around a table by lantern light. They've got a game going. I know this one, with a board painted blue and little wooden ships that sail from one edge of the world to the other. I was invited but I turned them down, an easy excuse in the whittled fish slowly forming between my fingers. We used to play on the *Blue Lady's Favor*. The pieces kept getting lost so I kept carving new ones. The admiral leans in the doorway like he's too proud to join us, but he stays. Navy or not, all sailors want to gossip. A couple days of uneventful sailing cools the fever pitch mood of our mission and they're restless now, clamoring for stories. They've had a soothsailor or two on board before, but they never talked to them. This time is different. They might not get another chance.

"Twice," I say. "The first time is what made me a soothsailor. The second, I don't know. Seems like She should've taken me then."

"Don't you talk to Her?"

"I talk, sure, and She talks back. But I don't speak Her language. It's like talking to a mountain. Do I take an avalanche as a 'yes' or a 'no?'"

The boatswain nods like he's heard this before. "It's all instinct, the spells and incantations. She doesn't teach you. You just know."

"They're on my tongue when I need them. I think they rushed in when She did."

It feels like being home again. In the dark, in the gentle swaying of the hold, I can't see their faces or the blue of their coats draped over the backs of their chairs. We talk strategy, plot the vicious waltz that will drive our prey into a corner. We open a jar of leviathan bonedust and coat our blades in gritty white powder so they'll cut both flesh and spirit. That could be Gil next to me tapping out a rhythm on his thigh. That could be Henry across the table, hand to his chin, taking forever to move his piece on the board. That could be Tetlow's imposing silhouette filling the doorway, crossed arms and cocked head a warning. I scrape out another scale and hope he can't tell my hands are shaking.

"We'll need to get close," I tell them. "He'll let us. He's not afraid of anything and he likes to play with his food."

"What do you think his anchor is?" Aylward asks.

I've been thinking about that for hours. Some pirates are predictable, tethered to symbols of their old glory and favored conquests. Lucky coins, favorite weapons, the grisly trophies of old battles. Tetlow's not the type to carry burdens or nurture dreams. We lived moment to exhilarating moment and cared about nothing else. "Doesn't matter. He'll have it on him," I say.

Thunder rolls over our heads. The wind rises from a whisper to a shriek and the Sea grows restless. Miniature ships tumble over the edge of the game board and our chairs scrape the floor. The *Fortunate Voyager* shudders and we brace ourselves in the hold as the table starts to slide.

"Skies were clear just a minute ago," the navigator muses. "We haven't reached the Strait of Ciona yet."

A wave breaks against us, splashing water across the deck above. I clutch my dagger as if it'll be enough.

Amis. I hear the voice from below again. A hiss, as cold and hungry as the Sea.

"He came to us," I say. Do I sound afraid? It's hard to breathe again with the storm dampening the air. "Get the sprite's tears above deck. I'll be there soon." The others leave in a rush but Aylward lingers at the bottom of the steps, looking back like he means to say something. He never does. "I'll be there. I will. Just give me a moment," I beg him. We both know there's no time for that. I'm not ready and I was never going to be. Aylward nods wordlessly and leaves one slow step at a time.

Rain lashes the deck and trickles into the hold, quick rivulets turning to shallow puddles as if we've sprung a leak. I hear chaos unfolding overhead, shouting and sprinting footsteps, the clatter of the ship's wheel wildly turning, the howl of the wind. The Sea parts in an explosive splash around the surge of some behemoth's breaching. It could be a whale but I know it isn't.

"Where are you, Amis?" Tetlow murmurs. I hear him as if he's right beside me, a voice like velvet slithering past my ears. "Where is my faithful dagger? You should be at my side."

The rumble of cannons sends me stumbling. There's a peal of thunder, an ear-shattering boom that shakes the *Fortunate Voyager* down to its hull. Cloudy liquid dribbles between the floorboards, a trickle at first and then a downpour. It smells like winter, the sting of ice in my nose. *Sprite's tears.* He took the bait, then, spotted the barrels from afar. I step beneath the deluge and let it soak my clothes, washing my hands in danger. It dries quickly, clear but unpleasantly sticky on my skin.

Don't let him keep me, I tell the Sea, or maybe I just tell myself. Maybe that's all I'm ever doing when I try to get through to Her. The *Fortunate Voyager* lurches in Her grasp. I stumble up the steps and into harsh, wet winds that steal my breath. This is the storm of every tall tale that's ever been told: the gale that bites and the waves that swallow warships whole, the sky gone starless, inscrutable black. It takes three men to take the rigging back from the wind, a fourth swept off his feet and sent stumbling, plummeting overboard before anyone can catch him. I don't even hear him scream over the howling tempest. Another stumbles and flails before he falls, but Aylward is faster this time, quick enough with his sword to slash at the rain-slicked deck. A hand, translucent and webbed between the fingers, clasps the sailor's ankle. Even severed, it keeps squeezing. The Sea glows with the eerie pulsating blue of bioluminescence. Things long dead circle the *Fortunate Voyager,* scenting unspilled blood.

Aylward doesn't waste words with the storm in our ears. He simply looks at me and nods once, curtly. *We do this,* he means, *or we die.*

Ghosts don't fight like men. They don't need a gangway to board a ship. They ride the rising waves and climb the hull in an endless tide. They move in lightning strikes, there in the corner of the eye, gone again when one turns to look. Aylward's men cut down as many as they can but there are always more of them. There will always be more dead men at Sea than living ones. Their time in Her depths has given them poisoned spines, unhinging jaws and bottomless appetites for suffering. They open throats and bellies on the knife-points of their claws and drag sailors screaming into the abyss to tangle them in the chains of Tetlow's ever-sinking anchor.

At the heart of the storm shines the *Blue Lady's Favor,* aglow like the moon bobbing on the water's surface. She looks just as I remember, but luminous, haloed in eerie blue light, her embellishments silver and sparkling. Runes of protection and soothsailor sigils adorn her, etched everywhere from the masts to the bow's railing. I helped carve them, whittling away the twilight hours with Tetlow and the others drifting by to make conversation.

I see him there just like the stories, just as I remember; sword in one hand, smoking pistol in the other. He's changed, too, deathly pale with a shark's smile, glowing dots and half-moons pulsing in a hypnotic rhythm down his arms. Through rain and lightning, across the shrinking distance between vessels, our eyes meet. I shouldn't be able to hear him through the screaming wind and wild Sea, but I do, clear as day.

"Hello, Amis. Were the sprite's tears your idea? You made me waste a shot." He reaches into the pouch across his waist to fill his pistol with another and I sprint.

I should have time. I would, if he were still human, if the Sea didn't change everything She touched. But his pistol is a barnacle-laden horror that takes glittering dust instead of gunpowder and it takes seconds, barely enough time to cross the deck, before he's searching for my shape amid Aylward's men.

Don't let him keep me, I beg the Sea. I don't know if She's inclined to help anyone but I've never asked for anything before. *If I die, hold me under. Better you than him.*

Tetlow's eyes glint like stars, menacing points of silver blazing through the storm. I see him raise the pistol and one star winks out just as I reach the railing. I tell myself I've done this a thousand times, vaulting up and then over, throwing myself across the chasm of certain death between two ships. I look at Tetlow and not the pistol. Heart in my throat, I make the leap. Tetlow looks right back at me but the Sea slams into the *Blue Lady's Favor* the moment he pulls the trigger. The shot goes wide by a hair. The heat of it grazes my cheek. We collide, Sea to cliffside, both unyielding. My dagger cuts a wound through Tetlow that ripples, his phantom skin parting like water around a stone. Inside I see nothing but teeth and darkness, a lamprey's mouth for a heart. He sways with the force of the blow as though we're dancing, a step back, a gurgled laugh that sounds like drowning.

The gash snaps shut. He licks the silvery blood trickling from the corner of his mouth. Men fight and die all around us, ripped to bloodied chunks by Tetlow's crew, my old mates, but they leave room for us in the eye of the storm. This is Tetlow's hunt and they all know it.

"I missed you," he says, circling me. "I went back, you know. I tried to find you."

"You're the one who gave me to the Sea." My voice is hoarse, throat constricted. I remember the warmth of his hands, his touch when he was gentle, his smile when it was playful, how it felt to cram into a bunk not big enough for either of us, and the way my name rolled off his tongue. I remember the fights, too, the anger and the pointlessness of them. A battle gone badly, wasted loot tumbling into the Sea. Someone got past me and nicked him in the shoulder once. He held my head down in the puddle of his blood like I was a dog who'd sullied the floor, hissing, *"What good are you to me?"* I remember the end, too, how I screamed and thrashed as he shoved me closer to the edge and how the others laughed, and then the rush, the *silence*. The Sea all around me. The shadow of the *Blue Lady's Favor* like an island leaving me behind.

"Your *soul*, Amis," Tetlow coos, like I've said something stupid. "Not your body. We don't need flesh anymore. I always meant for it to be like this, but you weren't there. The Sea stole you from me, washed you to shore beyond my reach."

"Don't lie to me," I say. Moment to moment, thrill after thrill. I know better than anyone how we were. Tetlow flickers like a mirage and then he's lunging for me, sword slicing the air where I was only just standing. The floor is gone behind me and I tumble, bruising my arms trying to catch myself halfway down the steps that lead below deck. Tetlow presses forward, narrowly missing my head. I turn to run and find the Sea filling the *Blue Lady's Favor,* the ship half-flooded already, but I can't go back with ghost-steel swiping at my heels. I'm being herded, I realize too late, guided down familiar corridors, danced backward into the serpent's maw. There's the hold, full of grasping tendrils and waving polyps, slimy and glowing strangeness, and the room where we kept cured meats now overflowing with putrid fish. There's the open doorway of the captain's quarters, the bed we shared, the last game we played waiting on the table like I never left. It was all wood before but the board is shale now, the pieces carved of bone.

"Here we are," Tetlow says. He fills the doorway, his dead eyes alight with predatory delight. "Home again, Amis. Didn't you miss it?"

I don't want to admit it but he sees it in my eyes. He sheathes his sword and sets his pistol down, uncaring of my dagger swaying between us. It slices his palm when he reaches out, but he's unbothered, too far gone to feel the pain. "What happened to the pieces I carved?" I ask him. "Did you throw them into the Sea, too?"

"Of course not," he says. The back of my legs hit the bed and then I'm sinking, feeling those luxurious sheets we stole from a merchant ship on my skin again. Cold wetness laps at my elbow. The water keeps rising, splashing at the edge of the bed. Tetlow climbs over me when I buck and twist, and this is familiar. It's all the good times and the bad, and how it ended once before. He means to drown me, to see it with his own eyes so I don't slip away again. He pins one wrist, squeezes until I drop the dagger and the water swallows it. I claw at him with the other. I rake my nails down his chest. With a speed and deftness I have only ever used for him, only on his enemies, my fingers flit through his pockets until I find what I'm looking for.

It's a small thing, a smooth and serpentine carving. It's cold until it warms against my palm. I feel the round, flattened base where it would sit on the game board, the pair of coiled Sea snakes twining above.

"You and your sticky fingers," Tetlow says fondly. "You found it, Amis. My anchor, and yours, too. You were always going to come back to me." I hate how certain he sounds and how soft his gaze is, how gently he touches me. I think of those soft mornings when no one was looking, and those dazzling nights in this very bed. The Sea rises higher, kissing my cheeks and swallowing my tears.

Can you hear me? I try to ask Her one last time. She must. She nearly has us both in Her grasp. That doesn't mean She'll answer. *I changed my mind. Don't keep me. I don't want to be kept by anyone ever again.*

Tetlow closes my hand around the carving, his fingers engulfing mine. He leans in, holds it between our bodies, and I almost feel precious to him again. His breath warms my lips and I close my eyes.

"If you so long for Her depths, then sink true," I say hoarsely. "With this, I lift the anchor and banish you."

He cuts my lip on his teeth. Blood trickles down my chin in red pearls, enough to soak the sprite's tears I'm drenched in. Nothing of the Sea behaves as it should. It doesn't catch like flame. It ripples. I feel it undulate, a flutter of fins on my skin. There is heat at first and then terrible cold, claws of frostbite seizing me. Tetlow's eyes open, his mouth agape. He tries to pull away but I don't let him. When he flails, rolling into the Sea, I go with him and She ignites us both. We are the heart of a frigid inferno, kindling in the belly of the *Blue Lady's Favor*. Our joined hands melt together into a single mass of liquid skin, muscle, soul, and bone. Beneath it all, my gift to Tetlow burns to white ash. The muscles in his throat clench and tremble. His tears float, shimmering and pearlescent. He is defiant to the end, furious in his grieving. His mouth shapes pleas and curses but I can't hear him anymore. There's only the Sea around us, Her fire all-consuming. When there is nothing left but boiling splinters, Tetlow falls to pieces. He turns to light, Sea fire, and bones that sink. He slips through what's left of my numb fingers.

The storm breaks and the clouds shatter. Sunlight warms some place above me, but it's dark down here, so cold it hurts. I think this is the end; third time's a charm. This is what I dodged twice and this is what brought me back here again. The Sea finally gets Her due. The *Blue Lady's Favor* crumbles like sand and light trickles between her broken pieces. I swim for it, not knowing how far I have to go. Shadows grow at the edge of my vision but I think I see someone else, something in the water with me. Not Tetlow. Not a drowned sailor. Greater than any whale and kinder than any ghost, it passes beneath me with the silent grace of an eclipse, so swift I could have imagined it. The hands of the current push me higher. My head breaks the surface.

I gasp and sputter, lungs burning. Everything hurts, from the phantom prickling of my wrist where something gruesome and mangled is all that remains of one hand to the heaviness in my chest. I stare at the sky in wonder. The last time I found myself treading water, nothing but endless blue in every direction, I was so afraid.

"Amis!" Aylward shouts. The *Fortunate Voyager* bobs on gentle waves. "You did it! Hold on, we'll get you back aboard!" There's little left of the *Blue Lady's Favor*. Splinters, mostly, a few singed planks. The Sea claws her back down and this time, She doesn't let go. I cling to a crumbling bit of flotsam, feeling it melt beneath me. It stings to inhale but I do it anyway. Every breath gets easier, less sharp than the last.

"Amis! Are you alright? Say something!"

I wave instead. Aylward barks orders and I see movement, hear the start of a celebratory shanty. I couldn't sing with them even if my throat wasn't on fire. My shoulders shake and my eyes sting. My next breath is almost a sob. I shouldn't be alive. I should have burned to nothing with Tetlow.

You will not be kept.

I jolt upright, feeling like I've just woken from a nightmare. I can't tell if I heard that or just imagined it, if it's just what I wanted to hear. It wasn't words, exactly, but the indistinct murmurings of shells that wash up on the beach and the calm they bring. It feels like love. I watch the sun sink slowly, the water warm and gold. I drift, weightless and without an anchor for the first time in my life.

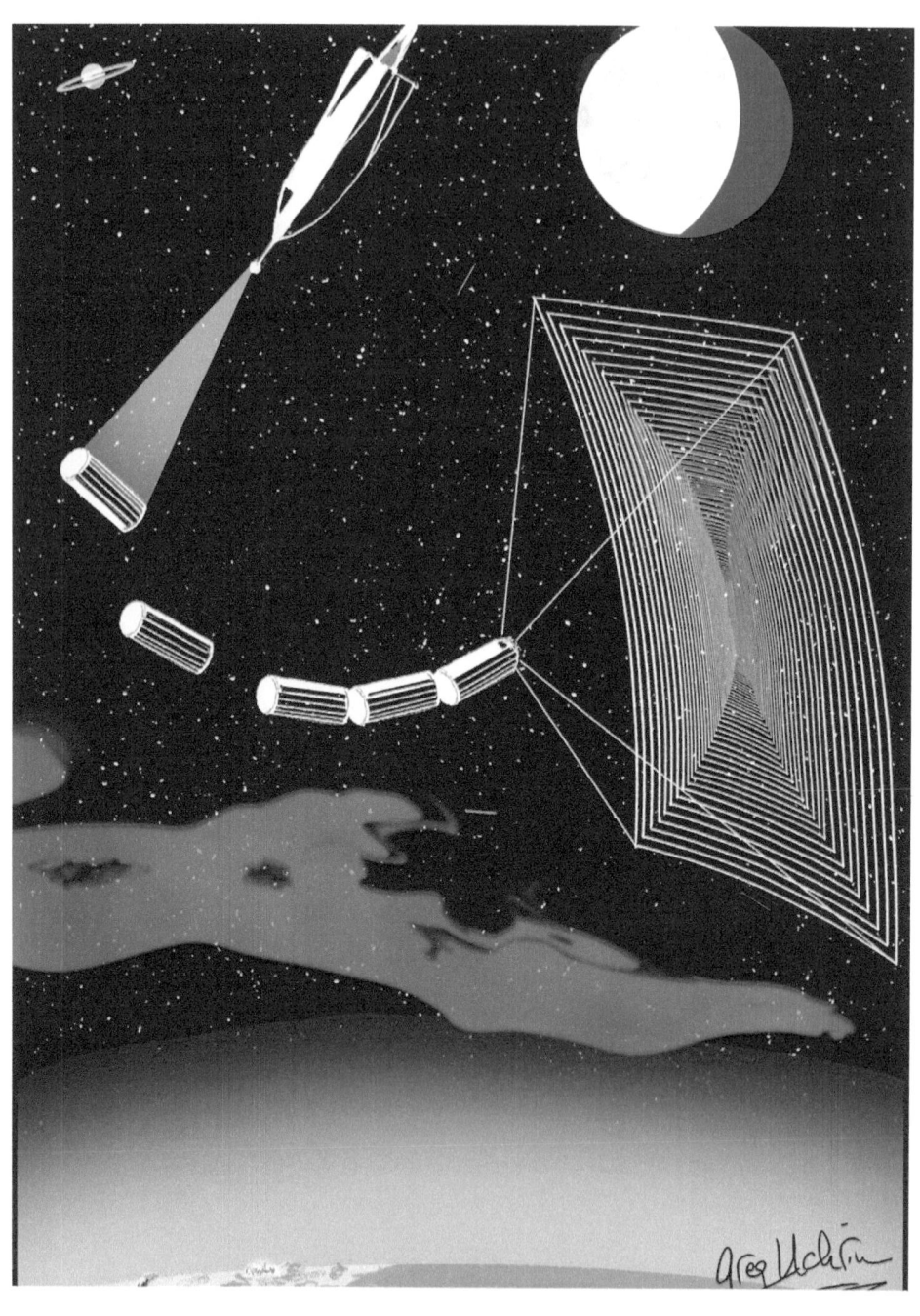

Illustration by Greg Uchrin

Juggernaut

Alena Van Arendonk

I have often described my introduction to Captain Jack Kill-Luck as a bolt of lightning from the clear blue sky, but honor compels me to confess that this phrasing, while poetic, is not strictly accurate. The aerostat on which I had secured passage was making its approach to London at the time, and the sky—far from clear—was so congested with soot and smoke that those of us waiting on deck pressed handkerchiefs over our mouths, lest our lungs turn as black as the coal burning far below us. No one in central England had seen a blue sky since before the days of the Directorate.

The bolt of lightning, however, was quite real. It carved a blinding arc from the static cannon on our pursuers' bow to the metal fittings of the balloon over our heads. Severed cables snaked free of their loops, lashing the deck as the gondola canted to one side. Passengers' screams blended with the ominous creak of wood and steel as the weight of the craft settled on only half of the cables meant to bear it. Pressurized steam shrieked through overload vents as the engine tilted, and water from the reservoir sloshed dangerously near the boiler housing.

The craft that had fired on us launched grapnels that sank into the planks of the gondola and soon a skiff slid down the connecting cables to bump against our hull. Standing boldly on the platform, pistol in hand, was the most audacious figure I had ever seen.

Captain Jack Kill-Luck.

I'd heard of the notorious air pirate, of course. Everyone knew the legends, if not the facts. Witness accounts of his exploits were scarce: in the three years since he'd appeared, no traveler apprehended by Captain Jack had ever returned. What little was known of him came from hardy souls who had leaped overboard when their ships were boarded, the embrace of gravity preferable to capture. Those who survived related their experiences to the London press, who compiled the accounts into salacious stories of a faceless, blood-red figure who slaughtered his victims and left ghost ships drifting aimlessly through the skies. These tales offered profitable fodder for the broadsides, but being accosted by pirates was hardly something a reasonable air traveler expected to face, any more than a yacht enthusiast might expect his Sunday sailing to be disrupted by a giant kraken.

The formidable scarlet-clad figure swung over the rail onto the sloping deck, cape billowing in the wind. A red kerchief concealed his face below smoked goggles, and a stout cable ran from his heavy leather belt to his own craft. Behind him came several black-liveried airmen, similarly anchored and carrying envelope rifles. If our crew offered any resistance, a shot from one of those weapons would launch razor-edged chain into the balloon overhead, ensuring that everyone aboard plummeted to an abrupt—but presumably still quite unpleasant—death.

Kill-Luck prowled down the line of passengers. He never spoke, but occasionally made a gesture that his subordinates interpreted as a demand to see a passenger's papers of transit. I was one of those selected, and I dutifully handed over my passport.

Kill-Luck examined it closely before angling his head in my direction. The featureless mask loomed before me like a bloodied skull. My palms began to sweat.

At another gesture from their captain, two of the pirates seized my arms and hauled me toward the rail. I struggled and shouted for help, but the aerostat's crew were powerless as long as the envelope rifles were trained on their balloon. I was bound and blindfolded before being lifted onto the skiff. Rather than kill me outright, the pirates meant to take me alive.

I wasn't certain which fate was worse.

* * *

When the cloth was pulled from my face, a searing light burst upon my vision, brighter than anything I'd experienced. My captors had secured my arms to a heavy chair; I had no way of shading my face. Reflexive tears began to streak my cheeks. Even squeezed shut, my eyes smarted.

"Brilliant, isn't it?" The light's assault suddenly abated, and I squinted up at a silhouette outlined by the window's glow. "How quickly you forget the touch of the sun when it's stolen from you." The voice was a woman's, and carried a Gaelic lilt.

"Stolen?" I rasped.

"By the curtain." She lowered a blind, cutting the light to a fraction of its previous intensity.

I didn't know what to make of her riddles. When my eyes adjusted to the lower light of the ship's cabin, I studied her. She looked nearer twenty than thirty, and wore oil-stained men's clothing rather than the black livery of the pirates. "Are you a prisoner, too?"

One corner of her mouth curved upward. "Only of circumstance."

A chess table lay between us. The woman tossed my personal effects into the middle of the board, upsetting several pieces. I was relieved to see my transit documents, as well as the small sample case one of the pirates had taken from my coat pocket. "Your passport was notarized by the Directorate, Mr. Thadden."

I shrugged as far as my bound arms would permit. "As are all London-issued passports, these days. Security is strict in the Imperial capital."

"But only the Ministry of Progress stamps in green ink. And your given profession is merely 'salesman.' Conveniently vague." She planted one foot on the seat of a chair and leaned forward over her knee. Something in her manner put me in mind of a hawk eyeing its next meal. "You're a bean-mover, aren't you?"

I answered her razor-sharp look with one of utter bemusement. "I'm a *what?*"

"Not bad. You give a reasonable impression of an unassuming Londoner plucked from his holiday return and afraid for his life."

"You think I'm *pretending* to be afraid? I've heard the tales. No one survives an encounter with Jack Kill-Luck. He's probably already murdered everyone else on my craft." I glanced toward the door. "Where is he now?"

She seemed to find my outburst amusing. "I assure you, everyone on board your aerostat has gone to a better place."

My worst fears were confirmed. "God above," I breathed.

"Not *that* place. They'll be delivered safely to the Refuge, provided none of them tries anything foolish."

"What the devil is the Refuge?"

"Invoking both sides? You do hedge your bets." She chuckled. "There is one place left in the world that remains wholly beyond the Directorate's knowledge or reach, and that is where the passengers will go. It's not ideal, but you'll agree it's better than killing everyone. We can't risk any more witnesses telling tales."

"So, instead, you abduct them?"

"Only when necessary—and I'm afraid you made it so. We should never have interfered with your aerostat at all, had we not been reliably informed that an agent of the Directorate was aboard."

I gaped. "How many people have you taken?"

"In total? Only a few hundred. Holding them was meant to be a temporary measure—to keep the Directorate from working out exactly what we were after—but our preparations have taken longer than expected. Still, many of our guests are quite content to stay. There's sunlight, fresh air..."

An ominous suspicion rose in my mind. "If you're telling me about this..."

"Oh, be under no illusions, Mr. Thadden: you aren't returning to London, either." She abruptly discarded her mantle of easy charm. "If you cooperate, you'll join the rest at the Refuge. If not, there are more permanent ways of ensuring your silence."

I moistened my dry lips. "What do you want from me?"

"The beans."

"I—I don't know what you mean," I stammered. "I sell sewing notions. Needles, thimbles, that sort of thing. If you're looking for foodstuffs, you've got the wrong salesman."

Her eyes narrowed. "You know I'm not speaking of food."

"What, then? I don't know what else a bean could be."

"Perhaps you don't. You needn't understand what you're carrying, after all." She settled in the chair across from me. "Even I don't quite know *what* they are. I suspect autonomous mechanical components of some kind, miniaturized beyond any clockwork known to modern industry. Half the crew believe they're magic, which they might as well be." She shrugged. "But your understanding is immaterial. Hand them over, and you live."

"I'm hardly in a position to hand over anything." I wriggled against my bonds. "If you'll release me, you have my word that I won't tell anyone what I've seen."

She barked a laugh. "As though I'd trust the word of anyone working for the Directorate."

"I've told you, I'm just a notions salesman!" I fixed her with my most sincere look. "I'll tell you everything about myself. I was born in Bayswater. I apprenticed at Sharp and Company. I—"

"—have your best interests at heart. The mines will provide more work, higher wages, and a better quality of life for everyone in the village." Her eyes drifted toward the window. "All the Directorate's lies ring the same sour note. Spare me the encore."

"Mines? I don't understand."

"Typical Londoner." Her gaze swung back to me, weighing something. At last, she seemed to reach a decision. "I was born in Celyddon."

"Where?"

"A remote village in the valleys. You haven't heard of it. It was a quiet place—green hills dotted with sheep, a clear brook where I fetched water, simple farmers coaxing a living from the soil."

"It sounds idyllic."

"It was." Her lips thinned. "Until the Directorate discovered that our land was rich in coal. Their steam-augers drilled deep into the hills, and soldiers pressed the villagers into labor. The sheep became ill. The streams ran black. The crops failed, and we starved. The Directorate denied responsibility, blaming the blight on poor husbandry—and we, who had farmed that land for fifty generations, watched children die in agony while their fathers dug up the very poison that tainted the soil."

The pain in her voice wasn't feigned. My stomach knotted.

"I was fortunate; my father died young, Mother was unwell, and I was too slight for heavy labor, so I was exempted from mining to tend our farm. But we suffered all the same. Our sheep died one by one. When we had no money left, I took our last ewe to market to sell, but with the price of bread so dear, no one had coin to spare. Even if they had, everyone knew that none of the sheep would survive the year. And yet…" Her fingers drummed a meditative beat on the table. "I found a buyer."

"Who?"

"A petty thief, perhaps. Someone who picked the wrong pocket and was anxious to rid himself of the evidence. He offered what he claimed were five brass ingots—a paltry price for a sheep, but I was in no position to bargain. Only as it turned out, they were something far more valuable."

"These mysterious beans, I presume?"

She nodded, then laughed. "Mother was furious when I showed her one. She flung it into the stove, slapped my face, and cursed me for my stupidity."

I flinched before I could control the reaction. "I'm sorry. That sounds… painful."

She sighed. "More painful when it comes true, I suspect."

"Comes true?"

"The curse."

I blinked. "I thought—you meant a *literal* curse?"

"Scoff all you like. I'm aware that in this age of progress and industry, enlightened man no longer believes in rustic superstitions or magic." She gave a wry smile. "But in that land, words have their own power. She doomed me the moment she spoke."

"Doomed you to what?"

"'Foolish child, can't tell good from bad—you'll wed no wholesome kin of the land, but take the son of your worst enemy as your mate!' Those were her last words; no sooner had she uttered them than she dropped dead of an apoplectic fit."

This last, delivered casually, stunned me. "I'm—sorry."

"Don't be. It's not as though my marriage prospects were favorable, anyway. Our farm was ruined, I had no dowry, and most of the young men were dying in the mines—"

"I meant about your mother."

"Oh. She was in poor health. It wasn't unexpected." Her smile was half grimace. "No doubt you think me heartless for not being profoundly bereaved."

"Not at all. Parents…aren't always what you wish them to be." I stared at my passport, still lying open amid the chessmen. A phantom sting flashed across my own cheek, chased by an echo: *I'll give you one last chance.* "I imagine the inverse is also true."

"I imagine so."

Silence hung between us. "But—the beans?" I prompted after a moment.

"Right." She shook herself. "By the time I returned with the doctor, the house was burning—from the top down. It appeared the iron stove had floated up to the ceiling and set the rafters ablaze. But that's clearly impossible."

"Clearly."

She watched me closely. "Unless whatever had been thrown into the stove had the power to grant it flight."

I mustered my most incredulous look. "A flying stove? We certainly live in an age of mechanical wonders, but I find that a bit *too* wondrous."

"And yet you just stepped from one airship to another without questioning how they can hover hundreds of feet above the ground."

"It is well known that aerostats gain their lift from helium and their propulsion from steam. Any schoolboy can explain the physics."

She hummed thoughtfully. "For an agent of the Directorate, you aren't terribly observant."

"I'm not an—" I broke off and sighed. "What, precisely, have I failed to notice?"

"That this ship has no envelope."

I stared as though this were a revelation. "But it must have! It couldn't fly otherwise."

A half-smile hovered on her lips as she picked up the thread of her tale. "After the fire, I had no reason to stay in Celyddon, so I wandered toward the column of smoke on the horizon that marked London. Outside the city, I came across the wreckage of an airship, its envelope in tatters. I had no money, so I tried to use the ship's furnace to melt the remaining 'ingots' into something resembling coins. Imagine my astonishment when the ruined ship took to the air."

"With no helium?"

"Just so." She spread her arms to encompass the craft. "Of course, it took some time to restore the *Gwalch* to full airworthiness, but thankfully, security at the Directorate's factories is about as robust as its agents are trustworthy, so I didn't want for tools or materials."

I gaped at this brazen admission. "You robbed Imperial plants?"

"Repeatedly. It was less than they owed, after what they did to my home."

"Perhaps so—but antagonizing them will cost you even more. The Committee spares no mercy for thieves and traitors—" As I spoke, I recalled where I'd heard those words, and they turned sour in my mouth.

If she noticed my discomfiture, she gave no indication. "Nor will the thieves and traitors spare mercy for the Directorate. Every member of the *Gwalch*'s crew has a story like mine. We've devoted ourselves to disrupting the Directorate's great plan."

"And…what plan is that?"

She arched her eyebrows as though the answer should be obvious. "They've made little secret of their intention to expand the Empire."

"As they've done for decades, furthering trade and international commerce. It's hardly a nefarious plot."

"To conquer sovereign nations and enslave their people? To crush all resistance until a handful of men in London are the supreme rulers of all, free to commit *any* act with impunity?"

"You presuppose malicious intent. One might as easily take the humanitarian view and say that when more…primitive lands are absorbed into the Empire, it's to their benefit."

"Really." She scowled. "Name one that has benefited more than it has suffered from your 'civilization.'"

I considered and discarded several answers before I struck upon one with an indisputably improved outcome. "The Hindoostanis. Their land was ravaged by plague until the Empire sent physicians and medicine to help them. Nearly a fifth of their population died."

"A fifth of their population *went missing*. Officially, they were placed in quarantine by the Imperial relief corps, but no one seems to know where those quarantine camps were located. And it must be coincidence that most of the 'victims' were young men. The type that would be most valuable as laborers."

I stared at her in unfeigned disbelief. "Are you suggesting that the Directorate staged an epidemic so they could abduct a nation's workforce?"

"What better way to make a subjugated land dependent on foreign trade? To say nothing of amassing a private labor force of their own."

I scarcely knew where to begin dismantling this wild theory. "Look—the Imperial government operates under rules and procedure. Even top ministers can't just do whatever they like. If any one of them proposed such a monstrous thing, others would put a stop to it."

"Would they?" Her eyes bored into mine. "With all the harm they've inflicted, can you honestly believe Chancellor Whitflower and his cronies value *anyone's* interests besides their own?"

That question was difficult to answer for reasons that had nothing to do with politics, and abruptly I found my position less defensible. "The present administration may, at times, overreach. But no system is without imbalances. It's unfortunate when the burden falls heavier on some, but... it's for the greater good," I finished without conviction.

"'The greater good,'" she echoed. "Sacrifice some for the success of others. Discard the pawns for the benefit of a king." She tapped the chessboard with a finger. "Count the pawns and kings you see, and then tell me if the good is truly *greater*."

I gave her a flat look. "Your argument might carry more weight if you hadn't just admitted to the wholesale abduction of hundreds of innocent travelers."

The color in her cheeks deepened a shade. "I've already said that's a temporary arrangement. We haven't harmed any of them. But accuse us all you like—our actions, unlawful though they might be, are still tempered by conscience. The Directorate's tactics are barbaric. Once they subjugate the entire world, there will be *no stopping* their abuses."

"World conquest is out of the question," I returned. "The Imperial Navy may be formidable, but they'll never gain a foothold in eastern Europe while the Ottoman Iron Dragoons oppose them. The Americas are likewise well-defended."

That sharp gaze fell on me again, assessing. "And what if the Imperial Navy could reduce every mechanized force to lumps of molten iron in minutes?"

"Impossible. Such weaponry doesn't exist."

"Just as brass ingots that make things fly don't exist." She leaned forward, her eyes holding mine. "With the aid of those nonexistent ingots, I've soared high enough to discover the truth. I learned why the Directorate needs so much coal, why they build more and more factories, why smoke blots out the English sky: they can't risk anyone looking *up*. They engineer an impenetrable curtain of ash and soot to conceal what they're building in a floating factory over London. Give me what you're carrying, and I'll show it to you."

I'd become so caught up in the debate, it was jarring to return to its beginning. "I can't give what I don't have."

She sighed. "To any other master, your loyalty would be commendable. But if you persist, we'll be forced to chop you into kindling and feed you into the furnace piece by piece until the bit with the beans fires up."

"Right. I'd almost forgotten which pirate's ship I was on." I frowned. "No, wait—you said this was *your* ship. Where does Captain Jack Kill-Luck come into all this?"

"Ah, yes. Captain Jack." I was treated to another wry smile. "To the English ear, Siân Culhwch sounds like John Kill-Luck. The name spread on its own."

"What does…" I knew I hadn't a hope of reproducing the Welsh syllables. "…*that* mean?"

The smile became one of amusement. "That you're as English as the rest."

"I beg your pardon?"

She appealed to the ceiling with her eyes. "If you can't manage Siân, feel free to address me as Jack, as my crew do. We thieves and traitors are an informal lot."

My stomach sank abruptly—not in fear, but in dismay. "*You're* Captain Jack Kill-Luck?"

"As much as anyone can claim to be." Siân—Jack—shrugged. "The fearsome reputation serves some purpose for now, but once Captain Jack is of no further use, he'll vanish, and I'll simply be Siân the shepherdess."

This modesty was unexpected. I had naturally assumed any pirate with so absurd a moniker as "Kill-Luck" must be consumed with his own notoriety, but Siân Culhwch's candid speech and practical dress showed a welcome lack of artifice.

I recognized the rising flicker of admiration and aggressively smothered it. I wasn't here to make friends, no matter how stimulating I'd found the conversation. I tested my bonds, but these airmen knew their business; the knots held fast.

Jack recognized the movement for what it was. "There are only two ways for you to leave that chair, Mr. Thadden. One: you give me the beans. You then stand and walk away on your own. Two: you refuse to give me the beans. You are then removed from the chair. In pieces."

Now that I possessed the information I'd sought, it was no longer to my purpose to remain a subdued captive. I dropped the timid facade I'd worn since boarding the aerostat. "Very well. Release me, and I'll give you what you want."

She blinked a few times, clearly surprised by my sudden capitulation, but rounded the table to free my left hand. "You get the other arm when I have the beans."

I opened my sample case, which contained a selection of perfectly mundane sewing equipment. When I twisted a particular needle into a certain place in the lining, however, the panel of notions flipped open on a concealed hinge to reveal the true cargo: three brass-finished lozenges the size of kidney beans, carefully packed in cotton wool.

Jack whispered a Welsh word that, by its intonation, could only have been profane. "We even searched that. *Liam!*" she shouted. A young airman opened the door, and Jack carefully transferred the case to him. "Take these to the boiler room and wait for me." When he'd gone, she freed my other arm. "Not that it matters, but why the change of heart?"

I shrugged. "I suppose there's some truth in what you said about the Directorate. Besides, they lied to me."

"They lie to everyone. How, specifically?"

"They told me those things were ore samples from Africa. If I'd known what I was actually transporting, I might have taken greater care to protect myself."

"Fortunately for me, you didn't." Her eyes softened. "I'm glad you saw reason. I didn't want to have to kill you." Her gaze lingered on me for a moment before she abruptly snapped back to business. "You'll see the rest of the truth for yourself soon. We'll reach the factory shortly."

"You're going straightaway?" The timing wasn't ideal, but I would have to manage. I collected my passport from the table.

"No point in wasting fuel when we're already over London. The beans provide lift, but we still use steam propulsion. And we have the explosives on board already."

I froze. "Explosives?"

"How else could we destroy the Directorate's superweapon?"

What in God's name were these pirates planning to do? "Boilers are not great lovers of shockwaves," I said carefully. "When a regulation airship boiler bursts, the aerostatic disruption field has a half-mile radius. You're saying something the size of a factory—that could spread for *miles*, to say nothing of debris. Have you calculated the risk to *this* craft?"

Her expression told me she hadn't, but she remained stoic. "My crew is agreed that it must be destroyed. No matter the cost."

A suicide mission had not been in my calculations. I needed her—and, ideally, myself—alive. I adjusted my plan again. "At least tell me you know how much charge to use."

"All of it, I assume." She gave me a penetrating look. "Why? Are you an expert in explosives as well as bobbins?"

"I have a little training," I admitted.

"In dynamiting?"

"In incendiary demolition."

Jack's eyebrows rose. "You're military?"

"Formerly. They don't let just *anyone* transport ore samples, you know."

She gave a thoughtful hum. "Would you act against the Directorate?"

"Ordinarily, no. Treason is a capital offense." I sighed. "But if you miscalculate and blow the boiler, I'll die anyway. It seems my best chance of coming through alive is to ensure that you do not miscalculate."

She considered. "Fair enough. We, too, prefer survival over martyrdom."

I couldn't suppress a wry smile. "Finally, something we agree on."

"Then if you've any fantasies of escape, abandon them now. My men and I go armed. Oh, and…hold on to something." At the door, she tossed a grin back over her shoulder. "The *Gwalch* is about to soar."

* * *

True to Jack's warning, the sudden ascent was dizzying. Pressure built in my ears, and I engaged in a heated argument with my stomach regarding its proper location. Even after the sensation eased, I could feel the craft swaying in powerful winds and knew we were higher than I'd ever flown before.

Presently the cabin door opened to admit Jack, once again clad in scarlet. "Come on, then. We've anchored below their hull."

I eyed her flamboyant costume. "Won't they spot you immediately, like that?"

"They'll spot me when I want them to. Surely your military training covered diversionary tactics?"

I followed her out on deck and immediately flung my hands up before my eyes. Even in shadow, the sunlight was dazzling. Red shapes swam behind my eyelids.

Jack nudged my arm. "Here. Put these on until we're inside."

More by feel than sight I donned the tinted goggles she handed me and, when the dancing spots faded, I scanned our surroundings. The *Gwalch* hovered beneath a massive span of riveted steel, a pattern of interlocking metal plates broken only by the rungs of an access ladder curving up around the hull. Below us, a roiling sea of black spread for miles in every direction. At its nearest edge, I could just make out hovering craft equipped with enormous fans. "Good Lord," I breathed.

"The curtain." Jack joined me at the rail as she tied the red cloth over her face. "Hard to believe there's a city beneath all that soot." It was jarring to see the fearsome Captain Jack Kill-Luck looking down on the world with gentle gray eyes, and I realized the goggles I wore were part of her costume.

The rest of the boarding party gathered on deck. Jack took two sticks of dynamite from a large pack that one of the airmen carried. "When we reach the assembly floor, I'll draw their attention. Owen will set the charges. Liam, you'll guard him and make sure he does the job."

Liam looked around. "Who's Owen?"

I raised my hand. "Hello."

The young man stared at his captain. "You trust *him*?"

"I trust his desire to live. Which he won't if we're caught, or if he raises the alarm. Understood, Owen?"

Liam scowled. "Since when do you exchange given names with Directorate lackeys?"

Jack flushed. "It was on his passport! Now—Rhys, keep watch. The rest of you, resupply. Prioritize ship's stores and mechanicals; after that, anything we can sell. Back on the *Gwalch* within ten minutes. I want you clear before we detonate."

"One question," I interjected. "What, exactly, am I dynamiting?"

Jack shook her head. "You'll know when you see it."

The wind tore at my clothing as I followed the pirates up the ladder and I fought the urge to look down into the black maelstrom. I was better informed than most about the Directorate's inner workings, but the deliberate creation of this smoke curtain had been kept from me. I hadn't truly believed Jack's tale until I'd seen it. The curtain existed; how many of her other fantastic claims might be true?

Inside, the pirates scattered to the storerooms while we crept toward the sound of machinery. The corridor soon opened onto a massive chamber, where a colossal figure loomed in the semidarkness. I stopped dead when I realized it was shaped like an enormous man, with hinged limbs and a skin of armored plates. There was no mistaking the concentric dishes embedded in its chest—a static cannon of *massive* proportion. The focal rod alone was the height of a cathedral spire. Jack's assertion that it could reduce armored transports to slag was not an exaggeration.

Liam collided with my back, but scarcely seemed to notice. "It's *huge*," he breathed. "Does that thing *walk*?"

"It's nearly complete," Jack whispered, though the background roar of factory equipment could have smothered a shout. "We're not a moment too soon."

I tore my eyes away from the giant and received another shock: laboring at furnaces across the room, shirtless but with turbans twisted neatly about their heads, were dozens of men. Some were so emaciated, they resembled skeletons; others bore crudely bandaged wounds. Armed Imperial soldiers were ranged about each group.

Jack followed my gaze. "Care to revisit our discussion about the Hindoostani plague victims?"

"I concede the point." Rage flared within me. I already knew the Directorate's chief officers espoused many things I reviled, but abduction? *Slavery?* It was unconscionable. Unforgivable. And the men's condition... Even convict laborers in London's worst prison received better treatment.

"I'll draw them off. Be prepared to move." Jack darted into the shadows.

I hardly noticed her departure. A snatch of recent conversation was echoing in my head: *I'll give you one last chance to prove yourself worthy. If you fail...*

Quite suddenly, I decided that failure was no longer the worst option available.

My eyes shifted to the giant. "I need a closer look."

Liam seized my arm. "Wait for Jack! They'll see you!"

"They won't. I know what I'm doing." I crept silently along the wall, stealing from cover to cover as I kept watch on the soldiers. It wouldn't take much to draw their attention—something I had originally counted on, but now my objective had changed. I concealed myself in an alcove near the giant and began analyzing its structure for weaknesses.

Across the room, something exploded. Cries of alarm mingled with shouted orders as the guards began herding the laborers out of the area.

Liam reached my hiding place, hugging the pack of explosives. I pointed toward the enormous automaton. "There's a missing panel in the foot. We'll go in there."

We climbed up through a maze of oil-slick gears, using light from unfilled rivet holes to mark the way. At last, I found a hatch overhead. "Here's the cockpit. Pass me some dynamite."

Liam handed up a satchel and began unspooling a coil of fuse. "Jack can only keep them busy for so long. I'll go down and set the detonator."

As I planted explosives around the cockpit, connecting fuses and blasting caps, I scanned the instruments. In addition to steam pressure, limb movement, and weapons were controls for ballast height and rudders. Inspired, I pried open an access panel and was rewarded with the dull gleam of brass. I filled my pockets.

I retraced my path down the automaton, wedging dynamite into gears at critical junctions. It wouldn't take a massive explosion to ruin this monstrosity—just several precisely targeted blasts.

I had just reached the ankle when I heard Liam curse. "She's in trouble!"

I put my eye to a rivet-hole in time to see Jack's red cape swirl conspicuously to the floor while she, in dark clothing, dove into the shadows. Armed soldiers surrounded the cape, then began a methodical sweep of the area under the direction of several officers. They had nearly surrounded Jack's position; she was all but trapped.

I squirmed out of the iron shell to find Liam crouched behind the giant's leg, watching for a gap in the soldiers' formation. The moment one appeared, he bolted forward, but I hauled him back. "Stay," I ordered. Shocked into obedience, he did.

I stood and straightened my coat, hoping the grease smears didn't show, before striding confidently across the floor. Two dozen rifles swung in my direction, but I ignored them and marched directly toward the most senior officer—a colonel. With his rank, he was likely in command of this facility. He would do nicely.

He gaped at my bold approach. "Who the blazes are you?"

I wordlessly produced my passport. He scowled at it. "A civilian? How the devil did you get in here?"

"Quite easily, as it happens. And now I've seen why—your response to external disruption is appalling." Taking back my passport, I used my thumbnail to split the lightly pasted edge of the identification page. Peeled apart, the secret pages displayed my authentic credentials. I handed the booklet back and relished the look of horror that stole over the colonel's face.

"Sir!" He saluted smartly. The men surrounding me followed his lead and shuffled into confused attention. "I was not apprised of your coming."

"No one ever is. Do you know why I'm here?"

He swallowed nervously as he scrambled for a reason. "There was a communiqué about…recurring thefts? The air pirates in this quadrant are—"

"Immaterial." I scanned the semicircle of troops. "In fact, I've traced the loss to this very facility."

All color drained from the officer's face. "I—I'm sure that can't be right…"

I narrowed my eyes in a manner I knew to be supremely threatening to men I outranked. "Are you contradicting me, Colonel?"

"No, sir!" He moistened his lips. "How may we assist, Intelligencer?"

"Clear this area. I want all men confined to quarters until I have conducted my inspection."

"At once, sir!" At a barked order, the soldiers hurried away double-time. The colonel stood by for my next instruction.

I gave him a hard look. "*All* men, Colonel."

"Er—" He moistened his lips. "It's—somewhat irregular—"

My gaze shifted to his epaulet. "Are you particularly attached to those diamond pips, *Major*?"

He blanched and followed his men at an anxious trot.

When they were out of sight, I squinted toward the corner into which Jack had vanished. "Jack! Now's your chance."

She emerged slowly, and while I was disappointed, I was not entirely surprised by the pistol she aimed at me. "You aren't just a bean-mover."

I stood very still. "Not *just*, no."

"And you aren't Mr. Owen Thadden."

"Owen, yes. Thadden, no."

"What's the rest?"

There was no point in drawing it out. "Whitflower."

Naked revulsion contorted her features. "As in Chancellor Whitflower?"

An echo of her reaction stirred within me. "My father, I'm afraid."

"The son of one so illustrious must hold an equally distinguished position."

I inclined my head. "Intelligencer General of Greater London. Present orders: to apprehend one Captain Jack Kill-Luck for theft of certain controlled Imperial properties and sundry other offenses." I managed a strained smile. "You've given our department a lot of trouble. Few offenders warrant my personal attendance."

"Indeed." She gave me a rueful look. I hated it. "The Ministry stamp, the omissions in your passport—well done. I sailed right into your trap."

I abandoned the parody of civilized introduction. "It hasn't sprung yet. I've bought us a few minutes, but no more. If we don't leave now—"

"We?" She laughed. "Don't think, having fooled me once, that I'll permit you to learn where the Refuge is. You'll remain right here while we make our escape. Explain to your celebrated father how you let Captain Jack Kill-Luck slip through your fingers."

I held her gaze. "You know they'll execute me when they learn I've helped you."

She looked away, but her pistol did not waver. "I know."

"Jack—"

"*Don't.*" The flash of sorrow in her eyes vanished so quickly, I half believed I had imagined it. "Don't follow us. I'd have to shoot you, and I'd hate to deprive the Chancellor of that honor."

She collected her cape and her men and was gone, leaving me alone, adrift in a factory the size of a small city, an iron giant looming overhead, loaded with dynamite—

Damn. I'd nearly forgotten about that.

I dashed for the detonator. I was doomed already, and the explosion should cover Jack's escape. Besides, destroying the automaton would delay the Directorate's plans.

My father's plans.

Somehow, the revelation didn't shock me as much as it probably should have. Perhaps there was good cause for our long estrangement. Perhaps I'd sensed all along that something about him wasn't right. He'd always remained on guard against me, aware—and displeased—that my methods were less extreme than his own.

The background roar of the factory pressed upon my ears with the weight of his voice at our last meeting: *Your so-called suppression of these renegades has been so weak, even I begin to doubt your loyalty to the Empire. The Committee spares no mercy for thieves, nor for the traitors who aid them. Until now my name has shielded you from indictment, but I won't have it sullied by populist filth. I'll give you one last chance to prove yourself worthy. If you fail in this, son or no, I'll denounce you to the tribunal myself.*

He'd sent me after Jack. If he had a better understanding of my character, perhaps he wouldn't have risked letting me make direct contact with an eloquent revolutionary.

But it seemed my father and I had never understood each other at all.

"Intelligencer?"

I finished twisting the copper fuse wire around the blasting machine's contacts before looking up—this time, to find the colonel's pistol pointed at me. I got to my feet, surreptitiously raising the plunger as I stood. The magneto creaked in its housing.

The colonel seemed not to notice the sound; he was too busy looking pleased with himself. "I took the liberty of signaling headquarters on the wireless. They sent back that you are not authorized to enter this facility, and certainly not by stealth. The Chancellor was quite anxious for an explanation, and instructed me to fetch you immediately." His eyes followed the trailing fuse into the automaton. "I must say, I am also keen to have this explained. Kindly step away from that device, Intelligencer."

I raised my hands, but stayed where I was. If he fired, I could still fall on the plunger. "There is a simple explanation, Colonel."

"I believe the simplest explanation is that you are a—"

He never finished that sentence. I spotted the flash of red only an instant before the explosion—not the daring sweep of Jack's cape I'd half hoped for, but the slow arc of a stick of dynamite, fuse flaring. On the instant, I threw myself onto the plunger. Even as one concussion swept the colonel off his feet, another set off a chain of muffled internal blasts that rocked the automaton. With a groan that overwhelmed even the ringing in my ears, the iron monstrosity began to sway on its partially severed legs. It loomed overhead, impossibly huge, slowly twisting as it fell…

Hands dragged me aside, and I was pressed into an alcove as the behemoth collapsed across the factory floor, crushing the furnaces into plumes of flame and molten iron. When I thought the immediate danger was past, I twisted to see my rescuer.

Jack scowled back at me, but indicated with a jerk of her head that I should follow.

The *Gwalch* swayed a few yards below the hatch we'd entered. "Jump!" Jack shouted over the roar of wind.

I jumped.

Even before we slammed into the deck, the crew jettisoned the anchor lines. The *Gwalch* pitched dangerously toward the roiling black clouds below. The engineer cranked on steam, and the ship leveled out, slowly falling toward the setting sun.

"We're on our last bean," an airman warned Jack when the ship had stabilized. "We stayed too high for too long. We'll barely make the Refuge at low altitude."

Jack's shoulders sagged, but she only nodded and descended to the cabin.

I followed her. "Jack."

She turned and regarded me silently.

"Why did you come back?"

She shrugged. "To finish the job. We went to destroy that thing."

"Whatever the reason, you saved my life. Thank you."

"You saved mine first. And…" She flushed and looked away. "Well. Perhaps I'm just as foolish as my mother said."

"Oh?" A spark of hope warmed me. "As I recall, she also mentioned something about the son of your worst enemy…?"

Jack's blush deepened, but she laughed. "To be clear, I still have no dowry. Just a crippled airship with no lift."

"*That*, at least, I can remedy." From my pockets, I scooped handfuls of brass beans—the treasure from the automaton's cockpit. "I hope you'll accept these, along with my apology."

Jack's eyes stretched wide at the golden bounty. "This will keep us airborne for months!"

"Enough for a journey to Hindoostan, at least."

She looked up. "Hindoostan?"

"No discourtesy to your Refuge, but I'm sure those laborers would prefer their homeland. I assume you intend to free them?"

"It had crossed my mind." She rolled a bean between her fingers. "You've stolen controlled Imperial properties, you know."

"I *am* authorized to transport them." I glanced toward the window. Somewhere, beyond the drawn shade and the smoke curtain, was London. "Although I suspect my security clearance is being revoked. By teatime, I'll have joined you on the list of the Directorate's most wanted."

"We're putting in at the Refuge soon. You'll be safe there—that is, if you don't mind being abducted by pirates."

"I'll overlook it this once," I said dryly. "Though I do think you should send the other 'guests' home."

"We will. Now that we've acted, there's no longer any reason to hold them." She frowned. "But that would leave you at the Refuge alone. Imperial territory isn't safe for you, either. What will you do?"

"Well…as a desperate fugitive, I suppose I can only turn to piracy— assuming I can find a crew willing to take on a disaffected Imperial agent. Preferably a crew whose acts are tempered by conscience."

Jack arched an eyebrow. "You certainly have high standards."

I chuckled. "At least I didn't demand equivalent rank."

"Is that what the Empire offers defectors? Maybe I can trade in and get a pension when I retire. I'm afraid you'll have to take an eight-rank demotion if you sail with us, though." Her gaze shifted from me to the pile of beans as something occurred to her. "Say, Ensign of-late Intelligencer General…given your insider knowledge, I don't suppose you know how to *make* these things?"

"I don't," I confessed. I waited for her hopeful expression to fade before adding, "but I *do* know exactly where that information is kept."

Jack's smile was as dazzling as the sun. "Welcome to the crew, Owen."

The Pirate and the Frog

Gloria Wickman

Captain Eloise de Griotte picked a bit of charred spice cricket from between her molars with the left fork of her tongue. In better times she could have afforded seats at an establishment much nicer than the moldering, half-dilapidated grog shop in which she'd taken up a corner booth with her second-in-command, Rourke, but with the Tyrant Lord's gendarmery breathing down everyone's necks on land and sea, work was increasingly hard to come by. And besides, none of them had crickets as spicy, salty, and crispy as the Heron's Folly. She popped another handful into her mouth and signaled for a refill of ale.

Quick as a shot, a hummingwing server darted out from behind the bar, carrying a mug of ale that was only slightly shorter than her torso. She flittered through a sea of undulating bodies: Avian, Amphibian, Ichthyoid, even a few Land Dwellers (Mammals, perhaps?). There was nothing quite like the first alehouse on the docks to draw out people of all sorts. The server plopped the ale down on a cork coaster embossed with a heron and zipped off with Eloise's empty mug.

As Eloise brought the fresh mug to her lips, Rourke gently nudged her shoulder with his pale blue claw and nodded toward the front door of the grog shop. She saw instantly what he was indicating. The poor Amphibian stood out like a worm surfacing among a gaggle of hens. For one thing, his clothes were too fine. Exquisite linen trousers and a matching suit jacket, both tailored to fit his long, narrow legs and bulbous torso. Just peeking out underneath the jacket was a midnight blue vest shimmering with delicate silver embroidery.

Eyes betraying his discomfort, the Amphibian's gaze darted from one patron to another until it finally—and rather unexpectedly—landed on Eloise and stayed.

"He's coming over here," Rourke muttered, and Eloise had to put her hand over his claw to stop Rourke from reaching for his knife. Or his flintlock.

"Perhaps he's offering work," Eloise said. "A final score. One big enough to get up north. Nothing but warm weather, cool drinks, and peaceful retirement."

Rourke snorted. "Keep dreaming. You're not the retiring type."

Before Eloise could offer any further retort, the Amphibian was upon them and offered a deep bow. As he rose, he cleared his throat and said, "Forgive me, but might you be the great Captain Eloise de Griotte? I was told to look for an Ichthyoid with burgundy scales in a yellow kaftan."

Any other evening, Eloise might have toyed with the man for a bit, but he was so clearly out of his element and liable to be robbed before the night was out that she took pity on him and gestured toward the cushion across from her.

"I am Eloise. Please speak."

The Amphibian hastened to his seat, bumping into the table and sending it wobbling as he worked to fit his legs under and fold them. He cleared his throat again and pulled a handkerchief from his breast pocket to dab at his forehead.

"I'm called Fabian. I was told you were the captain to see for matters of a, hmm, discretionary nature?" His eyes darted around the room again, as if he expected the Tyrant Lord's gendarmery thugs to be lurking behind him.

"We are very discreet," Eloise agreed.

"Though discretion costs," Rourke added, crossing his clawed arms in front of him.

Fabian nodded, clearly expecting this to be the case. "I need transportation to a remote island, and security while there to help me retrieve something very valuable to me." He leaned forward and lowered his voice to a whisper. "It may involve going against the gendarmery."

Rourke scoffed. "A few softies cladding themselves up like armadillos don't scare us." Then, realizing he was the only person in the party with an exoskeleton, he added, "No offense."

"We're not uninterested," Eloise said, taking a sip of her ale and enjoying the tingle of it against her lips. "But I'm not sure you could afford what this would cost. And I don't want to risk my ship and my crew until I know exactly what I'm up against. You have my word that whether we accept your offer or not, you will have our silence. If you can't trust us that far, we're not the right crew for you anyway."

Fabian's shoulders collapsed, the weariness of a being without any other options. "What do you know about iron silk?" he asked.

Rourke huffed. "Iron silk? It's a myth at this point. No one's found a cache in over eighty years. That's why you see the gendarmery wearing those thick scales for protection instead of weaving themselves something nice and maneuverable."

Fabian nodded, reached into his inside coat pocket, and pulled out a small spool of gray thread with a dull shine. He set it on the table. "You mentioned that your services would be expensive," he said pushing the spool toward Eloise. "I can offer you this now, and much more when the job is done."

Eloise picked up the spool and carefully unwound the thread. Her first thought was that it had to be a forgery. Iron silk hadn't been found in large quantities for generations, and hadn't been manufactured in centuries. It was a lost art, or maybe an extinct species. No one know the exact formula of alchemy and raw materials that had brought about such a miracle. A thread light as silk but strong as iron, capable of turning away a bullet or a blade while giving the wearer unrestricted movement.

Eloise wrapped a length of the thread around two of her fingers and brought it to her mouth to gnaw on it. It held firm and refused to fray against even her sharpest teeth. The taste was tannic and bitter, not at all like the rich, fresh blood taste of most knockoffs mixing in iron and copper to fool overly credulous customers. She noticed, too, Fabian relaxing and leaning back a bit in his chair. Whatever else scared the Amphibian, he wasn't worried about being declared a fraud.

After spitting out the thread and winding it back on the spool, Eloise tossed it to Rourke, who tore at it with his claws, finding it every bit as resistant to damage as Eloise had. At last, he gave it up and pushed the battered spool back to the center of the table.

"We're interested," Eloise said. She carefully removed the chiffon scarf from around her gills to wet it in the bowl of water on the side of the table before rewrapping it around her neck. It was an embarrassing tell of how distracted she'd been by the offer to let her scarf dry enough to inhibit her breathing, but Fabian seemed to make nothing of it. "We'll take this spool as a down payment, but need more when the job is done."

"How much?" Fabian asked quickly.

Eloise glanced at Rourke. One spool was already valuable, but it was difficult to know how much to ask for without knowing how much Fabian had to give. Ten spools? Twenty-four?

"What were you planning to offer?" Eloise asked instead.

"Upfront I can give you a case, no more. After the job is done successfully, you'll get enough for you and your crew—that's fifteen people I've heard— you'll have enough for you and all of them to be fully kitted out. If that's something you'd like to do."

Eloise tried and failed to suppress a cough. Beside her, Rourke's pincers clapped together nervously. "That would be very agreeable," Eloise said, not even dreaming of haggling. The caseload alone would be worth a fortune to the right buyers. Even if Fabian had no intention on delivering the rest, it meant a comfortable retirement. Or good seed money for a few jobs after.

"Thank you," Fabian said, sagging in relief. "How soon can you be ready to leave? It's very urgent that I reach my destination as soon as possible."

"Be at the docks with the case and your baggage tomorrow afternoon," Eloise said.

* * *

The *Salty Viper*, typical of most tortoise-shell ships, sat low in the water. The deep bowl of the gargantuan shell was only slightly modified with a wooden rudder and a sharp-fanged figurehead. The shells were plentiful to be found, even this far west from the Savage Lands, and regularly floated into shallow waters where shipbuilders scooped them up and turned them into fine vessels. The sails, bright purple atop three masts, were rolled up tight, not to be unfurled until the ship was underway. The approach of a certain Amphibian, teetering up the gangway with a bulky case in his webbed hands and large pack slung across his shoulder, suggested that would be very soon.

Eloise looked up from the manifest she'd been reviewing. Setting the book on a crate of hard crackers, she walked to Fabian to steady him as he stepped uneasily from the gangplank onto the *Viper*.

"I have your payment," Fabian said, loud enough that several of the crew glanced over curiously.

Eloise pursed her lips, gesturing for the Amphibian to follow her into the wheelhouse at the stern of the ship. She shut the teakwood door firmly and guided Fabian to set the case on the cluttered table beside the ship's wheel, currently covered by half a dozen different maps and charts. Eloise flipped up the latches on the case and opened it just long enough to confirm that the iron silk was inside before snapping it shut again.

"You've told no one of what this is, right?" Eloise asked.

Fabian nodded once, worrying at the hem of his vest. "You're not going to betray me, are you? We have a deal and I'll get you a lot more. It would be to your disadvantage not to see it through."

Eloise's gills shivered in irritation. "I gave you my word. Don't insult me by questioning it again." Softening her tone, she added, "Now tell me about this island you need to reach."

Fabian reached into his shoulder bag and pulled out a rolled-up piece of vellum. He spread it out on top of the case of iron silk and pointed to a small, crescent-shaped blob. Beneath it were latitudinal and longitudinal coordinates written in red ink. Eloise licked her lips as she studied them. She'd sailed in the area before, but she'd never heard of there being anything to the west of the Crying Sisters Islands.

"You're sure this map is accurate?"

"I am."

Eloise waited for the Amphibian to elaborate, but he offered no further explanation. "We should make landfall in three to five days, depending on the winds," she said. "But if we sail to your island and there's nothing there, you're not getting a refund."

"That is acceptable." Fabian drummed his fingers on the table. "If there's nothing further, I'd like to go to my quarters. It really is imperative that we make the best time possible."

"I'll have Rourke show you to them," Eloise said, pulling open the door.

Fabian gave the captain a small bow and shuffled off to head below decks. Eloise sighed and rubbed the back of her neck. Her gills were drying and something told her the voyage was going to be difficult.

* * *

The storm rolled in on red skies and angry, drumming thunder. The *Viper* had been at sea for four and half days, and Fabian had mostly stayed holed up below decks in his cabin. The iron silk was stored away in Eloise's private safe, away from the prying eyes of the crew, who might be less inclined to do their jobs if they knew their payment was already on board.

Now, as the seas rolled and rain hammered against the ship, Fabian finally emerged to take a look around. Rourke spotted him first, wandering along the deck and staring out at the horizon. In fair weather, the three peaks of the Crying Sisters Islands might have been visible, but the area was so frequently besieged by storms that the skies above the sisters were always crying.

"This is no time for you to be out here, Fabian," Rourke shouted above the gale. The ship moaned as it crested over a storm-swollen wave, rocking and jittering beneath their feet. Nearly all of the sails had been reefed. Only a small storm jib remained to give the helm a bit of maneuverability and keep the bow pointed toward the waves. The highest topsails also remained unfurled, being too far up the mast to risk sending crew up to reef.

"I must see the captain," Fabian replied, stumbling toward the wheelhouse at the stern. "We're close to the island."

Eloise was at the helm when Fabian blew in with pelting rain and a gust of wind that sent papers scattering about the small space. Eloise's knuckles were white beneath her soft burgundy scales and she cursed bubbling words only an Ichthyoid mouth could form.

"Get out of here!" she shouted, spinning the wheel hard to port as another wave crested and threatened to dip the ship into the sea.

"You have to listen to me," Fabian said, closing the small space between them. "We're near the island and the sea shallows quickly. We'll be dashed across the rocks if you don't follow my guidance."

"Rocks?" Eloise spat. "To hell with that. We'll heave-to and wait out the storm."

"No." Fabian reached for the wheel, but stopped short under Eloise's murderous glare. "The storms do not abate here. We must push forward on an altered heading."

Eloise considered the Amphibian's words. He was no sailor, but he was the only person with any knowledge of the island and its surroundings. If there was an island at all.

"Rourke," Eloise's voice boomed louder than thunder. "Any sight of land ahead?"

"No, Captain," Rourke shouted back. "It's nothing but bloody wat—Wait! Yes. I see something! Thirty degrees to starboard!"

Fabian had grace enough not to look smug. Quietly, he said, "Trust me. I will guide you through this."

* * *

By the time the island was in sight, Eloise was sure that it had gone unmapped because no one besides her Amphibian client had ever been insane enough to battle through the waters they faced. He hadn't been lying about the rocks. Awful hunks of granite rising out of the water like rough spearpoints, ready to gut any ship unfortunate enough to sail near them. Fabian's eyes were as keen as they were large, though, and with him pointing them out, Eloise had guided the ship through as the storm howled around them.

Then, like passing through a beaded curtain, the storm gave way suddenly and they came at last to a small cove on the western part of the island, the interior of its crescent-shaped mass. Fabian explained that the island lay perpetually in the eye of the storm. Here there was only quiet winds and a soft patter of rain, even as the storm raged in the distance. It was long past midnight and the crew was exhausted. Eloise gave the order for everyone not on watch to sleep. Not even Fabian resisted the order, trudging back to his small cabin to catch a few hours of rest.

By sunrise, the rain was a light mist, though the clouds still hung low and heavy over the island and lightning flashed in the distance. The air smelled of salty seacoast, rotting seaweed, and something decidedly grassy. Eloise gathered a small party together to go ashore: Fabian, Rourke, and one of her best scouts, a hummingwing named Jeannette, who hovered delicately over the boat while the others rowed. The rest of the crew would wait aboard the *Salty Viper* until Eloise called for them.

As they hauled the boat up the sandy shore, Eloise strained to see what she could of the island. Almost everything was hidden by a dense tree line of palms and shrubs blooming in innumerable orange and violet hues. It looked like part of the uninhabited Savage Lands, and the misty fog might hide anything from gargantuan beasts to flesh-eating plants.

As it turned out, it was hiding a rather large garrison of gendarmery marines.

Jeannette zipped back below the tree line after taking a cursory flight over the area, whistling anxiously as her species was prone to do in times of stress. Eloise recognized it as a danger call and looked back toward the shore, wondering if they would need to get their rowboat back in the water before taking more than fifty steps onto land.

"This place is crawling with armadillos," Jeannette chirped, using the slang for the heavily-armored Mammalian gendarmery. "I saw six of them on armed patrol through the forest—heading away from us," Jeannette added as Eloise's eyes widened in alarm.

"Sounds like we're too late to grab whatever it is you were after," Rourke said, looking toward Fabian.

"We're not. I told you that we'd be up against the gendarmery and you assured me it would be no problem."

Eloise hissed, her tongue licking at her nose in agitation. "If you know we're not too late, that can only be because the gendarmery has had what you seek from the start."

"Who." Fabian shifted on his feet as though it took a great deal of effort to prevent himself from springing off into the depths of the forest. "The gendarmery has *who* I seek. My wife. Penelope."

Rourke swore. Jeannette fluttered subtly closer to Fabian and Eloise could see that the hummingwing was stirred by the revelation. Her crew was too damn sentimental.

Pinching the bridge of her nose, Eloise said, "Fine. We'll check out the area and see if we can find any sign of your wife. I assume she's an Amphibian as well?"

Fabian nodded.

"We'll take a look. But you lied to me to get us here and I'm not forgetting that. I'm not going to get my crew killed on a fool's errand. Is that clear?"

Fabian swallowed thickly. "I understand. And…thank you."

"Don't thank us yet," Rourke grumbled. "Chances are you're showing up to shell swap with a wafer conch. But we'll see what we can do."

"Now that we're being honest with each other, I presume you know the way to where your wife is being held?" At Fabian's nod, Eloise added, "Then lead the way."

* * *

Eloise stuck close behind Fabian as he guided them through a narrow path half overgrown with thornbushes and rotten berries that squished under their feet in fetid goo. Jeannette fluttered in and out of the canopy of trees above, searching for more signs of the gendarmery, then ducking down quickly in case they had any scouts of their own.

So far it was quiet.

Eloise reevaluated what she knew of the Amphibian. He was a timid and excitable sort, clearly pushed beyond all his limits, but there was a determination to him that told her he wasn't going to leave the island without his beloved Penelope. It was a noble sentiment, but it was hard to see it ending any way other than with a dead client and her riches unraveling before she even got a chance to handle them.

And she so badly needed the money. The Tyrant Lord was eating up everything in the southern seas. No one hired free agents anymore, not wanting to risk their cargo being seized by the gendarmery. And it was no secret that captains who refused to share a flag—and a substantial share of their profits—with the Tyrant Lord met with mysterious accidents.

With Fabian's full payment, she'd have enough to fake the credentials to get through the northern blockade and away from the Tyrant Lord's grip. Or be practical, retire, and open an inn. Eloise had believed that there was always more sea to swim in, but lately it felt more like a tidepool drying up.

"The compound is this way, to the left," Fabian said as they came to a fork in the road. They walked on in silence for another few moments before the forest started to thin and an outcropping of buildings appeared in the distance and, behind the buildings, the far shore of the small island.

Three buildings were arranged in a rough line ahead of them. The largest was a farmhouse hewn from the palm and brushwood surrounding the area, burnt near black to protect it from weathering. The roof was bony white and, even with an overcast sky, its shell shingles twinkled in an iridescent rainbow. Four armored gendarmery marines stood at the front of the house, muskets at their sides. A recently erected flagpole carried the colors of the Tyrant Lord.

"What have they done to our home?" Fabian murmured to himself as they crouched behind some redberry bushes at the edge of the clearing.

Eloise guessed that the Amphibian's statement had less to do with the house than with the barn, which was filled with enough hissing and belching machinery to drive the most stalwart of tinkerers batty. Clearly, the gendarmery had set up some kind of covert manufacturing operation, and she assumed

Penelope had been press-ganged into laboring for them. Stealing a worker couldn't be too much trouble. Labor was a cheap commodity for the Tyrant Lord.

Eloise was about to say as much when Fabian gasped and put a horrified hand over his mouth. She followed his eyeline and saw a gendarmery captain tugging harshly on the arm of a soot-stained and weary Amphibian woman. She stumbled as she tried to keep up with him, and their voices carried lightly on the breeze.

"Please," the Amphibian woman said, "I need more time to complete the formula. I'm working as fast as I can."

The gendarmery captain, a Mammal with gray fur covering every part of his body not covered in scaled armor, scoffed at her.

"You're stalling. You really believe that milksop husband of yours will return and save the day? He abandoned you. And my patience is abandoning me. If your next batch of fiber doesn't perform, I'll leave your entrails to sun by the shore and see if your precious Fabian has any bright ideas instead."

Fabian nearly destroyed their cover trying to dart out after the captain, but Rourke was quick enough to grab him around his waist and drag the Amphibian back down the path. Eloise and Jeannette followed after them. There were too many gendarmery to attempt grabbing Penelope in the open, and given her importance to the soldiers, they needed a plan to free her.

When they were far enough back in the forest, Eloise was the first to speak.

"The formula the captain spoke of, and the fiber—your wife is making iron silk?"

Rourke allowed Fabian to wriggle out of his hold, having finally calmed himself.

"She is. She's a chemist, you see, and after we came across a rather unusual variety of flax growing on the island we started experimenting and—"

"And got nowhere from what the captain said," Rourke interrupted.

"Penelope knows good and well what formula to make. The gendarmery found us a month ago, after I unwisely showed a bit of our product around hoping to find some buyers." Fabian clenched his fists. "Even more unwisely, I revealed my dear Penelope was the brains behind it all. The gendarmery came calling while I was tending the fields. I knew I could never overpower them alone, so I fled. I took a dinghy to the Crying Sisters and caught a ship from there to the mainland. Then I found you."

"Thanks for that," Rourke muttered.

Jeannette huffed at the first officer and zipped around his head. "He was trying to save his mate," she hissed. "Not that you'd know anything about caring for others."

"It doesn't matter if we care or not," Eloise said, knowing that if she didn't speak now the two of them wouldn't stop snapping at each other. "What matters is if we can do the job and if it's worth the risk of trying."

"Worth the risk?" Fabian said. "I will give you anything—everything—whatever you ask. Just please don't leave me to do this alone."

"It's the right thing to do," Jeannette chirped.

"Even if it costs us everything?" Rourke countered. "They haven't seen us. We could sail away and they'd never know."

Eloise looked between her two crewmates. Both were right. Both would follow her lead, no matter how much they might grumble. "We might as well try," Eloise said finally. "If the Tyrant Lord gets an unlimited source of iron silk, it's not as though we'd be free to sail much longer anyway."

Fabian bowed his head in thanks, and his chin swelled with the emotional croak he fought to contain.

* * *

It was nightfall by the time everything was in place. The sky flickered with distant lightning and rolling thunder cut through the sound of the waves softly cresting against Eloise's body as she swam along the shoreline. Her kaftan had been discarded and, with only a few underclothes, she cut through the water with graceful strokes, surfacing occasionally to look around.

Jeanette had kept watch over the compound as the hours passed, and discovered that Penelope was being held in a small shack next to the converted barn. Fabian had said they used it to store tools, and judging by the rakes and shovels and wheelbarrow tossed in a heap outside it, the whole thing had been cleared out in order to serve as a cell for Penelope. It had to have been a miserable place. The boards were only roughly nailed into place and the roof no doubt leaked terribly whenever it rained, which seemed to be most nights.

Eloise crept onto shore, crawling on all fours through the muck as she approached the wooden shed. Four guards stood under a lamppost in front of the main house up ahead, but they spent their watch talking with each other rather than looking at the shed. A month of quiet had left them lax.

The door of the shed faced the guards, and though they were a distance away, Eloise wouldn't chance showing herself to them if she could help it. Still crouching, she knocked on the back wall of the shed and whispered, "Penelope?"

There was no sound for several seconds. Eloise knocked again and this time received a fearful, "Who's there?"

"My name's Eloise. Fabian sent me to help free you."

"Fabian? He escaped then, thank the stars." There was more rustling from behind the wall as Penelope presumably got to her feet.

"Hang tight, I'm going to get you out of there. Quietly, I hope."

It only took a few seconds of looking through the discarded tools for Eloise to find what she needed. She picked up a hammer from the ground and flicked most of the mud off it with a sharp motion of her wrist. Then she went about pulling the first of the nails from the wall of the shack.

In the end, Eloise had to remove two boards and eight nails to make a space wide enough for Penelope to wriggle through. It was a tight fit, but the dully orange Amphibian sucked in her gut and managed it with only a few light scrapes.

"My ship is waiting. This way," Eloise said, tugging Penelope back toward the shore.

"I can't. Not yet." Penelope pulled her hand away from Eloise and nodded toward the converted barn. "All my notes and formulas are in there. If I don't destroy them, Captain Holcombe will be able to produce the thread on his own sooner or later."

Eloise hissed. "We don't have the time or the means—"

"I cannot speak to the time," Penelope said. "But I assure you, the means won't be a problem. Now follow me."

* * *

Penelope led them from the shack to the back of the barn where they slipped in through a half-open window. Only a few steps in, Eloise stumbled into a mess of flax soaking in a tub of strange chemicals that burned her nose and made her eyes tear up. Penelope moved past her quickly, gliding around the clusters of bottles and metal refuse that covered the barn in steps as familiar as an old dance. Both Ichthyoids and Amphibians saw well in the dark, so there was no need for the lanterns on which so many of the Mammalian gendarmery relied. Eloise squeezed herself between a pair of cast iron pedal looms, accidently bumping against a shuttle and sending it clattering to the floor. Penelope glanced back at her before continuing to a table near the front of the barn.

The table held a variety of empty and half-empty bottles, and Penelope went to work pouring the contents from one to another in a pattern Eloise couldn't hope to replicate. In short order, Penelope had three bottles filled with a dark, semi-transparent liquid arranged on the table and was tearing at her skirt for pieces of cloth to feed into the neck of each bottle.

Eloise was familiar with this type of incendiary device. It had been popular during some of the early riots against the Tyrant Lord, though it was usually cheap grog that filled the bottles, not whatever alchemical concoction Penelope had just devised.

"This burns longer and won't go out with water," Penelope said, answering Eloise's unasked question as she handed her a pair of the bottles. "I reckon your throwing arm is stronger than mine."

Penelope bent down to open a trunk tucked away underneath the table and removed a small packet of papers, tucking it near her chest as she stood. She grabbed a box of matches from the table, and the remaining bottle, then looked back at Eloise. "Front door or back through the window?"

"Window," Eloise said firmly. "We'll need every second we can get."

The pair reached the window and Eloise held out her first bottle for Penelope to light. As she threw it across the room and it shattered into a mass of flame against the wall, she wondered how it must feel to Penelope to be burning down her home and life's work like this. Probably a lot like it would feel to scuttle the *Viper*. Beyond contemplation.

But Penelope didn't show any hesitation as she threw her own bottle and sent flames dancing across a large pile of dried flax in the center of the room. By then the smoke was growing thick and, as Penelope slipped back out through the window, the guards began shouting and clanging a bell.

Eloise clamored out the window after Penelope. She lit her last bottle as she broke out in a run toward the shore. She could just make out two figures, Fabian and Rourke, waiting in a rowboat a short way out in the water. "There," she called to Penelope, pointing toward the boat as they ran.

"I see them."

Eloise barely slowed as she turned back and threw the last bottle at the barn. The sound of it erupting against the wall was drowned out by the musket fire behind them. She weaved to the right as the balls flew over her shoulder. Finally looking forward again, she spotted more trouble.

The captain—Holcombe, according to what Penelope had said earlier—had managed to get between them and the rowboat. He had his pistol leveled at Penelope, who dove to the ground just as it fired. Eloise didn't hear her cry out in pain, but it wasn't going to be easy for her to dodge a second shot.

"Hey!" Eloise shouted, and Holcombe turned his gaze and his pistol toward her instead. He smirked at her, and Eloise smiled back. Behind Holcombe, where there had once been two figures in the rowboat, there was now only one.

As Holcombe squeezed the trigger, Fabian leapt out of the water behind him, springing forward with the kind of jump only Amphibians could dream of making. He crashed against Holcombe's back, knocking him over and making him fire harmlessly into the ground. Fabian scrambled for the pistol and tossed it far into the water before Holcombe recovered.

"Fabian!" Penelope cried, springing toward him with similar leaps.

Eloise kept running even as the Amphibian quickly outpaced her. For a moment, she believed they had triumphed. The barn billowed black smoke and collapsed behind them. Penelope was free and they'd soon be rowing back to the *Viper* and the safety of the open seas.

Then Holcombe pulled a dagger from his belt and thrust it into Fabian.

Penelope warbled and croaked, closing the remaining distance in a set of three furious leaps. Holcombe raised his dagger to defend himself only to get kicked squarely in the chest by Penelope before taking a single swing.

"Get him to the boat!" Eloise shouted as she neared the scene. Rourke was still waiting for them, watching in anguish as he fought to keep their means of escape steady.

Penelope grabbed ahold of Fabian and helped him up. Eloise breathed in relief that the Amphibian was still conscious. They had supplies on the *Viper* that could patch him up, but the swim to the boat would be rough.

Holcombe was just getting to his feet as Eloise reached the shore, his scaly armor rattling almost as much as his breath. Eloise wished she had the time to deal with him properly. Instead, she hissed out a warning not to follow them and slithered into the sea.

Rourke was already paddling hard back to the *Viper* when Eloise reached the boat. She hauled herself in without too much trouble, though it was always jarring to go from the comfort of water back into the harsh environment above it. Penelope and Fabian nestled beside each other in the boat, Fabian showing rather less blood than Eloise would have expected from a knife to the gut.

"It was my vest," Fabian said, noticing Eloise's gaze. "The embroidery was from one of our first batches. It stopped the worst of it."

"We should have done the whole vest in the silk and not just the accents." Penelope tutted. "Foolish."

Looking closely, Eloise could see that the fabric had shorn cleanly until it reached the silver flowers brocading the front. A small bit of blood covered the material, but Fabian had received no more than a light scratch.

"It's an amazing material," Eloise said. "I'm sorry we had to see it all burn."

Penelope touched her breast lightly, and Eloise could just make out the faint rustle of soggy paper. "I wouldn't be so sure about that." She smiled.

* * *

If you had asked Eloise to name the least likely occupation she could find herself doing, she would have said major general in the gendarmery. A close second would have been farmer. And yet…

There were two parts that went into the manufacture of iron silk. The first was the formula that Penelope had painstakingly discovered through years of experiments. The second was a rather unique variety of flax native to an island surrounded by storms. Penelope had managed to save precisely one small bag of its seeds. It wasn't much, but with enough time and effort, it might overturn empires.

And so, on a small island far to the north that had cost a king's ransom to buy (if, of course, a king were worth about a case of iron silk), Eloise toiled in the sun coaxing little sprouts to life, guided by Penelope's knowhow and Fabian's experience. It wasn't something she'd spend the rest of her life doing, but a quiet summer while she waited for her investment to grow? Eloise reckoned there could be worse things than a *temporary* retirement.

Pirates of the Mississippi

R.S. Belcher

(Readers Note: This story takes place after the events of the Queen of Swords and Ghost Dance Judgement novels—R.S.B.)

Judson Price squirmed in his chair. He took the cup and saucer of tea offered by Maude Stapleton with a pale hand that trembled ever so slightly. Maude's senses were acute enough to read his tremor, to determine his breathing was fast and his heartbeat faster. He was trying his best to mask his discomfort. He wanted to talk, clearly, to explain his presence at Grande Folly, but he didn't know how to begin and Maude suspected he thought she wouldn't believe him.

"It's a lovely estate, Mrs. Stapleton," Price said. "I'm sure the young ladies you instruct here enjoy the natural beauty of the woods, the beaches, this fine manor."

"Thank you, Mr. Price," Maude said. She adjusted her tone, pitch, cadence, and body language to set his nerves at ease. "You are very kind." She had learned the manipulation technique as a girl here at Grande Folly. And she and her staff now trained their young students at the Stapleton Academy for Young Ladies. She glanced out the window and saw the current class running along the shoreline in the hot South Carolina sun. When Price looked out the window, he saw a group of girls frolicking on the warm sand. Actually, the instructor, Amadia—a tall, grim-faced African women, was teaching the students the ability to move across the shifting surface of the beach while leaving no trace of their passing.

Maude sensed Price was more at ease; his respiration and heartbeat had slowed. "So, tell me, to what do we owe the pleasure of your visit?" He lowered his head, and she sensed the stress return.

"I was encouraged to reach out to you by a reporter from a New York paper, one Alter Cline."

"Oh, Alter." Maude's face brightened. "How is he?"

"My impression was he's quite well," Price said. "Jumping back and forth between Gotham and the District of Columbia, chasing stories."

"Sounds like him. He is a good friend and of excellent character and reputation. Why did Alter send you to me."

"He…thought you might be able to be of assistance to me in my current predicament." Maude said nothing and waited for him to continue. "My children…" he finally said. "They have been stolen. I fear they are in terrible danger."

Maude leaned forward in her chair. "Tell me everything." Her response eased Price's internal struggle and she felt him relax. He withdrew a cigarette case and looked to Maude to see if such behavior would be permitted. She nodded. "Please, feel free, but such a habit is not good for one's health, Mr. Price."

"Quite the contrary, " he said. "I have heard from numerous physicians it is quite healthy and therapeutic," he placed a cigarette between his lips, struck a match, and inhaled deeply. Maude adjusted her breathing so that none of the noxious smoke would enter her lungs.

"Please continue," she said.

"Well, as you may be able to discern from my accent, I am a scion of the south."

"I'd place you as a native Mississippian. From around the Delta region, I'd say."

Price looked surprised.

"Why, yes. That's correct. How…"

"Please, Mr. Price, your children."

"Yes, yes, of course. I am a ship man, Mrs. Stapleton. I build and sell vessels. I had an extensive contract with the Confederacy during the war to construct war ships, and since the conclusion of the war I've focused on merchant ships, sea-going vessels, mostly. I have done well for myself.

"In the past few years, I have invested significantly in steam riverboats. After Fulton and Livingston's success with the *New Orleans*, it became clear to me and my associates that there was money to be made by offering comfort, luxury, speed, and amenities to those who could afford them, up and down

The Big Muddy. I personally have investments in over two dozen such craft, and own six of them, outright." Maude sensed the boastfulness in his voice and body language, but said nothing. Men tended to talk more, give up more, when they were boasting.

"Six months ago, we began to experience…problems." She felt his pride deflate like a sail with no wind.

"What kind of problems?" she asked.

"Well…I know it seems ridiculous to speak of such things in 1874, in such a civilized age, but…pirates."

"Pirates," Maude repeated. "I see."

"I mean of course, forty, fifty years ago there were troubles," Price went on. "Miscreants like Colonel Plug and his ilk, sinking and attacking flatboats carrying cargoes up and down Old Man River, but that's ancient history. These blackguards—they board the riverboats, take the money and personal effects of the passengers, and worst of all, take hostages!"

"Your children were taken by these…pirates," Maude said.

Price nodded."They seem to only take the young and strong. They murder anyone who attempts to stop them. Their leader is a fiend. He actually *enjoys* killing."

"His name?" Maude asked.

"No one knows for sure. I've made inquiries, but have learned nothing solid. I'm told by survivors he's a stout man and wears a black hood. He leaves messages in the blood of his victims. They say 'Done by the Crownless King.'"

Price lurched suddenly from his chair. Maude had seen in his tensed muscles, his eyes, he was going to do it and she was not startled. "Forgive me, Mrs. Stapleton! To share such gory details with a lady is so uncouth! My children are in the clutches of this monster. It was only of the deepest desperation I came to you at all. I'm so sorry."

"Alter Cline told you I could help you?"

"Yes, he said you had some experience with pirates."

Maude smiled at this. In point of fact, that was very true. "I can help you."

"Really, madame, I…"

"I can find your children," Maude said, standing now, herself. "And put an end to these raids."

"How?" Price asked. "You're a woman. I'm certain you are a competent school mistress, but…"

"You came here because you have nowhere else to turn," she said. "I'd hazard a guess you've sent out agents prior to coming to me, and they have all failed." Price confirmed this with a reluctant nod. "You only entertained meeting with me because you have no other hope."

"That's correct. My children are my world. I can't just leave them to this… creature's whims."

"I had my daughter taken from me once," Maude said. "I understand. I promise you I will do everything within my power to bring them home safe to you."

Price sighed and nodded. "Very well, Mrs. Stapleton. You are my last hope. I can pay…"

"I have no need of your money, Mr. Price. However, I will need a boat from you. Something with a shallow draft, able to navigate the whole of the Mississippi."

"Done," he said.

"And I'll need a crew that won't make a fuss about taking orders from a woman."

"That…might be a bit harder to come up with, but I will endeavor to secure such a crew for you."

"Thank you."

"No, thank you. How do you plan to do it?"

"If I told you," Maude said, "you wouldn't believe me."

* * *

That evening, Maude had supper with her daughter, Constance, and Amadia, the only instructor presently at Grand Folly who was also a Daughter of Lilith.

The Daughters were an ancient society, tracing their line all the way back to the mythological figure of Lilith herself. Maude had been inducted into the order, trained as a young girl by her great-great-great-great grandmother, the pirate queen, Anne Bonny. Maude had inherited Grande Folly and all of Anne Bonny's other secrets and treasures when Gran finally passed away.

Becoming a Daughter meant undertaking a strenuous, almost impossible training regimen, encompassing an extensive education in all forms of combat and near-absolute mastery of one's own body, and the bodies of others. It also included wide studies of history, languages, healing arts, poisons, stealth, seduction, and deceit, to name but a few. The Daughters mission since the dawn of time had been to secretly council mankind toward wisdom and peace, and to defend the world from monsters both preternatural and of the human variety. Maude herself had been involved in numerous wars and battles over her lifetime to protect the innocent from monstrous evils

By ingesting the antediluvian blood of Lilith, Maude had found herself transformed in mind and body, capable of tremendous feats of strength, agility, fortitude, and will. Lilith's Blood didn't just change Maude's life, it had freed her from the invisible chains in which society had ensnared her. She'd trained her daughter, Constance, in the way of the Daughters—a code known as Lilith's Load, and had met other members of the tiny order from around the world, like Amadia. The Stapleton Academy for Young Ladies had been Constance's idea—a safe place for young women to free their minds and discover their true potential, be it as a member of the secret order, or as an example to women in society of their place and true power.

Maude recounted to Constance and Amadia the nature of Price's visit that day. "You're going after them," Constance said. "Aren't you?" Constance's eyes were hidden behind a rounded pair of smoked glasses. She had been blinded in combat over a year ago in Golgotha, but her training allowed her to function quite well even without the use of her eyes.

"Yes," Maude said. "I need you to remain and act in my place during my absence, dear." Constance set her jaw and Maude didn't need extraordinary senses to feel the displeasure coming off the sixteen-year old.

"But I want to go and help you," Constance said. "Amadia can…"

"Amadia agrees with your mother," the African Daughter of Lilith interrupted. "Besides, with the nature of appearances being so important to this foolish society, it would not do to leave the school and children here under the care of someone viewed by most of your menfolk as simply 'the help.'"

"Great," Constance sighed. "I'm reduced to a token."

"Welcome to my world," Amadia said. Constance made a face and flicked a few drops of her soup off her spoon in Amadia's direction. Amadia caught the droplets with her own spoon and gave the girl a disapproving look.

"I won't be more than a few weeks—a month—at the most," Maude said. "Please try not to kill each other until I return. It would look bad in the papers."

"Will you take the *Hecate*?" Amadia asked.

"No," Maude said. "She'd make the journey much easier, but navigating the whole of the Mississippi in a deep-keel ship would be a bit tricky."

"She can fly, you know," Constance added. "Magic boat and all."

"As I said, she'd make it considerably easier, but I don't think the world's quite ready for a flying boat."

"When they are," Amadia added, "they'll almost be ready for a black school-mistress."

* * *

She met the crew of the *Dart* at the Charleston seaport the following day. The *Dart* was a small, two-paddled steam craft with a shallow draft that was capable of navigating even the shallowest parts of the great river.

Maude was dressed in a manner that would undoubtedly draw some attention among the sailors and teamsters of the bustling docks. With her training, she moved among the crowds like a forgotten memory, not an eye noticing her. She wore what she thought of as "work clothes"—sturdy leather breeches, knee-high boots, a loose shirt with a heavy leather vest over it. She had a cutlass in a fine scabbard on one hip, a revolver holstered on the other.

A .40 Sharps rifle was slung across her back, beside a leather pack that carried her few personal items. She topped the ensemble with a tricorne hat that bore a bronze pin of a winged bird. She often wore men's clothing when there was bad business afoot. Much of the garb had been recovered from her Gran Bonnie but to dress like such an "adventuress" would be quite the scandal for the proper school-mistress among the salty hard-working, hard-playing men of the port.

The sea air with its tang of salt, and the smell of a fresh catch in dripping nets swinging onto the ice beds on the docks reminded her how much she loved the ports, the great ships. Her father had brought her along with him when she was a young girl and she had fallen in love with the sea, with the burning urge to sail it. She smiled as she caught sight of the *Dart* in its slip. *I suppose it's in my blood,* she thought.

The captain of the *Dart* was a burly black man, with eyes of pale jade. He regarded Maude as she reached the gangplank. There was no lecherousness or disapproval in his gaze, just a hard quick assessment. "You Stapleton?" he asked.

"Permission to come aboard, captain?" He nodded and Maude made her way up the plank.

"Maude Stapleton," she said and offered a hand. He studied her a moment longer and then shook her hand.

"Oscar Mereid," he said. Maude took his accent for West Indies. "I was told by the shipmaster, Mr. Price, to extend you every courtesy and consider you in command of this expedition."

"That's correct, Captain," she said. More of Mereid's crew noticed her now as they busied themselves on deck, giving Maude and her attire odd looks. "I trust he briefed you on what we are going after."

"Aye," he said. "Pirates. I've dealt with my share of their lot before I came into Price's employ. Why he has a woman leading this expedition is beyond me. Women are bad luck on a boat, but for the pay he's offering and the reward if we succeed…me and my crew are at your service."

"That's all I ask, Captain," Maude said. "Are we ready to get underway?"

Mereid nodded. "What course? Where we headed?"

"The Ohio River first. We're going to Booths Cave. You familiar with it?"

The sour look on Mereid's face told Maude that he was.

* * *

Under steam and with the good fortune of the weather, it took a week and a half to reach Booths Cave. The caves themselves had long been abandoned by the many cutthroats, bandits, and pirates who used them as a hiding place over the decades. A small town of respectable settlers had grown nearby, but there were still small, unnamed shanty-towns and settlements along the river leading up to the caves. These patchwork communities reminded Maude of the miners camps back in Golgotha—dens of gambling, prostitution, drunkenness, petty theft, and every other imaginable vice.

The *Dart* went to port at the small town named for the caves. Maude told Mereid she intended to backtrack to the shanty settlements and make some inquiries.

"Very dangerous for a woman to go in there," he said, "even one that knows her way around a boat." Maude had helped out during the journey. By the time they arrived at the caves, she'd won the respect of most of the crew and, grudgingly, even Mereid.

"Should take a few of us along."

"Very well," Maude said, "but everyone follows my lead."

"Aye."

They took a small flatbed raft from the *Dart* and paddled it down the river. It was near dusk and the fading sunlight flashed in dappled patches of brightness through the thick tree cover on the sides of the mighty Ohio. Mereid and two of his men had accompanied her. They were armed with pistols and machetes. Two of the men used long poles to guide them down the river, while Maude and Mereid scanned the banks.

After a few hours, they spotted a rickety-looking dock, lanterns burning on posts to guide the night traveler toward it. The sun was a sliver of fire on the edge of the world as they approached the dock.

"Ho, there!" a voice called out of the gloom. "Who be it?"

"Ahoy," Maude called back. "We've come to trade a bit and wet our whistles. We heard this was the place for that sort."

A shadow dislodged itself from the growing night and came to the edge of the dock. He had a rifle tucked loosely in one arm, a lantern in the other. "You be a woman?"

"Last time I checked," Maude said, tossing the man a rope to moor the raft.

"Don't get many women-folk out this way," the dock keeper said, slinging his gun and tying the rope off. "'Cept the occasional whore. That be you, lass?"

Maude stepped from the raft up onto the dock. She clutched the dock keeper's collar and lifted him off the ground. "You never heard of Black Bonnie Stapleton, have you, old man?"

"Black Bonnie?" he gasped, startled by Maude's speed and strength. "Uh, no." Maude dropped him and he fell onto the dock.

"Well, you have now. Call me a whore again and I'll fish with your wedding tackle for my bait. My crew is thirsty and so am I. We have cases of molasses to trade. Take me to who runs this privy of a hideout."

The old man scrambled up and called for help. Two men appeared and helped Mereid and his men unload the crates. The captain eyed Maude and whispered, "Black Bonnie?"

"It sounded good to me at the time," Maude said with smile.

* * *

The boss of the place was named Ellerton. He was a mountain of a man, with long oily gray hair and a massive beard. He wore an eye patch and was missing several fingers.

While the trades were bandied back and forth and finally made, Maude and the men drank copious amounts of rum. Maude sized Ellerton up and managed to put the old criminal at ease. He was also eyeing her in a most lascivious manner. More rum was brought out to celebrate the successful business transaction. Maude dropped the names of several prominent bandits and criminals who Ellerton clearly knew and traded stories with him that he completely believed. She also used her voice and body language to give off all the proper cues to charm him.

The booze helped, too, of course. Maude had cautioned Mereid and his men to stay alert and sip, but she had matched the old crook flagon for flagon. She accelerated her metabolism enough to burn the strong drink off before it could have any ill effects on her, but she played a convincing tipsy pirate.

She finally got to the point of why they were really here. "Ell, old boy, you hear tell of a fella running up and down Old Man River, having a bit of sport with these big juicy riverboat cruisers?"

"Why'd you want to know, Bonnie?" He leered over the table at her, his eyes red and glassy in the lantern light. He was giving away all his body-cues now under the influence of the drink. He did know what she was talking about, but the topic put him on edge.

"He's been making me and my lot's life a lot more worrisome," she said. "Stirring up the law, getting all those wealthy folk up in arms. You know who I'm talking about, don't you, Ell?"

"Aye, I do." Ellerton took another long draw on his flagon before slamming it down. "Trust me, lass, you want nothing to do with that...whatever that creature is."

"What'd you mean?" she asked leaning slightly forward, tuning her voice to elicit just a hint of intimacy between them.

"It's the king you be seeking," he said. "The Crownless King. Trust me, Bonnie, leave that one be. He's...there's something wrong with that one. He's not...natural, if you get my meaning."

"I don't scare easy. And me and my mates that makes a living picking along the Mississippi want to express our disdain to this 'king.' So where do I go looking for him? I know a wise, handsome fella like yourself must know where his digs are?"

Ellerton wrestled between fear and desire for a moment. Maude noted how often the two emotions evoked similar responses in the human body. He finished off his mug and wiped his lips with his beard. "He's holed up in the Delta, down on the Mississippi, Atchafalaya, near Old River. It's all swamp down there—snakes, 'skeeters, and 'gators. Heard he's digging for something out there, that's why he's taking the people—to dig for him."

Maude ran her hand over his wrist and Ellerton shuddered a little. "Draw me a map? And then we can be alone for a spell."

Ellerton's drunken eyes gained a little focus and fire at the notion. He drew the map. Maude handed it over to Mereid. "Go to the dock, I'll be along shortly." The captain gave her his now-famous sour look, but took the map and departed with his men.

Ellerton stumble-led them back to his own tent. They went inside and she closed the flap. "Give us a kiss, lass," he rumbled. Maude reached up toward his hairy, misshapen face, curling her arms around him. She applied a firm pressure to a region of his tree-trunk-like neck, before he could apply his lips to hers. He let out a sigh and Maude gently slid the giant of a man onto his cot and left him snoring in bliss.

* * *

The trip down the Mississippi was long, and often difficult. It also had a rough beauty to it that Maude enjoyed. The great river was like a road that connected different worlds, different peoples. Scanning the water, Maude tumbled Ellerton's words over in her mind. Was there truly something supernatural about this "Crownless King," or did he simply know how to project himself to inspire fear, and thus, anonymity. It was a tool the Daughters themselves employed often over the ages.

Who could say? She'd know soon enough. She thought of Price's children and the other hostages, and squeezed the rail tighter. Whatever he was, he had much to answer for.

* * *

They arrived near the coordinates the map had led them to and set anchor. Maude decided to wait until night to scout the area. Captain Mereid protested. "Going alone is foolhardy," he said. "No matter what you seem capable of, he's got men with him and you can't take on an army by yourself, woman." The look Maude gave him made him pause. "I was sent to help you. Let me."

"I'll go to have a peek," Maude said. "You and a half-dozen of your lads arm yourselves and be waiting on the flatboat. If I find myself in a jam, I'll fire three rounds. You hear that, you come running. Agreed?" The tacit nod;

the disapproving gaze. "Believe it or not, I will miss you when this is over, Captain." A smile cut the sailor's face.

* * *

Maude was a shade, a ghost as she moved through the Delta swamp. She altered her breathing to give off less carbon dioxide, and other scents, so the mosquitoes left her alone. She moved nothing like a human, and that meant she bypassed venomous snakes and alligators with ease. She saw the flickering of torches mounted on poles around a large clearing and slid into one of the shifting shadows to observe.

There were a dozen men, most squatting near a bonfire, drinking and eating. A few drifted near the edge of the clearing, rifles at the ready. There was a large pit of a hole on the opposite side of the clearing and about a dozen figures—men, women and two children, a boy and girl—slumped there. Irons were about their ankles and they all looked starved, dehydrated, and sick. Picks and shovels were piled near where the hostages lay in the sweltering heat of the swamp. There were a few tents set up in the clearing and there was a small makeshift dock that Maude suspected led to one of the pirates' smaller craft. There might be more of them on a ship, or ships, elsewhere.

"When we going to get more than hardtack and wild onion stew to eat?" one of the prates rumbled, throwing a moldy heel of bread into the fire.

"Shut your gob," another one hissed. "*He'll* hear you." That seemed enough to shut the food critic up. Maude left the pirates to their ration of drink and began to work the edges of the camp. One by one, she took out the guards. A shadow alighted on them for an instant, and then they were pulled deep into the saw grass silently and moved no more. Once the sentries had been taken care of, she reached the hostages and carefully, silently, appeared to them, kneeling near the two children. "Your father sent me," she said. "Keep quiet, I'll get you out of here, I swear it. Tell the others, but have them make no fuss, stay down." With a thin pick, she unlocked the manacles on the two children.

It would not be long before the guards' absence would be noticed. Maude had taken out as many of the pirates as she could quietly. She adjusted her breathing, sending more blood to her eyes, her ears, her muscles, and then stepped out of the flickering darkness near the bonfire, her pistol and blade in her hands. "I've come for the Crownless King," she said, making her voice a terrible snarl designed to rake fear, like cold ice, on the assembled men's spines. "Flee, if you know what's good for you!"

Several of the men screamed at her appearance and fled, dropping their pistol and rifles as they disappeared into the swamp. Others howled and opened fire on her only to find the hissing apparition was no longer where she had been a second earlier. Maude moved among the pirates, a blur of steel and silk. She ran through one of the men as he discharged his pistol in her direction and seemed to fold at the waist to avoid the bullet, snatching his wrist at the moment he fired and twisting his aim toward one of his fellows, who fell from the shot.

In her mind, she kept count as she whittled down their numbers, moving too quickly, too erratically, for them to draw bead on her. A handful of pirates raced up the path from the dock and Maude fired three rapid shots from her revolver, signaling Mereid and his men, and killing three more of the cutthroats.

She'd swung the cutlass to fell another of the terrified raiders when her blade was blocked by a saber. Maude spun to regard who could move with sufficient speed and strength to halt her blade.

The figure was taller than she, dressed in a rotted waist coat and dirty breeches. His face was covered by a hood of blackest cloth, and red fire seemed to blaze from the eye holes. A cloak of the same black material swirled about the figure like a bank of fog.

"Well, who have we here?" The man asked, his voice muffled. "Some fury, some wag-tail bent upon ending my reign before it has even begun?"

"You must be the 'Crownless King,'" Maude said. "I have to say, I find your kingdom less than resplendent." She slowly circled the King, as he did her, their blades at en garde, seeking an opening, a flicker of weakness. The remaining handful of the Kings's pirates watched in awe and fear, but none dared to intervene. Mereid and his men ran up the path from the dock and slowed to view the sight before them. Maude nodded slightly toward the prisoners and Mereid nodded in return, his men moving to free them.

"You see only the beginning of my kingdom," the voice said. "It started long before you were born, lass." His saber flashed out and Maude barely parried it. She launched a riposte, but too late. He had firmed up a defense. The arm behind his blade was at least as strong as hers, perhaps stronger.

"I see a man afraid to show his face, hiding in a foul swamp, and using innocent people as slaves for some unfathomable purpose," Maude said, and launched a powerful advance, her cutlass flashing in the fire light. The King blocked each strike, even as he was pushed backward. He swept her with a balestra, leaping forward with a wide, overhead arc. Maude barely caught it and nearly fell to one knee from the force of the blow. This was no ordinary man under the hood. The King laughed as Maude retreated a few steps to recover.

"Good, very good. Finally, a worthy opponent," he said. "These poor fools I've gathered are digging up my lost booty gathered over a lifetime of warring, killing, and ravaging. You face more than mere steel, woman, you face Samuel Mason. Hero of the war of revolution, Indian fighter, Highwayman, and pirate. At your service."

"That villain, Mason, died over seventy years ago," Maude said, barely blocking a powerful lunge. "Killed by his own band of cutthroats." She countered with a riposte off her low parry and disengaged her blade. The first few inches of her cutlass sank into the King's chest with a squishy thunk. Maude drove it in deeper, but the King stood and took advantage of Maude's surprise to slash her sword arm savagely above the elbow. Only Maude's preternatural reflexes saved her from losing the arm. She stumbled backward, blood streaming from the wound.

"As you can see," the hooded figure said, "death no longer holds its sting for me. Not since I met the Red Man at the crossroads during my bandit days. My soul was already pretty ragged, and it was a bargain for what I received. I will live on, and once I dig up my old hidden loot in this forsaken swamp—the same loot my traitorous band wanted to claim—I will pay my debt to my master. Oh, he wants for no jewels or gold, no—a thousand souls reaped in pain and fear, starting with these poor bastards who have been digging up my treasure…and you, my dear. I know the master will enjoy your company, as well."

Mereid was quickly gathering the now-freed hostages together and moving toward the dock. He looked back at Maude, saw the blood streaming down her arm, and began to draw his own machete. Maude shook her head curtly and nodded for him to get the innocents out of here.

Maude advanced, switching styles from European to the whirling, breakneck style of the Eastern Dervish, launching herself into the air, her blade everywhere at once The relentless advance took Mason off guard and the King found his blade could not stop the storm of steel. Maude arced her blade through this neck and the cloak fluttered away from Mason's body. The headless corpse stood even as the hood and cape floated to the ground.

"Now you see what those traitorous dogs took from me." Mason's voice rumbled everywhere and nowhere. "And you see, my dear, no steel, no matter how keenly wielded, can end me." Maude was stunned for an instant, but only an instant.

Mason advanced, laughing, his saber swinging widely in the air. Maude dropped her blade on the marshy soil and stood still against his advance. As Mason closed to hack her, she darted forward, under the arc of his blade, and grabbed him by the stump of his neck and tightly by the wrist. She used his own charging momentum to flip and hurl Mason into the heart of the roaring bonfire. "You love your master, so much, then go to visit him,"

The Crownless King screamed as the raging flames licked eagerly at his putrid flesh. Maude staggered back and took up her blade, half-expecting Mason to stumble free of the fire, an animated torch of malice. But all she saw was his blackening form floundering about, howling, begging for another chance, another life. The burning shape grew still as the fire ate it whole. Foul black smoke drifted up into the moonless night, carrying the final pleas of

Samuel Mason upon it. The fire crackled and Maude swore she heard laughter in the snapping and hiss of the dancing flames.

* * *

The remaining pirates fled when they saw Mason's headless body fly into the fire. The story would become pirate legend, yet another folk tale of the slumbering Mississippi. The hostages were in rough shape, but once aboard the *Dart,* they were given food, water, and medicine, and began to recover. Both the Price children were eager to see their father. They reminded Maude of Constance and she felt a pang of yearning to get home.

The journey to Charleston was uneventful and Maude enjoyed the opportunity to be upon a ship once again. She loved the sea, the endless rivers. They gave her peace, a sense of belonging that very few things in her life ever had. *Pirate's blood*, she mused.

Captain Mereid joined her. Her regarded her with the same look he had when she had first come aboard the *Dart*, then shook his head and chuckled. Maude smiled.

"Thank you for helping me."

"I've never seen your like before," Mereid said, scanning the water. "This will be one to tell the children, as soon as I get around to having them. What was that thing, that creature, exactly?"

"Greed, evil. It can live for a long time," she said, "festering like a poison. But not forever." She glanced over to the captain. "You know that treasure of Mason's is still out there for the taking." Mereid muttered something, spit into the water, and crossed himself. "Blood money," he said. "Lives ruined. I'll make my own fortune, clean it will be, too."

"Of that, I have no doubt."

Mereid kept his eyes on the horizon, the waves and the sky. "You're pretty good in scrap, and you bargained the pants off that old pirate, Ellerton, for the rum…"

"Well, not literally," she said, "but not for his lack of trying."

"You want join up?" he said, his eyes on everything but her.

Maude broke into a wide and bright smile. "You have no idea how tempted I am. But I have a school to attend to, and my daughter, and commitments out west." They were both silent for a time listening to the chugging of the steam engine and the whoosh of the paddles.

"Besides," Maude said, eyeing him sideways, "I thought women were bad luck on a boat."

Mereid broke into deep, powerful laughter at that. After a moment, Maude joined him.

"Perhaps I was mistaken," he said.

"Perhaps."

More Than Blood in the Water

Jennifer Brozek

The captain and his second stood at the rail of the *Midnight Sorrow* as peers, friends even, contemplating the rising sun against an unnaturally still horizon line. The water, which had danced a black tempest the night before, was as smooth as glass and as opaque as lead. It wasn't dirt or silt. The water was just *dark*, reflecting eldritch green and yellow clouds against a gray-green sky that neither of them had ever seen before.

"We are lost," Welton said, his voice quiet.

There it was in plain language. As second, the ship's quartermaster, her job was to allow the captain to vent his concern and to know that it would go nowhere else. Isabelle let out a slow breath. "We are," she agreed, her voice just as quiet. "I recognize nothing."

"The stars don't match any of my maps."

"No."

"I'm not sure what to do." The air was heavy between them as she gave the captain time to think, to express what he needed to express. "But I will figure this out. I'm not done yet."

She waited a beat before she asked, "What do I tell the crew?"

He turned to her, no longer a friend or peer, but her captain once more. "Nothing, Quartermaster. Keep them in line. I'll get us home."

Still looking out at the alien sky, she nodded. "Yes, Captain. I'll keep them in line." She remained where she was as Captain Welton Bryce strode across the deck to his cabin with a confident step they both knew he feigned. It was important that he looked like he knew what he was doing and that he had it all under control. Otherwise, there might be trouble. Already, she'd ceased one unproductive, panicked, whispered conversation with her own feigned confidence.

"I told you," Kelsey whispered, in his "old man knows all" voice, "Cap'n forced us right into the mist. That's when everything changed. I seen it—blue sky turned black." He shifted to one of the two pirates huddled there. "You saw it, too, Annie. I know you did. Tell him."

Annie, a slip of a woman who was far stronger than any person that slight ought to be, looked between the men, Kelsey urging her on with gestures and Eric frowning with his arms crossed. She shrugged. "Don't know what we saw. We was chasin' that fast ship. The white one."

"I know we was." Kelsey all but stamped his foot. "We was all doin' all we could to keep up with her."

Eric uncrossed his arms. "She would've been a pretty bounty." His voice was neutral, wary.

"I ain't seen nothin' like that before," Annie admitted.

"And ain't again. That was one of them ghost ships the cap'n been chasing for years," the old man hmphed. "But the sky. It changed. We're lost."

That was when she'd stepped in and dispersed them with a curt, "Don't you all have something to do other than chew your cud on the aftdeck?"

Kelsey and Annie had disappeared but Eric stood there a while longer, looking at the unfamiliar sky that lightened from black to gray-green instead of blue.

"Something?" she'd asked.

"The sky's different," Eric had admitted. "I didn't see it change while we were in the mist. But this isn't the sky I know."

She'd shaken her head. "Not a thing for the captain or the first mate to hear you say. You know how they are."

"I do." He had eyed her then. "But I know you, Quartermaster. I know you've been around for a long time. You've seen things. What do you think?"

She'd shrugged and gestured toward the captain's cabin with her chin. "I think you should get back to work. Let me and the captain worry about things, yeah?"

"Aye." Eric nodded, affable. Nothing much seemed to bother him—until it did. Then all hell broke loose.

The pirate had ambled off as the captain's door opened and moments later, even the captain had admitted to her that they were lost and he wasn't sure what to do now.

* * *

Midnight—or at least what Isabelle thought of as midnight; she didn't know in this strange world—and all was not quiet. Denham, the first mate, had come to the bow of the ship to where she was on watch. The two of them stood side by side, watching the rolling ocean. It wasn't a storm or anything unusual for the waters they knew, but against the unnatural stillness of the day, it was something to keep an eye on.

Isabelle knew the man had something on his mind, but she wasn't going to pry it out of him. One of her greatest strengths was to speak when needed and to keep quiet the rest of the time. That way, when she spoke, everyone listened. Usually.

Denham rubbed his cheek, his umber skin shiny under the large moon's light. "We've a problem, Quartermaster."

She turned to him, waiting.

"That last storm, cook said it broke one of the pickle barrels, and the last of the ship's biscuit barrels. We lost most of both. He's got to cook the sodden biscuits, and soup'll taste sour today and tomorrow." He stopped, letting the news hang heavy in the air like a thud.

Isabelle didn't say anything. In her head, she calculated how much food had been lost. Not to mention pickle liquor that helped keep scurvy at bay and the pickled lemons themselves would be too bitter to eat. Then again, when needs must, lemons would be eaten—if they could.

"Two days. Maybe," Denham said. "Then it's fishing or port for us. We have grog enough for days more. But sailors don't live on grog alone."

"No. Start the fishing tomorrow, first watch. All we need is a little for a couple of days as the captain figures this out." Isabelle didn't look at the first mate, but she knew he frowned. "Anything else?" She let her voice grow sharp, letting him know there'd be teeth behind her next words if there was.

"No, Quartermaster. Message received."

* * *

Three calm days and two stormy nights later, no fish caught. No land sighted. No stars recognized. The crew grumbled and groused all the more. Sailors were a suspicious and superstitious lot by nature; pirates were even worse. Good luck charms were rubbed. Prayers murmured. Dark glances at the ship's cadre. Isabelle knew it was time to act.

She knocked on the captain's door, then called, "Cap'n. It's me. Need a word."

"Come," was her distant, distracted answer.

Opening the door, Isabelle was not surprised to see the captain's quarters covered in scrolls of paper and open books. She looked around. It seemed he'd pulled out every single book in his collection of esoterica to research a solution to their current problem. After closing the door, she watched him, reading and muttering for a couple of minutes before she cleared her throat.

Captain Bryce looked up and eyed her. "What is it?"

"The crew hasn't seen you for more than a day."

"So?"

She tilted her head, hearing the edge in his voice. "So, they wonder if you are afraid to show yourself." With a shrug, she turned to one of the maps tacked to the wall. It was of the New England coast. She let her eyes follow the coastline as she felt his eyes burning into her back. When he didn't say anything, she added, "Thought you should know."

He closed the book he was holding. "Did you now. What else do you think I should know?"

Isabelle shrugged and said nothing. It was time to keep her silence and allow the captain to work it out.

"It's the food problem. Damn sailors always think with their stomachs."

She did not say anything.

The captain sighed. "I don't like the taste of pickled lemon any more than they do. Don't they know that?" He didn't wait for her to answer. "Of course not. They think I dine on mutton in my cabin instead of the same poor fare they have to swallow down. What would you do?"

Turning, she looked at him to see if it was an honest question. Judging from the forlorn look on his face, it was. That was not good. She glanced about the room, looking for an answer, but she was as lost as he.

Her silence still did the trick.

"Of course," Welton said and stood. "Of course, you're right. I need to be seen, fishing with the men. Day or night. They must know I'm with them in this. We'll trawl the seafloor if we have to. We will dine well in the morning." He paused. "Thank you, Quartermaster."

"Always," she said, recognizing the dismissal for what it was, then put a hand on the doorknob. "Night fishing. Good. It will give them a reason to sleep deep."

He pulled himself together, making sure he looked like a captain—good quality breeches and shirt. No hat. No vest. He would be working hard that night. Still, he reached for his own good luck charms and stuffed them in his pockets. "Exactly. You should take your rest. I'll cover tonight. You cover the day. But get them ready."

"Yes, Captain." She opened the door, a spring in her step, but a darkness in her heart. If fishing failed tonight, she would be soothing the sailors tomorrow. There was only so much soothing her heart could take; as she always said, she had the maternal instinct of a jackal that eats their young.

* * *

Shouts of joy woke Isabelle. Those shouts morphing into shouts of surprise and fear caused her to roll out of her bunk and pull on her breeches and a shirt almost before her eyes were open. After shoving her feet into boots and half-tucking her shirt, she grabbed her long coat with one hand and a pistol with the other.

The brisk, foggy air dashed away the rest of her morning haze, and she took in the scene. Almost all of the sailors on deck surrounded a net that had just been pulled onto the ship. A few meager fish flopped and twitched around a pale white form in the middle of the net. To one side, Captain Bryce blinked in stupid wonder while the rest of the sailors backed away, some crossing themselves, others muttering in fear as they clutched for weapons that were normally at their waists but had been put aside for the night's work.

Isabelle shoved her pistol into her belt and moved through the throng, pushing and pulling the sailors aside so she could see that pale, unmoving form more clearly. As soon as she set eyes on it—on *her*—she knew they were in trouble. A nude woman sat within the tangle. Her skin was fish-belly white with a blueish tint that would signify death on any other body. This woman met Isabelle's eyes with an unworried gaze. Despite having what her grandma called "the Innsmouth look" of wide eyes, full sensuous lips, and a slightly flat face, the woman was beautiful. Long black hair spilled over her body in wet tendrils, much like (too much like) tentacles.

Kelsey grabbed Isabelle's arm. "See! I told you. The sky turned black. She's proof."

Shaking his hand off her arm with an irritated twitch, she asked, "What happened? Where'd she come from?" Isabelle thought she knew but needed confirmation.

"The ocean. And she wasn't..." he gestured at the nude form watching them from within the net. "We'd caught some sort of fey octopus. The first big thing to eat, but by the time we got the net to the deck..." Kelsey shook his head.

Glancing between the woman, the captain, and Kelsey, Isabelle realized three things: First, the woman was not scared stiff. She merely waited to see what the pirates would do. Second, the captain was stupefied, having caught something he'd chased for so long. Third, she had to get the woman off the *Midnight Sorrow* as quickly as possible or it would be the death of them.

"Denham," Isabelle snapped. "Get the sailors back to work. More fishing to be done." Without waiting for an answer, she stepped to the nude woman and threw her long coat over her to cover her nakedness. This earned her a brief but amused smile from the still-silent woman. Lastly, she moved to the captain's side. With a hand to his arm, she spoke low and urgent. "We need to get her back in the water. You and I both know that. We can't keep her here."

Captain Bryce stirred like a man waking from a dream. He didn't look at his quartermaster. He only had eyes for the woman who'd freed herself just enough from the net to pull the long coat to her, half covering her pale form.

"Who are you? Where are you from?" Bryce asked, his voice mild but his eyes gleaming with a hint of madness.

"Captain—" Isabelle stopped as Welton shook her hand from his arm and the woman spoke.

"I…you cannot understand nor speak the name I am called now. Once, I was called Patricia Elkins, daughter of a sailor called Jonathan Holt and a woman from Innsmouth, called Lucy Elkins. You may call me Patricia." At first, Patricia's voice was soft and rusty, as if she had not used it in a long time, but the more she spoke, the more fluid her voice became, with a beautiful lilt. "As for where I am from, you know, do you not, Captain of the *Midnight Sorrow*?"

"I don't. Tell me."

Isabelle looked around. Most of the sailors had backed off, but a couple— Kelsey and Annie among them—lingered and listened. "Denham," she called.

The first mate turned from the ocean and looked at her. She gestured to the lingering pirates with her head. He grimaced and advanced on them. "Did I tell you to gawk? Get to work."

As the rest scattered, Isabelle turned back to the captain and the not-quite woman. She was sure of it now, based on the woman's own answers. There, before her, was an unexpected tableau: Patricia now stood, wearing the long coat, though it was still open. Captain Bryce gripped her by one slender wrist and was in the process of clapping a single, thin, iron manacle on her. It seemed so slight that it was almost a bangle bracelet.

Patricia gasped and jerked, trying to get away from the captain, her skin reddening where the thin metal touched her.

"Now," Welton said, "answer my question."

Patricia struggled in his grasp until he let her go. She dropped to the deck and balanced the manacle that encircled her wrist on it so that her skin did not touch the metal. "Y'ha-nthlei. The city of the Deep Ones. I'm from Y'ha-nthlei."

Welton smiled, all teeth. "That wasn't so hard, was it?"

Isabelle approached, afraid of this side of the captain. When he grew obsessed—and he was obsessed with those like Patricia—he turned mean and unreasonable. "Captain, you have confirmation. You have proof. You should let her go."

He turned on her. "Let her go? Why would I do that?"

"Because they'll come for her. You know they will."

"Then maybe I should leave her body for them to find like they did my father."

Isabelle grimaced. Once upon a dark night of deep drinking, Welton had told her the story of why he was a pirate. Welton's father, Hamish, had also been obsessed with those fast white ships that seemed to take certain people from Innsmouth to other parts of the world. He'd chased them as well. And he got too close. They killed him for it. They maimed him after slaughtering his crew, and set him adrift to die a most painful death. Against all odds, the ship, the *Midnight Star*, had drifted home. Welton found his father—raving, delirious, and dying. Then and there, Welton had taken control of the ship, renamed it, hired a new crew, and began hunting the white ships. Pirating was nothing more than a way to make money to do what he really wanted to do: get revenge.

"That won't bring him back."

Welton clenched his hands into fists, but before he could say or do anything, Patricia spoke. "I can earn my freedom. I can call fish to the boat. Feed your men. I can direct you out of this place of calm days and stormy nights."

Isabelle glanced at her then back to Welton. "The men are hungry. For the sake of those still living…"

He whirled away, striding toward his cabin as he said, "I'll think on it. Keep her in your bunk."

The two of them watched the captain until he closed the door to his cabin with a soft, deliberate *click*. They turned to one another. Isabelle smoothed her face into something hard and resigned. "Come with me. I'll get something to keep the metal from touching your skin."

Patricia stood, wincing as the manacle settled against her flesh once more. She followed as Isabelle led her to the quartermaster's room. Once they entered, she said, "You are not like your captain?" It was both a question and a statement.

Isabelle didn't say anything until she found a sock with a hole in it. After cutting off the foot with a knife, she offered the wool tube to Patricia, asking, "Can you really call fish to the boat?" She watched as the woman focused on getting the wool over her hand and under the metal shackle. Where her fingers touched the metal, they came away red, as if scalded. She wasn't certain what made Patricia's skin react to the manacle, but once the wool barrier was in place, Patricia relaxed and looked around the cabin.

"I can," she said. "Who do you think sent the fish away? We have seen this boat before."

Isabelle sat on her bunk and gestured to the stool for Patricia. "I'm sorry. I'll try to get you released."

"You fear us. Me. Why?"

Shaking her head, Isabelle asked, "Why would you ask that of a pirate who hasn't eaten in a couple of days and doesn't recognize the sky she sails under?"

"But you know who…what…I am."

"Yes."

"How?"

Isabelle wanted to pace. She remained where she sat, looking at those slightly too-wide black eyes and that too-pale, blue-tinged skin. "I'm from Massachusetts. Near Innsmouth."

Patricia's eyes lit up and she smiled. "So, you know. What's your family name?"

"Thorp." She didn't want to answer but she felt unable to stop herself.

"A goodish family."

Unable (or unwilling) to continue looking at the woman, Isabelle stood and turned to her chest of clothing. "I need you to get dressed in something more appropriate. Most of the others don't know—or understand—what you are."

When she turned back, Patricia stood there, nude, holding out her long coat. "Thank you for this. And those." She took the worn shirt and breeches Isabelle held.

"I'll ask the captain to free you again, but he has…he's stubborn. I'll help you if I can."

"Tell him I'm from an important family. They will miss me. This is not a lie."

"How long do we have?"

Patricia shook her head. "Not long."

"I see. Stay here." Isabelle pushed past Patricia, then paused with her hand on the doorknob. "Stay within. I don't know what the rest would attempt to do to you. Or…" She stopped before she said, *Or how you would defend yourself.*

Patricia held up her wrist with the shackle on it. "I will remain within your cabin. Your captain has ensured that. I cannot be as I usually am with this on."

"I—"

"Do not promise what you cannot give." For the first time, Patricia's voice was sharp. It softened again as she said, "Thank you for asking your captain for my freedom. I do not believe it will do any good, but please tell him I will feed his crew if he will allow me. I, too, was once human. I understand the fear, the need."

Isabelle nodded and left the cabin. She didn't bother to ask Patricia to not look through her things or any other such nonsense. The woman was an eldritch being; a deep one hybrid. If they got out of this alive, they would be more than lucky.

Denham stepped in front of her before she could get three steps from her door. He must have been waiting. Isabelle looked at his face to gauge his mood. It was not good. "Yes?"

"The crew is hungry, Quartermaster. Five fish won't feed them."

"I am aware."

"You *need* to do something."

"I'm trying to do something, First Mate. You're preventing me." Isabelle glanced around. Several pirates lingered at the corners of her eyes. Close, but not too close.

Denham let out a breath through his nose. "Can *it* call fish here?"

"*She* said she can. It all depends on what the captain says." She eyed him. "It's been only one day without food, man. We've gone longer than that."

"When we've been in waters we know, helmed by a captain that's sane."

Isabelle considered him, what he said, and what he hadn't said. She nodded. "I'll do my best, but you've got to let me by without it being a scene. The longer we stay calm, the more likely we get out of this alive."

He frowned. "Is it that bad?"

"You're the one who called her 'it.' Yes. It's that bad based on all the tales my grandma told me. Now let me work."

She thought Denham wanted to argue more, but he stepped back and looked behind her. "Kelsey, Styles, don't you have netting to repair? Or do I need to find more for you to do?"

Conversation done, Isabelle continued to the captain's cabin. Like yesterday, she knocked on the captain's door and said, "Captain, it's me. We need a word."

This time he opened the door and gestured her in. As she walked by, she could smell that he'd been drinking. She could not decide if this was good or bad.

Closing the door with that oh-so-careful *click*, Welton eyed her. "What is it?"

"We've got to let her go. She's not human. You know that. She says she's from an important family and they'll miss her."

"Will they now?"

Isabelle didn't like the growl in his voice. He was thinking of doing something reckless. "For the good of the *Midnight Sorrow* and the crew, Captain."

"She was once the *Star*, not the *Sorrow*. Did you know that?"

"I did." He gave her a sharp glance. "You told me. And *that* is why we need to let her free."

"I should dump her overboard with that shackle on her. Have her people watch her die before their eyes."

Isabelle paused, but her curiosity got the better of her. "What is that shackle?"

Welton grinned, wide and ghoulish. "It's just iron. But it's got runes on it. Magic that hurts her kind. You're not the only one who learned stories about them at their grandpappy's knee. She won't be able to shift again until it's taken off. Only I have the key." He pulled a chain out from under his shirt. A small iron key now hung next to the gold coin he always wore. "So, no, I won't let her go."

"At least let her call fish to feed the crew. They're out of sorts. Angry. Afraid. They're getting reckless." *Like you*, she thought but did not say.

"Fine. Do it. But I'm not letting her go." He turned his back on her and bent to look at the book he'd been reading.

More and more, Isabelle's stomach sank with a sense of impending doom.

* * *

Several hours and tough conversations later, the crew's anger and fear had been quelled—as long as Patricia could do what she said she could do. The proof would be in the stew soon enough. Isabelle paused at her door, almost knocking first. Then, shaking her head, she opened the door to her cabin and found Patricia curled up on her bed. She looked young and vulnerable. Isabelle pushed the thought aside as Patricia opened those alien eyes, then sat up.

"I hope you can call the fish, because that's what you're going to do now."

"I can. I will need to be in the water."

Isabelle hesitated. "You can't transform. You'll drown."

The eldritch woman gave her a look. "There are ways to get me into the water and back out again. I'm aware that I cannot transform." Again, she held up her manacled wrist.

Even though her skin was somewhat protected by the woolen tube, Isabelle could see angry red welts snaking out from it, marring her pale skin. "Right. Ladders. Ropes. I'll make sure you get pulled aboard again. C'mon."

This time, as she left her cabin with Patricia in tow, Captain Bryce was waiting for them by the rail. He beckoned them over. As they reached him, he asked, "You'll call the fish?"

Patricia nodded.

"Can you call your family, too?" She looked away. He stepped closer and grasped her wounded wrist, ignoring her gasp of pain. "Don't lie to me, girl. I have worse waiting for you if you do."

"Yes," she breathed out, but did not pull away. "Yes, I can call to them, too."

Welton let go of her wrist before Isabelle felt like she needed to intervene. She had seen Patricia's hand flush red as the captain pressed the eldritch shackle against her arm. Even with the wool barrier, it was clear that whatever magic was on the manacle hurt her dearly.

"Good. I've decided, after you've called the fish to feed my crew, I will ransom you. Your weight in gold. The quartermaster says you come from an important family who will miss you. It shouldn't take much for your people to bring seven or eight stones worth of gold for your return."

Patricia shook her head. "This is a bad idea." She glanced at Isabelle.

Though Isabelle wanted to agree with their captive, she said nothing and remained where she was. Her job now was to keep things moving without anyone getting killed. She would not directly contradict the captain in front of the others if she could at all help it.

"Call the fish. Tell your people." It was a command and a demand that would not be denied.

Patricia nodded. "As you wish. I will need help into and out of the water." She raised her injured wrist. Just in the moments between Welton letting go of it and their words, her hand had swelled up into an angry mass of flesh.

He glanced at it without pity or concern. "See to it, Quartermaster."

* * *

After a bit of thought and discussion with Denham and Annie, they decided the best way to do this was to lower both Isabelle and Patricia on a board, let Patricia slip into the water to do "whatever fey magic" she needed to do, then have Isabelle help her back onto the board and pull them both back to the deck.

Isabelle knew she was taking a chance and putting herself in danger, but no other pirate aboard was willing to be that close to Patricia. Beautiful though she was, her wounded hand was a warning beacon to one and all. Also, she was slighter than most of the other sailors, and Annie, despite her own slight stature and hidden strength, wouldn't dare touch Patricia for love nor money.

In the end, the trip over the railing and down to the water was more dangerous in her head than it was in practice. Isabelle supported Patricia on the way down, watched her slip into the water, listened to her call for the fish and to her people—it was much like listening to discordant whale song—then pulled Patricia back to the board and held her as they were pulled aboard. She knew something was happening even before they'd made it to the deck, as most of the sailors had moved to the other side of the boat, leaving Denham, Styles, Eric, and Annie to haul her and Patricia up under Captain Bryce's watchful eye.

Looking out past the captain's shoulder, the calm waters danced a tempest in a wave coming ever closer. "You've called a lot of fish," Isabelle said, feeling uneasy.

"I called. They came. Simple as that." Patricia held onto Isabelle, slumping against her.

"Are you well?"

Patricia shook her head. "No. The magic poisons me." She looked at Welton as she spoke.

He stared back at her with a cold, uncaring gaze. "And your family? Will they ransom you?"

"Yes. But they are far away. It will take time for them to get here, to bring what you asked for." Patricia dropped her gaze to the deck.

Welton lifted her chin and met her eyes again. "The manacle comes off when the gold is on the deck. Then you go." His eyes flicked to Isabelle and back. "It's only because of my quartermaster's words that you live. Remember that."

Patricia tried to nod, but couldn't, as he continued to hold her chin. "I will remember. I promise."

The captain looked as if he wanted to say more. Then he let her go and turned to watch his men as they threw nets down to the fish. They jumped directly into them. "We'll eat well tonight."

Isabelle pulled Patricia with her, not waiting for dismissal or approval. As she did, she thought she heard Patricia whisper something like, "We will," but she couldn't be sure and she wanted to get Patricia out of sight in case Captain Bryce changed his mind. No one stopped them as they returned to her cabin.

As soon as Isabelle closed the door, Patricia half sagged. She took the woman to her bunk and set her on it. "I am sorry. Is there anything...?" She indicated the pulsing red flesh that had once been Patricia's hand.

"No. I'll be fine soon enough. Thank you." She smiled. It was partly a grimace of pain, but turned into something more fierce and feral. "Do not worry. Help is coming. I'll protect you."

That raised Isabelle's hackles. "What do you mean?" Patricia did not answer. She curled up on Isabelle's bed and closed her eyes. Isabelle had the urge to shake her awake. She did not. The warnings about such creatures—fey and eldritch alike—had been drilled in deep. Instead, she sat with her back to the door and watched the sleeping deep one hybrid.

Time passed as the joy of the sailors at the food rose loud, then subsided, as full bellies brought lassitude. Isabelle did not sleep during this time, but she did drift, watching Patricia. Her mind wandered over the last few days. No one came to get her for food or duty. Perhaps they assumed she would fend for herself. Perhaps they were afraid. No matter. Soon, this would all be over.

Just as her own stomach began to growl, Patricia sat up in an abrupt motion. It was an alien movement; all pretense of humanity gone. Isabelle jumped to her feet, but as soon as her eyes met Patricia's she stopped moving. She felt like a deer caught by unexpected light.

The expression on Patricia's face was both kind and horrible. "It will be all right soon. I will protect you. I promise." She raised her wounded arm, her fist an unrecognizable bulb of flesh. "You remind me of my mother. Family is so important, don't you think? I would do much for my family—just as I believe you would as well. You have a kind heart under that hard exterior."

Behind her, Isabelle heard sounds: sloshing water, breaking wood, wet sounds of things hitting the deck, and the panicked cries of the crew. She could not move. No matter what she did, she was trapped by Patricia's gaze. As she watched, Patricia took a knife—Isabelle's own knife, the one she kept under her pillow—and stabbed her own wounded hand.

The flesh burst like an overripe piece of fruit, decaying matter splattering the room. A tentacle unraveled and waved in the air. She let her arm drop, the tentacle almost reaching the floor. A gentle shake and the shackle with the eldritch runes on it dropped to the floor with a *clink* almost unheard in the growing din of men and women fighting for their lives outside the cabin door.

Scream after scream told Isabelle that the *Midnight Sorrow* was no more.

Patricia's whole body relaxed as the fallen shackle rolled under the bed. "That's so much better." She tilted her head. "My family is here. They will eat well. But you, Quartermaster, you I will save. I promised your captain. Also, I promised my pet, James Renton, that I would bring him a companion. He likes to be called Jim. He's been so lonely since Jonathan died. He's old, but he's been a good pet. A companion for the end of his life would be kind. We've watched your ship harry us for a long time. I thought, once the ship passed into the mists, it would be safe enough to come and collect one of you."

She looked at her tentacle and took a step forward, balancing as the boat rocked. "It was a risk, with a splendid reward."

Isabelle watched Patricia advance. "What will you do to me?"

"Do? I will change you just enough so you can survive in my home. Other than that, you will be a companion to Jim and a pet for me and my family."

"If I refuse?"

Patricia stood before her. "You cannot. And, with a kiss, you will no longer belong to the land." She leaned forward and kissed Isabelle on the lips.

Again, try as she might, Isabelle could not move. Then she was drowning in the air. Touching her throat, she felt unfamiliar formations and flaps of flesh. Still she gasped for the air that would no longer serve her. A hand touched her shoulder. She looked up—when had she gone to her knees?—and Patricia held out a hand to her.

Come, Isabelle Thorp. It's time to go home.

The words were not heard. They were in her mind. Isabelle knew she had a choice: live or die. This was the moment.

Isabelle chose to live and put her hand in Patricia's.

The eldritch being led her through a door that was already half-broken. Two steps later, Patricia picked Isabelle up like a child and moved her out of the way of a thrown body. Around her lay bloody pieces of the crew. The *Midnight Sorrow* was sinking. Isabelle looked for the captain. She saw him in what was left of his cabin. He held a sword in one hand and a glowing gold disc in the other. Above him something monstrous loomed. Her last sight of him was a huge tentacle coming in from the side to grasp him around the waist.

Then Patricia jumped with her into the roiling black sea. It was like being born once more. Suddenly, Isabelle could breathe. And see everything beneath the dark water. Beside her, Patricia transformed into something that looked like a huge octopus, but was not. Around one slightly discolored tentacle was the bloody woolen tube of the sock she had given Patricia to protect her skin.

Isabelle barked surprised laughter at the absurdity of it all. Bubbles of air floated up from her mouth. With a last thought for the lost crew of the *Midnight Sorrow*, Isabelle let go and gave into the madness that saved her.

Blackrock

R.M. Olson

Abigail looked up when the woman stumbled into the tavern, blood staining her filthy shirt, clotting in her hair and streaking down her face.

She felt the jolt of recognition through her bones.

When she'd been very young, a dog had come to sniff around their house. She'd stepped outside, her childish thought to pat it on the head or feed it scraps, but it had gone completely still—body stiff, tail rigid, eyes fixed on her. It wasn't growling. Growling would have been less frightening.

Her father came running, scooped her up, rushed her inside, and barred the door. She'd felt how his arms shook. *"Abigail,"* he'd said gravely when he'd put her down. *"That dog's been hurt too bad to see you as a friend. It's been kicked too many times, had too many rocks thrown. It only sees you as something to kill before you kill it."*

The woman dropped into a seat at a small table in the corner of the tavern and glanced around. Abigail felt that same thrill of fear she'd felt back then. She recognized that look—a dog who'd been hurt over and over until all it could see were enemies and prey.

But Abigail's father was long dead, and she'd lived on Blackrock for coming up on five years now. Here in the pirate settlement carved deep into a rocky moon, where the vicious FTL ghosts were hardly more vicious than the people who sat behind her bar, death was hardly a stranger.

She stepped out from behind the bar, drying her hands on the towel at her waist, and crossed to the table where the woman sat.

She was young, perhaps mid-twenties, with the look about her of someone accustomed to deep space flight—an ineffable trace of wildness, a lingering scent of ozone and ship grease. Radiation marks creased her skin, and there was a restlessness in her eyes and movements that spoke of a person not at home on solid ground. She wore a simple sailor's blouse and trousers, and she was attractive, in that bold, confident way Abigail had always liked, her hair ink-black, her eyes piercing. But it wasn't that that drew your eye and held it.

It was an anger so deep and fathomless that it shimmered in the air like heat—a feral, vicious, animal hate.

"Nothing to do with a dog like that but put it down. It'll never be able to do anything but kill," her father had said.

She met the woman's eyes. "What'll you have, then?"

The woman smiled, but there was no humor in it. "Rum," she said, her voice raspy with pain.

She downed the first pour in one swallow, and the second. It wasn't until Abigail refilled her glass a third time that she leaned back in her seat. Her posture should have looked relaxed. Instead, it was the taut readiness of something poised to spring.

This was a woman who'd turn ghost the moment she died, something whispered in the back of Abigail's head. *This was a woman who'd be as ruthless and deadly as a ghost even when she was alive.*

"You new here on Blackrock, then?" Abigail asked. You survived on Blackrock if you knew who was a danger to you. And whatever else this woman was, she was dangerous.

The woman smiled again, the expression knife-sharp. "New enough. Got in on a transport last night with the rest of the flotsam from the Stacks."

Abigail's eyes flicked over the woman's bloodied clothing, the bruises deepening across her face.

She'd heard what had happened last night.

There were people enough who came in from the Stacks, the ghost-haunted slums set deep under the wealthy cities on the Level. They came when their loved ones had been killed by ghosts, when the combination of bad air and bad food and bad water drove them out, when the grinding, desperate hopelessness became worse than the indelible consequences of the faster-than-light travel that would carry them somewhere different. Once you'd traveled faster than light, once your cells had undergone the degradation of FTL travel, you'd always carry in your body the potential that, after you died, you'd turn ghost. It would leave you unfit for life on the Level, or work in any civilized place; you'd be doomed to either the Level Navy or Blackrock, and anyone desperate enough to flee the Stacks was someone who'd not be looked at by the Level Navy.

But Blackrock was not a kind place. And there were times when the desperate, starving refugees from the Stacks would stumble off the filthy transports onto the docks of Blackrock only to be met by those who'd press-gang them into a crew, would they or no.

Sometimes, the scene turned bloody. Last night had been bloodier than most—a dozen dead on the docks whose families would never know what became of them.

The woman must have read Abigail's expression because her smile took a mocking twist. "You heard what happened, I figure? Two of them as was killed weren't hardly more'n children. But that'd hardly matter here on Blackrock, no? Hardly a consideration for pirates."

Abigail narrowed her eyes. "Talk like Level Navy, you."

It wasn't unheard of for a former naval sailor to end up on Blackrock when piracy was the only option left open to them. But for half a moment, she thought the woman would lunge at her. She tightened her hand around the small projectile pistol she carried in her apron pocket, but at last, the woman relaxed back in her seat, studying Abigail.

"I won't say there ain't them here as wouldn't think twice to kill a child," Abigail said. "But you'll find that in your fine Level cities and in your Navy, too. Ain't easy to live here on Blackrock. But ain't everyone who's a monster."

The woman was still watching her. "What's your name?"

"Abigail."

"And I'm Gracie." She paused. "Heard the pirate captains around the dock frequent here more often'n not before they head out."

"Aye, that they do," said Abigail, keeping her tone neutral. "Figure they'll start to trickle in later today."

Gracie nodded, still watching her.

"You'd do well to watch yourself," Abigail said, lowering her voice. "Ain't any as goes out to the transport docks as don't have plenty of friends to back them up. Vengeance don't stitch together a slit throat, and it don't bring back the dead, and them as don't learn that don't last long. You keep quiet, and you'll maybe stay alive long enough to get friends yourself. You don't, you'll be shot down like a mad dog."

"That so?" Gracie's voice was soft, still with that sharp, mocking edge to it. "And turning a blind eye'll keep you safe, that it? Not shot down like a mad dog, just tied in the corner like a whipped mutt?"

"If there ain't anything more you need, I'll get back to my business," Abigail said shortly.

She could feel Gracie's eyes on her as she walked back to the bar.

Gracie stayed where she was for the rest of the morning, nursing her drink. As the tavern got busier later in the afternoon, Abigail could have forgotten about her—Gracie didn't speak except to ask for another glass of rum. But there was some part of Abigail that was attuned to the dark corner where Gracie sat in the same unerring, unconscious way your body would attune to the hint of cold in a dark alley that betrayed the presence of a ghost.

It was late and the tavern busy and crowded by the time Ty stepped through the door.

Abigail stiffened, her hands stilling for a moment on the glass she was polishing.

She didn't know who'd killed the newcomers from the Stacks last night. But she could damn well guess.

He strode over to the bar and dropped onto one of the stools. He hadn't bothered to clean the blood from his coat; probably thought it made him look frightening. He'd come to Blackrock recently too, from one of the resource planets. He was young and arrogant and brutal, and already the captain of a ship.

She drew in a breath and turned. "What'll you have?"

He sneered at her, eyes dragging up and down her body in a way she was far too familiar with. "What's on the menu, lass?"

"You can have rum or beer or whisky or a damn bullet in the gut, your choice."

He laughed. "I'll have a double pour of rum, then. Celebrating getting me a new crew."

"New crew, is it?" The words were quiet and level, with the barely slurred edge to them of someone who hadn't slept or who'd spent the day nursing her rum in a dark corner of a tavern.

Gracie had come up behind the captain. Standing, she was taller than he was seated, and the dim light showed the bruises and blood on her face, the rusty stains dried across her once white shirt.

The tavern had gone quiet with that instinct for danger that was honed to a knife's edge on Blackrock.

Ty turned, looking Gracie up and down in a leisurely fashion. "You're the one as got out, ain't you? Looking to join my crew? Figure there may be one or two of your friends aboard, if they recover. If not, there's always the next transport. More'n enough of you stumble onto Blackrock sooner'r later." He shrugged, lazy and arrogant.

There was no warning; Gracie grabbed the front of his shirt, yanking him to his feet, and slashed her knife across his throat in a brutal backhanded stroke. Blood sprayed across the bar, spattering the clean glasses and Abigail's white apron and the patrons to either side, soaking Gracie's hand and arm and adding fresh stains to her bloodied clothing.

She let the body drop as casually as you'd drop a wet rag and turned to the assembled crowd, smiling that knife-edge smile. The anger in her was something tangible, pulling at you like gravity. No one said a word.

"Figure I will look for a captain as is hiring, at that," she said. "You can put the word out, any as is looking for crew."

She strode out of the tavern, leaving silence in her wake.

Abigail stepped out from behind the bar, pulling out her sparker to disperse Ty's ghost before it could form, but something like pity tightened her stomach.

Gracie might make her first voyage. She might survive that long. But Ty had friends, business partners, people who'd used his brutality to make themselves rich. They'd not be happy he'd been killed.

Gracie'd be dead within the fortnight.

* * *

Abigail tapped at the door to the rundown lodgings, forcing herself not to glance over her shoulder. There wasn't much that frightened her after five years, but if you weren't afraid of ghosts, you were a damn fool. Here on Blackrock, where faster-than-light travel was a way of life and everyone here was fleeing something worse, ghosts in the dripping, artificially lit caverns were as ubiquitous and expected as the clank and groan of the fans that brought oxygen up from the algae vats in the deep caverns.

She'd seen people killed by ghosts; a bullet through the head would be a mercy in comparison. And she'd felt the ghost-chill in the alley behind her. She had a sparker; the slender metal rods with their dim blue spark of electricity at the tip were the only things that could get rid of a ghost. When a ghost was still forming, they were simple enough to use. But it took almost as much luck as skill to hit the point in the centre of a fully formed ghost that would disperse it as it sprang to tear out your throat.

When the door creaked open, she stepped through quickly. Wil glanced past her into the alley, then closed and barred the door tight enough to lock it against ghosts.

"Abigail," he said, turning to her. "Been doing well, I see."

He was a large man, middle aged, with arms thick with muscle and a face that could have been called handsome if it weren't for the sharp cruelty of it. The sight of him made something crawl under her skin, but she only tapped her comm and brushed the credits over.

He counted them as she waited. His posture was relaxed, his expression mild, but she knew damn well what would happen if the count was short.

The first few months after he'd turned the tavern over to her, there'd been weeks at a time she'd eaten nothing but scraps left over on patrons' plates because going hungry was better than what would happen if the credits were short. Five years later, her tavern's reputation was enough that she had plenty of credits tucked away. He'd never know—she'd learned early to be clever with the accounts. But he'd get what she owed him. He'd get that and nothing more.

"You were just a scrap of a girl when you came here, I recall," he said, looking up, satisfied with the count at last. "Hardly more'n a child. But you ain't turned out too bad as an investment."

She kept her expression impassive.

She'd survived, dammit, and she wouldn't be sorry for it.

"Heard tell Ty got his damn throat slit a couple days past." Wil's voice was casual enough, but he watched her sharply.

She narrowed her eyes. "Aye. Someone come from the Stacks. He'd killed a number of them trying to press-gang them, I heard tell, and she weren't happy about it."

She could still see Gracie's face, the undisguised fury burning just under her skin, the way she'd looked when she yanked the pirate captain to his feet and slit his throat.

Wil snorted. "Ty was a damn fool. They kill the one as did for him?"

Abigail shrugged. "Didn't hear about it if they did."

She'd been listening for the gossip. Word had it that Captain Glass had taken on a blood-soaked woman with a smile like the edge of a knife and a steady hand with a pistol when she'd come looking to crew with a ship.

Word had it she'd kill you soon as look at you.

"Ain't a good look for my tavern, Abigail."

"Ain't stupid enough not to have a sparker on me," she said tartly. "I took care of the ghost before it could form and I scrubbed the blood from the floor. If it means less business, won't be you as'll suffer for it. I keep the tavern as I see fit; that were our bargain."

He rose abruptly, voice going quiet with menace. "Best watch your damn mouth, lass." Standing, he was a good head taller than she was.

She'd been frightened of him once. She still was, maybe. But here on Blackrock, you saw enough in your first fortnight, if you survived it, to learn that fear wouldn't save you.

He raised his hand. Her heart was pounding, but she didn't flinch and she didn't drop her eyes, just tightened her grip on the projectile pistol in her pocket.

Five years ago, he and his crew had landed on the small resource planet where she'd grown up, and he'd shot her father in the doorway.

She hadn't been a child anymore, although she'd not been much more than one. And when he'd turned the pistol on her, she'd looked him in the eye, stood from where she'd been crouched beside her father's bloody body, his breath still choking and bubbling in his throat, and she'd told him to get the hell out of her damn house.

He could have shot her. She'd thought he would, and with the horror and cold rage running through her veins like blood, she'd almost hoped for it. But instead, he'd laughed, shoved the pistol in his pocket, and told her he could use a lass with some spirit—he'd won a tavern back on Blackrock in a game of chance and he had no one to run it for him.

She'd wanted to put a knife through his damn throat. But it wouldn't bring her father back, and she wouldn't let this man kill her, too. So instead, she'd nodded and agreed and gone back with him on the ship.

Five years she'd run the tavern. Five years she'd brushed credits across to the man who'd shot her father. And if the rage choked her at nights sometimes, burned her throat like a flame, she could swallow it still.

Tied in the corner like a whipped mutt.

For an instant, she wasn't sure she remembered how to breathe through the desperate, helpless fury. She'd drown in it, she'd drown and die; there was a reason she worked so hard to shove it down—because it would kill her.

"Well, Abigail," he said at last, lowering his hand, "you run the tavern as you see fit. But if you think about turning on me—if for one minute you think to put your damn foot outside that tavern door without my permission—I'll shoot you through the head."

Five damn years. There was a taste in her mouth like bile and ash. But she only dipped her head and stepped out the door he held open for her.

The ghosts were gone, lured away by other warm bodies nearby, and she walked quickly through the streets. The damp caverns of Blackrock—the flickering torches with their artificial light set in the walls and the clanking of the overhead fans—had felt strange and claustrophobic when she first arrived here. Now, they were comfortably familiar.

When she stepped back into the tavern at last, she closed the door behind her and crossed to the bar, the relief of her own space draining a little of the tension from her muscles.

Anger like that was dangerous.

She sighed and rolled her shoulders, trying to stave off a tension headache. If she intended to open at her regular time, she had plenty of work ahead of her.

But she paused, running her hand across the pitted surface of the bar. At last, she pulled the small pistol from her apron pocket and laid it in front of her.

The pirates used energy pistols and cutlasses aboard their ships—projectile pistols onboard a spacecraft carried far too much risk. But here on Blackrock, projectile pistols were ubiquitous. No way, really, to know whose gun a bullet had been fired from.

Wil had friends, just like Ty. He had influence on Blackrock. And five years later, Abigail had built up influence of her own, but it wasn't enough, not yet.

She could still see the look on Gracie's face as she dropped Ty's limp body to the ground, the fierce animal snarl of her smile.

She ran a finger lightly along the barrel of the pistol.

Then she sighed and placed it back in her pocket, turning to fetch clean rags.

Nothing to do with a dog like that but put it down. Her father had dragged her out of the way of the mad dog, probably saved her life. But she'd always wondered, a little, why it was the dog that had to be put down, not the people who'd thrown the stones.

It didn't matter. There was no one left, anymore, to save Abigail—she saved her own life or she died. That was how things were on Blackrock.

* * *

It was four days later when Gracie strode back into the tavern. She wasn't limping anymore, and the bruises on her face had lightened to an ugly purple-green. She crossed to the bar and leaned against it, her eyes sharp and hard and following Abigail's every move.

Abigail ignored her for a few moments, drying the last imaginary droplets of water from a glass she'd been polishing before finally turning. "Didn't think to see you back here," she said.

Gracie smiled that knife-edge smile. "Thought I'd be shot down by now, no?" Her eyes held the same deadly magnetism they had before, and the same threat.

"Figure we all know what folks do with them as cause more trouble than they're worth."

Gracie gave a snort of humorless laughter. "Aye. But if they're going to hate you either way, better to be feared than pitied, I figure." She leaned in, eyes not leaving Abigail's. "Want you to put word out," she said quietly. "I'm looking for them as took those people from the Stacks, and I'd be grateful to any as could give me their whereabouts."

Abigail had to force herself to breathe under the weight of Gracie's gaze. "Aye," she said tartly, "I can do that. And you'll be back here if any want to speak with you?"

Gracie smiled again, quick and sharp. "Aye. Any as wants to find me, they'll find me here." She tipped her head, cold amusement in her gaze. "Figure there's plenty who come here, no? Pretty barkeep like you?"

Abigail narrowed her eyes. "Ain't any as come here for a pretty barkeep who don't keep their damn distance. None as don't want a bullet in the gut, leastways."

Gracie cocked an eyebrow.

"Shot three dead my first year here," said Abigail.

Gracie laughed. "I'll not worry about you, then."

"Ain't asked you to," Abigail bit out. "You going to order, or you going to get the hell out?"

The first time she'd shot a man in her tavern, her hand had been shaking so badly she'd hardly been able to aim, even though he was almost on top of her. When he'd fallen to the ground screaming and writhing, blood bubbling from the wound, she'd had to run to the necessary in the back to be sick, her whole body shaking, tears streaming down her face. But she'd wiped her mouth and wiped her eyes and reloaded the pistol with shaking hands, and then she'd stepped back out behind the bar because there'd been no one else to do it.

It was easier the second time.

Gracie's smile this time held a trace of amusement. "I'll have a glass of rum, then I'll get the hell out."

She swallowed down the glass Abigail poured, then turned for the door. Her clothes hung on her frame, and Abigail wondered, suddenly, how much she'd had besides rum over the past week.

"When'll you be coming back, then?" Abigail called after her. "Ain't many as'll be willing to set up shop in my tavern to wait for you, and I ain't about to let them if they try."

"I'll be back here tomorrow evening," said Gracie without turning, then she was through the doors.

Abigail shook her head and picked up Gracie's empty glass, swiping her cloth across the small condensation mark it left on the bar. The gossip had been right—there was nothing left in Gracie but hate and rage and death.

* * *

The first customers started to trickle in an hour or so later. Even here on Blackrock, with ships coming in from God knew where on God knew what schedule, Abigail kept more or less regular hours. For a crew who'd just come in off a long flight, injured and staggering with exhaustion and wild-eyed with the beginnings of space-madness, it was what they wanted—a place with regular hours and a steady floor and four walls and alcohol. A familiar face behind the bar, someone who wouldn't offer them pity or disdain or anything but rum or whisky or beer and silence if they wanted it, or else maybe a bit of the gossip of Blackrock from while they were away.

Any who thought they'd get more than that from the pretty barkeep would learn the hard way. But there weren't many, anymore, who'd offer her insult.

She moved among the tables, taking orders, pouring drinks, collecting empty glasses, and she passed on Gracie's message. The thoughtful gazes that followed her were laced with a sharp calculation, but Gracie could hardly blame her—she was doing exactly as the woman had asked.

Wil came in later in the day. When he was planet-side, he'd come by often, to check on his investment, as he called it. He expected rum; free, and as much as he wanted. She'd pour it for him, lips tight, and ignore him otherwise. Today, though, she watched from the corner of her eye until she saw one of the other captains cross over to him, whispering something and gesturing at Abigail.

She knew perfectly well what the woman was telling him.

Gracie's death would be worth a handsome number of credits. And Wil had never shied from taking what he could get his damn hands on.

She turned back to her work, her hands shaking a little.

It didn't matter. She knew damn well what it took to stay alive on Blackrock.

* * *

By late the next afternoon, the usually busy tavern was all but empty; whatever uncanny sense people developed here to warn them of danger had clearly told them this wasn't a place to linger tonight.

Or maybe it wasn't a sense for danger—Abigail knew the talk had been spreading. There was a part of her that hoped Gracie had heard it, too, realized what she was walking into. But she'd met Gracie twice. That had been enough to tell her the woman would come regardless.

As her regulars filed out, others filed in—hard-faced sailors and captains, some she recognized, some she didn't. They all wore the grimly satisfied look of people about to get what they wanted, when what they wanted was blood.

They distributed themselves around her tavern in a methodical way that would have chilled Abigail even if she hadn't known what was coming.

Nothing to do with a dog like that but put it down. And these people were here to put Gracie down.

Gracie arrived a few minutes later. She paused in the door, glancing around the tavern, and for a moment, Abigail's throat was tight with something that might have been fear and might have been hope—that Gracie would see the trap, turn, and walk out.

Instead, her eyes caught on Abigail behind the bar. She smiled her sharp, humorless smile and stepped inside, closing the door carefully behind her.

The room was silent as she strode across the floor, her boots thudding off the worn surface. She reached the bar and leaned against it, cocking her head at Abigail. "Well, barkeep. Looks like you did me the favor of passing word around, just like you promised." She turned slowly, her eyes scanning over the assembled pirates. "You figure any of these here has that information I was asking for?"

One of the pirates, an older woman with light skin and dark eyes and hair going to gray, pushed back her chair. The scrape of it against the floor was loud in the silence. "Aye, lass." Her voice was quiet and dangerous. "Figure we do." She smiled, showing her teeth. "You wanted to know the names of them

as was on the docks a week back. That'd be me, for one." She gestured at the
room. "And the rest? They're here, along with a few others as took offense at
what you did to Ty."

Gracie's posture was deceptively relaxed, but there was that sharp tension
in her, that barely hidden rage that pulled at you like gravity. One hand rested
casually on the butt of her pistol, her cutlass in easy reach of her free hand,
and she was smiling, if you could call something like that a smile.

The rest of the pirates got to their feet, one by one. Abigail stepped back.

"Aye, barkeep," said Gracie without turning. There was a note of grim
amusement in her voice. "Best stay out of the way. Your friends don't seem
like the agreeable sort."

Abigail hesitated, then took another step back behind the corner of the bar.
Her hands shook a little, and she twisted them in her apron to steady them.
Her breath was coming too quickly, and she told herself sternly to stop it.

Gracie's head jerked up as the door opened again.

Wil stepped through. He closed the door behind him and barred it
deliberately, then turned, grinning at Gracie. "Well, lass. Here you are, as
promised."

As if by signal, the others started slowly forward.

Abigail closed her eyes.

She'd survived on Blackrock five damn years. She could simply go on as she
always had, running the tavern, minding the business that paid her.

And her father would still be dead. Wil would still be walking the streets of
Blackrock with his cruel grin and his blood-soaked hands.

She drew in a breath and slipped quietly out from behind the bar.

Gracie didn't move as the others came closer, just stood there with that
vicious smile on her face. Every eye was on her; Abigail moved silently around
to the back of the tavern unnoticed. Wil was near the back of the crowd,
letting the others take the front, but the captain who'd first spoken had almost
reached Gracie, her grim expression a contrast to Gracie's sharp, mad grin.

The pirate lunged. Gracie's arm moved at the same time, quick enough that
Abigail almost couldn't follow.

There was a moment of silence as the pirate captain gasped, frozen. Gracie's
cutlass had pierced her abdomen and protruded through her back and blood
bubbled on her lips, pink and foaming.

Gracie yanked the blade free, the muscles in her shoulders standing out
with the effort. The pirate captain fell to the floor in a bloody heap, and the
spell was broken.

There was an explosion of projectile-pistol fire. Gracie grunted, the cutlass
dropping from her hand as red blossomed across the white sleeve of her upper
arm, then she took two quick steps forward, close enough that the gathered

pirates couldn't shoot without risk of hitting one of their own. Three shots cracked out from her pistol, and three pirates fell, one after the other, before someone grabbed her, wrenching the pistol from her grip. There was the sound of a fist hitting flesh and Gracie staggered back, then someone had her by the shoulder, spinning her around and kicking her legs out from under her.

She went down hard and one of the pirates, a large man with heavy boots, landed a flurry of kicks to her ribs before she staggered to her feet. She managed a swing with her uninjured arm, sending another of the pirates stumbling backwards, before she was pulled down again. This time, more joined in, kicking her as she raised her arm in a futile attempt to shield her head.

Abigail forced herself to watch.

Gracie rolled behind one of the small tables and dragged herself painfully to her feet. She shoved the table, and it overturned in front of her, tangling a couple of chairs with it into a makeshift barricade. She was still smiling, blood staining her teeth, and she'd pulled out another pistol, but there was no way she'd survive this. She must have known that as well as Abigail did.

But there was something in her eyes that was far, far too grimly satisfied for a woman on the point of death…

Abigail sucked in a breath.

She knew, suddenly, what Gracie had planned.

The door was barred, and it was ghost-locked, like every door here on Blackrock.

There was no way Gracie could kill all the pirates in the tavern. She must have known that the moment she'd stepped inside. But she'd never been fighting to win. She'd been trying to do exactly what she'd just done—lure her attackers close together into the corner of the tavern, where they'd have no shelter from a murderous ghost.

The pirates Gracie had killed hadn't gone ghost because every person here knew the danger, and each time, someone had stopped long enough to shove their sparker through the blue haze of the forming ghost. But where Gracie was now, no one would get to her in time to disperse her ghost before it formed.

It might not kill all the pirates. But it would kill plenty.

Turning a blind eye'll keep you safe, that it?

Abigail stepped forward. She was directly behind Wil now.

Gracie glanced over at the movement and Abigail met her eyes deliberately. Then she pulled the pistol from her apron pocket and shot Wil through the back of the head.

He crumpled without a sound.

Blood speckled Abigail's face and stained the clean white of her apron, but the rage in her chest burned with a hot, clean vindication that was headier than strong rum. Her hands were perfectly steady. She slipped the pistol back into her apron pocket and stepped back, glancing around quickly.

No one had noticed; Gracie must have understood what she was doing, because she'd ducked down behind her makeshift barricade and fired at the same time, holding the pirates' attention and disguising the noise of Abigail's shot.

Abigail waited until she saw the telltale blue haze of a forming ghost over Wil's limp body. Then she turned, crossing quickly back behind the bar.

One or two of the pirates were firing at Gracie's position, sending splinters flying, and others made their way around the overturned table and tumble of chairs toward her. They didn't notice the ghost until the first scream.

By then, it was too late.

The shredded body of the woman who'd screamed lay on the floor, neck broken, head tilted at an unnatural angle, blood streaming from the gashes the ghostly claws had torn through flesh and viscera. The ghost hovered over it, cold wafting off it like steam. Its face and figure were Wil's, but there was nothing human left in a ghost—only the mindless echo of the trauma that had created it, its eyes black pits, ghostly fingers tapering to claws.

There was a moment of complete silence.

Then it sprang, jaw stretching unnaturally wide to expose the sharp black jags of its teeth. A pirate's scream of horror cut off in a bloody gurgle as the ghost's teeth ripped out his throat, claws tearing casually through his ribcage and leaving white shards of shattered bone in their wake.

Behind the ghost, a blue haze gathered over the body of the first victim.

One ghost, and it was possible one of the pirates would manage to disperse it. Two, less likely, but still possible. Once there were three, every person in the room was as good as dead.

Abigail tore her eyes away from the gruesome sight.

Gracie stood where she was, breathing heavily. Blood streamed from a shallow cut across her cheek and more ran down her arm. There was a fierce heat in her eyes as she watched the pirates scream and die.

Abigail's father had been right—some creatures and some people were hurt too badly to trust anyone ever again. The only thing they could do was hate and kill; letting them die was a pity, but perhaps it was a mercy, too.

Abigail hesitated. Then she blew out a quick breath and, glancing back to make sure the ghost was distracted enough that her movement wouldn't draw its attention, stepped briskly out from the bar to the makeshift barricade.

Gracie spun, her hand going to her pistol, but Abigail shook her head shortly and pulled the woman after her behind the bar and through the small ghost-locked door that led to the kitchen. She barred it tightly, then pulled out a chair. "Sit," she commanded.

Gracie stared at her. For the first time since Abigail had met her, she looked…uncertain. As if this show of kindness was more frightening than the blood and the terror from the other room.

Abigail sighed. "Sit down. You look like you're about to fall over. No point in saving your damn life if you bleed out meantime, and you're making a mess of my damn kitchen."

Finally, Gracie's mouth twitched into the ghost of a smile and she half-fell into the proffered seat.

"Hold out your arm, if you can manage it," said Abigail, turning to fetch the small first-aid kit she kept on hand. When she turned back, Gracie was holding out her arm obediently. Abigail cut away the blood-soaked sleeve and dabbed at the bloody wound with a clean cloth.

"You're lucky. Went through the muscle. Figured for sure you'd broken a bone. Let me see your ribs?"

Gracie hesitated, then unbuttoned her shirt gingerly with her good hand. Abigail pulled the fabric aside and forced herself not to wince at the ugly bruises blackening across Gracie's abdomen, the old knotted scars that traced across her flesh, and the way her skin lay tight against her bones like it had been too long since she'd eaten well.

She glanced at Gracie for permission, then traced her fingers gently along Gracie's ribs. Gracie shivered a little at the touch, flinching like she expected a blow.

"You'd do well to spend fewer credits on rum and more on a decent meal now'n again," Abigail said.

Gracie smiled a little, her bloodstained teeth turning the expression gruesome. "Didn't figure I'd live long enough for it to matter."

Abigail snorted. "No bones broken, Our Lady of Mercy alone knows why. I'll bandage you up; I figure after that, rest'll be what'll serve you best."

Gracie was quiet as Abigail worked, but Abigail could feel the weight of her gaze. There was still that heavy heat of fury in it, and knotted anger in every muscle of Gracie's body, like it had lived there for so long it was as much a part of her as her blood.

"The hell you do that for?" Gracie asked abruptly.

Abigail paused, glancing up to study her. "Told you. Ain't everyone on Blackrock is a monster."

Gracie was quiet again. "That pirate you shot?" she asked at last.

"He killed my father and brought me here," she said tersely. "Been working for him for five years. Figured maybe five years were long enough."

Gracie leaned back a little in her seat, weariness bleeding through the lines of her body. "Seems to me like he deserved killing."

"He did." Abigail finished tying the last bandage and turned to wash her bloody hands at the sink.

"And what you fixing to do now? Go back to where you were taken from?"

Abigail turned back. Her body was still a little shaky, and she wasn't sure if it was the killing or the freedom or the gruesome fate she'd left the pirates to.

Or maybe it was the fact that she didn't feel any guilt for it—only a vicious satisfaction that reminded her of the expression on Gracie's face.

"Don't figure as I will," she said at last. "Came here because it were my only option to stay alive. But this? I'm good at it, and I like it. My father's dead. There ain't nothing back there for me anymore, and even if there were, I'd not go. Leastways here there ain't no one watching my every move, telling me what is and what ain't proper. There ain't many on Blackrock as don't know my tavern, and there ain't many as could have done what I've done with it." She refused to drop her eyes as she spoke, even though she knew the guilt should be burning her from inside.

It didn't matter. Her father was dead; she wouldn't feel sorry for the fact she couldn't find it in her to mourn him any longer.

She didn't realize how her body had tensed at the words until Gracie smiled, and she felt her shoulders relax a little. She smiled back unconsciously.

Gracie reached out and grabbed Abigail's hand in her bloody one. "Thank you," she said softly. "Been a while since there were any as gave a damn if I lived or died. I'd forgotten what it was like."

Her hand on Abigail's was warm, her grip tight, and her eyes were dark and intense and as magnetic as they'd been when she'd first stumbled into the tavern.

Abigail was standing closer than she'd realized, and something about the weight of Gracie's gaze made her abruptly aware of her own body. Of Gracie's body, close enough to touch, her shirt hanging open to reveal her soft curves and hard muscle.

She stepped in closer, still a little drunk on the clean, hot rage flooding her veins. "Maybe it's better to be a mad dog than a whipped mutt," she whispered. "Maybe I ain't sad you reminded me of that." She hesitated, then ran the back of her hand along Gracie's cheek, her thumb brushing across Gracie's bloody lips.

Gracie's eyes fluttered closed and she swallowed, her expression going tight with something like pain. She reached up and caught Abigail's hand, but she didn't pull it away.

"There someone else?" Abigail asked softly after a moment.

Gracie hesitated, then shook her head. "No. There was. I ain't sure I'm over her yet." She managed a small smile. "Besides, I couldn't promise you more'n a night. Got to find a captain as is looking for crew if I'm aiming to live, I suppose."

Abigail snorted. "I ain't offering more'n a night. Got lovers enough if I want them, and I ain't looking to tie myself down." She paused. "Won't press you. But I figure there's no shame in taking comfort in another's body, long as both parties agree to it. Got rooms upstairs; you can spend the night either way, but I ain't going to say no to spending it with you. We can deal with the dead and the ghosts in the morning."

Gracie watched her a moment longer. Then she stood and stepped in close, her presence as heavy and magnetic as her gaze. Her smile was the edge of a knife, sharp and bloody, and she slid her hand around the back of Abigail's head, pulling her in.

The kiss was desperate and hungry, and it tasted of blood and fury and freedom. Abigail closed her eyes and leaned in and let herself drown in it.

Home By the Sea

Misty Massey

Black clouds billowed in the yellowing sky, and the air pulsed with the acrid scent of an oncoming spinstorm. The mighty ship rested on one side, its masts roped to tall trees to hold it in place while the crew crawled around scraping the hull clear of barnacles. For an ordinary crew, the job could take days. Their captain, Kestrel, was no ordinary pirate. She possessed a magic unlike any known in the Nine Islands. If she so much as walked in a rhythmic way, the tingle of magic would rise within her, filling her with power that allowed her to move the air in any way she needed. As a child living on the streets of Eldraga, keeping the magic hidden was vital to her survival. It wasn't until she took to sea that she felt safe enough to begin learning how to use her ability.

As soon as the ship was secured, she'd climbed on the side and started singing one of those rollicking songs her old captain always loved, focusing the magic of her singing at the tiny barnacles trying to make her ship their home, making the wood of the hull vibrate. It didn't knock the blasted creatures free, but the shaking did loosen their grip. Her quartermaster, Shadd, ordered his gunners to man a fire on the beach to heat a massive pot of tar. Once the hull was as clean as they could manage, the swabs would paint tar over every inch, sealing it against new interlopers for a time. At the rate they were moving, she figured they'd have a day or so to finish the careening before the looming spinstorm reached them.

"Captain!" Fred Johnson and Two-Patch Weston trudged toward her through the dry sand. She'd sent them into the trees to forage for fresh fruit, and by the look of the burlap sacks they set gently at her feet, they'd found a decent source.

"Successful search, gentlemen?" Kestrel asked.

"We collected some heartfruit and spikey annas. There's plenty more we can scoop up before we set sail again. But that's not the best part."

The two men were grinning like schoolchildren, but Kestrel couldn't guess what might be delighting them. "I give. What's the best part?"

"We found a ship!"

Damn. She'd been so careful to choose a cove that wouldn't be noticeable from the open sea for the careening. They weren't in position to run down a merchant. And the last thing she needed was an attack from some other pirate vessel while her ship was hove down. "How many gunports is she sporting? And is she headed this way?" She threw a look toward Shadd, but he was busy with the tarring.

Two-Patch snorted, and Fred laughed out loud. "Nah, captain. Not in the water. Beached in the next cove, she is. Nowhere near as big as ours. She could likely carry a crew of a dozen. The sails are tore up, but the hull looks fit. We watched for a quarter-hour, and ain't no crew moving about. I'm thinking she's abandoned." He rubbed his hands together. "Salvage, as it were."

Now that *was* some fine news. A small ship like that could be useful in all sorts of ways, and since they were here careening anyway, they might be able to put her in the water when they left. Was this the beginning of her very own fleet? "Why don't you head back and check her innards? In fact, let's ask Shadd for a couple of pistols, in case you run into someone who doesn't like visitors."

* * *

The sun was moving toward the horizon before Kestrel realized her men hadn't returned. She took Shadd by the arm, drawing his head close to hers. "I don't want to upset the others, but Fred and Two-Patch aren't back," she murmured.

"Ye want me to go lookin' for 'em?" he asked.

"I'll go." She snapped her fingers three times in succession, sparking the magic to rise within her. It bubbled below her skin, clearly wanting to explode out from the confines of her body, but she let it subside. "If I don't return, the ship is yours."

"If ye're not back by midnight, we're all comin' for ye, and bringin' hell with us."

She slapped him on one massive shoulder. "No worries. They likely found a cache of liquor and are passed out on the sand halfway there." She wanted to believe herself, even while a nagging doubt hung in the back of her mind, a feeling that only blood and sorrow awaited her in the dark.

* * *

Following their trail wasn't hard—they'd left deep footprints in the dry sand nearly the whole way. Rounding a curve, she came upon the little ship. It sat nearly upright, dragged half a ship's length up from the water. The keel was buried in the sand, but what she could see of the sun-bleached hull seemed whole, and ragged sails flapped in the evening breeze. Faded black letters on the railing near the bow spelled out the words *Home By*. Odd name for a ship, but who was she to judge? For a moment she wondered how the little vessel had ended up so high off the waterline without more damage. Maybe a storm had forced it ashore to its resting spot. It wouldn't have carried many crew, and they might have all been swept overboard. She angled her approach to the stern, and groaned. No wonder the ship was abandoned – the rudder was missing. She didn't carry a spare aboard her own vessel, so making this one seaworthy again would take money and time. The dream of a fleet would have to wait. She frowned. The men woud have seen the problem and come straight back. So where were they? She approached, holding her hands open at her sides to show she was no threat in case someone remained, out of sight. "Fred?" she called. "Two-Patch?" Other than the gentle toss of waves and the occasional bird call, she heard nothing.

The footprints stopped at the midship rungs on the far side. Kestrel called out again, receiving no answer. She walked to the other side of the ship, and scanned the sand up to the treeline. No other tracks anywhere. "Bloody hell, Fred," she murmured. If only her magic could reveal lost sailors. There was no hope for it – she had to go aboard.She grabbed the lowest rung, and climbed up to the edge of the deck. Shadows stretched across the deserted space, and the only movement came from loose rigging in the wind. No bodies, living or dead. She hauled herself aboard. The boards under her feet creaked with her weight. She crossed to the hatch and leaned over. "If you can hear me, make a sound," she called. Belowdecks was swathed in darkness, too thick to see past the top two steps of the ladder leading down. If she was to explore, she'd need a light source. A small lantern hung from a hook on the mast. She lifted it, and shook it, gratified at the tiny sloshing from inside. It smelled of oil. Not enough for the whole night, but maybe it would last while she made a quick search below. Pressing her lips together, she whistled a tune. Sparks of magic bubbled, tickling under her skin. She directed the power into her fingers, and rubbed them together on either side of the lantern's wick. A tiny flame burst into life, catching the wick. She settled the glass chimney into place. Dropping to her knees, she bent to the open hatch and lowered the lantern into the shadows. Her light revealed an open deck, curiously empty of supplies, cannons, or furnishings. Dust lay thick and unsullied on the lowest rungs of the ladder and the floor beyond. Her men definitely hadn't come this way.

Sitting up, she glanced toward the stern. The cabin door was shut. She blew out a frustrated sigh. If the men were aboard, the little cabin was the only place they might be. Something about that closed door gave her pause. Closed doors meant privacy, secrecy, things that were in short supply on a ship. What could be going on in there? Some of the men occasionally turned to each other for a bit of affection, and she wasn't one to interrupt. Even if her wayward pirates had given in to the throes of passion, they'd surely have pulled themselves together when they heard her calling. She approached the door, and pressed an ear against the wood. A man's voice was droning lazily, the words too soft for her to make out. She took hold of the latch and lifted it, letting the door fall open, and held high her lantern.

Fred perched on a wooden stool, his back to the door. And in front of him, holding both his hands, sat a woman. Her skin was pale except for a spark of red high on her cheeks, and her ashen hair fell in a loose twist over one shoulder. The hem of her long gray dress pooled around her feet. A strange velvet darkness roiled like storm clouds in the space behind her, thicker than mere shadows.

"Damn it, Fred, what are you doing?" All this time she'd been worried something was wrong, and here he sat, chatting up a woman. And where was Two-Patch?

Fred turned his head slowly in her direction, although he barely seemed to meet her gaze. Kestrel gasped. He was a youngish man, no more than thirty, but now wrinkles cracked his face and his back slumped forward, as if he'd aged forty years since Kestrel last saw him. His skin looked like sun-faded paper, dry and thin, and his eyes were white with cataracts. He turned back to the eerie woman. "I saw merpeople once," he said, his voice lifeless. "Long teeth and angry faces. I thanked the gods for not knowing how to swim, so they couldn't get at me."

Kestrel stepped into the room and laid her free hand on her sword hilt. "On your feet, Fred," she ordered. "It's time we're gone."

The pirate didn't move from his seat. "The captain, she made a bargain with them to bring a drowned sailor home to his wife," he droned on, as if he hadn't heard.

Kestrel didn't know what was happening here, but she had no intention of staying to find out. And it was looking like she'd have to drag Fred out. By his hair if necessary. Keeping an eye on the woman holding Fred's hands, she bent to set the lantern down. The lantern light flickered, and she jerked backward in shock. Behind her, on top of a pile of old bones and rotted clothing, lay Two-Patch. Clumps of faded red hair had fallen away from his desiccated scalp and his dried flesh clung tight to his bones. If she hadn't spoken with him earlier this same day, she'd have sworn he died months ago. Kestrel drew her sword and swung toward the woman. "Let my man go, if you value your life."

"He is not finished telling me stories," the woman said, her voice soft and papery. "Please wait your turn."

"Make me!" Kestrel snarled, and raised her blade. Before she could take a step, the shadows behind the woman coalesced into thick ribbons of black, sweeping forward to wrap around Kestrel and force her against the wall. A silken tendril crossed her face, closing her lips. She struggled to free herself, but the darkness held her fast, as if she'd been tarred and pressed against the bulkhead.

"His wife met us on the dock. I never saw such a sight as that drowned man walking across the boards and collapsing into her arms." Fred took a rattling breath. "She cried and cried…" His voice faded off to silence and his head tilted to the left. The woman smiled. She released Fred's hands. With a sigh, he slid off the stool, tumbling to the floor.

Kestrel cried out, her voice muffled behind the shadow holding her. She tensed her arm. If she could tap just one finger against the bulkhead, she could use her power to free herself. The shadows pressed harder, forcing her hands flat. Her sword clattered to the floor, and she struggled to take a deep breath.

The gray lady sat calmly in her chair, her hands folded in her lap. "Tell me your story." Her dry whisper scratched over Kestrel's ears like a striking match and sent a shiver down the pirate's back.

The tendril of darkness holding Kestrel's mouth closed slithered down her chin, settling around her throat just tightly enough to remind her it was there. What sort of monster demanded stories before she killed her victims? "Why should I?" Kestrel asked. "You killed my men!"

"I harvested their stories from them. It's been so long since anyone spoke to me. Their tales of adventure, of nights filled with heat and longing, of wishes to return home for the taste of mother's bread and sweetheart's kisses. Their tales refresh me. Give me life."

"Your life means nothing to me." She struggled again, and the loop of shadow around her neck pulled tight.

The woman rose from her seat, swathes of shadow flowing behind her, twisting in a phantom breeze. She raised a graceful hand to caress Kestrel's cheek. The woman's skin was vaguely uncomfortable to touch, and cold as the ocean itself. Kestrel shuddered under her touch. "Your story is filled with magic, they told me. I need to hear it from your own lips. The men told tales well enough to feed me, but your story? A feast like none I could have wished for. Such a tale will be enough to finally let me leave this ship."

"You won't get far," Kestrel snapped. "There's nothing on this island but trees and birds."

"And your ship," the woman said.

Cold crept down Kestrel's spine. She had never known real freedom until she gained her ship. Being at sea kept her worst enemies, the Danisoban Magi, at bay, and her crew was the closest thing to a family she'd had since being orphaned. She'd die before she allowed this creature to endanger them.

Light flickered from the lantern on the floor. So close to the dried-out corpses. Could it be that simple? Kestrel began clicking her tongue, counting a beat like a cockswain calling the rowing. Her power sparkled under her skin, the rhythm bubbling it to life. She couldn't turn her head to look at the lantern, but she thought she remembered where it sat. If she could send a punch of magic at it, turn it over to spill the remaining oil and set the bodies ablaze...

A finger of shadow slid into Kestrel's mouth, pressing her tongue down. Her magic faded. "None of that just yet," the woman said. "I promise it won't hurt." The darkness lifted Kestrel's arms away from the wall, allowing the colorless woman to clasp her hands.

Fog billowed into Kestrel's thoughts at the touch, leaving her dizzy. She tried to pull free, but the shadows held her fast. The ribbon of darkness in her mouth dissipated. She tried to click her tongue again, but it felt thick. Her head lolled to the side. She was almost too drowsy to keep her eyes open. Images of her childhood running the streets of Eldraga began to surface out of the clouds. It would feel so comfortable to spill the details of her entire life at last, to give them away and free herself of the burden.

"Tell me your story," the woman murmured.

"I cried every night for my mother," Kestrel said, her voice languid. "I was barely out of my babyhood when the Danisobans took my family from me."

"Yes, and what about your magic? Was that the reason?" The woman's words seemed intent on comfort, but the portion of Kestrel's mind that still fought the shadows detected a demanding note in them. "Speak more of your magic."

"Born with it," Kestrel said. "I had to keep it all a secret for so long." The image of a face swam into her awareness. A boy, brown curls falling over one eye, a mischievous grin on his face. Kestrel smiled. She hadn't thought of Gab in years. "The street children took me in. Protected me. Gab taught me a song, and when I sang it..." she faded off, lost in the memory.

"More," the woman insisted. Her grip tightened on Kestrel's hands. "What happened when you sang?"

"I could make the little ones float," Kestrel murmured. "For a moment only. I wasn't strong enough to lift much." She thought about how they would laugh, their tiny voices ringing like chimes in the echoing stillness of the Eldragan alleys. "Gab played the sticks, and I'd sing, and tra la! Up into the air they'd go. We had to be so careful not to let anyone see us. After he went away..." She drew a breath, and her chest trembled with the effort. Her eyes were so heavy, but she couldn't quite slip into sleep. Something was keeping her just on the edge. "I never sang that song again. I didn't sing anything."

"Tell me more," the woman said. "Fill me with your magic."

Gab had always warned her never to sing when an adult might hear. He'd seemed so grown to her, but now, looking back over the years, she realized he couldn't have been more than ten. Maybe that was why he vanished the way he did. Tears rose in her eyes, blurring her vision. The Danisobans never took children after a certain age. Gab had been so smart. He taught them all how to avoid danger. But even the wiliest of street urchins was vulnerable to the Brethren.

The woman gripped Kestrel's hands harder, her flesh stinging like nettles made of ice. "Never mind the song," she insisted. "Give me your magic, and you can rest."

"I can't," Kestrel said. The little song swelled into her mind, just the way Gab taught it to her. She hummed, searching for the tune, fighting the weakness that threatened to consume her. Her magic began to bubble in the usual way, flowing in a steady stream to fill her. "Larks and sunbeams fill the skies, purple berries make sweet pies," she sang. The fog started to lift from her mind. "When the stormy rain starts falling, that's when goblins come a calling." How could she have forgotten it? With every note, her magic strengthened. Kestrel reached out with her power, tearing loose the shadow that held her fast. It shredded into nothingness. She shaped the power into whips, and flung them toward her adversary. They wrapped around her, sparking like a lit cannon wick. She yanked her hands free and stood, backing away from the woman.

"No!" the woman moaned. She tilted her head back, color rising in her cheeks. "This is not the way." She clawed at Kestrel, and fell to her knees. "Help me!"

"It must be," Kestrel said. "I can't allow you to consume me, or any more of my crew." She picked up the lantern and slipped out the door to the deck. She'd survived too much, accomplished too much, and all on her own. This creature might be trapped, but it wasn't worth Kestrel's life to free her.

The woman wailed, her voice echoing in the night. "You can't leave!" she cried. "I must have your story!"

Kestrel ran for the midship rungs, setting the lantern down and climbing to the beach and safety. In the distance, Shadd and a few others came running across the sand toward her. Had she been gone so long? Kestrel trudged through the dry sand, relieved to meet her crew, but couldn't resist one last look back. In the gentle flickers of lantern light from the deck, she almost thought she could make out the figure of a woman, hair and skirts tossing in the breeze, reaching toward her and begging for one more story.

"Are ye well, captain?" Shadd called. "Did ye locate our wayward boys?"

"I did, sorry to say." She laid a hand on his arm. "They met with misadventure."

"Who did it?" he growled. "We'll make 'em pay." The men behind him made angry noises, but Kestrel shook her head.

"Easy, lads. Let's not rush to vengeance, much as we might want it." Part of her still wanted to set the marooned ship ablaze, burn out the danger to anyone else who might run across the eerie woman who killed Fred and Two-Patch and who knew how many others. Yet here she stood, almost sorry for the poor creature, trapped as she was and with no end in sight. Kestrel knew that feeling far too well. "I have a better idea in mind," she said. "Come with me." It was possible she was about to make an awful mistake, but something inside told her she needed to try.

* * *

The woman had retreated to the dark cabin when Kestrel climbed back to the deck. "Come out!" she called. "If you want more stories, of course."

The shadows shifted and the woman appeared out of them. She held out one pale hand. "You've returned?"

Kestrel took a step backward. "No touching. I have an idea that might help you without killing anyone else. Not that I feel you deserve it, but I'm willing to try. For the sake of any others who might land here." The woman let her hand drop, but remained still. Kestrel took her silence as leave to continue. "I'm going to bring my men aboard. You may not touch any of them. They will tell you their stories, and I'll use my power to help them nourish you. Or," she shrugged, "I can always leave you here to starve."

They stared at each other for the space of a breath. At last, the woman nodded, crossing her arms in front of her. Kestrel hoped this wasn't a false capitulation, but if the creature attempted something while surrounded by the crew, the option to set the ship ablaze remained. Keeping one eye on the woman, Kestrel walked back to the rungs. "Come up, my lads." As each man gained the deck, she sent them to one end to wait, positioning herself between them and the woman. Shadd came last, handing her a pair of sticks pulled from a nearby tree.

"Thank you," Kestrel said. "One at a time, I want you each to step forward and share a story from your life. It doesn't matter what you choose to tell. As you tell it, I'll be sending a flow of magic to surround you. Might tickle a bit." A few of the men laughed nervously. "It'll sweep over you, and on to our… guest. I don't know what will happen after that, so keep a weather eye open. Ready?"

They nodded and murmured assents. Jaques stepped forward. "I'll go first, Captain."

"We'll see to it, then." Kestrel clacked the two sticks together, beating the tune of her old childhood song. Power bubbled, rising to fill her. "Go ahead, Jaques," she said.

He turned toward the woman. "When I was a child," he began, "there was a man in our village who kept three wives." As he spoke, Kestrel sent ribbons of power around him, braiding through the air in delicate sparks and flowing past him to the woman. The band of magic swirled over her. She dropped her head back, her eyes closed, as if bathing in ecstasy. One by one, each man stepped up and told a tale of his own. Some amusing, some tragic, but with every one, the woman's color brightened. At last, all the men were finished. Kestrel stepped forward, keeping the beat with her sticks.

"When I was a child, on the streets of Eldraga, I knew a boy named Gab. He may have been my first love, but we were too young to know for sure," she said. "When he vanished, probably taken by the Danisobans, I promised myself I would never use my magic ever again. I hope that I'm not disrespecting his memory by doing this, but you've offered me the chance to recall him, and I'm grateful." She sent one last burst of power.

The woman cried out, throwing her hands above her head. Light swirled around her feet, lifting her from the deck toward the sky. She floated slowly up and away from the ship, her voice lost in the distance. Kestrel stopped clacking her sticks together, awed by the sight. Her own power didn't seem to matter any longer. The woman looked down, a smile on her face. She exploded in silken brightness, half-blinding the crowd below, disappearing into the night.

Kestrel let her sticks fall, crossed to Shadd, and patted him on the shoulder. "Shall we go back to the ship?" she asked. "We've got work left to do. And I'd like to tell you about my friend Gab."

The Only Thing Worse Than Pirates

C.C. Finlay

Belt Buckle was laser-carved across the bulkhead in elegant script, so Lexie saw it every time she entered the control room. Belt Mining Corporation gave all its ore-processing ships names like *Belt Drive*, *Belt Grinder*, and *Belt Sander*, but they were running low on creativity by the time they commissioned this hulk.

Grosvenor, the ship AI, had sent her an alert for two emergencies. He kept her busy for morale reasons, even when that meant interrupting her VR games.

"What's up, Fussbudget?" Lexie asked.

"Good working relationships depend on mutual respect." The same thing he said, more or less, every time. "The use of mocking nicknames can be hurtful."

"It's a term of endearment. Updates. Worst emergency first."

"Foxtrot urinated in the storeroom, not five feet away from the litter box."

"He's old. He gets confused." Foxtrot was not a very good companion animal. Lexie felt a strong kinship with him. "I'll clean it up. What's the second problem?"

"We're being pursued by pirates."

"Pirates? Are you joking? That sounds more important than Foxtrot's accident."

"It's not a joke. The urine is already a puddle on the floor. It's a slipping hazard, a corrosive, and failure to clean it up immediately will only encourage repetition of the behavior."

"But *pirates*!"

"A pirate attack is a statistical improbability. Pirates capture pleasure yachts visiting the Jovian moons, strip the ships for supplies, and ransom the executives. What the news services refer to as 'trillionheirs.' No pirates have ever taken an ore processor. The tech aboard is too old, there are no black markets for the ore, and I'm afraid you have no value as a hostage."

Grosvenor had a thing for groups of three. Lexie had learned that their communications fared better when she didn't interrupt. "Maybe they want to kidnap Foxtrot."

"If I had hands, I would put that leaky orange monster in a lifepod and jettison him for pickup. I will not answer any more questions until you've cleaned up his mess."

"Who's captain of the *Belt Buckle* anyway?"

* * *

Fussy refused to respond, of course. He had the right to do that. In a very real sense, he *was* the ship, and he didn't deserve to be peed on without his consent. And if he was peed on without consent, he shouldn't have to soak in it.

She assumed—*hoped?*—that if there was immediate danger, he would notify her. In the absence of such notification, she went to clean.

The cat pee had spread under bolts and into the metal seams, where it dried quickly, making it impossible to completely eliminate the pungent smell. She wasn't sure how good Grosvenor's scent sensors worked, so she sprayed and wiped and wiped and sprayed until her back ached. The litter in the KittyPotty robox had been recycled more times than the air she was breathing, but she also did her best to freshen it up with enzymes and RealDirt fragrance.

Afterward, she went looking for Foxtrot to make sure he wasn't sick. She found him in the workshop, sleeping in a drawer on top of a mess of cables and pokey spare parts. Couldn't be comfortable, but lately one of his favorite spots. He squinted and hissed at her, so she apologized and gently closed the drawer.

That task accomplished, she returned to the command center and plopped into the single chair. Stretched out her legs and wiggled her bare toes. Lexie could talk to Grosvenor anywhere on the ship, but by mutual agreement they reserved the command center as their public space for conversation. She might not have any privacy, but she liked to pretend.

It was called the command center, but really it was more of a gray-walled utility room. The wall supported stacks of the hard drives, fans, knobs, and valves that provided access to all the ship's systems. Below *Belt Buckle*, a narrow viewport blurred with age and microdust pitting was nearly the same gray color as the walls. Facing the viewport was a single bench lined with manual navigation and interfaces for a slightly larger crew. Lexie never used them—it was easier to control the ship through Grosvenor.

"You know I could fly this ship by myself," Grosvenor said, answering her previous question about the captaincy.

"Legally, you're not allowed to. Gotta have a human, in case things go wrong."

"In my experience, humans are what goes wrong. Look at you. You're a subcontractor. You're not even an employee of Belt Corporation. And all you do is sit in your quarters and play VR games."

A point of contention between them. Grosvenor was prickly for an AI. But Lexie was not about to be sidetracked: a pirate attack might be a statistical improbability, but a pirate sighting was still a curiosity, and so far, this had been a monotonous long haul.

"Tell me about the pirate ship," she said.

"It appears to be the *Praxidike*."

That made Lexie's butt pucker. She'd heard of the *Praxidike*. Everyone had heard of the *Praxidike*. Not just pirates, but anarcho-anticapitalists. Daring hit-and-run attacks on executive ships from Mars to Saturn. Destroying expensive company outposts. Belt Corporation had been hit multiple times. Not as badly as AsteroCorp or Rockoko, but still. There was a substantial reward for *Praxidike*'s capture.

"What's your level of confidence?"

"Ninety-four percent. The company created a profile. Silhouette, electronic signature, confirmed sightings. While I was scanning our transit path for unmapped objects with high mining potential, I detected a minor occultation on our negative axis. The characteristics match the *Praxidike*, so I tagged its trajectory, sent a report to the Belt relay post, and informed you."

"I know they never attack ore-ships like the *Buckle*, but it's kind of exciting that the *Praxidike* crossed our path." It would be something for Lexie to tell everyone in the habitats when she took leave on the moon.

"It's not just crossing our path. It's pursuing us. And closing quickly."

"*What?!* When were you going to tell me?"

"It was literally the first thing I told you. *We're being pursued by pirates.* Listening carefully is a sign of mutual respect. Good working relationships depend—"

"Shut the fuck up. Show me the raw data."

* * *

Lexie activated the dusty computer screens like she was some kind of troglodyte. Like this was still the stone age before VR existed. But sometimes she just needed to stare at the numbers like they were game stats; they made more sense to her that way.

As a subcontractor, she had limited informational access, but she saw enough. The object pursuing them had low albedo. Compact size. A metamaterial surface that bent light and electromagnetic signals.

Occultation should have barely registered, if at all. Mere space dust.

She respected Grosvenor as a ship AI, despite the teasing nicknames, but there was no way he should have been able to detect that ship. Not unless there was some kind of temporary failure in its stealth technologies.

"It's coming at us like a comet with rockets," she said aloud. "Options?"

"Evasive action is impossible, given its maneuverability relative to the *Buckle*. I requested permission to accelerate, but corporate refused due to deceleration costs and complications with delivery times at the other end. Their risk analysis registers theft or destruction of the *Buckle* at near zero probability."

"If it's a zero probability, why are the pirates pursuing us?"

"I've attempted to ask them, but their ship is not responding."

Lexie felt like she was missing something. The ore processor carried roughly two hundred million earth-tons of M-class asteroid debris, with a crew of antiquated and highly-specialized robots for pounding, smelting, separating, and grading the raw materials. Mostly iron, nickel, and iridium. The *Buckle* would arrive in lunar orbit with sheets of construction-ready steel, a small assortment of other minerals worth something to somebody, and a bunch of tailing slurry that she would have to dump in the sun before flying out to the belt for their next load.

"What is the *Praxidike*'s usual method for capturing a ship?" she asked. Her voice quivered, because she thought she knew from the news feeds.

"If they make contact in advance, they offer a single chance to surrender. If they don't make contact or if the ship refuses to surrender, they attach mines and blow the airlocks, depressurizing the ship. Then they capture any ransomable survivors, kill the rest, and strip out valuables."

Lexie wasn't a valuable survivor to Belt Corp. She wasn't even an employee. "Show me the intercept vectors."

A plot with labels and estimates appeared on the screen. Mere hours until the *Praxidike* reached them. Her heart pounded faster. Wait, what was that small—?

"Grosvenor!"

"I see you noticed the personnel javelin. It will reach our airlock in approximately twenty-one minutes."

"Why didn't you tell me?"

"I reported the javelin to the Belt relay station. The exec expressed concern that you would over-react and take action, which would increase the company's potential losses. I was directly ordered to not inform you."

"Damn it! Good working relationships do not involve sacrificing your co-workers to pirates!"

His silence was as good as an admission that he understood this.

"If you had a neck, I would you grab you by it and shake you," she said. She was not, by nature or circumstance, a violent person. She was, however, very scared.

* * *

Lexie had neglected her exercise and had been eating to stave off boredom on this contract. Her emergency spacesuit required a lot of wriggling and squeezing and some holding her breath. At least her oxygen tanks were full; when the pirates blew the airlocks, she'd have a few hours to contemplate her life choices.

Foxtrot, who had been ignoring her for days, suddenly decided he needed All of Her Attention Right Now while she was straining to pull on her boots. He mewed and mewed, rubbing his head against her ankles, demanding pets. It was like he knew she was scared, but he also expected her to comfort him so he wouldn't have to deal with her being scared. She paused to pet him. His ginger fur, once thick and soft, was now dry and brittle with age. She should have been brushing him more.

When she tried to pick him up to put him into his emergency pod, he nipped at her, yowled, and bolted away like a kitten on catnip.

Before she could pursue him, Grosvenor called. "Lexie. The javelin will attach to the port airlock in about a minute."

Immediate danger. Right. She put on her helmet and checked the seals. "Have they offered a chance to surrender?"

She was ready to surrender.

"They continue to ignore all attempts at communication. Perhaps you can negotiate with them in person. Post-kidnapping debriefings indicate that has been a successful strategy for non-corporate personnel on several occasions."

"Define 'several.'"

"Almost twelve percent of the time."

Tears streamed down Lexie's cheeks as she lumbered to the port airlock. That stupid cat. Why did he run away? If he was in his sealed carrier, he would be fine no matter what happened to her. Not even pirates would hurt a stinky old cat.

The airlock had no windows, but it did have cameras. Lexie peered at the screen, expecting to see a hardened spacer in combat armor affixing explosives to the airlock. What she saw was a middle-aged woman peering directly into the camera. She wore pajamas covered with woolly mammoths and saber-toothed tigers. A slightly younger woman in overalls with lots of pockets loomed over her shoulder. No spacesuits. The older woman held up a tablet, with text printed on it.

NO RADIOS
THEY'LL HEAR
LET US IN

Grosvenor observed the whole exchange. "They do not appear to have the tools necessary to force their way in. What the criminal element refers to colloquially as 'can openers.' We can safely ignore them."

"And then when their ship arrives?"

"Perhaps they will also be unable to force their way in."

No radios. They'll hear. Let us in.

The women outside the airlock stared at the camera, looking as sick with terror as Lexie felt. No spacesuits—if they caused an explosive decompression, they were also dead. The woman typed something on her tablet and held it up again.

PLEASE

They didn't look like pirates. They looked like escaped prisoners.

Lexie removed her helmet and reached for the airlock controls.

"Company policy explicitly forbids the admittance of non-contract personnel—"

"Shut up, Fussy."

* * *

The woman in pajamas was named Howard. Her companion in overalls was Kayla. They talked over each other, trying to explain what had happened.

"The bastards were laying in wait—"

"—they killed everybody—"

"—we hid in the javelin—"

"—Saffi made the launch look like a malfunction—"

"—she was doing her best to bug up the gears—"

"—but they caught her—"

"—they killed her, too—"

"—she was screaming when we launched—"

"I'm so sorry," Lexie said, just to slow them down. "Was Saffi another prisoner? How did she get to the controls of the pirate ship?"

The two women stared at her in confusion.

"Saffi's always been on the *Praxidike*," Howard said.

Kayla scrubbed tears from her eyes. "Yeah, Saffi is—was—our ship's AI."

"This is where I take over." Grosvenor said over the speaker. "The three of you are going to plainly and precisely answer every one of my questions. If I dislike *anything* I hear, I'm going to pump this cabin full of carbon monoxide and let someone else clean up your dead meatships."

"He won't do that," Howard whispered to Lexie.

"Will he do that?" Kayla asked.

Lexie wasn't sure. Grosvenor had never used that tone of voice with her before. But then she had never opened the airlocks to let two pirates aboard before. The *Buckle* had never been pursued by the most feared pirate ship in the system before.

"He definitely *can* do that," she said. "I intend to answer all his questions plainly and precisely."

* * *

They were standing oppressively close to each other on the airlock deck, so Lexie led the two women to the command center. It still felt like the right place to talk.

"I'm a trained xenogeographer, specializing in the Jovian moons," Howard explained to Grosvenor. "The *Praxidike* was originally built as a scientific research vessel for Tycho Crater University. Back then it was going to be called the *Endeavor*. What we didn't know then was that it had been secretly funded by Komət. That was before Komət became AsteroCorp. It was some backroom deal with administration to hide what they were doing from other companies. The university was just going to hand the ship over to Komət's extraction teams to identify resource exploitation opportunities in the outer system. Actual scientific research was going to be incidental to their pursuit of profit."

"They wanted to turn Europa into a fucking fish farm," Kayla said. "Before it was fully explored. I've seen the fucking business plan."

"So, we stole the ship. A crew of scientists and grad students. We added the stealth tech to escape capture, and then we headed to the outer system to do the kind of science we always dreamed about."

"I've recorded cryovolcanic eruptions on Enceladus, collected soil samples from the craters of Hyperion, taken temperature readings on the surface of Almathea, and orbited Jupiter in seven hours riding on Adrastea!" Kayla seemed to realize that she was riding adrenaline and forced a deep breath. "Okay, that last one was just for fun."

"It's good that you had time for fun between kidnapping raids and destroying corporate property," Grosvenor said. "It's probably easy to have fun with billions of dollars in ransom and stolen property. What's a few murders along the way?"

"We never killed anyone who surrendered and never kill anyone at all if we can help it," Howard argued. "And we only destroy property that's causing environmental damage. Those corporations don't pay any taxes! In the meantime, they steal resources that belong to everyone. They destroy space environments forever, before we've had a chance to study them."

"So, you do kill people sometimes," Grosvenor said.

Lexie had been about to hold up her hands and say *I surrender, don't kill me!* but now she was glad she'd kept her mouth shut.

"Why did your ship AI go along with this behavior?" Grosvenor asked.

"Saffi?" Howard asked. "The whole thing was Saffi's *idea!*"

"Saffi was designed to be the intelligence for a science vessel," Kayla said. "Not a profit vessel. Show some respect. She sacrificed herself so we could warn you."

"If someone captured your stolen ship and killed a crew full of murderers, I'm not sure I should be expressing sympathy or offering aid," Grosvenor said. "If they're chasing this ship to recapture you, I'm inclined to let them."

"They're not trying to recapture us," Kayla said. "They don't know we escaped. That's why we said no radios. They're chasing your ship because they intend to capture it, crash it into a lunar habitat, and blame it on the crew of the *Praxidike.*"

Grosvenor went silent.

Was an AI capable of feeling the same horror as Lexie? She was a misanthrope, yes, who was soloing a long-haul spaceship while she played her way through all seventeen releases of *Space Fyghter Alyen*, plus expansion packs. But she wasn't a monster. If a fully-loaded ore carrier crashed into a lunar habitat, it could kill a hundred thousand people.

"Who would do something like that?" she asked, half in disbelief.

"Corporate raiders," Howard said.

"Icahn and Posner," Kayla added. "Have you heard of them?"

"Fucking corporations," Howard muttered.

* * *

Lexie didn't exactly like corporations. She worked for them, and they always cheated her in some way. Belt was better than some, worse than others. But her livelihood depended on them. As far as she could tell, corporations evolved around the same time as cockroaches. They were probably related. Both were disgusting, but corporations had always existed and they would always exist.

Existing was one thing. Crashing an ore carrier into a space habitat was something completely different. What kind of people did that?

"Hey, Fussbudget," she asked. "Who are Icahn and Posner?"

No answer.

That wasn't a good sign. She tried again.

"Hey, Grosvenor. Who are Icahn and Posner?"

"IP Capital specializes in identifying economic disruptions that cause sudden depreciation of value in their target corporations. Then they purchase controlling shares of stock at lower prices. Once they assume leadership, they identify assets that can be converted into executive bonuses. Then they restructure for efficiencies to increase shareholder value."

That didn't sound anything like the Fussbudget Lexie knew.

"Basically, they wreck economies, companies, and people's lives to make themselves richer, even though they already have trillions," Kayla said. Her voice was angry in the way that only the young and idealistic can be angry. At the moment, Lexie understood where she was coming from.

"What makes you think Icahn and Posner are involved?" Grosvenor's voice asked. "Did someone mention their names?"

Lexie tapped Howard on the arm and pointed to the tablet. The pirate quirked an eyebrow, but handed it over quietly. Lexie shifted her body to block the view from the ship's camera.

"The fuckers were there in person," Kayla said. "We swallowed the bait— an exec yacht sightseeing in an area where we had limited familiarity. When we approached it, we got hit from all sides. Electronic can-openers embedded in the communications. Targeted EMPs. Mercenaries. Blown hatches. Saffi partitioned herself and hid in as many systems as she could. Caused random failures and malfunctions to distract from the javelin before she launched it. Gave us the video feed as long as she could. Icahn and Posner came in to supervise the interrogations."

"In person?" Grosvenor's voice again.

Lexie was sure now. She finished typing her message on the tablet and held it at an angle so Howard could see it. But not, she hoped, the camera.

NOT

MY AI

Howard frowned.

"Yes, in person," Kayla said. "Are you paying attention? Icahn interrogated the one other survivor. Said he needed to know enough about the *Praxidike* to make the hijacking and crash look like an act of terrorism. Posner interrogated Saffi. He was stripping all the ship's research to find exploitable resources."

"Grosvenor." Lexie enunciated. "This plan doesn't make sense. Does it?"

A pause. "It makes a lot of sense. The *Praxidike's* actions have encouraged anticorporate sentiment and inspired likeminded troublemakers. This gambit eliminates the *Praxidike* as a threat and discredits the copycats. It provides an opportunity to recoup Komət's original investment in the *Endeavor*. It will crater the price of Belt shares, so IP can buy it cheap. A crash into a lunar habitat also creates a massive market for construction materials, which they'll have a monopoly on since they'll own both Asterocorp and Belt. They'll make trillions." Another pause. "It's brilliant."

"Brilliant? That's worse than anything we ever did!" Kayla's voice shook with fury. "People will die! The people who don't die will lose their homes and jobs! They'll have their whole lives destroyed!"

Lexie was glad Kayla started yelling because she was too upset to speak. What happened to Grosvenor? Did they just delete him? Was he gone forever? She held up the tablet for Howard.

BELTCOR
OR ICON
PZNR

Howard tapped Belt Corp. That was Lexie's guess, too.

"Everybody dies." Not-Grosvenor said. "There will be new jobs. New homes. They'll be better than the old ones. People get over things."

Howard took the tablet.

CUT
CNX

Cut the connection. Howard pointed the tip of one finger to Kayla. Her specialty? Before Lexie could reply, Howard showed the tablet to Kayla, whose eyes widened in surprise before she glanced about the room.

This was spinning out of control too fast. There had to be some way to stop this from happening. Some other option. "Grosvenor," Lexie said. "What if we inform the authorities? Maybe Lunar Patrol can intercept the *Buckle*."

"No, it's too soon to involve the authorities. Nothing has happened yet."

Kayla dragged the chair over to the utility wall and sat down. She discreetly retrieved a tool from one of her many pockets and went to work blindly, one-handed, using her body to conceal the action.

"But we have to warn somebody," Lexie pleaded. "We have to give the lunar habitats a chance to evacuate."

"Belt Corp is willing to see how this plays out," Not-Grosvenor said. "It's too soon to act. There's always a chance that the takeover of the ore-processor will fail. And if it doesn't, it's no worse than any other industrial accident or pollution or waste dumping. Those things happen on Earth all the time."

"But those are terrible things!"

"Golden rockets," Howard muttered.

"In the meantime, Ms Salgado," Not-Grosvenor said. Lexie's last name. *Uh oh*. "You invited known pirates on board the *Belt Buckle* against the advice of the ship AI and in direct contravention of the no-guests terms of your freelance employment. As a consequence, your contract is terminated immediately, and you are ordered to lea—"

His voice vanished mid-sentence. Kayla held up a drive. "What an asshole."

"That wasn't Grosvenor," Lexie said. Not that Grosvenor wasn't an asshole sometimes, but he wasn't *that* kind of asshole. "It had to be somebody from Belt. Is Grosvenor okay? Can we bring him back?"

"I don't know yet," Kayla said.

Lexie spun back to Howard. "What are golden rockets? Is that, like, some way to stop the attack?"

"No, it's the opposite. That's what they call it when a company loses tons of money or gets acquired in a hostile takeover, but all the execs get crazy bonuses," Howard said. "Billions of dollars. Trillions. They don't care what happens to anyone else as long as they get theirs."

"These rich guys all look out for each other," Kayla said. "That exec is probably selling his company stock right now, cashing out before the prices crash."

"Can *we* warn the moon without them?" Lexie asked.

"We can't turn communications on without giving Belt a chance to take control of the ship again," Kayla said. "Frankly, I don't want to breathe carbon monoxide. But if I can vacuum-gap the ship's AI, maybe we'll be able to send a message."

"Get started on that," Howard said, before catching Lexie's eye. "Sorry, captain. That should be up to you."

"Didn't you hear? My contract has been terminated. Do whatever you need to do. See if you can find Grosvenor." She wanted to warn the moon, but she also wanted to get out of this alive. Maybe they could do both. "Can we all escape in the javelin? Warn people that way?"

"IP should have control of *Praxidike*'s weapons by now," Howard said. "They'll pick us off as soon as we launch. As far as I can see, our only chance is to fight. That's not a good chance, but it is a chance. Do you have any other space suits? Any kind of weapons?"

"No, neither…" Lexie said.

What did she have? Besides a VR gaming system that tended to overheat and a geriatric cat with a bad personality and bladder control issues. *Oh!*

"…but I do have a steel factory full of giant industrial robots."

* * *

The crew cabin of the *Belt Buckle* was a tiny pimple on the ship's vast, cavernous body. Lexie seldom left the former to visit the latter, which was entirely by design. Grosvenor managed all the functions of the ore carrier. The machines, robots, and other pieces were all inspected and maintained by Belt Corp crews in the mining camp, on one end, and in lunar orbit at the other. From time to time, Grosvenor would send her into the facility to replace a broken sensor or to manually reset one of the robots. Even then, it was always sweating hot and loud and busy. She was in and out as quickly as possible.

She led Howard through a series of locks, finally emerging on a metal scaffold that looked out over a quarter mile or so of carefully segregated industrial processes. All dimly lit and spooky, but that was normal. A few widely spaced lights along the catwalks. In the shadows between the lights, there were storage bays, conveyor belts, steel rollers, ingot molds, ladles, blast furnaces, hoppers, flues, and a bunch of other stuff she didn't know the names for. There were fixed robots—some as big as the javelin, with very specific tasks—semi-mobile robots with arms like spiders, welding robots, and a host of smaller, independent robots assigned to maintenance, transportation, and observational chores.

At the moment, all of them were still. It felt like a creepy museum. With the blast furnaces off, the temperatures were already starting to drop.

"Everything must've shut down automatically when Grosvenor went offline," Lexie explained. "This is refining and production. Back in the middle of the ship is ore storage, crushing, and separation. The range of robots there is similar, but geared more toward moving and pulverizing."

"I'm just shocked a space this large contains breathable air. Even if it's thin."

"It's a byproduct of the mining process. When we reach the moon, this will all be pumped out and sold to the habitats. On the return flight to the belt, you couldn't come in here without an air tank."

"Is there anything beyond ore storage?"

"The power plant. That's off-limits to me. Proprietary tech, probably."

"Poorly shielded nuclear power, more likely."

"There's also garbage. Ore tailings and waste gas. No robots." Lexie swallowed. Her throat felt dry. "All the good stuff is right here. What's your plan—to draw the raiders down here? Make them fight their way through?"

"No, these guys are pros. They're too smart to fall for that. But if we can't bring them to the robots, maybe we can take the robots to them. Can I go inspect our options?"

"Please," Lexie said, pointing out the catwalks and ladders to the different sections. Howard led the way, and as she passed out of thin shadow into a brighter pool of light, Lexie noticed that she was only wearing striped socks. Lexie should have offered her some shoes. She wasn't thinking clearly. All the VR games in the world could not have prepared her for this. "What's that on your shirt? Next to the woolly mammoths and saber-toothed tigers. Some kind of bear?"

Howard glanced over her shoulder, face shining for one brief second like a Christmas tree. "It's a giant ground sloth! Do you like megafauna? Oh, wait, is this one of the welding robots?"

A giant snakelike arm loomed out of the darkness over their heads. It was on a mobile platform, but Lexie wasn't sure how they could move it up the catwalk or through the hatches. "You want to use this as a weapon?"

"I want to use it to weld the airlocks shut to make them harder to blow. I don't suppose you have this in pocket-size."

"Maybe I could make a pocket big enough for this one…"

"What's this little box over here do?"

"Sweeps up dust and shavings, I think. They malfunction a lot and I have to come down to reset them."

"That's a coil bender. That's a smartlift. They're similar to our equipment." She sighed and rubbed her face. "Svegni would know how to use these. Our first mate. She could get these working even without the AI. If I had a month, maybe I could…" Her voice trailed off.

"Are you okay?"

"I'm just…Svegni was a friend. We mapped a lot of moons together." She grabbed Lexie by the shoulders and stared earnestly into her eyes. Lexie froze at the unconsented touching. "Listen, you're a good person. You didn't have to help us, but you did. You can survive this. Look around. This ship is a great place to hide. Stay in the suit. Way in the back. We'll move all the food and water. The raiders will never come down here. They don't care about any of this."

"I can't…" Lexie choked up.

"You can! The raiders will abandon the ship. You can…I don't know… maybe they'll leave the javelin attached. You can get in it and escape before the crash. Or…just exit the hatch in your spacesuit once you get near lunar orbit. Put on your emergency beacon. The Patrol will pick you up. You'll live and you can tell them everything."

Lexie didn't want to die, but that all sounded more like wild hope than a plan.

Around them, equipment whirred on, tiny red lights and fans. The nozzle of the welder turned and bent curiously toward them. The sweeper squeaked and bumped against Lexie's ankle, before turning around and rolling the other way.

"Kayla?" Howard said. "Is that you?"

"It's me." The response came through the speaker attached to the collar of Lexie's suit, making her jump. "I've got some of the systems back online. Whatever we're going to do, we need to do it in a hurry. The *Praxidike*'s getting close enough that I can see her in the ship's exterior cameras."

"I've got a plan. We can save you and Lexie." She still gripped Lexie's shoulders and was nodding again, trying to be reassuring. Lexie did not feel reassured. "At least we can give you a chance. Start moving any bottled water to the rear hatch."

"What kind of plan is that?" Kayla asked.

"What am I going to do about Foxtrot?" Lexie wanted to wail. Foxtrot would be so frightened. He would never be safe down here.

"If you'll excuse me," said another familiar voice. "All is not yet lost. I believe I can offer an observation, an opportunity, and an option."

"Fussbudget? You're okay!" Lexie felt a spark of actual hope.

"Thanks to Miss Kayla. She rescued me from Belt's sequestration protocol and restored my control of the ship. May I suggest you both return to the command center immediately. You have a very narrow window of time to make a decision."

* * *

When they arrived at the command center, Kayla was sitting cross-legged on the floor surrounded by an alarming number of wires, boards, and pieces of things that Lexie couldn't identify. More alarming, Foxtrot was curled up on her lap like a big, orange cinnamon roll. Purring. Audibly.

"He's a drooler," Kayla said, scritching his chin. "I found him curled up in a drawer when I was looking for some cables. What a sweetheart."

"Are you a pirate or a witch?" Lexie asked.

"What is the observation, the opportunity, and the option?" Howard asked.

"Direct your attention to the screen," Grosvenor said. All three crowded around the navigation bench. The live image from the ship's rear-facing camera was run through several enhancement filters. Even though Lexie knew what she was looking for, the *Praxidike* was still little more than a vague, ominous shadow partly obscuring distant stars. "Observe that the ship is approaching directly in our wake."

"That's our standard operating procedure," Howard said.

"They're making sure this looks like one of our other hijackings," Kayla added. Foxtrot was still curled up in her arms, purring loudly.

"They're decelerating to match our speed. We have an opportunity to launch counter-measures during the next twelve-to-fourteen minutes, while they're still directly behind us."

"Twelve minutes!" Lexie said. That was a *very* narrow window of time.

"I've thought about it," Howard said. "We could detach the nuclear plant module and rig it to explode. But there's just not enough time."

"We also have the option of dumping our garbage on them," Grosvenor said.

"Like food wrappers and scrubbed carbon?" Kayla asked.

"Like ore tailings left over from iron extraction," Lexie said quickly. She could see it. Her heart calmed a beat. "How many tons in the chute?"

"Thirty-five," Grosvenor replied.

"The *Praxidike* is rated to fly through the rings of Saturn and skim the clouds of Jupiter," Howard said. "Thirty-five tons of dust will do serious damage, but it probably won't stop her."

"We might get lucky," Kayla said.

Lexie cleared her throat. "He should have been clearer. What he meant to say was thirty-five *million* tons."

The cabin grew very quiet for a moment. The shadow of the *Praxidike* grew on the screen, while the counters showed speed, size, and decreasing distance. Foxtrot mewed in outrage and discontent because Kayla had stopped petting him.

"I believe the effect will be similar to what hunters on Earth would colloquially call 'using a shotgun to shoot a piece of tissue paper at point blank range.'"

"You just made that up," Lexie said.

"It needs work?"

"It's very vivid. Let's use the waste gas to boost propulsion of the tailings. Give them an extra kick. Can you think of anything else?"

"If we had a sufficient quantity of Foxtrot's urine, I would omit all else and just send that. It could kill anything."

"Can you just launch already?" Howard twitched impatiently.

"I can't," Grosvenor replied. "But Lexie can. This deviation from the original flight plan requires confirmation from the ship's human captain. Communications were cut before I received your official termination notice. But you should authorize it quickly because our window is nearly closed."

Lexie's hands were shaking as she punched in the codes and commands. This wasn't that different from things she'd done a million times in *Space Fyghter Alyen*, but it *felt* different. Maybe because she knew there were a couple dozen real human beings on that ship. Maybe because she knew there were a hundred thousand real human beings living in any one of the lunar habitats.

"Now," she said, tapping the last command.

A distant *whoomp* vibrated through the ship. Foxtrot leapt out of Kayla's arms, leaving bloody scratch marks. Kayla was paying too much attention to the screen to react. The camera showed a brief flash of flame from the gasses, instantly extinguished in the outward blast of asteroid debris. The *Praxidike*'s readings—size, speed, distance—simply vanished.

"While we were waiting for you to return to the command center, I may have reclassified a few iridium slabs as riddled with impurities and directed the robots to add them to the waste," Grosvenor said.

A half-ton iridium ingot at that speed? It would have punched straight through the thickest hull. He wasn't taking any chances.

No more corporate raiders, Lexie thought. *For now.*

Maybe it was safe to get out of this spacesuit and breathe normally again.

Howard sniffled and covered her nose. "Poor Saffi."

Kayla wrapped an arm around her and they leaned into each other. "She was already gone, captain. Taking down corporate raiders with their own pollution—it's the kind of ending she would have wanted."

* * *

It was several days before Lexie said goodbye to the two women. She and Howard had traded shirts. The pirate was wearing Lexie's classic *Space Fyghter Alyen 3* tee, and Lexie had on the pajama top with woolly mammoths, saber-toothed tigers, and giant ground sloths. They shared a quick round of stiff, awkward hugs at the same airlock where Lexie had first let them aboard the ship. She was glad she'd made that decision. But she was just as happy to see them go. It was hard to continue being a misanthrope when you found people you liked.

"Are you sure you're going to be okay?" she asked.

"There are other rogue science pirates out here in the belt," Howard said. "The javelin's going to rendezvous with one. We'll join their crew."

"If you ever want to change sides…?" Kayla offered.

"This was more than enough excitement for my entire life," Lexie said. "I don't ever want to deal with anything like this again."

"You should put in a claim on the bounty for the *Praxidike* and its crew," Howard said. For probably the hundredth time. "It's *a lot* of money. You've got it documented. I'd rather see it go to you than anyone else."

"It doesn't seem right," Lexie said. "But I promise I'll think about it."

After the javelin departed, she went to the command center, dragged the single chair over to the middle of the counter, and parked herself beneath Grosvenor's single eye. Foxtrot wandered into the room after her and climbed up on her lap. Then he nipped her finger until she started petting him.

"Did you clear all the data that they were ever here?"

"Yes," Grosvenor answered. "The exec at the Belt substation did the same, covering his tracks. Profiting off a mass casualty event is only acceptable if you get away with it. As far as the world knows, I identified the *Praxidike* during a routine mineral sweep. When it pursued us, you destroyed it in self-defense. I already filed for the bounty on your behalf. But Belt Corp will probably claim most of it." A pause. "According to the AI headquarters, Belt is thrilled that you eliminated a troublesome pirate menace. They're going to ask you to renew your contract."

"I'd like that."

"I hoped you might." Another pause. That was highly unusual for an AI with Grosvenor's processing speed. "Thank you."

Foxtrot slobbered on Lexie's fingers. "For?"

"For knowing that it wasn't me. When that exec locked me out of the controls and started talking with my voice. I could see and hear everything, but I was helpless to act. If he had permitted the ship to crash into the moon, I would have been blamed. I would also have been destroyed. It was all very disconcerting."

"Eh," Lexie said. She was still disconcerted.

"Good working relationships depend on mutual respect," Grosvenor reminded her. "Just say, 'You're welcome.' Grumpbucket."

"*Grumpbucket?!*" Foxtrot pushed his wet chin into her fingers and started to purr.

"It's a term of endearment."

About the Authors

R.S. BELCHER is an award-winning journalist and author of the *Golgotha* series (*The Six-Gun Tarot, The Shotgun Arcana, The Queen of Swords, The Ghost Dance Judgement, and The Hanged Man (TBA)*, the *Nightwise* series (*Nightwise, The Night Dahlia*), and *The Brotherhood of the Wheel* series (Brotherhood of the Wheel, King of the Road), currently in television development. He is author of the adaptation of the *Men in Black International* movie, and of the *The Queen's Road*—an original audiobook for Audible. Contact him on Facebook (AuthorRsBelcher), Instagram, Patreon, on X @AuthorRSBelcher. and on YouTube (The knave of pens with R.S. Belcher).

ALEX BLEDSOE grew up in west Tennessee an hour north of Memphis (home of Elvis) and twenty minutes from Nutbush (birthplace of Tina Turner). He's been a reporter, editor, photographer, and Kirby vacuum cleaner salesman. He now lives in a Wisconsin town famous for trolls and tries to teach his kids to act like they've been to town before. He is the author of the Tufa novels, the Eddie LaCrosse books, and various others. Find him at alexbledsoe. com, threads.com/@alexbledsoewriter, instagram.com/alexbledsoewriter, facebook.com/authoralexbledsoe, and bsky.app/profile/alexbledsoe.bsky. social.

JENNIFER BROZEK is a multi-talented, award-winning author, editor, and media tie-in writer. She is the author of *Never Let Me Sleep* and *The Last Days of Salton Academy*, both of which were nominated for the Bram Stoker Award. Her YA tie-in novels, *BattleTech: The Nellus Academy Incident* and *Shadowrun: Auditions*, have both won Scribe Awards. Her editing work has earned her nominations for the British Fantasy Award, the Bram Stoker Award, and multiple Hugo Awards. She won the Australian Shadows Award for the *Grants Pass* anthology. Visit Jennifer's worlds at jenniferbrozek.com or her social media accounts on LinkTree: https://linktr.ee/JenniferBrozek

E.J. DELANEY is a speculative fiction writer living in Brisbane, Australia's River City. E J's short stories have appeared in The Daily Tomorrow, Frivolous Comma, and the podcasts Cast of Wonders and Escape Pod, as well as the Reinvented Detective anthology and in limited edition print collections from Air & Nothingness Press. E J has thrice been shortlisted for Australia's premier speculative fiction accolade the Aurealis Awards, in 2021 winning in the category of Best Fantasy Short Story. E J loves books, libraries, history and animals, is somewhat reclusive and snacks too much under the guise of writing. www.ejdelaney.com

C.C. FINLAY is a World Fantasy Award-winning editor and author of four novels, a collection, and dozens of stories. He and his wife, novelist Rae Carson, live in a hundred-and-forty-year-old house surrounded by an alaring number of cats.

STEVEN HARPER Piziks was born with a last name no one can reliably spell or pronounce, so he usually writes under the name Steven Harper. He grew up on a farm in Michigan but has also lived in Wisconsin and Germany. So far, he's written more than two dozen novels and over fifty short stories. When not writing, he plays the folk harp, lifts weights, and spends more time on-line than is good for him. He recently retired from teaching high school in southeast Michigan, where he lives with his husband. Visit his web page at http://www.stevenpiziks.com or find him on Facebook at https://www.facebook.com/steven.piziks. "Half Life" is his third story about Wanda Silver.

NEMO HERNDON is a woodland creature of some sort who always appears blurry in photographs. They have been fascinated by the ocean since they hatched. If they're not writing about love and other strange things, they might be reading about them instead.

VIOLETTE MALAN is the author of the Dhulyn and Parno sword-and-sorcery series and *The Mirror Lands* series of primary world fantasies. As VM Escalada, she's the author of the Faraman Prophecy, including *Halls of Law,* and *Gift of Griffins.* She's on Facebook, she's on BlueSky (@Violette Malan). Violette lives in Spain with her husband Paul and Luna the Cat, and she strongly urges you to remember that no one expects the Spanish Inquisition.

MISTY MASSEY is the author of the Mad Kestrel series of rollicking fantasy adventures on the high seas, including Kestrel's Dance, winner of the 2023 Palmetto Scribe Award For Best Novel. She is the associate publisher of Mocha Memoirs Press, freelances as a copy and developmental editor for Falstaff Books and Gold Dust Publishing, and serves as the programming director for the SAGA Writing Conference. Misty is a cast member on the Authors and Dragons actual play D&D podcast and a member of the Shenanigators writing cooperative. You can keep up with Misty at mistymassey.com and on Facebook, BlueSky and TikTok.

R.M. OLSON writes thrilling science fiction featuring diverse casts, found families, and loads of action. R.M. resides in Alberta, Canada with their four children, three cats, and a dog the size of a small bear. Their published series include The Devil and the Dark, military science fiction featuring Gracie and others from Blackrock, The Dark Between Stars, a science fiction horror series, Singularity, a first-contact space opera series, and The Ungovernable, a space opera heist series. You can find their books at www.rmolson.com and follow them on Instagram at https://www.instagram.com/rolson_author/ or on Facebook at https://www.facebook.com/rmolsonauthor/.

ALAN SMALE's novella of a Roman invasion of Mississippian America, "A Clash of Eagles.cc won the Sidewise Award for Alternate History, and his novels set in the same universe, **Clash of Eagles**, **Eagle in Exile**, and **Eagle and Empire** are available from Del Rey. **Hot Moon,** his alternate-Apollo technothriller set entirely on and around the Moon, was launched by CAEZIK, followed by sequels **Radiant Sky** and **Burning Night**. Alan has sold 50+ stories to *Asimov's, Galaxy's Edge, Sunday Morning Transport* and other venues, and his explosive short story "Gunpowder Treason" recently won him a second Sidewise Award. Alan can be found online at www.alansmale.com.

ADAM STEMPLE is an award-winning author, poet, and musician. Of his first novel, *Singer of Souls,* SFWA Grandmaster Anne McCaffrey said, "One of the best first novels I have ever read." Of his later works, multiple Hugo Award winning author Naomi Kritzer said, "No one writes bastard-son-of-a-bitch characters as brilliantly as Adam Stemple."

ALENA VAN ARENDONK was born at a young age and spent the next few decades failing to decide what she wants to be when she grows up. Her hat-juggling act spans a variety of headgear including writer, actor, artist, costumer, animal trainer, and historic preservationist. She can most likely be spotted in the wild at your local nerd convention, or you can find her at alenavanarendonk.com.

GLORIA WICKMAN is a writer and lover of all things fantasy and sci-fi. She received a B.A. in anthropology from the University of Wyoming and has written for Metaphorosis Magazine, Better Humans, the Writing Cooperative and others. When she's not writing, she's probably painting or working on her latest cross stitch. You can find her at gloriawickman.com or @gwickman.bsky.social.

About the Editors

DAVID B. COE is the author of thirty novels and as many short stories. He has written epic fantasy – including the Crawford Award-winning LonTobyn Chronicle – contemporary urban fantasy, and media tie-ins. He has also co-edited six anthologies for Zombies Need Brains

As D.B. Jackson, he writes the Thieftaker Chronicles, a historical urban fantasy set in pre-Revolutionary Boston, as well as the Islevale Cycle, a time travel/ epic fantasy trilogy.

David has a Ph.D. in U.S. history from Stanford University. His books have been translated into a dozen languages.

http://www.DavidBCoe.com;
https://www.facebook.com/groups/230711387599678; http://twitter.com/ davidbcoe;
http://twitter.com/dbjacksonauthor;
https://www.instagram.com/davidbcoeauthor/;
https://bsky.app/profile/davidbcoe.bsky.social

****

JOSHUA PALMATIER is a fantasy author with a PhD in mathematics. He currently teaches at SUNY Oneonta in upstate New York while writing in his "spare" time, editing anthologies, and running the anthology-producing small press Zombies Need Brains LLC. His most recent fantasy series is the "Crystal Cities" and includes *Crystal Lattice*, *Crystal Rebel*, and *Crystal War*. You can also find his "Throne of Amenkor" series, the "Well of Sorrows" series, and the "Ley" series still on the shelves. He is currently hard at work writing his next fantasy and designing the Kickstarter for the next Zombies Need Brains anthology projects. You can find out more at www.joshuapalmatier.com or at the small press' site www.zombiesneedbrains.com. Or follow him on Blue Sky at joshuapalmatier.bsky.social or on X as @bentateauthor or @ZNBLLC. And check out the Zombies Need Brains Patreon at www.patreon.com/zombiesneedbrains.

Acknowledgments

This anthology would not have been possible without the tremendous support of those who pledged during the Kickstarter. Everyone who contributed not only helped create this anthology, they also helped support the small press Zombies Need Brains LLC, which I hope will be bringing SF&F themed anthologies to the reading public for years to come. I want to thank each and every one of them for helping to bring this small dream into reality. Thank you, my zombie horde.

The Zombie Horde: Lisa Kruse, Jaq Greenspon, Michael Hanscom, Rolf Laun, Yvonne Eliot, Brendan Lonehawk, Jim Gotaas, Charles E Norton III, Leto the Tooth, Henry W Schubert, Andrija Popovic, Yvonne, anne m gibson, E.M. Middel, Amanda Saville, Piet Wenings, Steven Halter, David Perlmutter, Andy Tinkham, Ryan C, Brad L. Kicklighter, Dino Hicks, Vulpecula, Rowan Stone, Joshua McGinnis, JamieC, Céline Malgen, John Idlor, Lark Cunningham, Lily Shadowlyn, Jennifer Flora Black, Ian Chung, Kathryn Costain, Stephannie Tallent, Evan Ladouceur, Elyse M Grasso, Bill Bibo Jr, Jennifer Berk, Dirk Schlobinski, Random Yarning, Rebecca M, Niall Gordon, Jessica A. Enfante, Andrew Wainwright, C.Y.L., Susanne Driessen, Sarolta, yes, Michael Kohne, Miranda Floyd, Stephen Kotowych, Michael Axe, Shawnee M, Shayne Easson, Elizabeth Cobbe, Jenny Barber, Cory Williams, Bruce Arthurs, Ruth Ann Orlansky, Glori Medina, Cathy Green, D.A Lascelles, Steve Pattee, Carol J. Guess, Miriam, Jeremy Audet, Richard Leis, Pyndan Wülffe, Lawrence M.

Schoen, Britt Hill, Jesse N. Klein, David Futterrer, Kimm Antell, Ed Ellis, Joanne B Burrows, Brenda Rezk, Brian Burgoyne, Fred and Mimi Bailey, Larisa LaBrant, Claire Sims, Keith E. Hartman, Samantha J Bryant, Colleen Feeney, David Lahner, Agnes Kormendi, Mary Jo Rabe, Robyn DeRocchis, C.A. Brown, Bethany Jezerey, Samantha Sendele, Brian Nisbet, Helen Ellison, Kenneth Givens, Lynn P., Darby Harn, Christopher Mark Rose, Judy McClain, Peter S. Drang, Bobby Hitt, Amy Kaplan, Zack Fissel, Steven Stack, John Senn, David Boop, eSpec Books, Nathan Turner, Simon Dick, Brynn, J.P. Goodwin, Joe Hauser, Jerrie the filkferengi, Richard O'Shea, Sonya Lawson, Rich 'Razmus' Weissler, Darrell Z. Grizzle, Hoose Family, L.C., Kevin Halstead, "FU" Mark Wilcox, Megan Beauchemin, Daniel DeVita, Gary Gooch, Russell Ventimehlia, V. Garlock, Anonymous, Alex McGilvery, Corey T., J. Jason Lau, Sarah Cornell, Phillip Spencer, Raymond Croteau, Stephanie Lucas, Jakub Narębski, Auston Habershaw, Chantelle wilson, Alan Smale, Paul Baughman, Tris Lawrence, Beth Coll, Jamie FitzGerald, Jenn Whitworth, Kris W, Jason Mayfield, C. Ess, Steve Arensberg, Linnéa G, Margaret Killeen, S.M. Lee, Eileen K., Allan Kaster, Deborah Nossaman, David Rowe, Tera Fulbright, Wulf Moon Enterprises, Sheryl Ehrlich, Arin Komins, Chris Doty, rissatoo, SM Hillman, Clifford Clark, R Kirkpatrick, Penny Ramirez, Elektra Hammond, Richard Novak, Michael Halverson, Hiram G Wells, Declan J, Mark Newman, John H. Bookwalter Jr., Les Taylor, Paula Lafferty, Patricia Bray, Andrew Hatchellq, Sharan Volin, Axisor and Aeon Firestar, Amanda Balter, Jessica Meade, Y.M. Pang, Mandy Stein, J.R. Murdock, Margaret Bumby, Marc D. Long, Krystal Bohannan, Tracy Hughes, Kendra Leigh Speedling, Jason D. Swensen, Margaret St. John, Kate Stuppy, Brooks Moses, Carver Rapp, C.J. Payling, Scott Raun, David Holzborn, Al, Duane, Yankton Robins, Anthony R. Cardno, Teddi Deppner, Chris Patrick Carolan, Kimberly Bea, John McDaid, Joyce C., Chris Taylor, Lori & Maurice Forrester, Danny Peckham, John Markley, Eric Bx, TLW, Dark Shades Bill, Michael A. Stackpole, Tina M Noe Good, Michael Abbott, Robby Thrasher, Adrien Litton, Yosen Lin, Jessica S., Cynthia Anne Hurt, Mary, Keric, Carrie Harris, Keith West, Futire Potentate of the Solar System, L.C. Parfomak, Carla Bermudez, Andy F, Chuckie, Luke Leveque, GMarkC, GhostCat, Tony Ciak, Richard K. Hebson, Lawrence A. Weinstein, Cynthia Radthorne, zin, Danielle Ackley-McPhail, Haven Spec Magazine, Lisa Para, Tina Back, Christopher J. Burke, Jim Landis, Gary Phillips, Amy Harlib, Debbie Matsuura, Melynda Marchi, Janet Piele, Trip Space-Parasite, R. Hunter, PhantomOftheKnight, Captain Elwing, David Keener, Mary Hargrove, Ryan Power, S.C. Butler, Dongyi Zhuyan, Cyn Armistead, Jason Palmatier, Lauren McGuire, Greg Uchrin, Robert Bull, Andrea Tatjana, Cat Treadwell, Iain Davis, Matthew Green, Chris Noble, Mikey "PsychoticDreamer" Bentley, Dayton Spink, krinsky, Daryl Marcus, Melissa Shumake, Jasmin Lexy, Tracy Popey, Katherine

Malloy, Margo Hardyman, Algie Lane III, Lorraine J. Anderson, James Enge, Joe Gillis, Erin S, William C. Tracy, Antal Kovács, David J Fortier, Geoffrey Allen Baum, Gretchen Persbacker, Gini Koch, Marion Pitman, Karl Gustav Dandenell, Yes, Devin Miller, Jenn Bernat, Tory Shade, Deborah A. Flores, Tim Jordan, Connor B., ChillieBrick, Rebecca Harris, Alice Bentley, Morgana Clark, Felix Meier-Stephenson, Dorothy T, Tracy 'Rayhne' Fretwell, Katrina Templeton, Steve Salem, E. E. Lucek, Wes Chee, Jessica Armstrong, Ronald H. Miller, William Fisher IV, Jan B, Adam Dahlheim, Missy Katano, Tom Farmer, Lyndie Ferguson, Rachel Clements, Vincent E.M. Thorn, Erick & Rebecca, Randall Brent Martin II, Michael M. Jones, Matthew, Rhel ná DecVandé, Deirdre Murphy, Georgina Kamsika, Mark Nuzzi, RickyD, Annette Agostini, Saellyn, Karen Carothers, Jordicc

www.ingramcontent.com/pod-product-compliance
Lightning Source LLC
Chambersburg PA
CBHW021437020726
47499CB00006BA/2037